The Physiology of the Novel

Reading, Neural Science, and the Form of Victorian Fiction

NICHOLAS DAMES

OXFORD

UNIVERSITY PRESS

OXFORD
UNIVERSITY PRESS

Great Clarendon Street, Oxford OX2 6DP

Oxford University Press is a department of the University of Oxford.
It furthers the University's objective of excellence in research, scholarship,
and education by publishing worldwide in

Oxford New York

Auckland Cape Town Dar es Salaam Hong Kong Karachi
Kuala Lumpur Madrid Melbourne Mexico City Nairobi
New Delhi Shanghai Taipei Toronto

With offices in

Argentina Austria Brazil Chile Czech Republic France Greece
Guatemala Hungary Italy Japan Poland Portugal Singapore
South Korea Switzerland Thailand Turkey Ukraine Vietnam

Oxford is a registered trade mark of Oxford University Press
in the UK and in certain other countries

Published in the United States
by Oxford University Press Inc., New York

© Nicholas Dames 2007

British Library Cataloguing in Publication Data

Data available

Library of Congress Cataloging in Publication Data

Data available

Typeset by Laserwords Private Limited, Chennai, India
Printed in Great Britain
on acid-free paper by
Biddles Ltd., King's Lynn, Norfolk

ISBN 978−0−19−920896−8

1 3 5 7 9 10 8 6 4 2

THE PHYSIOLOGY OF THE NOVEL

For my parents

Acknowledgements

This study of patchy, partial, rapid, and solitary reading has profited immeasurably from generous colleagues who, at various points in its development, gave this book patient, informed, acute readings, and provided support when I most doubted its direction. At Columbia University, Jonathan Arac, David Damrosch, Ann Douglas, and Bruce Robbins read different parts of this book at different stages and gave help, suggestions, and encouragement whose traces appear everywhere within; Sharon Marcus in particular gave the book a reading that was sympathetic in the best sense, as well as crucial to its development. David Kastan and James Shapiro assisted the book and its author in other, equally significant, ways. The wit, insight, and advice of Amanda Claybaugh, Sarah Cole, Andrew Delbanco, Eileen Gilloly, Erik Gray, Karl Kroeber, and Edward Mendelson, as well as the students in the Victorianist Dissertation Colloquium, helped make Columbia a place not only to write but to learn and, occasionally, to laugh. Outside Columbia I have been fortunate to find in recent years readers and listeners who have provided important clues and opened new paths of investigation, perhaps without even knowing how much help they were rendering: I want to thank Stephen Arata, Nancy Armstrong, Jay Clayton, Andrew Elfenbein, Kate Flint, Catherine Gallagher, Dorothy Hale, Alan Liu, Deidre Lynch, Andrew Miller, David Miller, Leah Price, Alan Richardson, Garrett Stewart, and Kay Young for believing in and assisting the project at crucial moments. Three anonymous readers for Oxford University Press provided detailed and imaginative readings of the book.

My gratitude extends as well to audiences at Berkeley, Indiana, Harvard, Princeton, Vanderbilt, and Yale, whose responses continually spurred my thinking. To Mark Allison I owe thanks for pointing me to a comment by Raymond Williams that illuminated much that had been murky; to Douglas Susu-Mago I owe thanks for his help with matters Wagnerian. Ana Keilson, Nikil Saval, and Ying Ling Tiong, quondam students and brilliant minds all, did invaluable work in unearthing texts, making bibliographical connections, and editing prose; this book could not have been completed in as timely and coherent a fashion without them. Sarah Rose Cole, Aman Garcha, David Kurnick, Caroline Levine, Kent Puckett, and Karl Saddlemire contributed more than they know, with friendship, discussions, and shared interests in the world of Victorian reading. This book could not have been started without the help of Irene Chang and Maren Hill; so much of my life outside writing was made easier by the kindness and humor of Joy Hayton and Michael Mallick, who never failed to smooth bumps in the road. Amy Jakobson helped me find the clarity to finish this book, particularly this very page. Lev Kaye, whose intellectual curiosity, humor, and generosity I've enjoyed in over twenty years of conversations and debates, did much to make the years of this book's writing less costly to its writer.

I was able to begin work on this book thanks to a Chamberlain Fellowship and Junior Faculty Development Fellowship leave from Columbia, which allowed me time to read widely in physiology and Victorian criticism with only the shadow of an idea to pursue. I was able to finish it thanks to a Charles Ryskamp Research Fellowship from the American Council of Learned Societies, which gave me time to give flesh to that early shadow. At Oxford University Press, Jean van Altena, Clare Jenkins, Andrew McNeillie, Tom Perridge, and Val Shelley were both patient with my inexplicable delays and swift in guiding this book through to completion. The staffs and resources of the British Library, Butler Library at Columbia, the Huntington Library, and the New York Public Library were essential to this project.

Amy Mae King deserves a paragraph of her own for the support, intellectual and otherwise, that she gave as this book took shape. She was this book's first and most dedicated reader, a believer in it and a skeptic when necessary, and a witness and participant in the struggle of its writing.

This book is dedicated to my parents, John and Louise Dames, who, particularly as this book neared completion, gave me examples of understanding and generosity that I hope one day to repay. To my son Stephen, who was born before a word of this book was written, I can only say that the daily marvel of his flourishing self brightened beyond measure the world that reappeared whenever my work was put aside.

Contents

List of Illustrations

Introduction: Toward a History of Victorian Novel Theory

À quelle discipline ressortit une théorie de la lecture?

Ricoeur, *Temps et Récit*

In the late-career interview series collected as *Politics and Letters* (1979), Raymond Williams responded to a question about the possibility of 'a legitimate materialist conception of the human' by disclosing an unfulfilled, perhaps unfulfillable, goal: an account of what he called the 'physical effects of writing'. As Williams explained it, 'there is a very deep material bond between language and the body, which communication theories that concentrate on the passing of messages and information typically miss: many poems, many kinds of writing, indeed a lot of everyday speech communicate what is in effect a life rhythm and the interaction of these life rhythms is probably a very important part of the material process of writing and reading'. Such a critical agenda, Williams added almost wistfully, is not yet possible, since 'only scientific investigations could arrive at such a finding. . . . Indeed, if I had one single ambition in literary studies it would be to rejoin them with experimental science, because of work that is now being done which would make it possible to do so.' He went on to specify:

Years ago I tried to set up some actual experiments of what happened to physical rhythms in certain reading contexts, but such was the atmosphere of specialization that the work was never done. I believe, however, that we have got to move towards active collaboration with the many scientists who are especially interested in the relations between language use and human physical organization. . . . What is needed is . . . an introduction of literary practice to the quite different practice of experimental observation. That would be the materialist recovery.[1]

Williams's unabashed enthusiasm for experimental science as an integral part of literary study is both surprising and poignant: surprising for so committed

---

[1] Raymond Williams, *Politics and Letters: Interviews with* New Left Review (London: Verso, 1981), 341.

a historicist critic, and poignant not only because he never subsequently pursued it, but also because he seemed already to feel, at the moment of its annunciation, that its pursuit was unlikely, mitigated by institutional barriers and conflicts of procedure and emphasis between humanistic and scientific disciplines.[2]

What this book will suggest is an irony more surprising still: that the utopian goal envisioned by Williams in 1979 had, in fact, already been practiced in Britain, a century earlier, by a loosely affiliated coterie of scientists, journalists, and intellectuals who brought the experimental study of human physiology to bear upon the facts of novel-reading, as part of an attempt to theorize the force of the novel form in culture. That Williams, still one of the most influential figures for the current shape of Victorian literary and cultural studies, might have missed this connection is in no way unusual; the force of experimental science upon nineteenth-century novel criticism and theory has been so consistently overlooked as to encourage the persistent illusion that the Victorians had no theory of the novel at all.[3] Williams's seemingly forward-looking desire for a juncture of science and literary criticism was more Victorian than he knew. In the mid to late nineteenth century some of the period's most eminent and prolific critics of the novel had already written on the 'life rhythms' of literary forms and reading practices, and had already tried to generalize from these rhythmic signatures some sense of the effects that certain narrative forms could have upon the 'human physical organization'; they had already speculated upon 'physical rhythms in certain reading contexts', particularly the context of novel-reading, and had arrived at a complicated sense of the social and political stakes of these rhythms. Figures such as G. H. Lewes, Alexander Bain, E. S. Dallas, Geraldine Jewsbury, and Vernon Lee would have immediately understood Williams's agenda, and would have been able to supply the missing term that, for them at least, conjoined scientific observation with literary analysis: physiology.

---

[2] One version, although with little humanistic input, did take shape shortly after Williams's remarks: Victor Nell's research in the 1980s into the physiological and cognitive conditions of what Nell terms 'ludic reading'. In a technologically, if not methodologically, advanced version of Victorian physiological studies of reading, Nell connected laboratory subjects—readers—to translucent goggles and multiple electrodes in order to measure heart rates, muscle activity, the electrical activity of the skin, and respiration rates. Not surprisingly, given the Victorian tradition into which he unwittingly fits, Nell's instances of 'ludic', or nonutilitarian, reading tend almost exclusively to come from prose fiction. See Victor Nell, *Lost in a Book: The Psychology of Reading for Pleasure* (New Haven: Yale University Press, 1988).

[3] Not entirely overlooked, however: Kate Flint's work on medicalized language about reading—particularly as it related to the consumption of women—stands out for its attention to the period's physiological sciences. See Kate Flint, *The Woman Reader, 1837–1914* (Oxford: Clarendon Press, 1993), 53–70.

That there existed for a period of time in the nineteenth century a literary theory that I will call 'the physiology of the novel' is the first claim of this book, and a large part of what follows is dedicated to tracing its most important practitioners, its central texts and influences, its methodological peculiarities, tendencies, and blind spots, its critical protocols, and its thoroughly reciprocal impact upon the novels produced during its most influential period. As much of this book will attest, a substantial body of major Victorian fiction was preoccupied, thematically and formally, with the questions about readerly comprehension and cognition that this body of theory posed. But a second, perhaps wider, and certainly more speculative claim animates my recovery of physiological novel theory: that our own theories of the novel could be refreshed by taking into account the practices, however historically and geographically distinct, of novel-reading that may be the novel's most significant contribution to modern culture. Williams's latter-day call for a scientific criticism is explicit about what 'experimental science' could do for literary theory: give both rigor and nuance to our accounts of reading by tying reading to the rhythms of the body, a goal that is by definition physiological. Left implicit is Williams's contention that contemporary literary theory fails to attend to reading in its material, social, and physical aspects. This attention to reading is still important for the future of novel theory precisely because, as we shall see, the psychological processes of novel-reading—most frequently, in fact, reading the nineteenth-century novel—are continually being recruited into contemporary debates about literature and civic virtue, which not only potentially distort and misrepresent the actual rhythms and practices of novel-reading, but also construct dubious ethical hierarchies (which are often hierarchies of taste, or class) of kinds of novel-consumption.

This is not to say that the methods of physiological novel theory should be resumed wholesale, as if Victorian novel criticism's protocols and angle of vision could simply be reactivated without any serious adjustment to our own realities and forms of knowledge. Physiological novel theory was, as we shall see, too limited in its historical reach, and too antique in its scientific tools, for anyone to wish its reanimation. I do want to suggest, however, that those methods offer us a compelling instance of how one vanished theoretical configuration imagined what the historian Adrian Johns has called 'the decisive moment of face-to-face confrontation between reader and read', and how that imagination was then incorporated into a theory of one literary genre's formal shape and cultural impact.[4] The following

----

[4] Adrian Johns, *The Nature of the Book: Print and Knowledge in the Making* (Chicago: University of Chicago Press, 1998), 386. Johns's important study of the early modern 'physiology of reading', which ranged from ocular physiology to the psychology of the passions, is perhaps

could be said to be the animating spirit behind my survey of the Victorian physiology of the novel: that a study of the intellectual resources brought to bear, at a given historical moment, upon the act of reading—here, the act of reading novels—offers possibilities of renewal for our own considerations of the social meaning of the novel form, and opens up areas of investigation that have been successively foreclosed by the author-centered novel theory of the past century. More particularly, the practices of physiological novel theory reveal cultural zones—nineteenth-century debates over the novel's role in shortening attention spans, diminishing the temporal reach of cognitive effort, and dangerously accelerating textual consumption—where the reach of the novel as a cultural technology is both profound and as yet little understood, today every bit as much as in the nineteenth century.

In other words, if in his famous article 'First Steps Toward a History of Reading', Robert Darnton has called for 'a juncture between literary theory and the history of books', physiological novel theory as Victorian critics practiced it presents us with a model—flawed, obsolete, and yet rich in its ambitions and often in its results—for what that might look like.[5] As a result, this book borrows much of its impetus from the diversely constituted field known as the history of reading, but in a particular vein. My study of physiological novel theory and its relation to Victorian fiction depends on the study not of bibliographical objects (although considerations of certain forms, such as the three-volume novel, will become important), nor of the recorded reactions of particular readers (except insofar as they took the form of published criticism), but instead of a 'reading formation', to use the term coined by Tony Bennett: a general consensus about the salient aspects of the reading act that made its way into novel theory and criticism in the mid to late nineteenth century.[6] The nineteenth century has long been the site where some of the most visible and influential Anglo-American work in the history of reading has been done, starting with Richard Altick's seminal *The English Common Reader* (1957) and continuing with work by John Sutherland, Kate Flint, Cathy Davidson, David Vincent, Jonathan Rose, and Leah Price, among many others; but the connection of this tradition of scholarly work to any literary-theoretical endeavor centered on genre or form has only recently been considered a

the most detailed and impressive study to date of the influence of scientific thought upon nonscientific conceptions of the reading act.

[5] Darnton, 'First Steps Toward a History of Reading', in *The Kiss of Lamourette: Reflections in Cultural History* (New York: Norton, 1990), 181.

[6] For Tony Bennett's definition of the term, see his 'Texts in History: The Determinations of Readings and Their Texts', in *Reception Study: From Literary Theory to Cultural Studies*, ed. James Machor and Philip Goldstein (London: Routledge, 2001), 61–74.

possibility.[7] Victorian physiological novel theory offers a potential image of what such a connection would look like. Its almost naïve willingness to hold in a triangulated tension observed facts about novel-reading habits, analyses of literary form, and large ideas about industrial society makes it a particularly fruitful place for a history of reading to turn. In many ways it can look like a Victorian version of the currently complex intersection between the history of audiences, media studies, and cognitive science, in which—as in the work of Mary Ann Doane, Elaine Scarry, and Ellen Spolsky—complex theories and histories of aesthetic reception as a mental act, particularly immersion or submergence in narrative, are attempted.[8]

---

[7] Any list of important sources for the history of reading, centered on the eighteenth and nineteenth centuries in Europe, must include the following: James Allen, *In The Public Eye: A History of Reading in Modern France, 1800–1940* (Princeton: Princeton University Press, 1991); Richard Altick, *The English Common Reader: A Social History of the Mass Reading Public* (Chicago: University of Chicago Press, 1957); Laurel Brake, *Print in Transition, 1850–1910: Studies in Media and Book History* (Basingstoke: Palgrave, 2001); Patrick Brantlinger, *The Reading Lesson: The Threat of Mass Literacy in Nineteenth-Century British Fiction* (Bloomington: Indiana University Press, 1998); Roger Chartier, *The Cultural Uses of Print in Early Modern France*, trans. Lydia Cochrane (Princeton: Princeton University Press, 1987); Darnton, *Kiss of Lamourette*; Cathy Davidson, ed., *Reading in America: Literature and Social History* (Baltimore: Johns Hopkins University Press, 1989); Simon Eliot, 'The Business of Victorian Publishing', in *The Cambridge Companion to the Victorian Novel*, ed. Deirdre David (Cambridge: Cambridge University Press, 2000), 37–60; Flint, *Woman Reader*; David Hall, *Cultures of Print: Essays in the History of the Book* (Amherst: University of Massachusetts Press, 1996); John Jordan and Robert Patten, eds., *Literature in the Marketplace: Nineteenth-Century British Publishing and Reading Practices* (Cambridge: Cambridge University Press, 1995); Jon Klancher, *The Making of English Reading Audiences, 1790–1832* (Madison: University of Wisconsin Press, 1987); Martyn Lyons, *Readers and Society in Nineteenth-Century France: Workers, Women, Peasants* (London: Palgrave, 2001); Jacqueline Pearson, *Women's Reading in Britain, 1750–1835* (Cambridge: Cambridge University Press, 1999); Leah Price, *The Anthology and the Rise of the Novel: From Richardson to George Eliot* (Cambridge: Cambridge University Press, 2000); Alan Richardson, *Literature, Education, and Romanticism: Reading as Social Practice, 1780–1832* (Cambridge: Cambridge University Press, 1994); Jonathan Rose, *The Intellectual History of the British Working Classes* (New Haven: Yale University Press, 2001); James Secord, *Victorian Sensation: The Extraordinary Publication, Reception, and Secret Authorship of* Vestiges of the Natural History of Creation (Chicago: University of Chicago Press, 2000); William St Clair, *The Reading Nation in the Romantic Period* (Cambridge: Cambridge University Press, 2004); John Sutherland, *Victorian Fiction: Writers, Publishers, Readers* (Basingstoke: Macmillan, 1995); David Vincent, *The Rise of Mass Literacy: Reading and Writing in Modern Europe* (Cambridge: Polity, 2000); William Warner, *Licensing Entertainment: The Elevation of Novel Reading in Britain, 1684–1750* (Berkeley: University of California Press, 1998). One very useful and representative anthology of such work is James Raven, Helen Small, and Naomi Tadmor, eds., *The Practice and Representation of Reading in England* (Cambridge: Cambridge University Press, 1996).

[8] See Mary Ann Doane, *The Emergence of Cinematic Time: Modernity, Contingency, the Archive* (Cambridge, Mass.: Harvard University Press, 2002); Elaine Scarry, *Dreaming by the Book* (New York: Farrar, Straus, Giroux, 1999); Ellen Spolsky, *Gaps in Nature: Literary Interpretation and the Modular Mind* (Albany, NY: SUNY Press, 1993). Much of this work centers on new media and the conditions of reception it demands; see, e.g., Janet Murray, *Hamlet on the Holodeck:*

A study of Victorian physiological novel theory is thus both a history of a theory of reading as well as, inevitably, a history of reading itself, insofar as both material and literary-formal changes to the Victorian novel were made, to a significant extent, on the basis of the scientized methodologies of the period's critics. Such a study is therefore also, in part, a history of science, at least in the intersection of various physiological sciences with literary criticism. While this book will not engage to any large degree with contemporary cognitive science, it does center on the history of neural science in the Victorian period in its relation to literary practices and critical protocols. In that sense, it is also part of the emergent interest in a history of literary criticism and theory, and by juxtaposing Victorian physiology and neurology with literary theories of the time, it provides an image of past interdisciplinary collaboration and friction that Williams, speaking in 1979, thought so unlikely for the future. Understanding the close relationship between experimental physiology and novel theory in the nineteenth century also provides new ways in which to think through a formal or technical history of the British novel, since writers such as Thackeray, Eliot, Meredith, and Gissing, to each of whom a chapter of this book is devoted, constructed their fictions in more or less overt ways around the topics that the Victorian physiology of reading was concurrently exploring.

How, then, did the readers of the past—for my purposes, the Victorian novel-reader—read? What transpired in mind and body as reading occurred? That deceptively simple question has been the chimera of a distinguished body of scholarship which has always come back to the melancholy conclusion that, in Roger Chartier's words, 'it must postulate the liberty of a practice that it can only grasp, massively, in its determinations'.[9] It was also the question, if more optimistically posed, of the Victorian neural sciences in their collaboration with literary criticism, for which a range of cognitive and physiological activities involved in the reading act seemed suddenly capable of study and definition. What quality of attention do certain texts or genres demand and receive? What rates of consumption and comprehension are normative for given genres? How does the mind make sense of elongated narrative forms? How does the eye traverse different texts differently? These were the questions which 'the physiology of the novel' sought to answer. Even if those questions, and the answers provided to them by Victorian

---

The Future of Narrative in Cyberspace (Cambridge, Mass.: MIT Press, 1997), which explicitly pursues comparisons between 'immersion' in traditional literary narrative, particularly novels, and 'immersion' in computer gaming.

   [9] Roger Chartier, *The Order of Books: Readers, Authors, and Libraries in Europe between the Fourteenth and Eighteenth Centuries*, trans. Lydia Cochrane (Stanford, Calif.: Stanford University Press, 1992), 23.

physiological novel theory, were no less subject to the limits of 'know.. ᴗ reading than the answers provided by the methodologies of the contemporary history of reading, they are nonetheless of great value to us for the ways in which they uncover the language used to discuss and evaluate reading in the Victorian period, particularly novel-reading. Furthermore, such questions, and the answers that physiological novel theory gave them, reveal the primary ways in which Victorian fiction was understood to have shaped the reading habits of its public.

I have divided those primary ways into four categories, each of which Part II of this book explores in connection with a major Victorian author: intermittency (the shape and quality of attention), periodicity (the duration of comprehension), discontinuity (the size of units of comprehension), and acceleration (the speed of comprehension). These are only semi-autonomous categories; it was of course difficult to write on attention span without also tackling the issue of duration, and issues of speed-reading, as we shall see, were inextricably intertwined with the kind of attention spans that accelerated reading could permit. Taken together, they offer a vision of Victorian fiction that, across the varied range of the Victorian physiology of the novel, was remarkably consistent, and can be expressed as follows: the novel of the nineteenth century trained a reader able to consume texts at an ever faster rate, with a rhythmic alternation of heightened attention and distracted inattention locking onto ever smaller units of comprehension. From the vantage-point of the physiological criticism that engaged it, the Victorian novel was a training ground for industrialized consciousness, not a refuge from it.

That this is not our usual sense of the cultural role of the novel is precisely the point: if anything, our profile of novel-reading is one of withdrawal, retreat, and even sanctified self-communion, an antidote to the assault of stimuli presented by modern, media-rich existence. An analysis of Victorian fiction through the terms provided by an overlooked body of novel theory contemporary with it is not just an exercise in 'reading the Victorians in their own terms' but in understanding what the stakes might be in the very difference between their terms and ours. Why, for instance, does novel theory after the 1880s largely eliminate novel-reading from its conceptual apparatus, and how might we heal the divide between novel theory and reading? Why does the picture of novel-reading as adaptation to industrialized, mechanized life jar so profoundly with our own habitual sense of reading novels as an escape? And what are the ways in which we unwittingly borrow from the work of Victorian physiologists of reading, to very different ends? We may not be able wholly to know how the novel-readers of the past read, but we can know how they were thought to have read—and how novels, engaged in a complicated interplay with the scientific criticism of the time, were shaped to reflect the reading habits that they were, in turn, thought to be shaping.

SOME AXIOMS FOR PHYSIOLOGICAL NOVEL THEORY

Asked by the editor James Hutton for an unspecified article in 1859, G. H. Lewes responded wearily but agreeably that 'as you seem to be counting on it, I will put the frogs aside, & set to work at once'.[10] Any perusal of Lewes's intellectual activity, from the 1850s up to his death in 1878, must account for this combination of interests: practical, vivisectionist physiological experiment alongside a wide range of literary and philosophical issues. Physiology formed a background to all of his mature work, a background that was shared with more traditionally literary concerns: finishing his *Life of Goethe* in 1855, Lewes wrote to a friend that 'I do nothing else but work at it, and chuckle like an old hen as it grows under my hands! By way of relaxation there is Shakspeare & Physiology'.[11] Life at the Priory, Regent's Park, at which Lewes and George Eliot settled in 1863, was composed of both literary production and frequent scientific work. Symptomatically, Lewes's early *Bildungsroman*, his 1847 novel *Ranthorpe*, is split between two main protagonists: Percy Ranthorpe, poet, dramatist, and journalist, and Harry Cavendish, medical student and surgeon, who initially meet in a London bohemia that spans both scientific and literary aspirants. Lewes was only the most vivid example of an intellectual formation of the mid-Victorian period: well-positioned and influential critics, often editors or in positions of authority in journals or newspapers, whose criticism was informed by the most advanced psychological theory of the day: namely, physiology, the study of the autonomic nervous system and its interrelations with cerebral functioning that sought a materialist and organicist basis for the associationism that dominated eighteenth- and nineteenth-century British theories of mind.[12]

The combination is odd and pervasive enough to call for some opening characterizations, which the bulk of this book will flesh out in detail and with

---

[10] *The Letters of George Henry Lewes*, ed. William Baker, i (Victoria, Canada: English Literary Studies, 1995), 284.

[11] Ibid. 236.

[12] For physiology's place within the history of British psychology, see Edwin Boring, *A History of Experimental Psychology* (New York: Appleton-Century-Crofts, 1957), and Kurt Danzinger, 'Mid-Nineteenth-Century British Psycho-Physiology: A Neglected Chapter in the History of Psychology', in *The Problematic Science: Psychology in Nineteenth-Century Thought*, ed. W. R. Woodward and M. G. Gash (New York: Praeger, 1982), 119–46.

reference to a set of key novelistic/cultural instances from the 1850s to the 1890s. While by no means exhaustive, the following axioms offer a general grounding in the landscape of physiological novel theory:

1. *Its figures were both part of and more than a coterie.*

The physiological psychology of Victorian novel theory is most visible, and most complexly elaborated, in the work of a small set of mid-Victorian male figures: G. H. Lewes (the intellectual polymath), E. S. Dallas (the novel critic and aesthetician), and Alexander Bain (the authoritative psychologist of his time, who dabbled in theories of fiction). Their cultural position was, with some minor differences of shading, unusually eminent, and their frequent biographical intertwinings demonstrate how well aware each was of the others' work and career; as a result, they can seem like a 'coterie' of sorts, unrepresentative of broader tendencies in Victorian literary production or scientific inquiry.[13] Investigate other theoretical and critical zones in the mid-Victorian literary field, however, and the quieter presence of their more explicitly announced methodologies is striking. Among critics whose investments and cultural profiles were radically different from the urban male bohemianism of Lewes, Dallas, and Bain, the language of physiology continues to inflect writing on the novel, whether for more conservative critics like R. H. Hutton, W. C. Roscoe, or Margaret Oliphant; for prolific, weekly reviewers of the vast field of Victorian fiction like Geraldine Jewsbury; or for later aestheticians like Vernon Lee.[14] The examples of Jewsbury and Lee in particular demonstrate how for female critics of very different political and cultural stripes the methodological tools of physiological novel theory had potent uses. Rather than any sense of a coterie theory or theoretical

[13] As early as 1845 Lewes and Bain had, alongside John Stuart Mill, collaborated in a futile attempt to convince Auguste Comte to allow them to translate his *Cours de philosophie positive*, and near the end of his life, in 1876, Lewes contributed an article to the first issue of *Mind*, the journal of which Bain was co-founder. Each was an occasional, and by no means uniformly positive, reviewer of the other's work. Dallas's position as anonymous novel critic for *The Times* in the 1850s and 1860s, as well as his friendship with John Blackwood, brought him to the attention of Lewes and Eliot both. For more details, see particularly Rosemary Ashton, *G. H. Lewes: A Life* (Oxford: Clarendon, Press, 1991), and Rick Rylance, *Victorian Psychology and British Culture, 1850–1880* (Oxford: Oxford University Press, 2000).

[14] The 'bohemianism' of Lewes—particularly with regards to his living arrangements with George Eliot—is well known; for contemporaries, however, Dallas might have best represented the free-thinking, and freely masculine, aspects of his circle. Dante Gabriel Rossetti's 1870 limerick survives to bear witness to an aspect of Dallas's social existence which a uniquely Victorian silence otherwise conceals: 'There is a poor devil named Dallas | Who tends, as I'm told, to the gallows | Yet if not so well hung, | He might never have swung, | For it's mostly along of his phallus.' See *The Correspondence of Dante Gabriel Rossetti*, ed. William Fredeman, iv (Cambridge: D. S. Brewer, 2002), 461.

'school', the following might be said: physiological novel theory was made coherent not by institutional location (which was still in formation), personal affiliations (which existed in certain but not all cases), or political/ethical programs, but by a shared set of assumptions about the function of novelistic narrative as a cultural technology best investigated with reference to categories of physiological response during reading.

> 2. *Its aim was a psychology of print consumption, with the novel as the ideal paradigm of 'print'.*

The interest of physiologists in novel-reading, and the interest of novel critics in physiological psychology, is no accident. Critics such as Dallas sought an understanding of the widespread appeal of the novel, and guessed that the appeal could be understood only via a psychological study of the conditions of reading; psychologists such as Bain sought a common form of consumption on which to test their theories of response, and the novel—read in solitude, yet culturally pervasive—presented itself as the ideal datum. For both, the novel, physiologically considered, did what all print does, only more so: condition the physiological apparatus of the reader for the temporal rhythms of modernity. Victorian novel theorists can be considered media theorists *avant la lettre*; like McLuhan would a century later, they would understand the novel as 'an extension of ourselves involving us in a state of numbness', a strategy of 'equilibrium for the central nervous system'.[15] Put another way: physiology is inherently a study of receptive states, and as such was an apt fit for a literary-critical practice oriented toward consumption rather than production, toward the reception of texts rather than the text-as-object. Like Marx in his gnomic introduction to the *Grundrisse*, physiological novel theorists held that production 'not only creates an object for the subject, but also a subject for the object'.[16] Their interest was in what kind of subject their chosen object, the novel, was creating.

> 3. *It was a processual, affective, reader-centered methodology whose notion of 'form' was thoroughly temporal.*

The word 'form' plays an important role in the chapters that follow, because its history within Victorian writings on the novel reveals important differences from our habitual use of the term. Physiological concepts taught the critics who adapted them for literary analysis that form, particularly novelistic form, must be defined temporally, as a rhythm or time signature, rather than a synchronic structure. In musicological terms, physiological novel theory was

---

[15] Marshall McLuhan, *Understanding Media: The Extensions of Man* (Cambridge, Mass.: MIT Press, 1994), 42–3.

[16] Karl Marx, *Grundrisse: Foundations of the Critique of Political Economy (Rough Draft)*, trans. Martin Nicolaus (London: Pelican, 1973), 92.

interested in horizontal, or rhythmic-melodic, analysis rather than vertical, or harmonic analysis. Temporal form, as critics such as Catherine Gallagher have noted, has long challenged literary formalism, which has preferred to find various ways (such as the influential theories of Percy Lubbock discussed in Chapter 1) to still time in order to detect structure.[17] Only occasionally in the history of twentieth-century formalism or narrative theory—as in Viktor Shklovsky's comment that 'the methods and devices of plot construction are similar to and in principle identical with the devices of, for instance, musical orchestration'—is time embraced with any comfort.[18] Even histories of the novel find time an embarrassment: Ian Watt's *Rise of the Novel* (1957) comments reluctantly on the prolixity of early British fiction, tying it to a range of economic facts, but the lengthiness of Fielding or Richardson fails to enter his famous catalogue of the features of 'formal realism'.[19] Physiological novel theory imagined novelistic form as produced by reading in time, particularly in the rhythms of attention and inattention, slow comprehension and rapid skipping ahead, buildups and discharges of affect. What it sought to specify was what Arjun Appadurai has called the 'structuring temporal rhythm' of a 'socially regulated set of consumption practices'.[20] It might be said, in fact, that in physiological novel theory the act of novel-reading seems like a performance—a performance enacted in and by the nerves—rather than an encounter with an object. As the following chapters will demonstrate, that temporal form could be stretched (as in Eliot and Wagner), or accelerated and retarded (as in late-century speed-reading and Gissing); but the sense of the novel as a process rather than a structure was a fundamental part of Victorian novel theory.

[17] See Catherine Gallagher, 'Formalism and Time', *Modern Language Quarterly* 61/1 (March 2000): 229–51.

[18] Viktor Shklovsky, 'The Relationship between Devices of Plot Construction and General Devices of Style', in *Theory of Prose*, trans. Benjamin Sher (Normal, Ill.: Dalkey Archive Press, 1990), 45. Other works in which the temporality of literary form finds some analysis is that of Wolfgang Iser, particularly his analysis of the 'wandering viewpoint' of the reader, and the more contemporary work of cognitive narratologists such as David Herman, Richard Gerrig, Manfred Jahn, and Mark Turner. See Wolfgang Iser, *The Act of Reading: A Theory of Aesthetic Response* (Baltimore: Johns Hopkins University Press, 1978); David Herman, 'Scripts, Sequences, and Stories: Elements of a Postclassical Narratology', *PMLA* 112 (1997), 1046–59; Richard Gerrig, *Experiencing Narrative Worlds: On the Psychological Activities of Reading* (New Haven: Yale University Press, 1993); Manfred Jahn, 'Frames, Preferences, and the Reading of Third-Person Narratives: Towards a Cognitive Narratology', *Poetics Today* 18 (1997), 441–68; Mark Turner, *Reading Minds: The Study of English in the Age of Cognitive Science* (Princeton: Princeton University Press, 1991).

[19] For his analysis of novelistic length, see Ian Watt, *The Rise of the Novel: Studies in Defoe, Richardson, and Fielding* (Berkeley: University of California Press, 2001), 56–7.

[20] Arjun Appadurai, 'Consumption, Duration, and History', in *Modernity at Large: Cultural Dimensions of Globalization* (Minneapolis: University of Minnesota Press, 1996), 68.

4. *It was an attempt to discover critical tools adapted to novels, not borrowed
   from epic, dramatic, or lyric art.*

No small part of the interest that Victorian novel theory has is the light it
sheds on the protocols of the period's literary criticism. As Mary Poovey has
recently argued, the 'model system' of contemporary literary criticism—the
object that functions as the exemplary instance upon which knowledge-
gathering techniques can be employed, such as the frog was for Victorian
physiologists—continues to be the romantic lyric, a choice tending to foreclose
any interest in readerly response in favor of organic wholes. As Poovey
writes, 'continued reliance on the trope of the organic whole keeps us from
developing a methodology that could analyze what this metaphor effaced in
the first place: reading'.[21] Physiological novel theory's most salient difference
from contemporary novel theory (as well as the Arnoldian criticism whose
visibility still obscures it) is its insistence upon reading as its focus, and
particularly the conditions of *narrative* consumption, making the novel not
just one of many possible genres in its purview but the necessary and sufficient
(i.e., model) genre for its methods. Ideas of 'the total structure' or 'the
logic of the whole'—familiar terms from Cleanth Brooks and Robert Penn
Warren's *Understanding Fiction* (1943), which not incidentally followed their
Understanding Poetry (1938)—are largely absent from physiological novel
theory, which instead hunted the moment-to-moment affects and processes
of reading prolonged narratives, despite occasional relapses, which I discuss
in Chapter 4, into an older discourse of organic form.[22] As this book's
first chapter will demonstrate, much early Victorian novel criticism was also
concerned with distinguishing the novel from drama, as part of an effort to
make solitary rather than collective consumption the standard upon which
criticism should be based. With this in mind, the distinctive and usually
derided practices of Victorian novel criticism, such as lengthy citations and
discussions of the reviewer's physical and psychological reaction to the work
in question (discomfort, boredom, excitement), gain new meaning. They
can be read as attempts to find a discursive form adequate to the task of
analyzing the act of reading novels. When, for instance, Dallas opens his
Times review of Dickens's *Great Expectations* with an analysis of the 'little
half-hours and quarters throughout the day which we sometimes know not
how to fill up', and how that half-attentive state is catered to by periodically
issued narratives like Dickens's, we have a criticism that to our ears sounds

---

[21] See Mary Poovey, 'The Model System of Contemporary Literary Criticism', *Critical Inquiry*
27 (Spring 2001), 438.

[22] Cleanth Brooks and Robert Penn Warren, *Understanding Fiction* (New York: F. S. Crofts,
1943), p. viii.

flippant, but that bears the marks of a pressure to find a neutral critical language for novelistic consumption and its usual modes.[23] One good way of categorizing a critical school or critical practice is to define the pitch, intensity, and duration of readerly attention that it employs and seeks to make normative. The attention requested by physiological novel theory, and so pervasively present in the period's criticism, is pitched toward the forward momentum of reading, its pure seriality, rather than large structural units or small felicities of language.

    5. *Its range of literary evidence was (remarkably, crucially) limited.*

Physiological novel theory was in no way a history of the novel, and furnishes insufficient tools for such a project. Resolutely presentist, its historical grasp of the novel rarely stretched back further than Scott, and in fact tended to be oriented solely toward contemporary fiction, particularly the towering examples of Dickens, who might even be thought of as (by virtue of his extreme popularity) the spur for the theory in the first place, and sensation fiction, which seemed an apt exemplification of the theory's interest in bodily responses. One might even say that physiological critics normalized both Dickens's popularity and sensation fiction's production of occasional readerly shock, making them both constitutive of the genre *per se*; as Alison Winter has noted, early reviews of sensation fiction were explicitly physiological, as was the fiction's thematic and material shape.[24] Precisely because of this normalization, this book will turn to neither Dickens nor any of the sensation novelists of the 1860s and 1870s for its literary evidence, although instances of physiological novel theory's readings of Dickens or sensation fiction are discussed in the following pages. Of more use are examples of self-conscious *response* to physiological novel theory's areas of concern, whether those responses were, as with Eliot's *Daniel Deronda*, nuanced evaluations of a body of physiological theory of reception, or, as with Gissing's *New Grub Street*, embattled and defensive reactions to the perceived threat of a newer version of the physiology of reading. I have found that the most provocative routes into physiological novel theory's impact tend to run through the more self-conscious and detached (if currently more canonical) novels that either resisted, partially embraced, or reformulated the concerns of the preexisting theory. That said, the historical amnesia of the novel theories formulated by physiological theorists is striking and symptomatic. The eighteenth-century novel, not to mention earlier fiction, vanishes entirely in its lens. This is

---

[23] E. S. Dallas [anon.], 'Great Expectations', *The Times*, 17 Oct. 1861, 6.

[24] See Alison Winter, *Mesmerized: Powers of Mind in Victorian Britain* (Chicago: University of Chicago Press, 1998), 322–31, for a vivid illustration of the physiological discourses surrounding the publication and reception of Collins's *The Woman in White* (1859).

perhaps in part a result of its positivist orientation: even late eighteenth-century and early nineteenth-century neural sciences, such as those evaluated by Coleridge in his *Biographia Literaria*, go largely uncited, as if for any purely scientific approach only the current horizon of knowledge matters.[25] It is perhaps also a consequence of its status as a kind of media theory, for which history, as Laurel Brake has recently noted, is often of little importance.[26] Regardless, this theory arises out of a narrow and specifiable range of literary evidence: the popular British fiction of the mid-nineteenth century, from Dickens's novels at its apex to more ephemeral novels at its base. This is a history of the novel only in the sense that Thomas Pavel has defined a 'speculative' history of the novel, one attuned more toward the inner dynamics of generic evolution than any extensive survey of important prior instances.[27]

6. *Its range of intellectual affiliations was (remarkably, crucially) varied.*

However limited its range of literary instances, physiological novel theory was promiscuous in its intellectual links to other cultural zones. As Chapters 2–5 will demonstrate, the study of novelistic reception engendered by physiology had intimate connections to a set of what one might call 'microsciences', or evanescent yet influential scientific formations, such as acoustic natural science (or scientific musicology), 'psychophysics' (the attempt to arrive at a unit measurement for consciousness), ocular or ophthalmological physiology (the study of eye movements), and 'psychometrics' (the attempt to time the speed of neural operations). Attached to these microsciences were a host of important cultural practices that physiology inflected, either directly or indirectly, from listening to music (particularly via the British reception of Wagnerian opera) to typography and page design. The litany of names mentioned in the following chapters who, now largely unknown to literary scholars, had important intersections with or contributions to

---

[25] The omission is even more curious given the evidence of British Romanticism's extensive interactions with theories of mind, most of which are invisible within Victorian physiological novel theory. See Alan Richardson, *British Romanticism and the Science of the Mind* (Cambridge: Cambridge University Press, 2001).

[26] See Brake, *Print in Transition*, pp. xiv–xv, for an analysis of 'the deracination of the study of media from its histories that has become a defining characteristic of the field of media studies and the training of journalists'.

[27] As Pavel defines it, with Lukács's *Theory of the Novel* (1920) as his prime example, '*l'histoire spéculative du roman . . . excelle moins dans l'exhaustivité de son survol*—apanage des histoires naturelle et sociale du roman—*ni dans la comprehension des formes*—spécialité des histoires de la technique—*que dans l'attention accordée à la maturation interne du genre*' (the speculative history of the novel . . . excels less in the exhaustiveness of its purview—the privilege of natural and social histories of the novel—and less in its study of form—the specialty of histories of technique—than in the attention it devotes to the internal maturation of the genre). See Thomas Pavel, *La Pensée du roman* (Paris: Gallimard, 2003), 38.

physiological theories of reception, such as the musicologist Edmund Gurney, the German physicist Gustav Fechner, or the French ophthalmologist Émile Javal, is itself testimony to the odd breadth of physiological criticism outside the range of histories of the novel. The lesson here is that physiological novel theory connected the novel more often to adjacent, or synchronous, cultural zones and technologies than to any lineage of past fiction.

7. *It could imply a politics that distributed values surprisingly differently from our own reflexive assumptions.*

'An immense public has been discovered,' Wilkie Collins famously announced in 1858: 'the next thing to be done is, in a literary sense, to teach that public how to read.'[28] Collins's mixture of openness and condescension to the new social fact of mass literacy is characteristic of much Victorian discourse on the mass reading public, at least for those who did not respond with outright fear or distaste. The evidence, from Altick's *English Common Reader* down to recent studies, tends to reveal that the growth of literacy in Victorian Britain was the occasion, on the part of more traditionally lettered segments of society, for either pure anxiety or anxious efforts to contain or reeducate that new public. The work of physiological novel theorists presents a different picture. Where we might expect fear of mass reading, we get celebrations of its spread; where we look for attempts to shape the tastes or practices of this 'unknown public', we get a tendency to treat those practices, insofar as they were understood, with neutrality. While by no means consistent—the methodologies of physiological criticism could be practiced at once by quasi-radicals like Dallas and conservatives like Oliphant—the politics of physiological criticism does tend to color social facts, particularly the kind of response given to novels, in surprising ways. In Chapter 2, we will see distracted or inattentive reading, a hallmark of conservative jeremiads about mass reading habits, marked out by theorists like Herbert Spencer as a practice of readerly liberty; in Chapter 4 we will see reading in short 'bits', usually associated with barely literate readers, reimagined as the foundation of George Meredith's polished and sophisticated novelistic practice, as a way to heal the division between high and low audiences. The reading practices that we have come to see as characteristics of intellectual seriousness and even civic virtue—elongated attention spans, careful, slow comprehension, alertness at every moment—bore very different values in Victorian literary theory and practice, as signs of class or economic oppression, as instruments of subjection, as elite tastes. The political stakes of physiological novel theory

---

[28] Wilkie Collins, 'The Unknown Public', *Household Words* 18 (21 Aug. 1855), 222.

are often opaque, and somewhat volatile, but continually challenge our usual
distribution of values.

SOCIAL NORMS OF COGNITION: READING, VIRTUE, AND VICTORIAN NOVELS

Any survey of writing on the cognitive impact of reading Victorian fiction,
from the nineteenth century to the present, immediately reveals one striking
historical irony: that the Victorian novel has progressed from being considered
a potentially disastrous fact in the history of consumption, enervating the
intellects of its readers and reducing their ability to concentrate, to being today
a monument to a rigorous kind of comprehension to which contemporary
readers can only vainly aspire. For many alarmist Victorian observers, the
novel's greatest influence was its toxic effect upon readerly cognition. Thus
Alfred Austin, in his 1874 assessment 'The Vice of Reading': 'Reading, as at
present conducted, is rapidly destroying all thinking and all powers of thought.'
Austin's condemnation is pointed specifically at what he calls the ' "realistic"
novel', that narrative form which is 'not read merely, it is devoured', and
which leads to an 'unstrung' will and a 'soddened' understanding.[29] That this
is not merely a Victorian position on the novel is amply demonstrated by the
influential work of Q. D. Leavis, whose *Fiction and the Reading Public* (1932)
charts a catastrophic decline in the quality of the consumption habits of the
British public, for which the Victorian novel is largely to blame. In Leavis's
account, Victorian serial plots destroyed assimilative consciousness ('to read
on a kind of penny-in-the-slot-machine principle is to lose the ability to read
in any other way'), made prolonged attention seem wearisome ('Victorian
popular novelists accustomed the reading public to habits of diminished
vigilance'), and led directly to the culture of the cinema, the magazine, and
popular jazz music, which provides 'a set of habits inimical to mental effort'.[30]
Leavis's history of reading echoes a strain of Victorian thought: namely, that
the Victorians were the first bad readers in Western history, and their novels
were the primary instrument of their lazy, inattentive, patchy, and immature
reading.

   All the more interesting, then, that the Victorian novel occupies a very
different role today as a common locus for reading as an engaged, fully alert,

---

[29] Alfred Austin, 'The Vice of Reading', *Temple Bar* 42 (1874), 252–4.
[30] Q. D. Leavis, *Fiction and the Reading Public* (London: Chatto & Windus, 1932), 157,
230, 224.

and politically sensitive activity, for cognition as heroism.[31] Most frequently, these accounts come from contemporary ethical and political philosophy, which, via a lay cognitive science, recruits the nineteenth-century or realist novel as a training ground for philosophical maturity. Richard Rorty has argued for the novel as a key way in which sensitization 'to the pain of those who do not speak our language' now occurs.[32] Rorty's very general claims are specified and amplified by Martha Nussbaum, who in recent years, most notably in *Love's Knowledge* (1990) and *Poetic Justice* (1995), has made numerous claims about the ethical benefits of novel-reading based on the cognitive processes of consuming Victorian novels, or what she calls the 'readerly activity built into the form'.[33] For Nussbaum, the projects of human sympathy and ethical imagination are engendered by encounters with the *form* of novels, particularly their prolonged duration and descriptive fullness: 'we seem to require a text that shows a temporal sequence of events (that has a plot), that can represent the complexities of a concrete human relationship, that can show both denial and yielding; that gives no definitions and allows the mysterious to remain so.'[34] Thus Nussbaum turns to the Victorian novel, in particular to the Dickens of *David Copperfield* and *Hard Times*, to instantiate her claims of how a reading practice 'that demands both immersion and critical conversation' is best produced by Victorian fiction's temporal amplitude and luxury of circumstantial detail, and how that reading practice is urgently needed: 'If we think of reading in this way, as combining one's own absorbed imagining with periods of more detached (and interactive) critical scrutiny, we can already begin to see why we might find in it an activity well suited to public reasoning in a democratic society.'[35] Why the equally lengthy and detail-rich eighteenth-century novel is never brought forward in these contemporary ethical philosophies of reading is a question of some interest, since this statement is, one might reasonably feel, an updated version

---

[31] The term 'heroism' comes from one of Edward Said's final texts, his essay 'The Return to Philology', in which he writes of 'heroic first readings'—readings characterized by an attentiveness that 'requires alertness and making connections that are otherwise hidden or obscured by the text'. Said's willingness to use the herm 'heroic' stands in useful contrast to other contemporary accounts of reading, which, despite their often exalted claims for the social and psychological benefits of novel-reading, shy away from the language of heroism even in the act of defining reading as such. See Edward Said, 'The Return to Philology', in *Humanism and Democratic Criticism* (New York: Columbia University Press, 2004), 67.

[32] Richard Rorty, *Contingency, Irony, and Solidarity* (Cambridge: Cambridge University Press, 1989), 94.

[33] Martha Nussbaum, *Poetic Justice: The Literary Imagination and Public Life* (Boston: Beacon Press, 1995), 4.

[34] Nussbaum, 'Love's Knowledge', in *Love's Knowledge: Essays on Philosophy and Literature* (Oxford: Oxford University Press, 1990), 281.

[35] Nussbaum, *Poetic Justice*, 9.

of eighteenth-century defenses of the novel, with a language of the moral
sentiments replaced by the language of cognitive science.

Nussbaum's analysis of the form of Victorian fiction as a training process in
ethically valuable cognitive habits depends to a large degree on the separation
of novel-reading from other experiences of consumption and other practices
of everyday life. The novel is not music, for instance, which she argues
'is in its very nature dreamlike and indeterminate in a way that limits its
role in public deliberation'.[36] It is a non-dreamlike escape from what she
elsewhere calls 'daily life, with its routines, its inattentions, its patches of
deadness', into 'the more concentrated attention that produces and animates
the literary text'; this is a form of attention that produces the kind of reflective
yet sympathetic cognition that, Nussbaum would have us believe, democratic
society vitally requires and which, given its usual absence, amounts to a kind of
demotic heroism.[37] And the obverse? Nussbaum's more optimistic orientation
toward the ethically valuable possibilities of novel-reading prevents her from
producing a jeremiad about other consumption habits; but elsewhere a
vibrant strain of contemporary cultural criticism does just that. Sven Birkerts's
Gutenberg Elegies (1994) evokes a world in which textual consumption is
rapidly being eclipsed by visual media, and while he admits that this shift may
have some gains—among them, a 'tolerance' and 'global perspective' that
sound much like the virtues of Rorty's novel-reader—the inevitable losses are
cognitive and also, necessarily, political: 'a fragmented sense of time and a loss
of the so-called duration experience, that depth phenomenon we associate with
reverie'; 'a reduced attention span and a general impatience with sustained
inquiry'; and 'a shattered faith in institutions and in the explanatory narratives
that formerly gave shape to subjective experience'.[38] We cannot think critically
or productively, Birkerts argues, because we have lost touch with the cognitive
habits of reading long narratives—Birkerts prominently mentions Henry

---

[36] Nussbaum, *Poetic Justice*, 6.

[37] Nussbaum, 'Introduction: Form and Content, Philosophy and Literature', in *Love's Knowledge*, 9. Here and elsewhere Nussbaum's argument cites Wayne Booth's *The Company We Keep* (1988), which makes an explicit case for the ethical value of immersiveness in reading, often in language that is far from problematic: 'When a story "works," when we like it well enough to listen to it again and to tell it over and over to ourselves and our friends... it occupies us in a curiously intense way. The pun in "occupy" is useful here. We are occupied in the sense of filling our time with the story—it takes over our time. And we are occupied in the sense of being taken over, colonized: occupied by a foreign imaginary world.... Whenever that does not happen, we can hardly say that we have responded to—that is, behaved responsibly toward—the implied author.' See Wayne Booth, *The Company We Keep: An Ethics of Fiction* (Berkeley: University of California Press, 1988), 139–41. Booth's pun on 'occupation' merely makes explicit the usually buried political problematics around attention, which I explore by way of Thackeray in Ch. 2.

[38] Sven Birkerts, *The Gutenberg Elegies: The Fate of Reading in an Electronic Age* (New York: Ballantine, 1994), 27.

James and Thomas Hardy along with Dickens—that once made critical thinking possible. The argument is familiar and has been produced, in various forms, by many others in recent decades: Geoffrey Hartman complains in *The Fate of Reading* (1975) that we now 'experience and read scanningly', while Alvin Kernan writes in *The Death of Literature* (1990) of the 'episodic, brief, and ephemeral' images of television as against the durative intricacies of narrative art.[39] So influential are these arguments that they have filtered down into our default alibis for the continued teaching and study of Victorian fiction: giving students a cognitive skill set that will enhance their ability to act responsibly (i.e. attentively, immersively) in democratic society.

The ironies here ramify. It is not just that the Victorian novel (in Nussbaum particularly) is employed as a central site for engaged and responsible cognition, but that the media it is now seen as a bulwark against—film, television, electronic technology—are described in precisely the same terms as an earlier tradition had explained the novel itself: as a piecemeal, 'episodic', lazily consumed form that sacrifices mental effort to the dubious pleasures of inattentive, uncritical intake. The irony is increased by the fact that the very same texts and figures—such as Nussbaum's chosen example of Dickens—perform diametrically opposite functions: enervating the mental fabric of the public, or training them in the kind of sympathetic alertness upon which healthy democracies rest; exemplifying a culture of immature and distracted consumption, or offering a passage into a world of strenuous, even athletic imagination. This would seem to suggest the following: that from its time to ours, the reader of Victorian fiction, in the cognitive activity she supposedly undergoes, is a charged political figure, capable of extreme embodiments of virtue and vice. Furthermore: that the supposedly neutral cognitive activities of reading are anything but. And lastly: that if we are truly to understand the cultural work of the novel, in its time or in ours, we need much more careful, historically specifiable ways to think about its effect upon the cognitive activities of its readers, ways that read the novel not as merely directly indicative of culture at large (as in Leavis), or as a refuge from it (as in Nussbaum or Birkerts), but in a complicated set of exchanges, compromises, and local engagements with other forms of consumption, aesthetic and nonaesthetic both. We need, that is, nuanced and evenhanded accounts of what I might call the *social norms of cognition* of given historical moments, and how various artistic forms (like the novel) enter into social history by inflecting and revising those norms. Without any understanding of social norms of cognition, we will inevitably be

---

[39] Geoffrey Hartman, 'The Fate of Reading', in *The Fate of Reading and Other Essays* (Chicago: University of Chicago Press, 1975), 251; Alvin Kernan, *The Death of Literature* (New Haven: Yale University Press, 1990), 150.

stuck with narratives of decline, in which the novel either precipitates decline or acts as our last, best hope.

These accounts should be evenhanded, because the cognitive activities of reading are so embedded in social reality—thus *social* norms of cognition—that to describe them apart from their social context is to inevitably produce a tendentious or distorting vision. This was Raymond Williams's point in *The Long Revolution* (1961), in a response to the Leavisite condemnation of the post-Victorian reading public:

> Reading as this kind of easy drug is the permanent condition of a great bulk of ephemeral writing. But the question still is one of the circumstances in which the drug becomes necessary. . . . The kind of attention required by serious literature is both personally and socially only variously possible. The conditions of social variation ought to command our main attention: the association of railway travel with an increase in this kind of reading is obviously significant. More difficult to analyze is the evident distinction between ways of living which stimulate attention and allow rest, and ways which produce neither attention nor rest, but only an unfocused restlessness that has somehow to be appeased.[40]

Cognitive categories like attention or duration, in other words, do not have stable ethical and political meanings over time, however much the tradition of thought about Victorian fiction's cognitive impact may assume that they do. They gain their political meaning from specific intersections of material, social, artistic, and even physical practices, in which hierarchies of status and taste play an often obscured role. Williams stops short of describing the full range of social context coloring the cognitive activities of reading, but we might supply a partial list that extends his patent concerns with class and education level: adjacent forms of consumption, from other artistic media (music, visual art) to other nonartistic textual media; the characteristics of the textual object, its cost, size, portability, ease of use; the likely settings and milieux of reading, along with prevalent physical habits associated with reading; language competence in more globalized, multilingual societies; the presence or absence of leisure, and the cultural norms at any given moment that valorize or devalue it; and—not to be ignored—the literary form of the textual object, the ways in which it solicits or forbids certain kinds of consumption, the ways in which it refers to, models itself on, or contrasts itself with other experiences that compete for a reader's time and energy.

This is where a look back at the physiological novel theory of the nineteenth century provides assistance. It offers us a language through which the novel was connected to other consumption practices in Victorian culture, as well as to the

---

[40] Raymond Williams, *The Long Revolution* (New York and London: Columbia University Press, 1961), 193.

physical and material routines of reading. By virtue of its attempt, at its higher reaches, at a value-neutral description of novel-reading, it unexpectedly lays bare some of the hidden political ironies of the cognitive virtues discussed from Leavis to Nussbaum, and demonstrates that seemingly unproblematic qualities like 'alertness' and 'attention' have complicated histories. As one of the most influential discourses about the novel and reading of its time, physiological novel theory helps ground otherwise abstract and potentially tendentious arguments, which can be both misleadingly gratifying and unwarrantably pessimistic, about what Victorian novels 'do'. Its way of imagining the 'social forms of cognition' proper to the novel form invites us to rethink, in a fashion more responsive to social history, our habitual notions of the virtue, or lack thereof, involved in the consumption of long novelistic narrative.

That theory's broad assumptions, metalanguage, major sites and practitioners, critical protocols, and significant variations are sketched in this book's first chapter, which is intended as both a recovery of a largely vanished way of theorizing the novel and an explanation of why that version of novel theory was largely abandoned by the twentieth century. Specific applications of physiological novel theory, and vexed points within it, are raised in the book's subsequent four chapters, and it is in its intersection with specific novelistic practices that its potential, and problems, become most evident. The physiological explanation of human attention and its limits, in relation to Thackerayan social anatomies like *The Newcomes* (1853–5) in Chapter 2, helps illuminate a fictional style suspicious of rapt absorption and willing to explore the potential liberations of distraction. The problem of elongated artistic forms—forms whose length makes continuous, heightened attention impossible and acts of recollection difficult—is explored in Chapter 3 by triangulating Richard Wagner's impact upon British musical culture, George Eliot's role in that relation, and the physiological musicology that was the primary language through which Eliot, among other observers, approached Wagnerian opera, and that served to bridge novels like *Daniel Deronda* (1876), and music drama, as parallel temporal experiences. Chapter 4 explores physiological novel theory's vexed relation with notions of 'organic form' by exploring the discourse of psychophysics, a theory of the discrete building-blocks of consciousness, and how its description of 'units of consciousness' made older notions of organic wholeness untenable, as reflected in both Vernon Lee's essays on the novel form and George Meredith's ostentatiously fragmented *The Egoist* (1879). Chapter 5 relates the development of speed-reading, as both a technique and a field of scientific investigation, to the three-volume novels of George Gissing, particularly *New Grub Street* (1891), which registers and resists a cultural desire for accelerated comprehension. Together, these final four chapters, by contextualizing, testing, and probing the limits of what physiological novel theory could and could not encompass, offer a historicization of novel-reading's cognitive horizon that tries to avoid the pitfalls of condemnation and celebration. Such a historical recovery should—it is the gambit of this book—bring to light many of the novel's prior, and often surprising, complicities with and resistances to social norms of consumption and cognition, and help us to reconceptualize the novel's place in our own culture, our own teaching, and our own reading.

Part I

Theories of Reading

A Critical Prehistory

1

Mass Reading and Physiological Novel Theory

> Are we therefore reading automata?
>
> Lewes, *Physical Basis of Mind*

Novel theory—that loosely defined field of attempts to codify the generic uniqueness of a notoriously protean form—has often undertaken inquiries into the origins of the novel, even critiques of the idea of its origin; but it has nonetheless been prey to its own myths of First Causes and creations *ex nihilo*. Among the most tenacious of those myths has centered on the heroic period of novel theory's supposed birth and first efflorescence, book-ended by Henry James's 1884 polemic 'The Art of Fiction' and the twin masterworks of, respectively, Continental and Anglo-American novel theory, Georg Lukács's *The Theory of the Novel* (1920) and Percy Lubbock's *The Craft of Fiction* (1921). Between James and Lubbock, this familiar account runs, foundational methodological steps were taken: the novel's artistic dignity was successfully defended, major analytic categories were defined and explored, and a canon of representative examples, from Richardson to Flaubert, was implicitly agreed upon. One of the enabling rhetorical gestures of these novel theorists, in fact, was an assertion that no theory of the novel preexisted them, and that therefore no serious debate with any predecessor was necessary by way of ground clearing. So successful has this strategy been that even the most otherwise acute and suspicious of historians of literary criticism have failed to rebut these claims to origin and, despite evidence to the contrary, have tended instead to reinforce our picture of a *fin de siècle* heroic age.[1]

---

[1] Much of the archival work of excavating the pre-Jamesian history of novel theory is contained in two valuable histories and one important anthology: Richard Stang's *The Theory of the Novel in England, 1850–1870* (New York: Columbia University Press, 1959), Kenneth Graham's *English Criticism of the Novel, 1865–1900* (Oxford: Clarendon Press, 1963), and John Charles Olmsted's three-volume *A Victorian Art of Fiction: Essays on the Novel in British*

Traces nonetheless exist, even contemporaneous with the period of novel theory's Jamesian formation, of an earlier strain of theorizing about the novel's generic uniqueness, one which owes nothing to either Lukács's Hegelianism or the formalism of James and Lubbock. It is this hidden species of novel theory that this chapter will pursue. Long after it had vanished—a defeat for which the success of James and Lubbock was partly responsible—we can catch a marvelously condensed version of this earlier variety in Paul Valéry's 1927 lecture 'Propos sur la poésie'. Valéry's task, to differentiate prose fiction from verse, is underwritten by a psychological, even physiological, consideration of each genre's effect upon its reader:

Considérez les attitudes comparés du lecteur de romans et du lecteur de poèmes. Il peut être le même homme, mais qui diffère excessivement de soi-même quand il lit l'un ou l'autre ouvrage. Voyez le lecteur de roman quand il se plonge dans la vie imaginaire que lui intime sa lecture. Son corps n'existe plus. Il soutient son front de ses deux mains. Il est, il se meut, il agit et pâtit dans l'esprit seul. Il est absorbé par ce qu'il dévore; il ne peut se retenir, car je ne sais quel demon le presse d'avancer. Il veut la suite, et la fin, il est en proie à une sorte d'aliénation: il prend parti, il triomphe, il s'attriste, il n'est plus lui-même, il n'est plus qu'un cerveau séparé de ses forces extérieurs, c'est-à-dire livré à ses images, traversant une sorte de *crise de crédulité*.

Tout autre est le lecteur de poèmes . . .

En somme, entre l'action du poème et celle du récit ordinaire, la différence est d'ordre psychologique. Le poème se déploie dans un domaine plus riche de nos fonctions de mouvement, il exige de nous une participation qui est plus proche de l'action complète, cependant que le conte et le roman nous transforment plutôt en sujets du rêve et de notre faculté d'être hallucinés.[2]

Consider the comparative attitudes of the reader of novels and the reader of poems. They may be the same man, but he is entirely different as he reads one or the other work. Watch the reader of a novel plunge into the imaginary life his book shows him. His body no longer exists. He leans his forehead on his two hands. He lives, moves, acts, and suffers only in the mind. He is absorbed by what he is devouring; he cannot

---

Periodicals (New York: Garland, 1979). However, as Homer Brown has claimed, both Stang's and Graham's accounts cannot entirely evade the power of James's categories, and are therefore 'written toward the telos of the Jamesian novel'. See Homer Brown, *Institutions of the English Novel: From Defoe to Scott* (Philadelphia: University of Pennsylvania Press, 1997), 196. One exemplary recent history of novel theory, Dorothy Hale's influential *Social Formalism: The Novel in Theory from Henry James to the Present* (Stanford, Calif.: Stanford University Press, 1998), is paradigmatic in its reassertion—albeit in fresh terms—of James's foundational role; for Hale, James's concentration on 'point of view' determines novel theory's status as, essentially, an epistemology of alterity. What seems certain is that the myth of Jamesian origination—as Hale puts it, 'the Anglo-American scholarly record is virtually unanimous in crediting James and Lubbock as the forefathers of novel theory'—is as durable as it is flawed; however often it has been historicized, contested, or even debunked, it rises again. See Hale, *Social Formalism*, 22.

  [2] Paul Valéry, 'Propos sur la poésie', in *Œuvres* (Paris: Gallimard, 1957), 1374–5.

restrain himself, for a kind of demon drives him on. He wants the continuation and the end; he is prey to a kind of madness; he takes sides, he is saddened, he is no longer himself, he is no more than a brain separated from its outer forces, that is, given up to its images, going through a sort of *crisis of credulity*.

How very different is the reader of poems . . .

In fact, between the action of a poem and that of an ordinary narrative, the difference is of a psychological kind. The poem unfolds itself in a richer sphere of our functions of movement, it exacts from us a participation that is nearer to complete action, whereas the story and the novel transform us rather into slaves of a dream and of our faculty of being hallucinated.

If we stand within the usual institutional and discursive parameters of what, after James and Lukács, goes under the term 'theory of the novel', we mean by 'novel' either an object—a loosely distinct kind of prose narration—or a compositional practice, one given over to a set of formal assumptions about ordinary experience and its narrative expression. If we mean the latter, we can extend our consideration of the 'novelistic' or 'novelesque' to other media (cinema, television, even, lately, computer gaming), but we still root ourselves within a familiar theoretical network, one which privileges either an objectivist account of the novel (this is the kind of thing a novel is) or an account oriented toward production (this is how the 'novelistic' is written or socially propagated). What, however, is Valéry's speculation but a theory of the novel extrapolated from the manner in which it is usually consumed? Put another way, Valéry here outlines a genre theory based on modes of consumption, one which would necessarily take the form of a psychological, or more properly *physiological*, investigation. No longer the study of an object ('the novel') or a compositional practice ('the novelistic'), Valéry's novel theory is the study of the affective and physiological responses called forth by the novel's form. Remarkable as Valéry's shift of attention is—from the object, or the composer of the object, to the person holding the object—it is not unique. It is, in fact, belated: it is a last, isolated, and condensed expression of physiological novel theory as it was practiced in Britain and France, a theory that, in its combination of scientific/positivistic investigation and literary analysis, presents us with a vanished interdisciplinary formation.

That earlier strain of novel theory sought to determine the 'physiological' (what we might now call 'cognitive') dimensions of the response that a given form elicits, and as such engaged in a serious effort to link the aesthetic dis-tinctiveness of the novel with the habits of mass reading. The head-in-hands obliviousness that Valéry dismissively evokes is central to nineteenth-century novel theory—it is, in fact, the datum from which it begins; and therefore the delineation of what Valéry calls 'récit ordinaire' must find the tools to describe a *lecteur ordinaire*. Such is the embedded methodology of nineteenth-century physiological novel theory, which can be detected scattered across Western European writing on the novel, but that had its moment of greatest concentration from roughly 1850 to 1880, when a host of eminent proto-scientific theorists—G. H. Lewes (1817–78), Alexander Bain (1818–1903), E. S. Dallas (1828–79), Hippolyte Taine (1828–93), and Émile Hennequin (1858–88) most notably, followed later in the century by Vernon Lee (1856–1935)—as well as influential critics such as R. H. Hutton (1826–97), Geraldine Jewsbury (1812–80), and Margaret Oliphant (1828–97), produced the variety of novel theories and critical practices that took novel-reading as their inspiration, and consumption as their primary analytic category. Envisioning novel theory before James necessitates describing an intellectual task so different in its emphases—positivistic, experimental, relatively nonjudgmental about the habits, tendencies, or social effects of the expansion of literacy, largely neutral on the merits of various novelists and novelistic schools—that its invisibility is almost guaranteed.

Many additional factors contributed to this posthumous concealment. Not the least is the absolute contemporaneousness of the term 'novel theory', which, in the effort to expand beyond the more limited purview of 'the theory of the novel', covers a wide range of intellectual endeavors: narrative theory in the tradition of Lubbock, Wayne Booth, and Gérard Genette, theories of social subjectivity in the manner of Lukács or Lucien Goldmann, and theories of language such as those of Mikhail Bakhtin.[3] Insofar as nineteenth-century critics fit none of these categories easily, it has been difficult to discern how they might feed into our sense of novel theory's contours. Furthermore, as this chapter will argue, both the institutional and disciplinary boundaries of nineteenth-century novel theory are far different from what the post-Jamesian tradition has led us to expect. Genre theories of the novel were produced by an only incipiently institutionalized, loosely affiliated collection of journalists, physiological and psychological scientists, aestheticians, and even occasionally early examples of academics in English literary studies, who—far from the image of the Victorian critic as conservative moral censor—were often engaged in radical causes of various sorts and tended to represent the intellectual Left of their time. In their work we can find a strange alignment of disciplinary stars. A positivist physiological psychology met aesthetic theory, which in turn linked up with a sociology of a mass reading public to produce a remarkably consistent, if locally varied, approach to theorizing the novel form. Although the period saw the first signs of an academicizing of novel studies—David Masson, professor of English literature at University College, London, issued

---

[3] Much of the work of adumbrating and defending the wider category of 'novel theory' has been carried out by Hale, who offers an invigorating capsule history in *Social Formalism*, 2–19.

his pivotal *British Novelists and their Styles* in 1859—the work of most novel theorists was as likely to appear in reviews, periodical essays, or psychological textbooks as in literary monographs or surveys.[4] Furthermore, the 'theory' these writers produced was resolutely ahistorical; unlike such earlier works as Clara Reeve's *The Progress of Romance* (1785), Anna Barbauld's 'On the Origin and Progress of Novel-Writing' (1810), or John Colin Dunlop's *The History of Fiction* (1814), no attempt was made to write a literary genealogy of the novel, which was assumed to be not the offspring of some prior genre (such as 'romance' or epic) but instead something closer to *a mode of contemporary consumption*.

Put simply, what nineteenth-century theorists invite us to consider is what novel theory would look like if we restore the peculiarities and specific features of consuming novels to its set of analytic categories. Indeed, the methodological horizon of nineteenth-century novel theory suggests an intriguing revision of the usual aims and tools of the history of reading. We might summarize their wager as follows: what if the history of reading could be discovered not (solely) in records of individual reading acts—marginalia, journal reviews, histories of criticism, commonplace books, and autobiographies—but ossified in the very form of texts themselves, in the genetic code, so to speak, of genre itself, which evolves in a reciprocal relation with the reading modes they determine and are in turn determined by?[5] Put more simply, can genre ever be considered without a study of the peculiar responses (mental, physiological, social) that each genre uniquely elicits? Can we speak of generalized (and generalizable) responses to a genre, and can those responses be detected within the forms of literary works? In short, to paraphrase Valéry's question, instead of asking

---

[4] Masson's work has received renewed attention as an example of what Homer Brown has called 'institutional' histories of the novel, although it has gone unnoticed that the institution Masson represented—academic literary criticism—was far less influential in the formation of nineteenth-century novel theory than several other institutions, such as experimental physiology or periodical reviewing. Other mid-Victorian novel histories, such as John Cordy Jeaffreson's *Novels and Novelists from Elizabeth to Victoria*, 2 vols. (London: Hurst and Blackett, 1858), were written outside the academy by writers specializing in general matters of cultural taste. The tendency of recent work to equate institutionality *per se* with the university elides competing visions of what 'institutions' may have looked like, and as a result obscures our view of the wide range of disciplinary and institutional streams that nourished the study of the novel.

[5] 'Form' is, in fact, the missing determinant in most formulations of the methodology of the history of reading. Finding a *via media* between the liberty of individual readers and the determinations of social context has been a constant preoccupation of those historians and critics working, like Roger Chartier, in the wake of the *Annales* school. While several possibilities have been raised—such as Tony Bennett's 'reading formation', or 'a set of discursive and intertextual determinations that organize and animate the practice of reading'—genre, or some concept of literary form, has never been part of the solutions offered. See Tony Bennett, 'Texts in History: The Determination of Readings and their Texts', in *Reception Study: From Literary Theory to Cultural Studies*, ed. James Machor and Philip Goldstein (London: Routledge, 2001), 66.

what a novel *is*, can we ask what a novel *does*?[6] Can we, with nineteenth-century novel theory as an incitement, reimagine the novel as a technology? To end the novel's sequestration from other modes of consumption and other cultural technologies may mean to end its strange priority within much contemporary theory—its status as, for instance, the epic of alienated man or the form of bourgeois society *tout court*—but may offer us, by way of compensation, a clearer picture of its cultural impact at various historical moments.

SON CORPS N'EXISTE PLUS: THE DISAPPEARING READER

Within the field of late-nineteenth-century aesthetic theory, 'The Art of Fiction'—James's pivotal 1884 review, and dismissal, of Walter Besant's short study of the same name—presents itself as a fresh departure: 'Only a short time ago it might have been supposed that the English novel was not what the French call *discutable*. It had no air of having a theory, a conviction, a consciousness of itself behind it—of being the expression of an artistic faith.'[7] While it will become clear that James's annunciation is more an enabling blindness than an accurate description of the critical surround by the 1880s, the success of his historical account of novel theory—that prior to his moment there has been none to speak of—has been abiding. Part of this success can be traced to his choice of antagonists. Besant's essay is weak in precisely the places James identifies: his 'rules' of fiction are vague, his exhortations on behalf of the novel's moral purpose are bland and unnuanced, and his advice on narratorial personality ('in story-telling, as in almsgiving, a cheerful countenance works wonders, and a hearty manner greatly helps the teller and pleases the listener') approaches self-parody.[8] Perhaps most damningly, Besant's attitude toward the market power of the novel is riven with contradictions. While his essay defends the aesthetic status of the novel with reference to its popularity and cultural influence, and at times constructs

---

[6] This phrase, which so aptly expresses Valéry's brief novel theory, is borrowed from Deidre Lynch and William Warner, who describe the novel studies of the 1990s as a redirection of critical attention 'from refining the definition of the novel as a literary type to understanding how novels produce social divisions: from *what a novel is* to *what novels do*'. See their introduction to *Cultural Institutions of the Novel* (Durham, NC: Duke University Press, 1996), 2. Lynch and Warner's sense of novelistic agency is quite different from the senses of nineteenth-century novel theory, but they nevertheless share a commitment to genre as an agent, not merely as a taxonomic category.

[7] Henry James, 'The Art of Fiction', in *Henry James: Literary Criticism: Essays on Literature, American Writers, English Writers*, ed. Leon Edel (New York: Library of America, 1984), 44.

[8] Walter Besant, *The Art of Fiction* (Boston: Cupples, Upham, 1885), 37.

a liberal argument that the publishing market is an infallible guide to aesthetic value, he is at other moments uneasy about such an equation:

Unfortunately, there has grown up of late a bad fashion of measuring success too much by the money it seems to command. It is not always, remember, the voice of the people which elects the best man, and though in most cases it follows that a successful novelist commands a large sale of his works, it may happen that the Art of a great writer is of such a kind that it may never become widely popular. . . . So that a failure to hit the popular taste does not always imply failure in Art. How, then, is one to know, when people do not ask for his work, if he has really failed or not? I think he must know without being told if he has failed to please. . . . The unlucky dramatist can complain that his piece was badly mounted and badly acted. The novelist cannot, because he is sure not to be badly read.[9]

What we might glean from this passage and others like it in Besant is the following logic: the market (which is the reader writ large) is a reliable test of novelistic success, except when it isn't. Value may pass unrecognized or unrewarded, yet novels cannot be 'badly read'; their virtues and defects are not opaque to any or all readers. The qualified liberalism of Besant's essay—that the people know best, with exceptions—expresses an unresolved ambiguity characteristic of his moment: how to relate the great social fact of the novel, its popular success, with any appraisal of merit or analysis of technique. James's solution is to free novel theory from its obligation to consider popular response by directly contradicting Besant's premise: virtually the pertinent social characteristic of the novel, for James, is the certainty that it is (has been, will be) badly read.

The peculiar aspect of James's polemic with Besant is that it refuses to supplant Besant's vague 'rules' with any more specific technical precepts, and refrains from working out the implications of the social-ethical responsibilities of fiction that Besant adduces, but repeatedly insists upon pressing the case for the poor consumption habits of novel-readers. For James, those habits become more than an incidental fact—they are a key to a methodology. Ventriloquizing the public in order to ridicule its (rather Besant-like) confusions becomes a rhetorical move of some power:

Literature should be either instructive or amusing, and there is in many minds an impression that these artistic preoccupations, the search for form, contribute to neither end, interfere indeed with both. They are too frivolous to be edifying, and too serious to be diverting; and they are moreover priggish and paradoxical and superfluous. That, I think, represents the manner in which the latent thought of many people who read novels as an exercise in skipping would explain itself if it were to become articulate.[10]

---

[9] Ibid. 38–9.   [10] H. James, 'Art of Fiction', 48.

For the reader who wants 'incident and movement, so that we shall wish to jump ahead', no considerations of form are possible.[11] *Il veut la suite, et la fin, il est en proie à une sorte d'aliénation*: Valéry's maddened reader is close indeed to the *lecteur ordinaire* who appears in James's attack on Besant; both imagined that novel-readers suffer from an illness of sequence, an inability to either retard the temporal flow of narrative or to sublate that flow into some synchronic idea of 'form'.

In his 1899 piece 'The Future of the Novel' James presses the attack again, this time more explicitly:

> The book, in the Anglo-Saxon world, is almost everywhere, and it is in the form of the voluminous prose fable that we see it penetrate easiest and farthest. Penetration appears really to be directly aided by mere mass and bulk. There is an immense public, if public be the name, inarticulate, but abysmally absorbent, for which, at its hours of ease, the printed volume has no other association.[12]

The sexualized interaction between novel and public here is abetted by yet another shortcoming of that public's reading habits: the tendency to total, nearly aphasic absorption. *Il est absorbé par ce qu'il dévore*: once again, like Valéry's novel-reader, James's novel-public combines an accelerated desire for plot with an uncritical engrossment, the first a temporal dilemma, the second a slippage of consciousness into something approaching a sleepwalking creduli-ty. The terms of the condemnation are, of course, socially coded—James elsewhere lays some blame on national education and its diffusion of litera-cy—and this aspect of the matter has often been noticed.[13] What has received much less attention is their cognitive dimension. Whatever the social causes behind the geometrical increase in the novel-reading population, what is of more analytic moment to James is that population's cognitive habits, which are so poor as to require explicit disowning. The standpoint of the reader must be abandoned, and the standpoint of the producer must be taken up; of genre distinctions, James adds that they 'have little reality or interest for the producer, from whose point of view it is of course that we are attempting to consider the art of fiction'.[14]

'Of course': perhaps Besant would assent, since his article was also, in a sense, an advice manual for aspiring novelists. But the function of that 'of course' was precisely to obscure the more powerful, far more implicit antagonists of James's work: quasi-professionalized novel critics for whom a careful analysis

---

[11] H. James, 'Art of Fiction', 48.

[12] H. James, 'The Future of the Novel', in *Henry James*, 100.

[13] See, e.g., Jonathan Freedman, *Professions of Taste: Henry James, British Aestheticism, and Commodity Culture* (Stanford, Calif.: Stanford University Press, 1990).

[14] H. James, 'Art of Fiction', 55.

of novel-reading would yield both aesthetic rules for the novel and a generic definition. We might, therefore, think of 'The Art of Fiction', so long lionized as the birth of novel theory, as a deft evasion of more formidable claims, worked out through a clever sideswipe at a defenseless opponent. If, in other words, we have mistaken James's target as moralistic, belletristic Victorian criticism in the mode of Besant, we might do better to consider his true target as the positivistic novel theory of the century's middle decades; by using Besant as a straw-man to achieve a denigration of the cognitive shortcomings of novel-reading-as-usual, James upends the central methodological prop of that more entrenched version of novel theory.

We can detect in James's key novel-theory texts, then, the discarding of any theorization of reading, a gesture which was given a more thoroughly philosophical, even metaphysical, justification by his successors. The most important refinement of James's condemnation of novel-reading is Percy Lubbock's disowning of reading, in *The Craft of Fiction*, as a datum at all useful to the theorist. Lubbock's methodological dilemma is announced with unparalleled explicitness:

To grasp the shadowy and fantasmal form of a book, to hold it fast, to turn it over and survey it at leisure—that is the effort of a critic of books, and it is perpetually defeated. Nothing, no power, will keep a book steady and motionless before us, so that we may have time to examine its shape and design. As quickly as we read, it melts and shifts in the memory; even at the moment when the last page is turned, a great part of the book, its finer detail, is already vague and doubtful. . . . The experience of reading it has left something behind, and these relics we call by the book's name; but how can they be considered to give us the material for judging and appraising the book?[15]

The problem here is twofold, and remarkably close to James's critique of novel-reading-as-usual: the inescapably temporal facts of reading, and the psychological facts that obscure judgment (forgetting, selective attention). It has now been posed, however, as an epistemological problem common to any temporal form, rather than an aspect of half-educated mass consumption. In elevating what was for James largely a social problem (or a problem of certain socialized forms of consumption) into a transhistorical question of the apprehension of temporal data, Lubbock has already provided himself with his solution: a transcendence of temporality that, metaphorically, calls for *distancing*: 'So far from losing ourselves in the world of the novel, we must hold it away from us, see it all in detachment, and use the whole of it to make the image we see, the book itself.'[16] The problem of novel theory for Lubbock

---

[15] Percy Lubbock, *The Craft of Fiction* (New York: Viking, 1957), 1–2.
[16] Ibid. 6. Dorothy Hale's term for Lubbock's position here, 'noetic materialism', is an apt description of his attempt to make the substance of narrative a synchronic mental idea; we

is an epistemological one—how can we make a whole out of a temporal succession?—and can be solved only by eliminating, through 'detachment' (literally and figuratively holding the novel 'away from us'), the affective and psychological factors that are, Lubbock admits, unavoidably part of reading itself. In essence, the job of the critic is *not to read*, but to extract data from the novel that make up mental wholes, to avoid everywhere the temporal flow and affective identifications that infect novel-reading. Plot summary (the précis, the master map) is one way in which that temporality can be suspended, and therefore it becomes a familiar aspect of novel theory after Lubbock.

A battery of images of reading is then marshaled by Lubbock to display their inherent futility: 'Not as a single form, however, but as a moving stream of impressions, paid out of the volume in a slender thread as we turn the pages—that is how the book reaches us. . . . The impressions that succeed one another, as the pages of the book are turned, are to be built into a structure.'[17] In yet another influential and creative metaphorization of James's earlier practice, Lubbock writes a novel theory from the standpoint of the producer, although now to 'write' a novel instead of to 'read' it is a purely mental act available to any attentive participant in a fiction. It has, in fact, become a property of any truly critical reading: a rewriting of the novel in question with an eye to dissolving its temporal, or narrative, aspects. Lubbock here points the way to the *lisible/scriptible* distinction that would take such root in more contemporary theory. It is worth noting that this rather abstract epistemological point arises out of a distaste for the common characteristics of novel-reading, a distaste which in turn is a matter, first and foremost, of disgust at the novel's social ubiquity.

If novel theory therefore can not pursue any of the experiential, or phenomenological, questions of novel-reading—note how Lubbock prefaces his work with a phenomenology of reading in order to prove its ultimate uselessness—it cannot pursue any of the social questions of the novel's mass success. Here James's theoretical work, dotted throughout with dismayed considerations of the novel's wide dissemination and the disparate composition of its usual audiences, stands in stark contrast to Lubbock's silence on

---

might also reflect upon the strange recurrence of Lubbock's own metaphor, the book held 'away from us . . . all in detachment', in Franco Moretti's recent call for 'distanced reading'. If Lubbock's primary dilemma is the temporality of fiction, his secondary dilemma—the too-focused engrossment common to consuming temporal forms—has again, at the end of the twentieth century, become a critical sore point. See Hale, *Social Formalism*, 62; Franco Moretti, 'Conjectures on World Literature', *New Left Review* 1 (2000), 56–8. For a compelling recent attempt to rehabilitate the language of 'detachment', see Amanda Anderson, *The Powers of Distance: Cosmopolitanism and the Cultivation of Detachment* (Princeton: Princeton University Press, 2001).

[17] Lubbock, *Craft of Fiction*, 14, 19.

the subject. To disown reading *per se* means to reject any consideration of market power, popular habits of consumption, or material aspects of book publication, sales, and use; whereas James could comfortably muse on the sheer bulk of the average novel and the possible aesthetic significance of that fact, Lubbock shields novel theory from the contaminations of materiality or social agency. The resolutely dehistoricized tone of novel theories written in the wake of Lubbock is a testament to the power of this methodological move. Unlike the genealogies of Reeve's *Progress of Romance* or Barbauld's 'Origin and Progress of Novel-Writing'—works whose very titles bear witness to their historicizing energies—Lubbock's followers abandon history, literary or otherwise, for abstraction. Such post-Lubbock textbooks as Edwin Muir's *The Structure of the Novel* (1928), Van Meter Ames's *Aesthetics of the Novel* (1928), Carl Grabo's *The Technique of the Novel* (1928), and Pelham Edgar's *The Art of the Novel* (1933) depend largely upon an enabling silence about the novel's social role, rooted in an even firmer silence about the act of novel-reading.

This is not merely to recycle familiar observations about Lubbock's formalism and the impact it had upon prewar Anglo-American studies of the novel; it is to resituate our sense of that formalism as a purposeful evasion of response theory as a whole, of reading in particular, and specifically of the affective and cognitive dimensions of reading. Lubbock's solution, again borrowed from James, is well known: a concentration upon 'point of view': 'The whole intricate question of method, in the craft of fiction,' he famously proclaimed, 'I take to be governed by the relation in which the narrator stands to the story.'[18] The best way *not* to read is to center investigations on those aspects of novels where knowledge—a sudden cognition of a whole—is revealed; the moments when characters have revelations, when new information is imparted by the narrative voice. Novel theory therefore becomes a species of epistemology: how we learn, in other words, not how we encounter a succession of incidents (which would necessarily partake of the misleading temporal flow to which mere reading submits). Lubbock is interested in how we *know*, not how we *react*; he is writing not only against the 'inarticulate, but abysmally absorbent' public, but also against a 'reactive' form of reading. There is, however, a lurking dialectical consequence to this choice: by transforming novel theory into an epistemological theory and away from any affective dimension, Lubbock risks making novel-reading, even the abstract brand he discusses, an 'informational' process, which would be uncomfortably close to the commercialized, everyday forms of consumption that he and James began by rejecting. There is, in fact, a peculiar sense that novel-reading is, by virtue of the purely communicative role of 'point of view', not very distant

---

[18] Ibid. 251.

from newspaper-reading or advertisement-reading, other modes of textual consumption that depend more upon the transmission of information than the diffusions of affect. Take his analysis of how 'point of view' operates in James's *Wings of the Dove*:

Presently her great hidden facts have passed into the possession of the reader whole, so to speak—not broken into detail, bit by bit, not pieced together descriptively, but so implied and suggested that at some moment or other they spring up complete and solid in the reader's attention. Exactly how and where did it happen? Turning back, looking over the pages again, I can mark the very point, perhaps, at which the thing was liberated and I became possessed of it; I can see the word that finally gave it to me. But at the time it may easily have passed unnoticed; the enlightening word did not seem peculiarly emphatic as it was uttered, it was not announced with any particular circumstance; and yet, presently—there was the piece of knowledge that I had not possessed before.[19]

In the process of demonstrating the delusiveness of reading—that the temporal flow of reading obscures the brilliance of James's presentation—Lubbock transforms Milly Theale's 'great hidden facts' into a 'piece of knowledge', or in other words, information. That James's informative technique is particularly subtle sets his text apart, but does not in essence distinguish it from more directly, or crudely, informative texts.[20] That without any theory of affect Lubbock's formalism risks turning the novel into an indirect or convoluted informational technology was a danger largely unforeseen by his enthusiastic adaptors. In many ways this risk fit comfortably enough into significant strains of earlier literary theory, be they the many accounts of the novel's reliance upon realism or Matthew Arnold's attempt to make *truth*, not affect, central to the critical enterprise.[21]

Turning pages (or sequence), burying one's head in a book (engrossment), becoming oblivious to the outside world (what Valéry called *une sorte d'aliénation*): whether we think of these as physical or mechanical facts, cognitive or psychological facts, or social facts, they are nonetheless all barred from

---

[19] Lubbock, *Craft of Fiction*, 176.

[20] It is Benjamin, in 'The Storyteller', who first explicitly links the narrative mode of the novel to the emergent culture of 'information', but in the work of the early post-Jamesian formalists that same link is made implicitly, without a sense of its theoretical consequences; Benjamin's comment that information appear 'understandable in itself' is close to Lubbock's idea that novelistic information—once flashed upon the mind of the reader—requires no complex past to be comprehensible: it is felt to be immediately *true*. See Walter Benjamin, 'The Storyteller', in *Illuminations: Essays and Reflections*, trans. Harry Zohn (New York: Schocken, 1968), 89.

[21] One persuasive account is that of Poovey, who seeks to link Arnoldian 'disinterestedness' to his formation of a 'procedural objectivity' that would base itself on 'metaphysical claims about "truth"'. See Mary Poovey, 'The Model System of Contemporary Literary Criticism', *Critical Inquiry* 27 (2001), 424.

novel theory at the moment of its supposed foundation and throughout the age of its efflorescence. It is perhaps too much of a generalization to claim the continued reliance of all twentieth-century novel theories upon this excision, but the pattern of most later novel theories, be they formalist, structuralist, even psychoanalytic, is evident already by the time of Lubbock's revision of James: the novel is separated from the matrices of response it evokes (either 'mass' reading or critical reading) in order to become a spatialized form dedicated to epistemological processes—getting us to *know* something or someone.[22] This twentieth-century pattern—what we might call epistemology over affect or temporality—is most evident, however, when matched against the form from which James detached himself: the physiological novel theory that took reading itself—the facts of speed, pace, attention span, engrossment, mental concentration, and drift—as the central data whereby to construct a generic theory of prose fiction, and which employed an experimental science in the hope of achieving rigorous analytic results.

L'ACTION . . . DU RÉCIT ORDINAIRE: THE GOALS OF PHYSIOLOGICAL NOVEL THEORY

'The prosperity of a book', G. H. Lewes wrote in 1865, 'lies in the minds of readers.'[23] In isolation, the comment sounds much like Lubbock's notion of form: a synchronic re-creation of a temporal process, produced within the consciousness of the reader. But Lewes's notion of the interaction between text and reader is both more specific, and more abstract, than Lubbock's. In the simplest sense—one that has often been overlooked in accounts of Victorian critical theory—Lewes expresses a belief in the theoretical importance of popular success, a willingness to treat publication numbers and the vaguer data of fame as indications of value. A liberal non-judgmentalism even less qualified than Besant's is Lewes's starting point, but to it is added a positivist faith in the ultimately physical grounding

---

[22] Exceptions to this general picture do, of course, exist, from the reader-response theory of Wolfgang Iser and Hans-Robert Jauss to the psychoanalytic narrative theory of Peter Brooks; both the Cologne School theorists and those who work in the vein of Brooks's analysis of desire and narrative bear intriguing similarities to their now-forgotten nineteenth-century predecessors. See Wolfgang Iser, *The Act of Reading: A Theory of Aesthetic Response* (Baltimore: Johns Hopkins University Press, 1978); Hans-Robert Jauss, *Toward an Aesthetic of Reception*, trans. Timothy Bahti (Minneapolis: University of Minnesota Press, 1982); Peter Brooks, *Reading for the Plot* (New York: Knopf, 1984).

[23] G. H. Lewes, *Principles of Success in Literature*, 3rd edn., ed. Fred Scott (Boston: Allyn and Bacon, 1891), 28.

of literary success: a grounding in the psychological sciences, particularly physiological psychology. Attempting to expound some aesthetic guidelines for fiction, Lewes continues: 'Our inquiry is scientific, not empirical; it therefore seeks the psychological basis for every [literary] law, endeavouring to ascertain what condition of a reader's receptivity determines the law.'[24] The statement could stand as a summary of the methodological presuppositions of an entire school of mid-nineteenth-century critical work, both British and French. It was a position with wide influence, as demonstrated by the sheer reach of the piece from which it is quoted, *Principles of Success in Literature*, which began as a series of articles in the *Fortnightly Review* in 1865, but would eventually be issued in book form and later commissioned by the University of California in 1891 as a textbook for class use; one pivotal figure in early American literary-critical professionalization, Charles Mills Gayley, employed Lewes's text as a foundation for his courses.[25]

What Lewes expresses here can be summarized roughly as the following set of operating assumptions: a physiological study of the cognitive act of reading can furnish a theorist with key rules of literary genre, since each distinct genre produces (and is intended to produce) different kinds of 'receptivity'. Careful study of literary genre should therefore balance what we might call 'top-down' analysis, working from observed facts of literary form to the kinds of response they produce, with 'bottom-up' analysis, working backwards from the observed facts of reading protocols to the literary forms that seem to be adapted to precisely those protocols. Any effective or valuable literary theory must, therefore, take into account facts of response, precisely 'psychological' or cognitive facts of response, as a way of explaining which features of a given genre are pertinent and unique. The theorist must, in fact, become a skilled physiologist of reading, attentive to the length and pitch of attention, the poses of the body, the pace and rhythm of progress, the speed of comprehension. Matching a valid general profile of a given style of reception to an equally valid general profile of a literary genre's typical form, and explaining each with reference to the other, becomes the working definition of an advanced critical practice.

---

[24] G. H. Lewes, *Principles of Success in Literature*, 128. Lewes's neutrality, at an earlier point in his career, was often expressed as a liberal faith in the beneficence of mass literacy, as in his 1847 novel *Ranthorpe*, where the narrator celebrates the new 'aristocracy of intellect': 'The learned languages are no longer written; the living speech utters the living thought; and cheap literature, in some of its myriad channels, conveys that thought even to the poorest cottage.' See G. H. Lewes, *Ranthorpe* (Leipzig: Tauchnitz, 1847), 93.

[25] For a description of Gayley's place within American literary studies, see Gerald Graff, *Professing Literature: An Institutional History* (Chicago: University of Chicago Press, 1987), 102–4.

In this there is much that would have been deeply familiar, linked in significant ways to an entire tradition of aesthetic philosophy, and much that would have seemed remarkably new. Using descriptions of audience affect and cognition as a ground for explaining artistic technique is a cornerstone of baroque aesthetics, and had been a familiar method for more then 200 years; such pivotal works as Matteo Peregrini's *Delle acutezze* (1639) and Emmanuele Tesauro's *Cannocchiale aristotelico* (1654) based theories of ornament on the presumed boredom or inattention of audiences, notions extended by Jean-Baptiste Du Bos's *Réflexions critiques sur la poésie et la peinture* (1719), which claimed boredom, and the need for distraction, as the fundamental cause of art, and which produced what we might call a theory of 'sensation management'—a mediation between the pain of excess excitement and the lassitude of quiescence—as the office of art.[26] Insofar as audience response was a necessary consideration of baroque and classical rhetoricians, its continued dominance in a more scientized, positivistic critical moment is perhaps not surprising. But by placing physiological psychology at the center of their enterprise, nineteenth-century critics and aestheticians fundamentally changed the notion of what 'audience' itself might mean—which cognitive processes go into reception, and which characteristics bind audiences, particularly the virtual audiences of mass literary publication, as opposed to the intimate audiences that Peregrini and Tesauro discussed. Indeed, physiology provided a useful tool for extending reception study to invisible audiences, the heterogeneous crowd of solitaries that made up the novel-reading public.

It is necessary to remember that, in ways both obvious and hidden, physiology was the metalanguage of nineteenth-century novel theory, as perhaps linguistics is of twentieth-century literary theory. The foreignness and rebarbative texture of that metalanguage for us has had several effects. It has first of all blinded us to the locations, both institutional and textual, of pre-Jamesian novel theory. The mainstream of Victorian novel theory found outlets in a variety of formats, none of them quite equivalent to the essay as practiced by James or the treatise as practiced by Lubbock (and expanded in such later versions as Wayne Booth's *The Rhetoric of Fiction* (1961)). Typical locations of novel theories include manuals of composition such as Lewes's *Principles of Success*, Alexander Bain's *English Composition and Rhetoric* (1866), and Herbert Spencer's 'The Philosophy of Style' (1852); physiological handbooks such as Bain's *The Emotions and the Will* (1859), which could also appear

---

[26] One excellent summary of baroque and classical theories of affect and audience cognition is Robert Montgomery's *Terms of Response: Language and Audience in Seventeenth- and Eighteenth-Century Theory* (University Park, Pa.: Penn State University Press, 1992). His consideration of 'the ways in which attention to affect can turn into attention to form' (p. 91) is particularly valuable as a prelude to the similar but recast efforts of physiological novel theorists.

serially prior to book publication in the manner of novels, as for instance sections of Lewes's *Physiology of Common Life* (1860) appeared in *Blackwood's* in 1858; or brief, usually anonymous reviews in periodicals ranging from the intellectual Left's house organs, the *Spectator* and the *Westminster Review*, to more skeptically conservative venues such as the *Saturday Review, The Times*, or the *Athenaeum*, in which Geraldine Jewsbury's weekly 'New Novels' section, in the 1850s and 1860s, offered a version of physiological novel theory adapted for general readers. Where historians of Victorian novel criticism have often looked to find important theoretical statements—primarily in the long essayistic evaluations that occasionally followed a major author's death—little in the way of adventurous thinking can be detected; while generally cautious imitations of Sainte-Beuve seem to be the norm in these commemorative appreciations, the avant-garde of nineteenth-century literary theory found its most comfortable means of expression in far less familiar, and certainly more scattered, places.[27]

The result has been a picture of British critical isolationism and anti-theoretical emphasis that has long obtained in Victorian literary history. René Wellek's 1965 assessment still stands largely unchallenged; Wellek asserted that 'the idea of a coherent literary theory disappears almost completely' with Coleridge's death, and that 'it would not be unfair to say that around 1850 English criticism had reached a nadir in its history'.[28] Edwin Eigner and George Worth, in their 1985 anthology of Victorian novel criticism, make a similar claim for the xenophobia of Victorian critical practice, which in their assessment resulted in a hostility toward 'theory': 'It is necessary frequently to read between the lines to find English theory almost reluctantly put forth

---

[27] For a useful précis of the influence that Sainte-Beuve had on English critics, see Chris Baldick, *The Social Mission of English Criticism, 1848–1932* (Oxford: Clarendon Press, 1983), 10–15. Part of the explanation of what we can call the scattering and resultant shortening of most Victorian literary theories—which could not announce themselves as such—was a familiar hostility to the idea of theory itself. Even fairly 'theoretical' pieces often felt obliged to disown any grandiosity of approach or scope; Edgar Dowden's 1865 piece for *Fraser's, Magazine*, 'Fiction and its Uses', begins by lampooning an apocryphal work-in-progress, a 'Philosophy of Fiction', which 'will take at least three thousand years to complete, with a century or two more to be allowed for unforeseen delays in the publication': Edgar Dowden. 'Fiction and its Uses,' *Fraser's Magazine* 72 (1865), 746. An earlier, anonymous *Fraser's* piece is even more direct: 'Does anybody want an aesthetical development of the art of telling a story? We sincerely wish he may get it. . . . If there be any such people, they constitute a special class in themselves, and should live apart in a particular world of their own. They have no right to trespass on the green fields of fiction, where people should take their pleasure at their ease, without stopping to ask questions as to whether they should be pleased or not': Anon., 'The Art of Storytelling', *Fraser's Magazine* 53 (1856), 723. Needless to say, both pieces are long attempts to produce the very theory they ridicule.

[28] René Wellek, *A History of Modern Criticism, 1750–1950: The Age of Transition* (New Haven: Yale University Press, 1965), 86, 141.

in arguments whose avowed purpose was to protect the English novel from theoretical foreigners and their misguided native disciples.'[29] Both seem to take their lead from comments like those made in 1871 by Edith Simcox, who lamented that 'there are no general principles of criticism recognised at once in the production and the appreciation of fiction'.[30] Simcox, however, was discussing standards of value rather than concepts of analytic practice, and the physiological novel theory of her time was indeed, as we shall see, wary of value judgments; but its 'theoretical' nature—that is, its orientation toward formulating general concepts of literary mechanics—has yet to receive sufficient notice.

As far as the institutional location of novel theory, the picture is similarly opaque. A partial but incomplete academicization of literary studies kept these critics only loosely linked to scholastic settings; those who, like Bain, held university positions tended to belong to the sciences, although—as the instance of Lewes illustrates—academic credentialing was not necessary for a high scientific reputation. With disciplinary boundaries between experimental science and literary journalism so dislimned, our more familiar models for literary-theoretical pursuit (either early academic critics like Masson or pivotal cultural critics like Arnold) are not entirely useful for tracking down the locations of early novel theory. E. S. Dallas presents a key example of the complicated institutional profile of Victorian novel theory: from 1855 to the late 1860s a salaried, if anonymous, critic on *The Times* and a major metropolitan cultural figure—a friend of Dickens, Collins, Ruskin, Rossetti, and Eliot—he nonetheless attempted to convert this unprofessionalized eminence into institutional power, applying for the Chair in Philosophy at Edinburgh, a position that implied some investment in what we would now call psychological theory.[31] After the failure of this move, Dallas largely fades from view, particularly as various forces of institutionalization gained ground in the later decades of the century.

The quasi-professional, largely physiological dream pursued by most mid-century novel theorists was, in short, a theory of silent, individual reading's impact upon genre. As a result, most of these theories, when not ignoring altogether the question of the novel's 'rise', turned backward not to the

---

[29] Edwin Eigner and George Worth, 'Introductory Essay', in *Victorian Criticism of the Novel* (Cambridge: Cambridge University Press, 1985), 1. See also Harold Orel, *Victorian Literary Critics: George Henry Lewes, Walter Bagehot, Richard Holt Hutton, Leslie Stephen, Andrew Lang, George Saintsbury and Edmund Gosse* (London: Macmillan, 1984), for a similar view of the supposedly anti-theoretical, or anti-doctrinal, emphasis of Victorian literary criticism.

[30] Published under Simcox's usual pseudonym, 'H. Lawrenny', in 'Recent Novels', *Academy* 2 (15 Dec. 1871), 552.

[31] See the biographical analysis offered by Jenny Taylor in '*The Gay Science*: The "Hidden Soul" of Victorian Criticism', *Literature and History* 10/2 (1984), 189–202.

romance or the early modern prose epic in the manner of Reeve or Barbauld, but instead to drama. The gesture is so characteristic, and so persistent throughout the century, that it calls for some explanation. As early as Bulwer-Lytton's 'On Art in Fiction' (1838), the private scene of novel-reading is adduced as a key factor in the differences of plot construction between fiction and drama:

In our closets we should be fatigued with the incessant rush of events that we desire when we make one of a multitude. Oratory and the drama in this resemble each other—that the things best to hear are not always the best to read. In the novel, we address ourselves to the one person—on the stage we address ourselves to a crowd: more rapid effects, broader and more popular sentiments, more condensed grasp of the universal passions are required for the last. . . . In the novel it is different: the most enchanting and permanent kind of interest, in the latter, is often gentle, tranquillising, and subdued. The novelist can appeal to those delicate and subtle emotions, which are easily awakened when we are alone, but which are torpid and unfelt in the electric contagion of popular sympathies.[32]

The generic difference here is an affective one—dramatic 'passion' supplanted by novelistic 'emotion'—yet it is rooted in the situation of the audience: crowd versus closet. Bulwer-Lytton's terms would become part of a familiar, if nonphysiologized, tradition in nineteenth-century critical theory; they reappear in much the same form in later textbooks such as Walter Raleigh's *The English Novel* (1894) and Wilbur Cross's *The Development of the English Novel* (1899), which both find in the novel a fundamental affective shift from drama: a slackening of the duration of feeling and a softening of its power.[33] In the hands of conservative critics, such a theory engendered a diminishing-returns lament, contrary to Bulwer-Lytton's intentions, about the catastrophic effects upon literary form of widening literacy. Talented critics like Walter Bagehot found the drama-into-novel analysis useful for constructing a narrative of cultural decline: Bagehot theorized the existence of a 'ubiquitous' novel, one which 'aims at describing the whole of human life in all its spheres', and which found its exemplar in Scott, but which had died prematurely because 'the genius of authors is habitually sacrificed to the tastes of readers', which, in becoming a more

[32] Edward Bulwer-Lytton, 'The Critic.—No. 2: On Art in Fiction', *Monthly Chronicle* 1 (1838), 144–5.

[33] Raleigh's account is perhaps the most frankly hostile to the mass reading public: 'To read a play with full intelligence is at all times difficult for an untrained reader, and the law of least possible effort can be as effectively illustrated from literature as from language. A new form of literature that had all the interest of the drama, but imposed only the slenderest tax on the reader's attention and imagination, was predestined to success.' Walter Raleigh, *The English Novel: Being a Short Sketch of its History from the Earliest Times to the Appearance of* Waverly, 5th edn. (New York: Scribners, 1905), 142–3.

properly *mass* taste, had turned wholesale to the domestic and sentimental.[34] For Bagehot, Scott represented an intermediate point between drama and novel, after which the novel succumbed to its audience's debilitating predilections.

The drama/novel distinction usually worked, therefore, to implant in mainstream Victorian criticism a fundamental paradox: a hostility toward mass readership, which expressed itself as a lament for the novel's atomization of sociability, or shared reception, into scattered private consumers. A further paradox ensued: mass readers could be castigated for either their indulgence in sentiment for its own sake or their too-vibrant tendency to be roused to action by their reading. The solution was a compromise formation that W. C. Roscoe, one of Bagehot's early patrons, called 'a sort of movement in subordination to the aesthetic faculty, a sort of voluntary submission to emotion with an undefined consciousness that it is not pure and simple feeling we experience, but feeling excited for the sake of the pleasure there is in the movement of the feelings'.[35] While we can be forgiven for mistaking Roscoe's tone for an Arnoldian defense of 'culture', Roscoe's formulation is far more hesitant and riven with doubt. Having tackled the subject of popular novelists (Roscoe wrote influential pieces on Thackeray, the Brontës, Bulwer-Lytton, and Dickens), he has already implicitly joined forces with the phenomenon he is so concerned to limit; and his solution—a private disinterestedness, an aesthetic faculty that is cut off from all but self-communion—looks uncomfortably like the solitary consumption of the ordinary novel-reader. The possibility of a *virtual sociability*, a social field constituted by habits of consumption rather than physical proximity or class affinity, is the specter that more conservative Victorian criticism is anxious either to deny or to castigate. The visibility of this more dismayed brand of criticism has led many critics, in persuasive ways, to identify it as representing the totality of Victorian thinking about the novel and mass readership: fear mingled with a confused jealousy.[36]

[34] Walter Bagehot, 'The Waverly Novels', in *Literary Studies*, ed. R. H. Hutton (London: Longmans, Green, 1895), ii. 87–8. Bagehot's article was originally published in the *National Review* of April 1858; under the editorship of W. C. Roscoe, the *National Review* became a major organ for a more conservative brand of literary criticism—one that preferred a man-and-mores assessment of major authors and tried to bring together the moralist with the connoisseur in its critical tone. Bagehot's work was perhaps more sophisticated in its attempts to describe and theorize the faults of mass taste, but it was nonetheless consistent with the journal's usual output.
[35] William Caldwell Roscoe, 'Sir E. B. Lytton, Novelist, Philosopher, and Poet', in *Poems and Essays*, ed. R. H. Hutton (London: Chapman & Hall, 1860), ii. 357. One of Roscoe's influential career assessments, this piece appeared initially in the *National Review* in April 1859.
[36] For the most recent and thorough account of anxieties about mass reading and their impact upon novelistic thematics and form, see Patrick Brantlinger, *The Reading Lesson: The Threat of Mass Literacy in Nineteenth-Century British Fiction* (Bloomington: Indiana University Press, 1998).

Physiological novel theory, however, was an equally powerful force, and its attitude toward sociability or the social field as a whole was far different in tone and method. For these theorists, a narrower but more easily specifiable definition of the social obtained: the cognitive styles of different consumptive modes are the primary means whereby social facts (industrialization, national education, economic liberalization) are inscribed upon the individual. The solitary reader is not a sign of the atomization of preindustrial sociability, but the very location of contemporary sociability; furthermore, an index of social change can be read through the automatic, or preconscious, styles of consumption that the most popular contemporary genre (i.e. the novel) tends to demand. Put more simply, a novel-reader's engrossment, physiologically considered, is exactly where 'the social' can best be observed. If conservative literary criticism noted engrossment in order to bemoan both its ubiquity and its iniquity (as a proto-sexual self-indulgence, as an abdication of responsibility, or, in a Platonic vein, as an indication of a culture's drugged slippage into second-order illusions), physiological novel theory, as we shall see, took it for better or worse as the location of modernity.

Engrossment, in fact, is exactly where the tools of physiology met the methods of literary criticism. Bain, Britain's preeminent physiological psychologist throughout the 1850s and 1860s, attempted to relabel the novel 'the literature of pursuit', and provided a capsule description of the novel-reader as a definition of the novel itself:

On the physical side, the situation of pursuit is marked chiefly by the intent occupation of one or other of the senses, accompanied with a fixed attitude generally, so far as the concurring active exertions will allow. The fixed stare of the eye, the alertness of the ear, the groping touch, are well known manifestations . . . we are 'all eye, all ear,' all observation; the attitude being one of stillness, and of suitability to the process of seeing, hearing, touching, or other sensibility engaged . . . there is a strong and concentrated activity; the stray currents of energy are recalled for a special effort; recipiency of impressions is reduced to a point; the system is open at a single avenue and closed at the others. . . . According as we are engrossed with things beyond ourselves, self-consciousness is in abeyance; and if the engrossment attains an extreme pitch, there is an almost entire suspension of feeling or emotion; pleasure and pain, even though arising out of the situation, cannot be felt, until there is some intermission or relaxation of the attention to the objects.[37]

---

[37] Alexander Bain, *The Emotions and the Will*, 2nd edn. (London: Longmans, Green, 1865). Originally published in 1859, the text's 2nd edn. became a standard reference work in Victorian psychology and is the edition most often cited. Bain revised the text wholesale for an 1899 edn., altering all his physiological explanations to evolutionary ones and eliminating his adventurous physiological literary theories; this was, however, a failed attempt to regain relevance at a moment when psychology was moving away from the kind of philosophical *chef d'œuvre* for which Bain

A crucial example of the tone and procedure of physiological novel theory, we can read in Bain here a dramatic contrast to the sort of pre-Arnoldian work turned out by Bagehot, Roscoe, and others. Bain's *The Emotions and the Will*, a magisterial summary of mid-Victorian physiological psychology, presents us with a new possibility: a literary theory without any necessary attention to literary language, specific instances, or even any citation. Instead, Bain's analysis is pitched at the level of genre, and focused on reception, observed from the standpoint of the objective psychological scientist. Rather than working within the traditional terminology of literary taxonomy, Bain (like so many of his colleagues) attempted a large-scale description of genre, in which it might be possible to rename 'the novel' as 'the literature of pursuit': in other words, to detach the genre from its historical origins and relabel it as *a mode of cognitive activity*, even (perhaps) a mirror of modern cognition itself. That activity, moreover, borrows its significance from its social pervasiveness, and in fact is observable in a host of other receptive activities, not all of them literary; literary criticism, in the hands of Bain and his like, is less properly 'literary' and more broadly cultural or social, even if specifically positivist in its methodology. The dream of Bain's approach might even be described as the attempt to make literary form physically accessible and experimentally verifiable—a dream that Percy Lubbock, sixty years later, would consider a prime theoretical fallacy.

It would be easy, in other words, to read this crucial faultline in Victorian critical practice as a 'two cultures' clash, between the scientifically trained and the journalistically inclined, or between physiological proto-professionals and aesthetically inclined gentleman critics.[38] Those cultures were, however,

---

was noted and toward more statistical, laboratory-controlled results. Originally in the vanguard of 'hard' psychological positivism, by the end of the century Bain's work—particularly his interest in literary questions—seemed quaintly belletristic.

[38] That Bain and Lewes represented a 'scientific' moment in Victorian literary criticism is not in doubt, but the extent of their positivism—and what it meant to be 'scientific' in their period—is open to a variety of accounts. For many contemporary observers, a 'scientific criticism' was a real desideratum; the classic formulation was offered by John Robertson, a leading *fin de siècle* Shakespearean scholar: 'What is really wanted in literary criticism is that there should be this statement of data and process of proof, the demand for that much being exactly what arose generations or even centuries ago in the case of the physical sciences.' John Robertson, *Essays Towards a Critical Method* (London: Unwin, 1889), 105. That broader definition of 'scientific criticism' would seem inarguably to animate Bain's and Lewes's efforts. For nuanced readings of how reductively somatic, or relentlessly positivistic, their efforts might have been, see: Rick Rylance, *Victorian Psychology and British Culture, 1850–1880* (Oxford: Oxford University Press, 2000); Jane Wood, *Passion and Pathology in Victorian Culture* (Oxford: Oxford University Press, 2001), 132–5; and, for the prehistory to mid-Victorian physiology, Alan Richardson, *British Romanticism and the Science of the Mind* (Cambridge: Cambridge University Press, 2001). An analogous reading of the influence of critical positivism (especially via Hippolyte Taine) upon the American academy is provided by Graff, *Professing Literature*, 61–74.

much less sharply defined than we might think, and figures like Bain and
Lewes repeatedly crossed the divide between literary journalism and scientific
research. What truly separated the conservative and liberal/physiological critical camps was the importance—social, methodological, even ethical—they
accorded novel-reading, which for each group was essentially identical to
mass reading. One might even add that 'science', in literary-critical contexts,
came to imply attention to the psychological and broadly cognitive factors of
reception. A useful place to look for this implicit sense is in the work of Émile
Hennequin, the French critic whose very brief career—his most important
work, *La Critique scientifique*, was published in 1888, the year of his death
at age 29—culminated in the manifesto that the more cautious, or genteel,
English physiological critics refused to write. Hennequin's critical theory is
unashamedly scientific in its referentiality: he cites Spencer, Wundt, Taine,
Bain, and Maudsley rather than any purely literary critics, and insists that all
literary facts have 'une signification psychologique'.[39] His term for the school
for which he is writing a (largely belated) manifesto is 'esthopsychologie',
which he explains as follows:

En termes plus brefs, l'esthopsychologie n'a pas pour but de fixer le mérite des oeuvres
d'art et des moyens généraux par lesquels elles sont produits; c'est là la tache de
l'esthétique pure et de la critique littéraire. Elle n'a pas pour objet d'envisager l'oeuvre
d'art dans son essence, son but, son évolution, en elle-même; mais uniquement au
point de vue des relations qui unissent ses particularités à certaines particularités
psychologiques et sociales, comme révélatrice de certaines âmes; l'esthopsychologie
est la science de l'oeuvre d'art *en tant que signe*.[40]

Put briefly, estho-psychology doesn't have the goal of deciding the merits of either
artworks or the general means by which they are produced; that is the task of pure
aesthetics and literary criticism. It doesn't have as its object the conceptualization of
the artwork in its essence, its purpose, its internal logic, in and of itself; but solely
from the point of view of the relations which unite the artwork's characteristics
with certain psychological and social characteristics, as revelatory of certain souls.
Estho-psychology is the science of the artwork *as a sign*.

'Science' in Hennequin mediates between a psychological science—the study
of receptive consciousnesses—and a social science, since in Hennequin's
understanding of the physiological tradition, every physical or cognitive
response is caught in an ultimately social circuit of communication. 'Esthopsychologie' is a science, but a science both for its positivist methodology (the
physicalizing of literary form via the study of reception) and for its value-
neutral approach to the reception of literary works.

---

[39] Émile Hennequin, *La Critique scientifique* (Paris: Perrin, 1888), 75.
[40] Ibid. 21–2; emphasis mine.

The novel as a temporal form directed toward a receptive consciousness which in turn was shaped, at least in part, by the exigencies of that form: that is the formula, broadly put, under which nineteenth-century physiological novel theorists worked. Their conclusions about novelistic form, therefore, were far different than those of the post-Jamesian tradition, and had surprising internal variances; their sense of how individual readers might form a community was far more sophisticated than one might suspect. As we shall see, working out the characteristics of the *lecteur ordinaire* led inevitably to working out the social function of ordinary reading, or the ways in which ordinary reading was already creating new forms of social organization. This is, ultimately, the significance of the physiological-critical school which Hennequin named 'esthopsychologie': an attempt to place the solitary reader at the very heart of modern social interaction. And at the center of that reader was a nervous system upon which everything—including the novel itself—hinged.

UN CERVEAU SÉPARÉ DE SES FORCES EXTÉRIEURS: THE READER IN NINETEENTH-CENTURY NOVEL THEORY

In a famously dismissive passage in *The Great Tradition* (1948), F. R. Leavis asserts of Thackeray's novels, essentially a metonym for mainstream Victorian fiction, that 'for the reader it is merely a matter of going on and on; nothing has been done by the close to justify the space taken—except, of course, that time has been killed (which seems to be all that even some academic critics demand of a novel)'.[41] Space and time: Leavis touches on, and recoils from, some of the key terms of physiological novel criticism. Lubbockian 'noetic materialism' placed the form of a novel in a space-that-is-no-space, a purely mental geography which annulled as well the troubling temporality of narrative reading; but the large, loose, baggy monstrosities of Victorian multi-plot fiction were less amenable to such dematerializations, and tended to highlight their own insatiable colonization of shelf space and readerly time. For Leavis, as for most of his post-Jamesian cohort, the sheer obviousness of the spatiotemporal maximalism of Victorian fiction was an embarrassment, and was treated with disdain, as if it was scarcely worthy of critical notice or theoretical comment. The result is a certain abstraction to the post-Jamesian notion of 'form'.

'Form' is conceptualized entirely otherwise in the nineteenth-century physiological tradition, however, and it is here that a serious survey of that work

---

[41] F. R. Leavis, *The Great Tradition* (Garden City, NY: Doubleday, 1954), 21.

must begin: with that tradition's interest in the temporality of novel-reading.[42]
It might be possible to speculate on the influence of serial publication and
serial reading habits upon the development of this theory, but nowhere within
the work of Lewes, Bain, and others is serial reading specifically mentioned.
For physiological novel theorists, the variable times of *actual* reading (a year
for serial publications, a few weeks for book publication) are less important
than the unarguably temporal process of *any* reading. This interest in temporal
form manifests itself first in a sensual alignment with sound rather than sight.
The nineteenth-century physiological tradition prefers musical analogies over
pictorial ones: the language of James's or Lubbock's novel theory ('point of
view', 'perspective', 'showing' over 'telling') replaced a discourse of 'theme',
'rhythm', and 'order'—a language of duration, repetition, and sequence. Even
as late as 1895 one can find pertinent examples of such vocabulary, as in
Vernon Lee's little-known but illustrative study 'On Literary Construction':

> Construction—that is to say, co-ordination. It means finding out what is important
> and unimportant, what you can afford and cannot afford to do. It means thinking out
> the results of every movement you set up in the reader's mind, how that movement
> will work into, help, or mar the other movements which you have set up there already,
> or which you will require to set up there in the future. . . . You must remember that
> in every kind of literary composition, from the smallest essay to the largest novel, you
> are perpetually, as in a piece of music, introducing new themes, and working all the
> themes into one another.[43]

Lee's 'construction' is a temporal viewpoint, looking both back and ahead,
an art of unfolding effects. If the energies of form in Lubbock are oriented toward condensation—toward the truly telling event, the imparting of
knowledge—in the discourse of 'construction', the energies are dynamic and
radiating, borrowing the terms ('movement', 'theme') of symphonic composition. Although belated, and not specifically oriented toward physiological
explanation, Lee's essay reminds us that nineteenth-century definitions of
such categories as 'form' and 'construction' tended to be diachronic. George
Eliot's brief notebook piece from 1868, 'Notes on Form in Art', makes the

---

[42] Perhaps the most intriguing precursor to this nineteenth-century interest is Diderot's 'Éloge
de Richardson', with its defense of Richardson's length; Diderot's method—remarkably similar
to that of Victorian critics—sets the novel among a host of cultural experiences of *duration*:
'Vous accusez Richardson de longeurs! Vous avez donc oublié combien il en coûte de peines, de
soins, de mouvements, pour faire réussir la moindre entreprise, terminer un process, conclure
un mariage, amener une réconciliation' ('You accuse Richardson of being long and drawn out!
You must then have forgotten how much trouble, pain, and activity it takes to see through
the smallest undertaking, to finish a lawsuit, to arrange a marriage, to set up a reconciliation').
Denis Diderot, 'Éloge de Richardson', in *Œuvres esthétiques*, ed. Paul Vernière (Paris: Garnier,
1965), 34.
[43] Vernon Lee, 'On Literary Construction', *Contemporary Review* 68 (1895), 406–7.

claim explicitly: 'Poetic Form was not begotten by thinking it out or framing it as a shell which should hold emotional expression, any more than the shell of an animal arises before the living creature; but emotion, by its tendency to repetition, i.e. rhythmic persistence in proportion as diversifying thought is absent, creates a form by the recurrence of elements in adjustment with certain given conditions of sound, language, action, or environment.'[44] Formal investigation, in the discourses of Victorian aesthetics, was usually grounded on the identification of recurrent units (sounds, themes, effects) over time, rather than the attempt to form a spatial map of such units or to shape them into a totality. Even the late-century physiological aesthetics of visual art of Vernon Lee and Clementina 'Kit' Anstruther-Thomson used the temporality of music as a basic analogy: visual patterning, as they explained in their 1897 essay 'Beauty and Ugliness', 'adds by its regularity the power of compelling the eye and the breath to move at an even and unbroken pace. Even the simplest, therefore, of the patterns ever used have a power akin to that of march music, for they compel our organism to a regular rhythmical mode of being.'[45]

These are fairly abstract tendencies, but they are ultimately derived, like so many of the methodological assumptions of mid-Victorian criticism, from physiological, even vivisectionist, experiment.[46] The ability of psychological theorists to test an organism's response to a varied order and rhythm of stimuli produced the desire to specify and make exact the relation between a particular rhythmic signature and the response displayed—in other words, to make form (literary or otherwise) experimentally, physically present, even quantifiable. That this was no obscure point is demonstrated by the many places it is announced, such as Lewes's important 1859 article on Jane Austen:

The art of novel-writing, like the art of painting, is founded on general principles, which, because they have their psychological justification, because they are derived from tendencies of the human mind, and not, as absurdly supposed, derived from 'models of composition,' are of universal application. The law of colour, for instance,

---

[44] George Eliot, 'Notes on Form in Art', in *Selected Essays, Poems, and Other Writings*, ed. A. S. Byatt (Harmondsworth: Penguin, 1991), 235.

[45] This essay, first published in the *Contemporary Review*, is collected in Vernon Lee and Kit Anstruther-Thomson, *Beauty and Ugliness, and Other Studies in Psychological Aesthetics* (London: John Lane, 1912), 185. For a contextualization of Lee's and Anstruther-Thomson's collaboration in relation to contemporary psychologies, Paterian aesthetics, and *fin de siècle* lesbian cultural formations, see Diana Maltz, 'Engaging "Delicate Brains": From Working-Class Enculturation to Upper-Class Lesbian Liberation in Vernon Lee and Kit Anstruther-Thomson's Psychological Aesthetics', in *Women and British Aestheticism*, ed. Talia Schaffer and Kathy Alexis Psomiades (Charlottesville: University Press of Virginia), 211–29.

[46] See Richard Menke's perceptive discussion of Lewes's use of vivisection in relation to his literary criticism in 'Fiction as Vivisection: G. H. Lewes and George Eliot', *ELH* 67/2 (2000), 617–53.

is derived from the observed relation between certain colours and the sensitive retina. The laws of construction, likewise, are derived from the invariable relation between a certain order and succession of events, and the amount of interest excited by that order.[47]

Because 'order' is both a property of any temporal art (the novel included) and an observable, testable datum, it is the object of a properly scientific criticism, as valid as the science of color. In fact, what Lewes is proposing is a science of narrative: one that would take sequences (of events) and responses (of readers) as the two analytic poles in need of simultaneous definition. The aspirations of this physiologized method were nothing if not high. One year after his 'Jane Austen' proclamation, Lewes adds this about Fielding: 'A great deal is said about the "construction" of *Tom Jones*. In this quality it is declared to surpass all other novels. This is a statement which admits of very definite argument; the quality can be tested as accurately as the perspective of a picture, or the proportions of a statue; it is one which may be placed beyond dispute.'[48] These passages annex reading—and therefore literature itself—to the sphere of everyday activities that might be fully explained with recourse to a study and measurement of the nervous system's reaction to various stimuli. Seen from this point of view, it is less of a surprise that the period's major physiological psychologies include a theory of fiction: what more 'everyday' than the reading of novels?

Two such sequential, or order-based, physiological novel theories deserve more extended comment. The first is Lewes's, which is spread between a series of major literary-critical articles written in the late 1850s and 1860s, his 1860 *Physiology of Common Life*, the aforementioned *Principles of Success in Literature*, and his unfinished attempt at a scientific magnum opus, *Problems of Life and Mind*, published in separate volumes from 1874 to 1879.[49] Put in general terms, Lewes's descriptions of novelistic form are closely tied to his descriptions of consciousness: both are periodic processes—that is, linear processes interrupted at more or less regular intervals by heightened

---

[47] G. H. Lewes, 'The Novels of Jane Austen', *Blackwood's Edinburgh Magazine* 84 (1859), 108.

[48] G. H. Lewes, 'A Word about Tom Jones', *Blackwood's Edinburgh Magazine* 87 (1860), 333.

[49] Perhaps the least well-known of the Victorian period's many omnidisciplinary intellectual projects, G. H. Lewes's *Problems of Life and Mind* had a complex organization and publication scheme; it was divided into three 'series', entitled *The Foundations of a Creed, The Physical Basis of Mind* (London: Trübner, 1877), and *The Study of Psychology: Its Object, Scope and Method* (London: Trübner, 1879); the first and third were divided into two volumes each. I am indebted to two excellent discussions of the many contexts surrounding its composition and publication: Peter Allan Dale, *In Pursuit of a Scientific Culture: Science, Art, and Society in the Victorian Age* (Madison: University of Wisconsin Press, 1989), 59–84; and Rylance, *Victorian Psychology*, 251–71.

sensation—with no necessary endpoint. A 'wave theory' of consciousness is Lewes's starting point:

We may compare Consciousness to a mass of stationary waves. If the surface of a lake be set in motion each wave diffuses itself over the whole surface, and finally reaches the shores, whence it is reflected back towards the centre of the lake. This reflected wave is met by the fresh incoming waves, there is a blending of the waves, and their product is a pattern on the surface. This pattern of stationary waves is a fluctuating pattern, because of the incessant arrival of fresh waves, incoming and reflected. Whenever a fresh stream enters the lake (*i.e.*, new sensation is excited from without), its waves will at first pass over the pattern, neither disturbing it nor being disturbed by it; but after reaching the shore the waves will be reflected back towards the centre, and these will more or less modify the pattern.[50]

The 'pattern' described by Lewes—what we might as well call his notion of form, literary or cognitive—is, first of all, temporal, constantly changing, and incapable of fixed or synchronic representation; it is a collision of sensations creating a kaleidoscopic image that cannot be stopped or put in reverse. It is, secondly, a *surface* pattern, a distinction that is important to keep in mind. The pattern is a record of recent excitations, with past stimuli being made fainter (or 'modified') by more recent ones, not a palimpsest pattern where temporally or spatially distant excitations are nonetheless visible. Here Lewes's account is of a moment-to-moment seriality, a kind of pure present of consciousness. Unlike Lubbock's image of consciousness, where static mental wholes are formed by the amalgamation of various temporally scattered stimuli, Lewes's consciousness is trapped by time, a creature of passing units of sensation. For Lewes, adjacent units of sensation may slightly modify others, but like the inexorable flow of waves, the fading of early excitations and the emerging of stronger, newer sensations is a constant fact of consciousness.

The broadly scientific importance of Lewes's claim is his attempt to erase the line between conscious action and unconscious sensation: differences of degree exist, but 'there is no real and essential distinction between voluntary and involuntary actions. They all spring from Sensibility. They are all determined by feeling.'[51] Excerpted from *The Physical Basis of Mind*, this is an argument against so-called Reflex Theory, which Lewes had been advocating since the late 1850s; but for our purposes that local fact of Lewes's intellectual history is less pressing than the ramifications of it for what I call 'early novel theory'. The literary importance of the theory is, first, that reading enjoys the status of the most telling mental action through which to demonstrate the erasure of conscious/automatic distinctions; and secondly, that the novel, by providing a perfect field for the exercise of silent reading, starts to shape itself more and

---

[50] Lewes, *Physical Basis of Mind*, 366.   [51] Ibid. 373.

more closely to the form of consciousness itself—that is, the novel's 'patterns' become identical to the 'patterns' of a wavelike consciousness, because silent reading is where the flux of consciousness is most evident.

'We learn to read with conscious effort,' Lewes explains; but by the time reading is a habit, 'the process passes so rapidly and smoothly, that unless there be some defect in a letter, or the word be misspelled, we are not "conscious" of the perceptions. Are we therefore reading automata?'[52] The answer for Lewes is both yes and no: insofar as all supposedly higher acts of cognition are rooted in automatic repetitions of lower acts of cognition, Lewes asserts that we are reading automata; but since the line between automatic and conscious cognition is actually a ruse, a semantic barrier, we are simply *readers*, relying on the nervous system's coordinations to carry out our comprehension. Lewes took an interest in acts of what we might call 'preconscious' reading—falling asleep while reading, absorption so total that it becomes trancelike—as extreme instances of what reading always in some sense is: a mental submission to the rhythms of consciousness, to pure seriality. What technology better suited to respond to this serial consciousness than the novel—the novel that is read in private, and that is long enough to require some (necessarily occasionally interrupted) mental absorption? Here Lewes gives a physiological tweaking to the drama/novel distinction of Bulwer-Lytton, Bagehot, and others. Insofar as private, silent reading is a primary feature of the novel as a technology, novelistic form is free to mimic more closely the rhythms of consciousness, which are unidirectional and sequential: a series of more or less vivid sensations, not necessarily some greater whole or a buildup to a closural sensation or climax. *Principles of Success* makes this claim most vividly:

The novelist is not under the same limitations of time [as drama], nor has he to contend against the same mental impatience on the part of his public. He may therefore linger where the dramatist must hurry; he may digress, and gain fresh impetus from the digression, where the dramatist would seriously endanger the effect of his scene by retarding its evolution. The novelist with a prudent prodigality may employ descriptions, dialogues, and episodes, which would be fatal in a drama.[53]

The loose bagginess of the Victorian novel that James's novel theory existed to correct is, in Lewes's criticism, exactly its virtue—more than that, its generic distinctiveness. That generic distinctiveness of the novel receives its importance in Lewes's work from its close similarity to consciousness itself, mediated via a readerly consciousness that is a receptiveness to pure seriality rather than a critical attempt to form some kind of non-narrative monad.

---

[52] Lewes, *Physical Basis of Mind*, 397.   [53] Lewes, *Principles of Success*, 137.

Matters are so interwoven in Lewes's work that it is difficult to tell, among the three major categories—consciousness, reading, and the novel—which category governs the other two; perhaps it is closer to the tone of Lewes's thought to say that each helps explain the form of the other two. An act (silent reading) that takes us close to the constant inner workings of the mind (a wavelike consciousness) is best studied with reference to a form (the novel) that asks of us nothing but a submission to the rhythms of that wave. Looked at one way, Lewes's project is an attempt to rehabilitate the often-noted deficiency of the novel, its formal shapelessness, by redescribing its form as the form of the mind itself. If mimesis, or questions of realist representation, are central to his critical canon—Lewes's current reputation, such as it is, rests on his discussions of realism—the effect of his physiological work was to make him understand literary form as psychologically mimetic, as a small-scale instantiation of the workings of the human mind.[54] Lewes's work remained scattered, however, his theories of the novel segregated from (although of an intellectual piece with) his theories of consciousness or of reading; as Peter Allan Dale has suggested, Lewes was perhaps 'too burdened by the criterion of verifiability' to produce an entirely coherent theory.[55]

With Alexander Bain, physiological novel theory is more explicitly of a single piece. *The Emotions and the Will* does the work of amalgamation and summary that Lewes never attempted, perhaps because Bain's simpler institutional profile—a Professor of Logic at the University of Aberdeen, a recognized physiological authority writing largely from within a single discipline—necessitated a more synoptic approach to his varied interests. Which is to say that Lewes's wave theory of consciousness, and its analogies to his descriptions of novelistic form, become in Bain a unified theory: a wave theory of physiological affect that carries with it a precise redefinition of what a novel does. As Gillian Beer has suggested in relation to the work of Victorian physicists John Tyndall and James Clerk Maxwell, wave theory 'seems to make a single process a sufficient explanation of all phenomena'—even, as in Bain, merging novel-reading and novelistic form into one wave signature.[56]

Bain's 'wave' is even more linear than Lewes's; it is defined by 'the alternations of fulness and discharge', or a 'periodicity' between sensations that 'are liable to weariness after a time, while by repose they become

---

[54] Here I am attempting to nuance Peter Allan Dale's claim that Lewes was more interested in 'mimesis or representation rather than expression and effect'; I would suggest instead that for Lewes, the 'effect' of novelistic form is itself mimetic of the structures of mental processing. See Dale, *In Pursuit of a Scientific Culture*, 65.

[55] Ibid. 62.

[56] Gillian Beer, 'Wave Theory and the Rise of Literary Modernism', in *Open Fields: Science in Cultural Encounter* (Oxford: Oxford University Press, 1996), 296.

charged with new vigour'.[57] What is compelling about Bain's version is that 'periodicity' is explicitly ascribed not just to consciousness in general but to aesthetic reception in particular; as divided into the two facets of 'Novelty' and 'Variety', or the intensity of the sensation and the varied interval between sensations, aesthetic reception and everyday cognition are understood as identical in shape: 'Novelty in incidents and events, is furnished by the ongoings of life, and by the pages of story.'[58] Even if Bain's 'periodicity' of consciousness is a constant fact of cognition, he finds it particularly useful in describing one literary genre in particular, the novel, which in its new guise of 'the literature of pursuit' is essentially *a form of interruption*. 'Pursuit'—which for Bain allies the novel with hunting, combat, sports, industry, and amorous affairs—propels the reader through the narrative, but the action of the narrative must be a kind of periodically interrupted sensation:

Ordinarily the feeling [of the reader] is some good or evil in the distance, an ideal end prompting us to labour for realizing it; the regards are intent upon the end, and more especially when its approach is rapid and near. Such a moment is favourable to that entranced attention, under which the mind is debarred from feeling, and from all thoughts extraneous to the situation. Nevertheless, we remit, at short intervals, the objective strain, falling back into emotion or self-consciousness; we then experience the full intensity of the primary motive, until such time as we are once more thrown upon the outward stretch.[59]

That there is an overriding interest—a closural interest, essentially—Bain does not deny, and in part that helps define the novel as 'the literature of pursuit'; crucially, however, the peculiar power of the novel is not in its closural energies but in its 'periodic' energies, its ability to relieve a tired mind with small 'discharges' and to build into its form moments of relaxation or lassitude. 'The struggles that have preceded vast changes, contests, revolutions, keep the reader in a state of thrilling expectation; while the inner plots and minor catastrophes serve to discharge at intervals the pent-up currents, and vary the direction of the outlook.'[60]

Bain's account of the varied reading commitments and modes within the same narrative gesture toward a novel theory that is not simply a historical curiosity, but rather one that, in the wake of James's sweeping dismissal of Victorian critical work, feels unexpectedly compelling. Although a species of excitation, for Bain the novel's real strength is its ability to subside reliably into something like quiescence; put more simply, the novel's time signature (which is essentially, more than any thematic fact, its generic signature) is equally dependent upon boredom and placid dilations as it is upon the

---

[57] Bain, *Emotions and the Will*, 33.   [58] Ibid. 44.   [59] Ibid. 151.   [60] Ibid. 160.

suspense of closure. Insofar as this is a felt need of modern existence—some intervals of mental rest between increasingly violent assaults upon the nervous system—the novel is the preeminent contemporary literary form. For Bain, the novel's place in modern life is cemented by its rhythmic signature, which is identical to the rhythmic signature of brain waves in the modern individual confronted with a ramifying set of stimuli: constant 'periodicity' between minor shocks, or 'discharges', and moments of lassitude, or 'relaxed intermissions'.[61]

These wave theories are theories of the novel as sequence, and more particularly as a sequence that effectively mirrors the functioning of everyday, solitary consciousness. But other peculiarities—particularly some differences from more recent novel theories—become apparent once the novelty of their concentration upon temporal progression is removed. The first is that they are completely unsubstantiated by any examples or citations; 'the novel' for Lewes and Bain is so obvious a category that there is no need to provide instances. Were we to look for apt data for these theories, however, the serial Victorian novel could hardly be bettered. In fact, both Lewes's and Bain's theories seem uniquely suited to the serial novel, particularly for the rhythm of 'discharge' and 'quiescence' necessarily built into an intrinsically interrupted form of publication. That neither theorist troubled to provide a narrowly critical instantiation of the broadly theoretical nature of his enterprise has, perhaps, helped prevent their later recognition; but the perfect match between the serial novel and the 'periodicity' of their wave theories is readily apparent.[62]

A second effect of these theories is not only to diminish the role of closure, but in fact to level 'plot' and 'subplot' altogether into the categories 'excitation' and 'relaxation'. Although this novel theory seeks to describe a *dynamics* of plot, it nonetheless differs in a key way from later plot-dynamic theories such as Peter Brooks's psychoanalytic textual motor: whereas in Brooks there is a clear division between plot, which seeks an end, and 'subplot', which retards or deviates from that end to form the 'arabesque' of desire, in physiological wave theory we might say, in a deconstructive mode, *il n'y a pas de sous-récit*: there's no such thing as subplot. There is only one level of plot, a kind of alternation

---

[61] The modernity of the novel's rhythmic signature has, by Bain's 1899 edn. of *The Emotions and the Will*, undergone a distinct change.

[62] What has received attention is Bain's short warning that the appetite for pursuit 'sometimes becomes too great, and requires to be restrained' (*Emotions and the Will*, 468)—the most frequently cited passage of his novel theory. While the sentiment was important enough to Bain to survive even into his revised 1899 edn., it is nonetheless an aside in a much more complex argument about the pervasiveness of mental excitation and the pleasures of its arousal. Bain's liberal theory of the novel and of mass reading has been obscured by the highlighting of his warning, which makes him seem much more like the mythical censorious Victorian than was in fact the case.

between relaxation and nervous discharge, a form of temporality that is not unidirectional but possible, like all musical rhythms, to play in reverse, or at least to play without a necessary reference to a tonic conclusion.[63]

Neither Lewes nor Bain wrote his theory as novel criticism; the theory is pitched at too high a level of generality for any instances. But what might this theory look like *as* criticism? As it appears in the work of several noted Victorian critics, it would resemble an interest in what we might call 'affective mechanics': the peculiar affective contours of a given writer's procedure, with particular attention to the quasi-emotive, quasi-automatic effects of sequence and speed. Take, for instance, two critical accounts of Dickens by otherwise dissimilar writers: the noted editor R. H. Hutton and Hippolyte Taine. Hutton's major piece, 'The Tension in Charles Dickens', appeared in the *Spectator* in 1872 as a belated career assessment; rather than a survey of the novels, however, Hutton identifes in Dickens's narratives a 'constant strain', a forced, too-rapid succession of events, which overwhelms his humor and sentiment to become the primary quality of the works.[64] In claiming a certain nervousness as Dickens's central affective quality—rather than the commonplaces of Dickensian robustness or Dickensian bathos—Hutton places the nervous system at the center of reading Dickens while also making this nervousness a formal effect of the fiction. Taine offers, in his *Histoire de la littérature Anglaise* (1863–70), a more expansive, slightly jaundiced account of the same process in his description of reading Dickens:

The contrast, the rapid succession, the number of the sentiments, add further to [our soul's] trouble; we are immersed for two hundred pages in a torrent of new emotions, contrary and unceasing, which communicates its violence to the mind, which carries it away in digressions and falls, and only casts it on the bank enchanted and exhausted. It is an intoxication, and on a delicate soul the effect would be too forcible; but it suits the English public; and that public has justified it.[65]

Again, similar formal qualities are singled out: Dickens's unequalled *velocity*, and the *violence* of his affective shifts (or what Lewes and Bain might call the shortening of the relaxation interval). Both are issues of duration, or

---

[63] Bain did, however, attempt to describe 'subordinate streams' of plot occurrence in his 1866 textbook *English Composition and Rhetoric*. Here he alludes to 'Concurring Streams of Events' and taxonomizes the different kinds of concurrent plot events, asserting that 'the art consists in upholding the prominence of the main stream of the narrative'. See Alexander Bain, *English Composition and Rhetoric: A Manual* (London: Longmans, Green, 1866), 132–3. That subdivision between mainstream and subordinate stream, which would be so crucial for later novel theories (particularly psychoanalytic theories), is nonetheless missing from the more physiologically inflected literary theories that Bain condenses in *The Emotions and the Will*.

[64] Richard Holt Hutton, 'The Tension in Charles Dickens', *Spectator*, 45 (16 Nov. 1872), 1456.

[65] Hippolyte Taine, *History of English Literature*, trans. H. Van Laun (Edinburgh: Edmonston and Douglas, 1874), iv. 134.

temporality, and with Hutton's and Taine's practices in mind we might hazard a guess that sequence and speed were, to nineteenth-century critics, what 'point of view' would become to critics after James and Lubbock.[66]

One consequence follows for the form of novel criticism: insofar as the sequence and speed studied by physiological critics (or those working in the wake of physiological novel theory) is relentlessly forward-directed, the need to refer back and forth to the web of plot is discarded. The importance of plot summary to twentieth-century novel theory—in order to condense the plot into a Lubbockian mental monad, it must first be summarized—is not at all felt by nineteenth-century critics, who replace it with a sense of plot as what we might call 'pure contiguity': a one-thing-then-another sense of plot which opens up the importance of small, reflective moments within the sequence of the narrative rather than the importance of readerly connections across wide expanses of plot. If Lubbock and his followers prized the long-term memory of readers and their ability to synthesize recollections into wholes, physiological novel theory posits a short-term-memory-only reader, who experiences the narrative as a series of affective 'moments', or, in other words, as a rhythm.

For Taine, this kind of 'affective mechanics' study led to generalizations about the receptive propensities of various nations, particularly about the 'grosser moods' of the English, which require 'strong emotions' in their entertainment 'to set these nerves in motion'.[67] For Hutton, it led to differentiating among the affective styles of various novelists, rather than any race- or nation-based taxonomies. But each receives its impetus from a physiology which looked not to race, nation, or individual, but to genre: to a generically specific affective function. In this, physiological novel theory stands firmly in the Aristotelian tradition, far more firmly than those later theorists, such as Wayne Booth, who received the label 'new Aristotelians'. The crucial move in Aristotle's theory of tragedy, as earlier novel theorists understood it, is not its theory of mimesis but its affective reception theory, centered on its description of *katharsis*. In the nineteenth-century reading, tragedy is for Aristotle a machine constructed to make its consumers feel *katharsis* through an only slightly variable, and certainly perfectable, order of events, which went under the names 'recognition' (*anagnorèsis*) and 'reversal' (*peripeteia*). Similarly, the novel is a machine constructed to make its reader feel through an only slightly variable, and possibly perfectable, order

---

[66] Although duration has been largely eclipsed in novel studies since James, a recent article by Garrett Stewart takes up the issue in a study of the 'duration envy' that painted scenes of secular reading evince for the temporality of the reading act. See Garrett Stewart, 'Painted Readers, Narrative Regress', *Narrative* 11/2 (2003), 125–76.

[67] Taine, *History of English Literature*, 175.

of events, which goes under the name of a periodic alternation between shock and lassitude.[68] In each instance, a theory of plot order leads to a theory of generically specific affects, which can be used to summarize a literary genre.

That physiological novel theory took from Aristotle a theory of affect rather than a theory of mimesis is one of its signal peculiarities; its concern is with how readerly attention is compelled, or what readerly emotion is like, rather than with how readerly belief is inspired. E. S. Dallas, in his *The Gay Science* (1866), puts it most explicitly: 'His [Aristotle's] leading principle, which makes all poetry, all art, an imitation, is demonstrably false, has rendered his Poetic one-sided (a treatise not so much on poetry, as on dramatic poetry), and has transmitted to all other criticism a sort of hereditary squint.'[69] Dallas, for whom 'at the stage which criticism has now reached there is nothing so much wanting to it as a correct psychology', instead calls for an aesthetics based on 'pleasure', or affect: 'All the accredited systems of criticism therefore take their rise either in theories of imitation or theories of the beautiful. It is not difficult, however, to show that both of the suppositions on which these systems rest are delusive, and that neither is calculated to sustain the weight of a science.'[70] Psychology for Dallas—which, as for most of his colleagues, is virtually synonymous with physiology—is not concerned with comparisons between the outside 'real' and the readerly 'fictional': it is concerned only with the cognitive activities of a mind submitted wholly to a sequence of fictional events, unconcerned with the verification of those events as 'probable' or 'likely'. The practical effect of this methodological turn is to make an earlier interest of novel theory—the potentially harmful effects of novelistic representations—inoperable. Thus the monitory tone of Reeve's *Progress of Romance* or Barbauld's 'Origin and Progress of Novel-Writing' is nowhere felt within the work of physiological critics; the reader is for them, in Valéry's phrase, a brain separated from its outside forces, entirely self-communing, entirely asocial, or, perhaps, part of an entirely new virtual sociability, where any questions of the 'real' are useless (see Figure 1.1).[71] The only 'real' for physiological critics consists of the data of individual response.

The necessary variations in these data become a challenge to any sense of physiological 'aesthetics', as is most evident in the late-century novel theory

---

[68] Few critics have noted the similarity between Aristotelian aesthetics and what we might call post-Renaissance response theories; for the account of one who has noticed, see Montgomery, *Terms of Reception*, 128–40.

[69] E. S. Dallas, *The Gay Science* (London: Chapman & Hall, 1866), i. 25–6.

[70] Ibid. 42, 78–9.

[71] For an account of the cultural function of Reeve's and Barbauld's monitory novel theories, see Anne Mellor, *Mothers of the Nation: Women's Political Writing in England, 1780–1830* (Bloomington: Indiana University Press, 2000), 85–102.

Fig. 63.

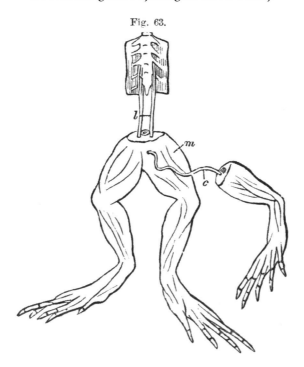

Figure 1.1. The virtual sociability of physiology: a non-cerebral network of nerves (here represented by the lumbar nerves of one frog connected to the leg of another frog) links individuals, who then produce identical responses when offered the same stimulus. G. H. Lewes, *The Physiology of Common Life*, ii (New York: Appleton, 1860), 243. General Research Division, The New York Public Library, Astor, Lenox, and Tilden Foundations

of Vernon Lee, whose articles on the novel produced in the 1890s read as a self-conscious reworking of Lewes's and Bain's theories, continually aware of the difficulty of reaching summary statements based on individual response, although response—contrary to James, whom Lee largely admired—is insisted upon as the only datum worth considering.[72] Lee's 1899 piece 'Aesthetics of the Novel' claims a range of 'non-aesthetic' attractions of the novel, such as suspense, gossip interest, emotional excitement, and affective or social

[72] Vernon Lee's articles are collected in her *The Handling of Words, and Other Studies in Literary Psychology* (London: John Lane, Bodley Head, 1923). For a prolonged discussion of her novel criticism and theory starting in the mid-1890s, see Vineta Colby's recent biography of Lee, which argues for their importance as an overlooked prefiguration of I. A. Richards, Russian formalism, Roland Barthes, and Wolfgang Iser; see Vinēta Colby, *Vernon Lee: A Literary Biography* (Charlottesville: University of Virginia Press, 2003), 200.

education; as far as a definition of 'the specific aesthetic quality of literature', Lee can only wonder:

What this is, I do not, and I suppose nobody nowadays does, know; a charm due to the complex patterns into which (quite apart from sound) the parts of speech, verbs and nouns and adjectives, actives and passives, variously combined tenses, can be woven even like lines and colours, producing patterns of action and reaction in our mind, our nerve tracks—who knows? in our muscles and heartbeats and breathing, more mysterious, even, than those which we can dimly perceive, darkly guess, as effects of visible or audible form.[73]

Moreover, it is never exactly specified by this neo-Aristotelian physiological theory what the novel reader is meant to feel, or what the novelistic counterpart to tragic *katharsis* might be. The content of novelistic feeling is registered by a number of vaguely similar terms ('tension', 'pursuit', 'engrossment', 'periodicity'), but no one term stands out to unify these disparate guesses. However, one might attempt a convergence of these various physiological terms. With reference to the central Aristotelian question—what does the tragic audience feel?—one might similarly ask, what does the novel-reader feel? The most accurate answer would perhaps be: the reader feels *nervous*, alternating between sensation and its lapse, momentary arousal and a return to quiescence, 'action' and 'reaction' in Lee's terms. This, however, is an almost tautological claim, given that nervousness is all that the organism *can* feel in Lewes's or Bain's physiologies; as we shall see, affect is for both of these novel theorists the output of the highly mechanical nervous system. Thus the strange interest of this field of novel theory in describing not unique, pleasurable, or dangerous narratives, or authorial careers, but novel-readers, engaged in a mental act that is somewhat less than fully conscious, part of a large social machine of novelistic consumption.

   This is a methodological preference visible throughout the field of Victorian novel criticism, even in a figure like Geraldine Jewsbury, now usually regarded, if misguidedly, as exemplifying the morally monitory Victorian hack reviewer. Jewsbury operated in a manner radically different from the abstract, scientized literary theories of Lewes, Dallas, or Bain; her niche, more readily open to female critics than the physiological textbook or long, signed literary assessment, was anonymous reviewing. In her most active period, from 1854 until the gradual loss of her eyesight in the early 1870s, Jewsbury routinely reviewed more than 100 novels a year in the unsigned 'New Novels' section of the *Athenaeum*, and as a result covered a breadth of Victorian literary production unlike that referenced by Lewes's or Dallas's theories; her other

---

[73] From Vernon Lee, 'Aesthetics of the Novel', *Literature* 5 (11 Aug. 1899), 100.

occupation, consulting reader for the publisher Bentley from 1858 to 1880, situated her firmly in the mainstream of British novel publishing.[74] Her prolific, if still largely invisible, presence within the Victorian critical field has usually been read as a 'middlebrow' one, a term which has largely served to cordon her off from the work of male critics such as Hutton or Roscoe. As Jewsbury's most thorough student describes them, her 'verdicts emerge as the epitome of conventional, middlebrow Victorian taste', and her reviews 'contain relatively few comments on narrative technique', concentrating instead on 'questions of readability'.[75] These assessments are accurate to an extent, although they paradoxically demonstrate Jewsbury's affinities to the physiological novel theory of Lewes and Bain rather than her differences from them. If Lewes, Dallas, and Bain generally avoided questions of value in favor of analytic descriptions of genre, Jewsbury's catholic taste in novels is similarly averse to constructing canons of high or low fiction; and as we have seen in the more explicitly physiological theorists, 'questions of readability' are, in the mid-Victorian period, essentially matters of 'narrative technique'. Only after Henry James can the two be easily distinguished.

In essence, Jewsbury's pervasive interest in the physical and cognitive responses of readers, particularly her insistence upon what we might call a readerly comfort zone that novels either solicit or disregard, is an interest in technique, and is at bottom a physiologically informed criterion of judgment. Throughout her reviews for the *Athenaeum*, Jewsbury used 'readability' or 'readableness'—terms for a comfortably enlivening nervous affect, her version of 'affective mechanics'—as her primary evaluative tool. In an 1865 review of Ellen Wood's *Mildred Arkell*, Jewsbury writes that Wood's novels 'in different degrees possess a quality that covers a multitude of sins. Their *readableness* is recognized by those who are most alive to their faults; and to the undiscerning and not fastidious people who form the majority of novel-readers they are sources of keen excitement.'[76] 'Readableness' is both a formal category—one that can be understood through a study of plot, characterization, and style—and also a matter of physical response; the

[74] Jewsbury's career is amply covered by Monica Fryckstedt's assessment of her work for the *Athenaeum*. Alongside a general analysis of Jewsbury's work, Fryckstedt provides the only index to Jewsbury's many reviews, and I have relied upon Fryckstedt's research to determine which 'New Novels' installments were written by Jewsbury. See Monica Fryckstedt, *Geraldine Jewsbury's* Athenaeum *Reviews: A Mirror of Mid-Victorian Attitudes to Fiction* (Uppsala: Acta Universitatis Upsaliensis Anglistica Upsaliensia, 1986). For Jewsbury's work for Bentley, see Jeanne Fahnestock, 'Geraldine Jewsbury: The Power of the Publisher's Reader', *Nineteenth-Century Fiction* 28 (1973), 253–72, and Royal Gettmann, *A Victorian Publisher: A Study of the Bentley Papers* (Cambridge: Cambridge University Press, 1960), 194–6.

[75] Fryckstedt, *Geraldine Jewsbury's* Athenaeum *Reviews*, 13, 49.

[76] Geraldine Jewsbury, 'New Novels', *Athenaeum* 1966 (3 July, 1865), 12.

primary work of the term in Jewsbury's criticism is to connect the literary form and the readerly body. Jewsbury often assesses novels through their failure to achieve this value, either by an excess of stimulation or a deficiency of stimulation; both the 'spasmodic' and the 'relaxing' fall short of readability, which seems to be a state of pleasurable, periodic nervous discharge. Her more theoretical statements criticize both kinds of failure:

> The love of idle excitement—an excitement fed at the smallest possible expenditure of emotion—seems to be on the increase, if we are to judge from the novels constructed to meet the taste of the day. Idleness, as shown in a desire to reach the result without the labour of encountering the means, is confessed alike by the writer and the reader. . . . Now, a taste for foolish, easy entertainment, that requires no effort of mind, deteriorates the moral strength and vigour which ought to underlie even the amusements of responsible and rational creatures. Without any positive immorality, the modern class of novels is pervaded by a vague, relaxing element, in which no brave or strong principle of virtue can exist. There is a low tone of thought and feeling, which, like a low tone of physical health, renders the individual liable to any form of disease which may be prevalent.[77]

This might certainly be taken as an instance of Jewsbury's conservatism, but her moral/political bias is grounded in a physiologized language that criticizes both excess 'excitement' and an equally debilitating 'relaxing element'. The result in Jewsbury is an evaluative terminology whose very familiarity obscures its affinities with physiological theories of readerly response, and has led her later readers hastily, as if in embarrassment, to label her standards 'middlebrow'. Terms like 'pleasant', 'comfortable', and the ever present 'readable'—all as descriptions of a reader's affective response—dot her reviews even of still-canonical novels. Eliot's *Silas Marner* is called 'comfortable reading'; *Adam Bede* is praised for its lack of 'startling, unequal or spasmodic' effects; Meredith's *Ordeal of Richard Feverel* is assessed in the following comment: 'The only comfort the reader can find on closing the book is—that it is not true. We hope the author will use his great ability to produce something pleasanter next time.'[78] As Jewsbury often insists, these affective qualities are results of novelistic technique and are linked to terms like 'construction' or 'workmanship'. Her 1867 review of Trollope's *The Claverings* claims that 'there are none of his books which show better or more artistic workmanship'; the outcome of this workmanship is not any greater depth of psychological understanding, but a more physically and cognitively pleasant experience: 'There was room in "The Claverings" for deeper studies in

---

[77] Geraldine Jewsbury, 'New Novels', *Athenaeum* 2066 (1 June, 1867), 720.
[78] From the following 'New Novels' installments: *Athenaeum* 1745 (6 April, 1861), 465; *Athenaeum* 1635 (26 Feb., 1859), 284; *Athenaeum* 1654 (9 July, 1859), 48.

human nature; but the book in that case might not have been so pleasant to read.'[79]

From a post-Jamesian standpoint, Jewsbury's interest in the 'pleasant' or 'comfortable' can seem like the apotheosis of lazy, and lazily conservative, approaches to fiction, and the fact that her most famous review today is her notoriously hostile attack in 1867 on Rhoda Broughton's *Cometh Up as a Flower* has only strengthened this sentiment.[80] An understanding of Jewsbury more situated in the physiological methodologies of her time produces a different picture of her work. What has earned her the condescension of later scholars, more than any particular political or social presupposition, is precisely what makes her so important an example of the impact of physiology upon novel theory in the mid-Victorian period: her concentration upon the comfort zones of readers, and how novels adapt themselves to those comfort zones. Jewsbury demonstrates that physiological novel theory was not carried out solely in the largely uninstantiated literary theories found in psychological textbooks, but also found a home in the wider world of weekly reviews, where its usual political leanings (such as Lewes's and Dallas's radicalism) often received different inflections. Both the explicitly scientized theory of Lewes and Dallas and the more coded methods of Jewsbury's criticism indicate a grounding in the affective mechanics of readerly nervous systems, and in the mechanics of how novels impact those nervous systems. Bain's 'periodicity' and Jewsbury's 'comfort', however institutionally separate (the academic psychologist and the weekly reviewer), are nonetheless of a piece.

SUJETS DU RÊVE: THE READER AS MACHINE

The machine: it is never far from the thoughts of nineteenth-century novel theorists, and in reading them one is struck by their tendency to describe the novel-reader as the most advanced and subtle of recent technological advances. Dallas insisted that 'many lines of action which when first attempted require to be carried on by distinct efforts of volition become through practice mechanical, involuntary movements of which we are wholly unaware. In the act of reading we find the mind similarly at work for us, with a mechanical

---

[79] 'New Novels', *Athenaeum* 2068 (15 June, 1867), 783.

[80] As instanced by the recent anthology *A Serious Occupation: Literary Criticism by Victorian Woman Writers*, ed. Solveig Robinson (Peterborough: Broadview, 2003), which reprints the Broughton review as an example of Jewsbury's work alongside the comment that she was 'an upholder of middle-class morality' (p. 139).

ease that is independent of our care.'[81] Soliciting the mechanical reception of readers is, for Lewes, the writer's first care, as in this telling analogy:

What is the first object of a machine? Effective work—*vis vita*. Every means by which friction can be reduced, and the force thus economized by being rendered available, necessarily solicits the constructor's care. He seeks as far as possible to liberate the motion which is absorbed in the working of the machine, and to use it as *vis vita*. He knows that every superfluous detail, every retarding influence, is at the cost of so much power, and is a mechanical defect though it may be an aesthetic beauty or a practical convenience.[82]

Both Lewes and Dallas take an interest in examples of purely automatic reading—particularly examples of reading during sleep—as outlandish instances of an everyday fact: textual consumption is less a matter of conscious construal than of unconscious absorption.[83] Caught in the dream of her novel, the reader is not far from dreaming itself, from the physiological state known as automatic functioning, and therefore not far from becoming machinery. As the master metaphor of physiological novel theory, the machine marries a kind of formalism (the novel *as* a machine, as in Lewes's analogy) to a physiologized theory of affect (the reader's mechanical responses) in order to produce what we might call a *novelistic hydraulics*: an elaboration of the novel's ability to mechanically move its mechanical readers, as well as a theory of the novel's place within the larger machine of consumption.

In this, theorists like Lewes and Bain were taking with unexpected seriousness a more flippantly dismissive metaphor that circulated throughout Victorian criticism. R. H. Hutton warned in 1862 of a new kind of novel-reader, one who takes 'a sort of disinterested delight in the technical machinery of novels quite apart from the human interests which that machinery used to subserve. . . . Ineffectual novel-machinery, like ineffectual money, may, after all, inspire a deeper and more abstract and concentrated passion than their legitimate use has ever inspired.'[84] Concentrated particularly around the 1860s

---

[81] Dallas, *Gay Science*, i. 223–4.   [82] Lewes, *Principles of Success*, 128.

[83] The passages on sleep-reading are remarkably similar: for Dallas's attestation to 'cases of readers overtaken with sleep and continuing to read aloud', see *Gay Science*, i. 224, while Lewes's account—in his case, of listening to a reading with full comprehension while nonetheless asleep—is in *Physical Basis of Mind*, 415–16. Both passages are part of a larger discourse on 'reverie', for which see G. H. Lewes, *The Physiology of Common Life* (New York: Appleton, 1860), ii. 169 ff. An interestingly inconsistent claim is made by Dallas in his well-known *Times* review of *Great Expectations*, which asserts that 'modern stories are intended not to set people to sleep [as in the example of Scheherazade], but to keep them awake', i.e. to provide regular shocks to a public lulled by the movement of the railway carriage or bored by everyday mundanity. Nonetheless this waking function, which Dallas sees as the intrinsic purpose of serial publication, needs a pervasive background of automatic lassitude for its success. See E. S. Dallas, 'Great Expectations', *The Times*, 17 Oct. 1861, 6.

[84] Richard Holt Hutton, 'Ineffectual Novels', *Spectator*, 35 (22 Feb. 1862), 219.

vogue for sensation fiction, a discourse of machine disgust proliferated, the most notable (because most histrionic) instance being H. L. Mansel's 1863 attack on the sensation novel: 'A commercial atmosphere floats around works of this class, redolent of the manufactory and the shop. The public want novels, and novels must be made—so many yards of printed stuff, sensation pattern, to be ready by the beginning of the season.'[85] Insofar as the demeaning analogy to mechanics was never entirely clarified—is it the fact that novels are machine-made, or that readers read them mechanically, or that those readers might themselves work in mechanical industry, that so upsets Mansel?—its explanatory power was largely inert. Margaret Oliphant's 1862 assessment of sensation fiction situated it amidst the military industry of the Crimean War and the American Civil War, among 'Merrimacs and Monitors', describing it as attempting 'a kindred depth of effect and shock of incident'; but it is difficult to determine whether a militarized readership, or an industrialized literary form, is to blame, or which might have caused the other.[86] Instead, 'the machine' seems in much of this critical corpus to have spread like a virus, infecting reader, text, and social setting alike, and becoming even more dangerous in its eerie similarity to the Arnoldian 'disinterestedness' which would seem to be its opposite.[87] A free play of the faculties, or the frictionless operating of a system: for many Victorian critics, the difference was becoming increasingly difficult to maintain.

It is here, perhaps, that the positivistic neutrality of physiological novel theory is most evident. In transforming a metaphor of conservative jeremiads into a methodological tool, it managed to do what no other novel theory prior to it—or, for that matter, subsequent to it—could envision: take the novel's mass success as a theoretical datum rather than an embarrassment or an accident. It attempted not only to place the novel within a wider cultural matrix of industry and industrial modes of production and consumption,

---

[85] Henry Mansel, 'Sensation Novels', *Quarterly Review* 113 (1863), 483. Mansel was not by profession a critic—he was an Oxford philosopher and professor of ecclesiastical history, a High Church Tory of a particularly strident kind—but his omnibus review quickly became a small masterpiece of the anti-novel genre, and it is still quoted and anthologized today as an example of mid-Victorian critical outrage.

[86] Margaret Oliphant, 'Sensation Novels', *Blackwood's Edinburgh Review* 91 (May 1862), 564–5.

[87] By the end of the century this more unfocused fear of machine reading (reading like a machine, reading as a machine, reading machines) sharpened into a series of sociological studies of mass reading tastes and habits which became a vibrant periodical genre. For some pertinent examples, see: Anon., 'What and How to Read', *Westminster Review* 126 (1886), 99–118; Edward Salmon, 'What the Working Classes Read', *Nineteenth Century* 20 (1886), 108–17; Anon., 'The Reading of the Working Classes', *Nineteenth Century* 33 (1893), 690–701; Joseph Ackland, 'Elementary Education and the Decay of Literature', *Nineteenth Century* 35 (1894), 412–23; Arnold Hautain, 'How to Read', *Blackwood's Edinburgh Magazine* 159 (1896), 249–65.

but to explain the novel's agency within this matrix: its ability to create the mechanical mass reader who, paradoxically, had helped call it into being. To elucidate this last, and perhaps most adventurous, aspect of physiological novel theory, it is necessary to return to one of its more salient features: its concentration upon *plot*. Much like later structuralisms of the novel, the physiology of Lewes, Bain, and Dallas turned the novel into a sequence of actions (or a sequence of receptive moments) rather than any encounter with characters; indeed, little is said of character at all in these novel theories, which are as suspicious of the very category of 'character' as any poststructuralist account. If a novel is a string of happenings with a generally specifiable rhythm, then character is nothing more than an occasion for those happenings, a kind of sporadic melody set above the form's rhythmic foundation. That concentration upon plot would seem to be necessitated by physiology's interest in temporality and the order of sensations, as explained earlier. In Dallas's work in particular, it takes a further theoretical path: toward the ability of plot machines to make secondary not only novelistic characters but the 'characters' of readers themselves. A literary machine, that is, produces sequences that appeal to a suddenly mechanized audience that is as characterless, as purely abstract, as the lexical ciphers that go under the name 'characters'.

This, at least, is Dallas's surmise: the novel is the form of mass identity. In the final pages of *The Gay Science* he offers his theory of the novel as a new kind of aesthetic pleasure, one based on 'the withering of the individual as an exceptional hero, and his growth as a multiplicand unit'.[88] Taking *Vanity Fair* as his key instance, Dallas ventriloquizes Thackeray's method as follows: 'Let any two characters be as dissimilar as possible; let the circumstances in which they are placed be as opposite as the poles, I will prove that their natures are the same, and I do not doubt that, spite of our censures, we in their places would have acted precisely as they did. . . .'[89] Thackeray, however, functions in Dallas's theory only as a kind of paradigmatic instance, not at all as an exceptional one; in the kind of field-sweeping move for which Dallas had a talent, he goes on to explain that the fictional school seemingly farthest from Thackerayan melancholic realism, the sensation novel, produces exactly the same effect of character dissolution. In either subgenre, at opposite ends of the mid-Victorian spectrum, individuality is reduced to the status of function within a larger production process that we usually call plot. Oliphant agreed, at least as far as the sensation novel was concerned, and insisted that paradigmatic moments in such novels took the form of 'simple physical effect' which was 'totally independent of character'.[90] If Dallas starts

[88] Dallas, *Gay Science*, ii. 287.   [89] Ibid. 289.
[90] Oliphant, 'Sensation Novels,' 572.

his account of the novel with a definition of it as 'gossip etherealized, family talk generalized', as the domain of the 'private individual . . . in the public regard', that gossip has less and less to do with individuality, and that private individual yields to a sequence of sensations. Thackeray may efface the individual deliberately, with the sardonic brio of a lecturer, while the sensation novel may do it far more thoroughly if less obviously, but the outcome is identical.

It is no wonder, then, that the ultimate 'author' of the novel is for Dallas not even human:

The stereotype, the photograph, wood-engraving, the art of printing in colour, and many other useful inventions have been perfected—making the printed page within the last thirty years what it never was before. At the same time the railway and the steamship, the telegraph and the penny postage, by daily and hourly bringing near to us a vast world beyond our own limited circles, and giving us a present interest in the transactions of the most distant regions, have enormously increased the number of readers, have of themselves created a literature, and through that literature have had a mighty influence upon the movement of the time.[91]

Ultimately this art of individual-withering, the novel, is born of technology, which at one stroke creates both readers and a form to satisfy them. Dallas starts from the standpoint of physiological psychology and follows that standpoint to the same terminus which Lewes and Bain reached, which is a redescription of the novel as a particular kind of rhythmic exercise. But from here Dallas goes further. If the 'withering of the individual' was in Lewes and Bain only implicit, suggested by the largely identical functionings of the human nervous system, in Dallas it has become the rationale for the genre of the novel. Physiological psychology's interest in *standard* responses (i.e. those felt by a nervous system in good working order, those replicable by laboratory experiment) still spoke of individuals as the unit of experiment; for Dallas, the novel is the literary form of standard reponses, the form that, through a mechanical, even industrial, perfection of its working parts creates a reliably similar response through a population, thus effacing the idiosyncrasies of individual reading. Simply put, for Dallas the individual novel-reader *is* the general novel-reader.[92] The

---

[91] Dallas, *Gay Science*, ii. 312.

[92] Here Dallas seems to be echoing a recent argument put forth by William Warner on behalf of what Warner calls 'the general reader', a reader without specific identity contours or ideological preferences, somewhere between 'a perversely polymorphous being' and 'an automaton'. Warner specifies the emergence of the 'general reader' in the early novel of amorous intrigue (Aphra Behn, Delarivier Manley, Eliza Heywood), while for Dallas the 'general reader' is the consequence of the novel *per se*, regardless of its subgeneric differences. See William Warner, 'Formulating Fiction: Romancing the General Reader in Early Modern Britain', in *Cultural Institutions of the Novel*, ed. Lynch and Warner, 279–305.

conclusion is hinted at by Lewes and Bain, but made axiomatic by Dallas at the conclusion of his aesthetic treatise.

It is picked up once more in the nineteenth century, in Hennequin's *Critique scientifique*. For Hennequin, one methodological problem of 'esthopsychologie', a familiar one still for historians of reading, is the necessary variation of individual response: 'une perception n'est nullement un acte simple, passif, constant pour tous devant un objet identique; les facultés les plus hautes, la mémoire, l'association des idées y participent...les differences individuelles deviennent énormes' ('a perception is not at all a simple, passive act, the same for all those facing an identical object; the highest faculties—memory, the association of ideas—take part...individual differences become enormous').[93] But Hennequin suggests that the problem can be sidestepped neatly by finding a solvent, one that can dissolve the large and unpredictable differences of individual response and leave behind only a residue of identical sensation: the novel. 'Nous avons pris le réalisme et le roman comme bases de notre raisonnement, car ces cas sont ceux où le caractère individuel, les facultés, les capacités du lecteur paraissent réduits à jouer le moindre rôle' ('We have taken realism, and the novel, as the foundations of our argument, because in these cases the individual character, mental faculties, and capacities of the reader seem reduced to their smallest importance').[94] If 'esthopsychologie' takes reception as the starting-point of an aesthetic theory, it is because the novel works as an effective control for the experiment, guaranteeing a large percentage of identical responses, its readers washed away into the vaguer and more statistically reliable contours of the reading public. Again, the novel-reader is the general reader, produced by the machinery of the genre that consumes her: a form of sensations that is registered by the most mechanical aspects of our cognitive apparatus.

The claims here, particularly in Hennequin's manifesto, are extreme enough to have started a movement; what they call for is a scientific study of the novel, for it is the novel they find the most apt of all literary genres for such a treatment. The efforts of Lewes and Bain—of which Hennequin seems to have been aware, given his respectful mention of Bain and other British psychologists—seem by the 1880s to be only a prologue to some more methodical, persistent tracking of the influence of literary form upon cognition, and upon the formation of identical mass cognitions. That eventual literary/scientific pursuit, of course, never arrived, and the dream of Dallas and Hennequin—a truly synthesized interdisciplinary theory of reading and the novel—was foreclosed by a host of cultural and disciplinary forces: evolutionary science

---

[93] Hennequin, *Critique scientifique*, 136.   [94] Ibid. 137.

(which subsumed associationist psychology's role as the master discourse of popularized science), literary formalism (which considered any discussion of reception a chimerical pursuit at best), and, perhaps most obviously, an increasing disdain for the general readership which made its theorization less and less consequential. That disdain is most visible in a later popularization of Bain's aesthetic theories, Grant Allen's 1877 *Physiological Aesthetics*, in which physiology is mobilized to explain both the vagaries of and the somatic basis for taste; in Allen, physiological study helps explain 'those varieties which differentiate the artistically minded few from the inartistic masses'.[95] Allen's evolutionary application of physiological literary theory turned more explicitly on issues of taste and canons of judgment than did the notably value-reticent work of Lewes, Bain, or Dallas, and not surprisingly marginalized the novel (called throughout by the consciously antique term 'Romance') as a species of daydreaming, a 'cheap and easy amusement, giving free play to certain of the faculties without much risk of serious ultimate disappointment'.[96] In Allen's work, physiology ratifies the evolutionary hierarchies, which are necessarily hierarchies of taste, of savage, child, and civilized adult, in which earlier physiological novel theory had shown no interest. Allen's evolutionary physiology may have been instrumental for late Victorian aestheticism, as critics such as Regenia Gagnier have suggested, but it signaled the beginning of the end of physiology's contribution to novel theory.[97]

One might also suggest a particular seed of failure hidden within physiological novel theory itself: the more its findings turned both novel and reader into machines, the less necessary (or, for that matter, interesting) its procedures seemed, and the more ancillary to other technologies the novel became—a melancholy conclusion that cut short some of the theoretical innovations that the theory had promised. The supposedly anti-theoretical, anti-systemic field of Victorian criticism seems in fact to have generated a theory that presented too strong a system—that of the machine—to encourage further development along the lines that physiological novel theory suggested. But in an age when 'technology' and 'media' are live terms of theoretical debate, the work of those whom we might describe as the first media theorists of the novel, the first theorists to understand the novel as a technology, can renew its plea to be included in the tradition of novel theory from which it has been so consistently excluded and forgotten. The following four investigations into

[95] Grant Allen, *Physiological Aesthetics* (London: Henry King, 1877), 47.   [96] Ibid. 206–7.
[97] See Regenia Gagnier's *The Insatiability of Human Wants: Economics and Aesthetics in Market Society* (Chicago: University of Chicago Press, 2000), 136–40, for an acute and spirited critique of Allen, if one that too readily ascribes to physiological literary theory as a whole faults evidenced in Allen's work.

the temporal, and physiological, form of selected Victorian novels attempt to demonstrate the impact that this novel theory had in the second half of the nineteenth century, while implicitly arguing for the viability of an updated, historically aware version of its approach in our future study of the novel form.

Part II

Practices of Reading

Four Cases

2

Distraction's Negative Liberty: Thackeray and Attention (Intermittent Form)

> Persisting, Bella gave her attention to one thing and forgot the other, and gave her attention to the other and forgot the third, and remembering the third was distracted by the fourth, and made amends whenever she went wrong by giving the unfortunate fowls an extra spin, which made their chance of ever getting cooked exceedingly doubtful. But it was pleasant cookery too.
>
> Dickens, *Our Mutual Friend*

More often than any other Victorian illustrator, Thackeray depicted scenes of solitary reading, with enough variety of scenic backdrops and textual material—newspapers, letters, books—to suggest an interest in the profusion of variables involved in the reading act. Yet the possible variations in these images tend, in fact, to resolve themselves into two fairly stable and recognizable types, to which Thackeray returns persistently across his career: raptly attentive reading, and its seeming opposite, the leisured, distracted perusal. The first is the image of pure engrossment: the reader turned inward, buried in a book, oblivious to the sensory surround which the illustration itself often presents in full detail. Take, for instance, the initial illustration to Thackeray's 'Roundabout Papers' series, which opened with 'On a Lazy Idle Boy' in the first issue of the *Cornhill* in 1860. The sketch's eponymous figure is depicted leaning on the railing of a bridge, turned away from the viewer's eye, holding a printed page of some kind close to his eyes, his head directed away from the mountain scenery which Thackeray's text places in the Swiss town of Chur (see Figure 2.1). As Thackeray narrates it, the lazy boy reads 'a little book, which my lad held up to his face, and which I daresay so charmed and ravished him, that he was blind to the beautiful sights around him; unmindful, I would venture to lay any wager, of the lessons he had to learn for to-morrow; forgetful of mother waiting supper, and father preparing a scolding;—absorbed utterly

A LAZY IDLE BOY.

Figure 2.1. Illustration to 'On a Lazy Idle Boy', the first of Thackeray's 'Roundabout Papers'. *Roundabout Papers* (London: Smith, Elder, 1869), opposite p. 1. General Research Division, The New York Public Library, Astor, Lenox, and Tilden Foundations

and entirely in his book' (*RP*, 4).[1] That absorption, the extreme attention for which the lazy idle boy is an emblem, is signaled by a series of iconographic traits that Thackeray's engrossed readers typically display. Most prominent is the figure's refusal to face the viewer, so that the look of readerly submergence is invisible, as if the inward-turned consciousness of the reader can best be troped by its unavailability for public inspection; instead the page being read faces us, inviting our curiosity about what those illegible lines might mean. Similarly, the depth-of-field focus of the image's background, which looms so impressively over the reader, only makes that reader's obliviousness to it all the more powerful; this is, one might plausibly feel, an attention so directed and intense that no competing visual information can possibly distract the act of textual construal. Finally, the lazy idle boy's proximity to his book—so close as to almost merge with it or obscure it from our view—reveals an absorption that desires something close to sheer physical consumption, as if to read attentively meant, in some fashion, to ingest the book. It comes as no surprise, then, that in the text itself Thackeray pursues the comparison between book and food, linking novels—for it is, we are told, 'a NOVEL that you were reading, you lazy, not very clean, good-for-nothing, sensible boy' (*RP*, 4)—with sweets as agents of voracious, if ultimately wearied, appetites.[2]

If this type-scene of rapt attention forms one aspect of Thackeray's pictured readers, his other version seems to offer the opposite. In one of the nineteenth century's most well-known images of novel consumption, an illustration from the first chapter of *Vanity Fair* depicts a considerably more comfortable, less strenuous relation to the pursuit of narrative (see Figure 2.2). Having just delivered a series of details of Amelia Sedley's tearful parting from her school friends, Thackeray deflates the scene with the following: 'All which details, I have no doubt, JONES, who reads this book at his Club, will pronounce to be excessively foolish, trivial, twaddling, and ultra-sentimental. Yes; I can see Jones at this minute (rather flushed with his joint of mutton and half-pint of wine), taking out his pencil and scoring under the words "foolish, twaddling," &c., and adding to them his own remark of *"quite true"*' (*VF*, 8). Jones's leisured, dismissive perusal, rather than being screened from our eyes by a face turned toward a page, is flagrantly open to inspection; his posture and bodily

---

[1] Citations from Thackeray are given parenthetically in the text, using the following abbreviations: *N: The Newcomes: Memoirs of a Most Respectable Family*, ed. Andrew Sanders (Oxford: Oxford University Press, 1995); *RP: Roundabout Papers, Little Travels, and Roadside Sketches*, in *The Works of William Makepeace Thackeray*, Kensington Edition, xxvii (New York: Scribners, 1904). *VF: Vanity Fair: A Novel without A Hero*, ed. John Sutherland (Oxford: Oxford University Press, 1983).

[2] For a polemical exploration of this figural exchange, so common in Thackeray, see Janice Radway, 'Reading is Not Eating: Mass-Produced Literature and the Theoretical, Methodological, and Political Consequences of a Metaphor', *Book Research Quarterly* 2/3 (Fall 1986), 7–29.

Figure 2.2. 'Jones, who reads this book at his Club', from chapter 1 of *Vanity Fair*, in *The Works of William Makepeace Thackeray*, i (London: Smith, Elder, 1883), 7. General Research Division, The New York Public Library, Astor, Lenox, and Tilden Foundations

arrangement suggest an invitation to be seen. His arrogation of one of the room's other chairs for his feet, and the very posed quality of his legs, indicates that he is 'striking an attitude', a reading attitude that displays a distanced attention from the text that he reads from behind an almost literally upturned nose, that foot, foot-and-a-half gap between his nose and his book expressive of a similarly large critical distance from its narrative. This is a reading looking for a momentary distraction, and all too happy to be distracted even from that search. Unlike the lazy idle boy's disembodied absorption, the focus of Jones's attention is not on any unraveling of plot—not, that is, pitched toward the long term, toward waiting or suspense—but is instead oriented toward the miniature: the individual unit or phrase which he highlights, from amidst the bored distraction of his gaze, with that marker of the phrase-fetishizer, the pencil. Where the lazy idle boy's hunched body signals the tensed but unconscious attitude of expectant attention, Jones's reclined slouch expresses an incipient inattention, a constant readiness to put his book down in preference for some more diverting entertainment.[3]

---

[3] Not surprisingly, the importance of Jones's image as a way of thinking through Thackeray's relation to the reading act has been stressed in two recent, influential pieces: Garrett Stewart's account of Jones's image as 'a fun-house mirror in which you resist recognizing the image of your

The polarity offered by these two images, repeated with slight variations in a host of Thackeray's novels and sketches, turns on the issue of attention: the lazy idle boy emblematizing the kind of engrossment which Valéry, as we have seen, described as a 'crise de crédulité', a disembodied and prolonged state; Jones standing for what we might think of as an abjected or 'bad' reading, distracted, distanced, unable to focus for long. This binary, however, is ultimately an illusory one, and it is the opening contention of this chapter that Thackeray's complex and career-long engagement with the issue of his readers' attention spans tended in fact to see both tense, directed focusing and relaxed, vagrant mental drift as components of the same process: a rhythmic oscillation between attentiveness and distraction, or alertness and obliviousness, that characterized all reading, particularly all reading of novelistic narrative. 'Attention', in Thackeray, is constantly in danger of slipping into its supposed opposite, distraction or obliviousness; or, perhaps more pertinently to these images, riveted attention is for Thackeray one kind of inattention.

This is most apparent in the way in which both images of reading are haunted by the possibility of interruption. If Jones wants to be seen—if he seems to invite the distraction that will lead him to stop reading—the fate that awaits the lazy idle boy is the revenge of the world that, while reading, he holds in suspension: 'the anger, or it may be, the reverberations of his schoolmaster, or the remonstrances of his father, or the tender pleadings of his mother that he should not let the supper grow cold' (*RP*, 5). Although the reading boy is alone in the frame of the illustration, the explanatory text of the sketch, as well as the detailed background to the image itself, insists upon the very mess of details (scenic beauty, family obligations, everyday mundanity) that the lazy idle boy is only temporarily managing to still and that will soon, we are promised, force themselves upon him. The schoolboy hunched over a book is also, not coincidentally, the schoolboy who will soon be beaten for *not* paying attention. If, that is, Jones is raising an ironic eyebrow over his play-acted attention to his book—showing us how unabsorbed he really is—the unironic absorption of the lazy idle boy is presented, oddly, as a species of distraction. As Thackeray seems at pains to point out, it is not so much that his emblematic boy is paying attention to something; it is more accurate to say that he is *not* paying attention to *many* things. Rapt

own readerly impatience', and Kate Flint's argument for the complexities of gender identification in this scene. See Garrett Stewart, *Dear Reader: The Conscripted Audience in Nineteenth-Century British Fiction* (Baltimore: Johns Hopkins University Press, 1996), 50; Kate Flint, 'Women, Men, and the Reading of *Vanity Fair*', in *The Practice and Representation of Reading in England*, ed. James Raven, Helen Small, and Naomi Tadmor (Cambridge: Cambridge University Press, 1996), 246–62.

attentiveness of one kind, in Thackeray, is only an alternative version of distraction.

Put another way, the stress in Thackeray's descriptions of reading—and, as we shall see, of any absorptive solitary act—is on what it misses, from what it is distracted, to what it is oblivious. It might be the text that is barely attended to, or the text might, although only temporarily, preclude attention to the world; but in either case, distraction is the pervasive mental state in Thackeray's frequent descriptions of solitary consumption. Attention of any kind, as we learn in Thackeray, has necessary limits, either by a blurring out into some less focused consciousness, or by being jerked back to the provisionally ignored world; attention seems to be just a periodic or rhythmic punctuation—as intense as the lazy idle boy's gaze, or as sharp as Jones's pencil—in a general wave of what we might call cognitive drift.⁴ This is a paradox well known to contemporary students of attention; as Jonathan Crary puts it, attention is 'continuous with states of distraction, reverie, dissociation, and trance', and is 'haunted by the possibility of its own excess—which we all know so well whenever we try to look at or listen to any one thing for too long'.⁵ For students and scholars of the novel, however—even, perhaps, for general readers—this amounts to a scandal. If attention is both temporally limited and also only partial, only part of some greater inattention, how then to read long, detail-rich narratives without sloppiness? Is Thackeray, simply put, a cynic or a defeatist when it comes to the question of how to read well?

The exigency of the question derives from matters of both literary form and social ethics. While we have some theories of attention and reading, such as Peter Rabinowitz's concept of 'rules of notice', what we have most of are scattered and even gnomic asides, and we have no account of how particular literary forms or genres seek to structure readerly attention—and certainly no account of how, specifically, the novel either sought, produced, enticed, or resisted the full attention of readers, or even of how it may have defined

---

⁴ In an alternative context and with slightly different emphases in mind, I have discussed the concept of periodic or punctuated attentiveness in Nicholas Dames, 'Reverie, Sensation, Effect: Novelistic Attention and Stendhal's *De l'amour*', *Narrative* 10/1 (Jan. 2002), 47–68. While not entirely dissimilar from the images of attention that Stendhal offers, Thackeray's example leads to different political, ethical, and formal considerations of the value of attention in reading.

⁵ Jonathan Crary, *Suspensions of Perception: Attention, Spectacle, and Modern Culture* (Cambridge, Mass.: MIT Press, 1999), 46–7. Crary's book is the most thorough and inventive study of attention as a connection between aesthetics and social psychology. Other valuable studies include Alison Winter's discussion of the physiology of attentiveness in the Victorian sensation novel in *Mesmerized: Powers of Mind in Victorian Fiction* (Chicago: University of Chicago Press, 1998), 326–9; and Stephen Arata's recent account of late nineteenth-century resistance to the claims of attention in 'On Not Paying Attention', *Victorian Studies* 46/2 (Winter 2004), 193–205.

the concept of 'attention'.[6] More precision is needed, in relation to both novelistic form and cultural norms of attentiveness, in order to determine what kinds of attention certain genres (such as, for instance, the mid-Victorian serial or multi-plot novel) demanded, or how certain genres managed readerly attention, and how those generic formations of readerly attention related to wider cultural notions of what qualified as mental alertness. Thackeray's position in relation to these questions is immediately provocative. Ever since Henry James's famous description of *The Newcomes* as exemplary of a class of 'large loose baggy monsters'—later echoed by F. R. Leavis's far more dismissive comment that reading Thackeray is 'merely a matter of going on and on'—he has been taken as an example of Victorian fiction's embarrassing reluctance to require strenuous attention.[7] Something about Thackerayan form pushes against expected, valorized norms of readerly alertness and concentration, in ways that dismayingly seem to code novel-reading as pure frivolity, something to be dipped into at leisure, rather than a heroic, sophisticated, or arduous process of sense making.

That 'something' has often been ascribed to the roots of Thackeray's mature novels in the processes of sketch writing, which seem to invite a discontinuous grazing rather than a focused consumption.[8] Another possible culprit has been multi-plot narrative, which—however complex a cognitive process of comparison and differentiation it may involve—nonetheless raises the problem of distraction. Peter Garrett's explanation is exemplary for the discomfort it voices: 'To multiply plots is to divide the fictional world, to disrupt the continuity of each line in order to shift from one to another, to disperse the reader's attention. We cannot even name or conceive of the form without implicitly raising this problem.'[9] Thackeray's comments on how he

---

[6] For Rabinowitz's helpful concept, see Peter Rabinowitz, *Before Reading: Narrative Conventions and the Politics of Interpretation* (Ithaca, NY: Cornell University Press, 1987), 51–6. On the gnomic, one might cite Roland Barthes's assertion that 'we do not read everything with the same intensity of reading; a rhythm is established, casual, unconcerned with the *integrity* of the text . . . has anyone ever read Proust, Balzac, *War and Peace*, word for word?'; or D. A. Miller's parenthetical remark, apropos of *David Copperfield*: 'Another open secret that everyone knows and no one wants to: the immense amount of daydreaming that accompanies the ordinary reading of a novel.' See Roland Barthes, *The Pleasure of the Text*, trans. Richard Miller (New York: Noonday, 1975), 10–11; D. A. Miller, *The Novel and the Police* (Berkeley: University of California Press, 1988), 215.

[7] See Henry James, 'Preface to *The Tragic Muse*', in *The Art of the Novel*, ed. R. P. Blackmur (New York: Scribners, 1934), 84; F. R. Leavis, *The Great Tradition* (Garden City, NY: Doubleday, 1954), 21.

[8] See, e.g., Richard Pearson's account of the noncontinuous reading modes imagined by Thackeray's travel sketchbooks: *W. M. Thackeray and the Mediated Text: Writing for Periodicals in the Mid-Nineteenth Century* (Aldershot: Ashgate, 2000), 101–2.

[9] Peter Garrett, *The Victorian Multiplot Novel: Studies in Dialogical Form* (New Haven: Yale University Press, 1980), 2.

imagined the consumption of his own novels only confirm this unheroic sense
of reading; his frequently voiced opinion is that the most pleasurable reading
is one closest to sleep: 'I should like to write a nightcap book,' he writes in 'On
Two Children in Black': 'a book that you can muse over, that you can smile
over, that you can yawn over . . . a dip into the volume at random and so on for
a page or two: a nod and then a smile; and presently a gape; and the book drops
out of your hand, and so, *bon soir*, and pleasant dreams to you' (*RP*, 12–13).

   Here, however, Thackeray is more than disarming; he is touching upon a
prevalent concern within the physiological study of the reading act. In the vein
of the sleep-reading interest of Lewes and Dallas seen in the previous chapter,
Thackeray's interest in sleep and reading signals an important reconfiguration
of the reading act: the mind's inattention at moments of consumption signals
a freedom, even a liberty, that is at war with constant, strained attentiveness.
If sleep and reading were linked for physiological literary theorists because
of their shared root in unconscious physical performance, for Thackeray
both sleep and reading offer the mind emancipation from rigid control.
The rapt attention of the lazy idle boy, seen this way, is less valuable as
a state of concentration than as a state of willful inattention to the social
and familial controls that reading is a distraction *from*; and the haughty
distractedness of Jones's reading is offensive only insofar as it flaunts a
freedom from authorial control that is not always easy to feel. Garrett
Stewart's recent claim that the Victorian novel is characterized by a 'relentless
micromanagement of reaction' becomes tricky when applied to Thackeray,
who seems to prefer micromanaging his readers precisely in order to release
them from the subjection of micromanagement—to encourage them to be
irresponsible in their consumption.[10] Sleep, as the *sine qua non* of readerly
irresponsibility, thus occupies a privileged space in Thackeray's gallery of
reader portraits.

   Thackeray's insistence upon distracted readings and readers is more than just
weary self-deprecation. As this chapter will argue, it is part of a characteristic
mid-Victorian liberal discourse on 'liberty' and its enabling conditions. If we
balk at this linkage between distraction and liberty, it is perhaps because of a
long, familiar tradition of thinking that equates reading and social ethics by
locating attentiveness as the primary way in which textual construal becomes
good citizenship. Not coincidentally, this tradition, which allies cultural
conservatives and culture-industry Frankfurt School theorists, tends to read

---

[10] Stewart, *Dear Reader*, 21. As Stewart later writes, that micromanagement is usually applied
to the goal of having the reader 'alert and on call, always potentially *at attention*'—a claim whose
persuasiveness is, I would argue, only buttressed by Thackeray's frequent insistence that he is
not asking for the kind of attention that it might otherwise seem like he should. See ibid. 46.

the Victorian novel as the tragic moment in a history of modern consumption. Q. D. Leavis's blunt assessment, in *Fiction and the Reading Public* (1932), is exemplary: 'Victorian popular novelists accustomed the reading public to habits of diminished vigilance, provoked an uncritical response and discovered the appeals which have since made the fortunes of Sir James Barrie and Mr. A. A. Milne, the reputation of the Poet Laureate, and the success of most later nineteenth-century and twentieth-century bestsellers.' What Leavis described as the 'mental alertness' of the Elizabethan theatergoing audience is irreparably damaged by the Victorian serial novel, which abandoned 'cumulative effect for a piecemeal succession of immediate effects'.[11] Theodor Adorno, in a similar vein, read the 'popular or semi-popular novels of the first half of the nineteenth century' as the progenitors of television, and as the historical agent of the lowering of 'middle-class requirements bound up with internalization', such as, prominently, 'concentration'. The accounts of distraction found in Siegfried Kracauer and Walter Benjamin tell a similar story: the fragmentation and temporal shortening of attention (produced by prose fiction) of modernity, which makes sustained political or ethical thought impossible.[12] So powerful has this line of thinking been that defenses of the mid-Victorian multi-plot novel must inevitably reassert, against Leavis or Adorno, the attentiveness required by the form, as when Michael Lund and Linda Hughes argue that serial novels demanded 'long-term commitment and sympathy, expanding structures of thought, the ability to connect distant pieces of a whole . . . [and] regular, disciplined effort'.[13] The morality of attention—a social morality, concerned with the ability to act knowingly and responsibly—remains unquestioned here, either in attack or defense of the novel. We might, in fact, hypothesize a tradition of thinking called 'cognitive

[11] Q. D. Leavis, *Fiction and the Reading Public* (London: Chatto & Windus, 1932), 230, 85, 157. Leavis's use of the word 'vigilance' as a synonym for politicized attention is telling; the term is primarily associated with psychological or 'human factor' research into attention-span limits carried out during and after the Second World War, when the cognitive processes involved in such work as radar scanning were put under close observation. See L. S. Hearnshaw, *The Shaping of Modern Psychology* (London: Routledge & Kegan Paul, 1987), 206–9. Much of modern attention studies, such as the influential information-processing theories of British psychologists Colin Cherry and Donald Broadbent in the 1950s, originates from this wartime study.

[12] Adorno, 'How to Look at Television', in *The Culture Industry: Selected Essays on Mass Culture*, trans. J. M. Bernstein (London: Routledge, 1991), 161–2. For Kracauer, see 'Cult of Distraction', in Siegfried Kracauer, *The Mass Ornament: Weimar Essays*, trans. Thomas Levin (Cambridge, Mass.: Harvard University Press, 1995), 323–8; for Benjamin, see his description of the readership of Baudelaire's time, for whom 'the reading of lyric poetry would present difficulties. . . . Will power and the ability to concentrate are not their strong points': 'Some Motifs in Baudelaire', in *Illuminations: Essays and Reflections*, trans. Harry Zohn (New York: Schocken, 1968), 155.

[13] Linda Hughes and Michael Lund, *The Victorian Serial* (Charlottesville: University Press of Virginia, 1991), 275–6.

ethics', which reads attention as 'vigilance' (Leavis's term), and which reads literary form's place in social life as the ability or failure to inculcate habits of mental concentration. It is not surprising that the recent claim, made by his son, that Lionel Trilling had Attention Deficit Disorder (ADD)—and that the disease influenced his interpretive style—has been so controversial; inattention and reading have not, in the twentieth century, been a comfortable fit.[14] The place of the novel form in this line of thought has been slippery, but in general it has been more castigated than praised, even if recent accounts of the virtues of attentiveness have tried, however hesitantly, to reclaim novel-reading.[15]

If novel-reading can be reclaimed, according to the terms of the prevailing tradition and its assumptions, it is by becoming labor: vigilant, disciplined, alert, concentrated. Here Thackeray's relation to distraction becomes clearer by contrast, as does the status of 'attention' in mid-Victorian discourses on literary form or human psychology. Victorian physiology, as we shall see, continually stressed the limitations of attention, to such an extent that their picture of attentiveness seems far closer to our contemporary category of ADD: a wavelike, in-and-out, temporally restricted capacity that, if stretched beyond its naturally small boundaries, ceases to become attention at all and instead becomes distraction. This scientific conceptualization of attention was often spurred on by the conditions of Victorian factory labor, where the perdurability of concentration was so evident: the longer that attention must be paid, the less effectively it will be paid. Victorian physiology's goal here might be considered the explosion of the myth—a myth of capital, as Marx saw it—that 'more' attention was always possible. Attention's enemy, for Victorian physiology, was duration—and therefore any temporally expanded form, such as the novel, could cohere only if it stopped resisting distraction and started instead

---

[14] See James Trilling, 'My Father and the Weak-Eyed Devils', *American Scholar* 68/2 (Spring 1999), 17–41.

[15] See, e.g., Julian Johnson's recent *Who Needs Classical Music?* (Oxford: Oxford University Press, 2002), which argues for the 'concentrated attention' necessitated by Western classical music's discursivity, in contrast to the distracted modes of listening created by modern forms of recording and listening technology. Johnson attempts a clarification by claiming that in 'some ways it [classical music] is comparable to a rather involved novel or film'—a clearly hesitant analogy, in which it remains unclear whether the novel, which after all can, as Johnson admits, suffer little damage from some skipping or from putting it down for a while, is more like classical music or its distracted, distracting opposite. See ibid. 35–6. For a polemical argument against the kind of 'concentrated attention' that Johnson admires, see Ross Chambers's defense of 'loiterly literature', which cleverly and innocuously displays a 'recalcitrance to the laws that maintain "good order" . . . it incorporates and enacts—in a way that may be quite unintended—a criticism of the disciplined and the orderly, the hierarchical and the stable, the methodical and the systematic, showing them to be unpleasurable, that is, alienating'. Ross Chambers, *Loiterature* (Lincoln: University of Nebraska Press, 1999), 9–10.

to allow for, even encourage, mental drift. This notion of a form permitting or supporting distraction is the central operating hypothesis of this chapter. Thackeray, in line with the Victorian physiological thinking that subtended discussions of literary form in the period, attempts in his novels—particularly *The Newcomes*—to manage distraction, not by combating it but by offering it material upon which to work, or spaces to 'opt out' of attention. His novelistic form is openly non-laborious: instead of offering an expanse of abstract, undifferentiated time, that of the factory worker, he offers rhythmically punctuated oscillations, or an intermittency between attention and reverie, concentration and drift. This is apparent in the largest movements of his plots as well as in the operations of small scenes, in which even moments of rapt, directed consciousness are bracketed by a descriptive procedure that insists upon the emptiness of attention in contrast to the vibrant fullness of a distracted mental wandering. Thackeray's thinking-through of the question of readerly attentiveness does at times center on the different-yet-similar conditions of visual art reception, which accounts for the large number of illustrations that this chapter discusses; this is hardly a surprise, given that the most accomplished analyses of modern attention, such as those by Crary and Michael Fried, take visuality as the locus of attention studies. But in visual art Thackeray finds not only a way to 'interrupt' text—although that is certainly one effect of his illustrations—but also a way to represent half-attentive states that become one of the primary cognitive and ethical values of his fiction. To read Thackeray's distraction, then, we must push past the unofficial moralities of attention as they have been handed down to us, and consider instead a fictional form that solicits its readers only in order better to leave them alone, free to drift.

EMPTY ABSORPTION: *VANITY FAIR*

There can be no doubt that, as Kate Flint remarks, Thackeray's first major novel 'persistently draws attention to the process of reading itself'.[16] Yet reading in *Vanity Fair* is an activity situated within a larger category to which our attention is even more insistently drawn: attention *per se*. Absorptive states are so common in *Vanity Fair* as virtually to dictate the composition of illustrations as well as the visual presentation of character depth; unlike the comic-dramatic group tableaux of Dickens's illustrators, Thackeray prefers

---

[16] Kate Flint, 'Women, Men, and the Reading of *Vanity Fair*', in *The Woman Reader, 1837–1914* (Oxford: Clarendon Press, 1993), 247.

isolated portraits of characters engaged in reverie, silent thought, and solitary
musing, oddly refusing to take advantage of the space that full-page illustrations offered for novelistic crowds to gather.[17] The example of Amelia Sedley's
protracted waiting for a visit from George Osborne is paradigmatic: Thackeray's illustration depicts her leaning on one hand, sitting before a window,
gazing absently—or attentively?—across Russell Square (see Figure 2.3). It
is a characteristic instance of mental immersion because of several factors,
most notably its presumed duration; we are allowed to infer that this is her
habitual pose while George is away at his Rochester barracks.[18] Its primary
affective qualities—namely, waiting (for George) and suspense (when will
he next come?)—are further typical qualities of the attentive state, and we
might even characterize this kind of attention as a narrative drive, since her
thoughts are presumably tending not only to his next arrival but also to the
possible marital consequences of that hoped-for visit.[19] It is an image, and
a set of affective relations, that is familiar not only from the genre paintings
of Greuze and Chardin in which Michael Fried detects the origin of modern
absorption, but also from a similar series of Pre-Raphaelite works whose force
derives from the reverie displayed by a solitary female figure. It is, in short,
one very common model for reception: a disembodied, projected interest,
disembodied enough that Amelia's thoughts, we are told, 'sped away as if
they were angels and had wings, and flying down the river to Chatham and
Rochester, strove to peep into the barracks where George was' (*VF*, 146).
At this point Thackeray closes his considerations of Amelia's absorption. He

---

[17] The extent to which this is true of Thackeray is amply demonstrated by how untrue it
becomes when he turned to Richard Doyle to illustrate *The Newcomes*. Doyle's images restore
a more Dickensian crowdedness to Thackeray's pages, centering on the climactic moments of
confrontation in the text that Thackeray's work for *Vanity Fair* and *Pendennis* usually avoid in
favor of moments of solitude. On solitude in general in *Vanity Fair*, see esp. Andrew Miller's
description of a Thackerayan 'solitude so deeply rooted that it rarely recognizes itself as such',
in *Novels Behind Glass: Commodity Culture and Victorian Narrative* (Cambridge: Cambridge
University Press, 1995), 38.

[18] In the same vein, Michael Fried notes of Chardin's genre paintings that their depictions
of absorptive states 'come close to translating literal duration, the actual passage of time as one
stands before the canvas, into a purely pictorial effect: as if the very stability and unchangingness
of the painted image are perceived by the beholder not as material properties that could not be
otherwise but as manifestations of an absorptive state—the image's absorption in itself, so to
speak—that only happens to subsist'. See Michael Fried, *Absorption and Theatricality: Painting
and Beholder in the Age of Diderot* (Chicago: University of Chicago Press, 1980), 50. For an
analogous investigation of nineteenth-century iconographies of reading that use it to project
duration, see Garrett Stewart, 'Painted Readers, Narrative Regress', *Narrative* 11/2 (May 2003),
125–76.

[19] For a recent study of suspense in Victorian realism that stresses its epistemological relation
to dubiety, the suspension of judgment, and therefore heightened attention, see Caroline
Levine, *The Serious Pleasures of Suspense: Victorian Realism and Narrative Doubt* (Charlottesville:
University of Virginia Press, 2003).

Figure 2.3. Amelia's blank absorption, from chapter 13 of *Vanity Fair*, in *The Works of William Makepeace Thackeray*, i (London: Smith, Elder, 1883), 144. General Research Division, The New York Public Library, Astor, Lenox, and Tilden Foundations

closes it, at least ostensibly, because of the less-than-genteel language of the soldiers of George's mess hall, where Amelia's thoughts threatened to enter. He also closes it because every scene of absorption within *Vanity Fair* suffers a similar fate: a premature interruption.

No small part of the force of this interruption is to restore a temporal rhythm to a moment that has become spatialized: Amelia's reverie is figured not in terms of its duration—although this has no doubt been long—but in terms of the geographical length it can travel; it is as if, in her immersive state, she can imagine the narrative of her courtship with George as a series of spatial relations (to Rochester and back) rather than the continually deferred temporal process she might otherwise have to acknowledge. The spatial stasis of her immersion, most vividly figured by the illustration, can be usefully compared to a reading habit that seeks a total, spatialized comprehension of a text, such as that advocated by Percy Lubbock; much like the reader of poetry who can see the poem's complete relations at once, or the orchestra conductor who, having memorized a score, can see its internal mechanics in one act of cognition, so Lubbock's 'noetic materialist' reader creates a set of spatial relations though a rigorous process of immersion, a blocking out of any perceptual surround. Against this atemporal absorption Thackeray restores a rhythmic pulse, primarily through the ironizing text surrounding the illustration's reverie. The illustration is prefaced by George's complacent comment to Dobbin about Amelia that 'I believe she's d—d fond of me', and followed by his obviously half-hearted promise to think more of her: ' "I should have liked to make her a little present," Osborne said to his friend in confidence, "only I am quite out of cash until my father tips up" ' (*VF*, 146–7). No absorptive state in Thackeray is permitted to escape this kind of immediate satirical juxtaposition, an interruptive rhythm that carries a static moment back into a progression of dispersed pulsations.

This is equally true of reading, and it is through the looming fact of interruption, which ironizes the state of absorption, that reveries like Amelia's are linked to moments of textual consumption. Our first glimpse of Dobbin is of a large boy buried in the *Arabian Nights*, an image which bears a strong resemblance to the lazy idle boy whom Thackeray would depict thirteen years later. Here Dobbin, having found a quiet corner of a playground, immerses himself in his book, while in the immediate background two schoolfellows—the very young George Osborne and Cuff, the resident bully—prepare to fight (see Figure 2.4). 'William Dobbin had for once forgotten the world', we are told, 'and was away with Sindbad the Sailor in the Valley of Diamonds, or with Prince Ahmed and the Fairy Peribanou in that delightful cavern where the prince found her, and whither we should all like to make a tour; when shrill cries, as of a little fellow weeping, woke up his pleasant reverie; and, looking up, he saw Cuff before him, belabouring a little boy' (*VF*, 51). Thackeray's refusal to specify exactly *where* Dobbin is in his *Arabian Nights*—as if respecting the privacy of his absorptive state—is made irrelevant by the violent interruption that brings that state to a close. Dobbin's *crise de crédulité* quickly becomes a more mundane, if narratively productive, crisis of combat, which permanently allies him to George. The scene is prefaced with an elaborate display of respect for Dobbin's immersive reading and a request that its sanctity be maintained:

If people would but leave children to themselves; if teachers would cease to bully them; if parents would not insist upon directing their thoughts, and dominating

Figure 2.4. Dobbin's interrupted reading, from chapter 5 of *Vanity Fair*, in *The Works of William Makepeace Thackeray*, i (London: Smith, Elder, 1883), 49. General Research Division, The New York Public Library, Astor, Lenox, and Tilden Foundations

their feelings . . . if, I say, parents and masters would leave their children alone a little more,—small harm would accrue, although a less quantity of *as in praesenti* might be acquired. (*VF*, 51)

That respect, however, is misleading, since it is not parents or teachers who conspire to interrupt Dobbin's reading, but rather a fellow child; and it is not teachers who 'bully' Dobbin but a child bully who forces Dobbin to put the book down.[20] The lesson is mismatched to its instance, the desire for a liberty of solitary absorption ('leave children to themselves') made curiously

---

[20] Although admittedly the violence of elders, hinted at in 'On a Lazy Idle Boy', does feature in Thackeray's image repertoire of reading and interruption, as in this description from 'De Juventute', also from the 'Roundabout Papers', of a boy attempting to read novels at school: 'As he reads, there comes behind the boy, a man, a dervish, in a black gown, like a woman, and

irrelevant by the way the scene actually operates. Dobbin is not led to abandon reading by the threat of parental or supervisory violence, as the lazy idle boy is; he instead selflessly confronts an act of ordinary violence that the book had prevented him from seeing initially. The freedom from interruption, as we shall see, is in Thackeray of far less moment than the liberty provided *by* interruption.

Amelia's patient reverie and Dobbin's absorptive reading belong together because they signal something important about attention states in Thackeray: they are less paths to understanding than states of temporary delusion, less intent than obtuse. We might say of both characters that their ability to understand or manage their respective worlds is in an inverse relation to their ability to focus strongly on any one part of it. We could also say that their single-minded, even anesthetic, focus ends up shading into a kind of aphasic stupidity; and that the narrative in which these attentive trances are encased will always either slide this absorption into a literal aphasia or interrupt it with a more scattered, but also more *engaged*, perception. Amelia and Dobbin offer us attentiveness as a state less of being occupied than of being preoccupied: in other words, distracted, distractable, not quite aware of what surrounds them. The result, for at least one major Victorian critic, of this insistence upon a preoccupied consciousness—the depiction of characters with their minds pitched elsewhere—was their lack, rather than surplus, of subjective richness. W. C. Roscoe, writing in the *National Review* in 1856 of Thackeray's career in general, complained about Thackeray's characters that 'not one of them is complete; each is only so much of an individual as is embraced in a certain abstract whole'.[21] This 'abstraction' of his characters is, through a logic that we might call genteel physiological theory, guaranteed by their states of physical and cognitive 'abstraction': as Roscoe noted, Thackeray 'paints men entirely in their moments of relaxation' and refuses to describe 'a man carried out of himself by strong practical aims and interests'; he 'produces his characters on the stage generally only in their hours of idleness or amusement; and though he may indicate external occupation, he never . . . indicates an absorbing external interest. All of his characters are self-engrossed, most of them self-seeking'.[22] The implicit conclusion of Roscoe's analysis is that to be self-engrossed means to have less of a self. Thackeray's preference, so pronounced in *Vanity Fair*, for describing his characters in moments of solitary

---

a black square cap, and he has a book in each hand, and he seizes the boy who is reading the picture-book, and lays his head upon one of the books, and smacks it with the other' (*RP*, 80).

[21] William Caldwell Roscoe, 'W. M. Thackeray, Artist and Moralist', repr. from the original 1856 *National Review* version in *Poems and Essays*, ed. R. H. Hutton (London: Chapman & Hall, 1860), ii. 267.

[22] Ibid. 295–6.

absorption, or mental 'abstraction', was even in his own time understood as a process of washing away subjectivity in general, as if the blank stares of their reveries accurately reflected a blank consciousness. E. S. Dallas, a far more explicitly physiologically inclined critic than the conservative Roscoe, similarly viewed Thackeray's procedure of character description as 'a method which tends to monotony of result', in which the solitudes of his individuals can evoke only an interiority much like everyone else's.[23]

Even though Roscoe was a more traditional man-and-morals critic than Dallas, he nonetheless understood Thackeray in temporalized, even physiologized terms, and equated the blank abstraction of Thackeray's characters with the wavelike attentiveness of his readers, who can only stay absorbed at the cost of a frustrated or tired recoil:

The impression left by his books is that of weariness; the stimulants uphold you while you read; and then comes just such a reaction as if you had really mingled closely in the great world with no hopes or ambitions outside it; you feel the dust in your throat, the din and the babbling echo in your ears. Art may touch the deepest sources of passion; awe and grief and almost terror are as much within her province as laughter and calm; she may shake the heart, and leave it quivering with emotions whose intensity partakes of pain; but to make it unsatisfied, restless, anxious,—this is not her province.[24]

Our engrossment with Thackeray, such as it is, results in the tired, blank state of mind that Roscoe calls 'weariness'. The conceptual chiasmus in Roscoe displays a careful thinking-through of Thackeray's images of absorption: one encounters characters in moments of 'relaxation', Roscoe argues, yet the reader leaves the fiction with a sense of exhaustion. It is as if the attentive, 'self-engrossed' states of Thackeray's characters must result in weariness; or, perhaps, that weariness and self-engrossment, or preoccupation, are essentially no different. Enlivening, and masculinized, engagement with the world, what Roscoe describes as 'a man carried out of himself by strong practical aims and interests', can only happen by coming out of this absorptive state; Dobbin must put down his book, Amelia rise from her window seat. And perhaps we too, Roscoe suggests, must put down our book—or at least our copy of Thackeray.

What Roscoe's account of Thackerayan absorption suggests to us is the following: states of attention in Thackeray are neither descriptive (a way to 'do' subjectivity) nor prescriptive (a moral desideratum). Thackeray, like Roscoe, seems to doubt that attention equals subjectivity, despite our sense—in many cases mirrored by contemporary cognitive research—that attentive states are

---

[23] E. S. Dallas, *The Gay Science* (London: Chapman & Hall, 1866), ii. 289.
[24] Roscoe, 'W. M. Thackeray', 281–2.

necessarily egotistical.[25] Instead, 'character' seems most vivid at moments when absorption has been disrupted, such as when Dobbin's immersive reading is interrupted by his hearing the call of duty and defending a weaker child against a stronger. Similarly, Thackeray seems to doubt that absorptive attention is either wise, or even necessarily ethically positive; Amelia's patient reverie is as blinkered as it is faithful, and Dobbin's childhood heroism comes at the price of his leaving his solitary pursuits behind. Attention can be neither descriptive nor prescriptive, precisely because it is so limited: the escape into absorption, either through private reverie or the printed word, is always in Thackeray a temporally limited and largely incomplete escape from the social world. The interplay of text and illustration—where, as in the above examples, illustration performs the absorption that text will ironically bracket and undo—mirrors the back-and-forth movement (moving into the world, then back out of it, for a while) that Roscoe found wearisome. Indeed, the process of reverie interrupted is one of *Vanity Fair*'s primary *topoi*, registered from the novel's opening meditation, 'Before the Curtain':

A man with a reflective turn of mind, walking through an exhibition of this sort, will not be oppressed, I take it, by his own or other people's hilarity. An episode of humour or kindness touches and amuses him here and there;—a pretty child looking at a gingerbread stall; a pretty girl blushing whilst her lover talks to her and chooses her fairing;—poor Tom Fool, yonder behind the wagon, mumbling his bone with the honest family which lives by his tumbling;—but the general impression is one more melancholy than mirthful. When you come home, you sit down, in a sober, contemplative, not uncharitable frame of mind, and apply yourself to your books or your business. (*VF*, 1)

This movement into the Fair and back out again—to which Roscoe's description of reading Thackeray as the process of mingling with the world, and then retreating from it exhausted, seems a commentary—obviates any kind of strict attentiveness. At the Fair, the narrator's gaze wanders idly and refuses to linger, in a kind of preoccupied, almost distracted disappointment; at home, the reading that then takes place ('apply yourself to your books') seems less absorptive than dutiful, a screening *out* of sensations—particularly of the Fair—rather than any immersion in new ones, as if the 'books' are a welcome anesthetic, an after-work drink, after the chaos of the Fair.

---

[25] The necessary egotism involved in attention is most famously demonstrated by the British psychologist Colin Cherry's pioneering work—in large part the origin of modern attention studies—on the 'cocktail party effect': the way in which subjective factors determine, when an individual is presented with competing stimuli, what gets 'heard' or mentally processed. See Colin Cherry, 'Some Experiments on the Recognition of Speech, with One and with Two Ears', *Journal of the Acoustical Society of America* 25/5 (Sept. 1953), 975–9.

In the language of modern cognitive science and information theory, what is continually disrupted in Thackeray, either by the back-and-forth movement inevitable between book and world or by some more sudden interruption, is 'flow': a seemingly effortless and atemporal focusing of consciousness on one task, a pure and unburdened state of immersion that is not exhausting so much as enlivening.[26] The disappearance of time produced by flow—the 'I didn't realize it had taken so long' experience—is undone by the frequent interruptions of Thackeray's form, whether those interruptions occur between text and illustration (what we might call the phenomenological level), between issues of serial numbers (what we might call the material, or social, level), or between temporary immersion in the book and reentry into the world (the imagistic level).[27] Indeed, our very difficulty in determining whether the 'books' in the above passage are the world, or a refuge from it, is telling; obviously the Fair is very much *Vanity Fair*, a busy, but melancholy, succession of sights, yet the narrator describes retreating from this Fair to read—perhaps even to read *Vanity Fair*. To those readers who, like Wolfgang Iser, read Thackeray's interruptions as an almost Brechtian practice of forcing readers into critical alertness (what Q. D. Leavis would call 'vigilance'), we might counter with Thackeray's constant description of alertness as a state of inattention *to something else*.[28]

Furthermore, despite frequent attempts to distinguish between characters in *Vanity Fair* on the basis of kinds of response habits—whether by gender codes, as in Kate Flint's study, or as different affective types, as in Peter Garrett's—no major character in the novel is unsusceptible to being described

[26] 'Flow' is defined by the psychologist Mihaly Csikszentmihalyi as 'optimal experience', or the feeling of order in consciousness provided by the ability to establish 'control over attention'. See Mihaly Csikszentmihalyi, *Flow: The Psychology of Optimal Experience* (New York: Harper & Row, 1990), 39–41. Of interest to students of nineteenth-century culture is Czikszentmihalyi's willingness—derived, perhaps, from information theory's desire to optimize the speed and efficiency of mental processing—to situate moments of flow in manual labor, even assembly-line labor, which places him in a tradition of Victorian thinking about attention of which he seems unaware. It is as if Czikszentmihalyi's workers want to experience 'flow', while Victorian factory workers are condemned to do so.

[27] On the temporal experience of serial reading, see Hughes and Lund, *Victorian Serial*, 5–8: 'If the publication of works a part at a time met the needs of increasingly rushed readers who were not free to devote continuous hours to reading, the serial dovetailed even more with the new awareness of time's extended duration.' Hughes and Lund do, however, claim a continuity to this duration—a stretching across interruptions, or a sustained quality to serial form—that my account of Thackerayan attention implicitly contests.

[28] See Iser's reading of *Vanity Fair* in Wolfgang Iser, *The Implied Reader: Patterns of Communication in Prose Fiction from Bunyan to Beckett* (Baltimore: Johns Hopkins University Press, 1974).

or pictured through the mechanics of mental drift.[29] For all her acute plotting and ability to concentrate on the tactical matters at hand, even Becky Sharp is caught in moments of inattention, such as her evident boredom during the daily routine of governessing depicted in Thackeray's illustration (see Figure 2.5). Her reverie is the result of exactly the kind of supervisory neglect that Thackeray had advised so strongly in relation to Dobbin's reading: 'She did not pester their young brains with too much learning, but, on the contrary, let them have their own way in regard to educating themselves; for what instruction is more effectual than self-instruction?' (*VF*, 106). The sudden ironizing, through Becky, of an educational philosophy that had been so urgently pressed chapters before is perhaps less surprising than that Becky's pose so neatly forms a diptych with Amelia's pose of reverie; each is depicted in a moment of mental absence which, rather than performing the work of differentiating their personalities, blurs them together. Characters in *Vanity Fair* may not all act alike, and their social personae may be carefully distinct, but in moments of private absorption (which are identical to moments of mental blankness), they look the same.

Absorptive states, then, can look indistinguishable from boredom, a boredom that Patricia Meyer Spacks reminds us is the affective sign of an oppressive social control in Thackeray.[30] If attentiveness in *Vanity Fair* can seem at all more alive than the submissive or distracted gazes of Amelia and Becky, it is only for children. As the final pendant illustration to Chapter 7 suggests, the pleased and rapt attention of a child engaged in a difficult task is a fondly recalled, if by virtue of its miniaturization rather precious and even ironized, state (see Figure 2.6). Not coincidentally, the illustration follows one of the narrative voice's longer divagations, one which, apropos of Becky's stagecoach journey to Queen's Crawley, loses itself in memories of vanished coach travel. The work of the illustration is ostensibly to belittle the narrator's nostalgic laments—'Alas! we shall never hear the horn sing at midnight, or see the pike-gates fly open any more' (*VF*, 87)—by comparison with the self-occupation of children building similarly flimsy edifices. But a key difference remains, and opens up an unbridgeable space between focused child and discursive narrator; the comparison is deliberately imperfect. What the child performs unconsciously, the narrator performs as an attempt at communication; what is absorptive for the child has, to use Michael Fried's terms, become theatrical for the narration. As Eve Sedgwick has argued in relation to Henry James, the

---

[29] See Flint, 'Women, Men, and the Reading of *Vanity Fair*'; and Garrett, *Victorian Multiplot Novel*, 105–6: 'we postulate a narrative whose figures function first of all as registers of experience, instruments for establishing a characteristic relation to the world.'

[30] See Patricia Meyer Spacks, *Boredom: The Literary History of a State of Mind* (Chicago: University of Chicago Press, 1995), 201–8.

Miss Sharp in her School-room

Figure 2.5. Becky's bored inattention, from chapter 10 of *Vanity Fair*, in *The Works of William Makepeace Thackeray*, i (London: Smith, Elder, 1883), opposite p. 106. General Research Division, The New York Public Library, Astor, Lenox, and Tilden Foundations

Figure 2.6. The absorptive state of the child, from chapter 7 of *Vanity Fair*, in *The Works of William Makepeace Thackeray*, i (London: Smith, Elder, 1883), opposite p. 85. General Research Division, The New York Public Library, Astor, Lenox, and Tilden Foundations

novelist theatricalizes the nonperformative absorption of an 'inner child'.[31] As the famous illustration of Jones at his club suggests, once absorption becomes performative, it ceases to be absorption at all. While the child building a card house is occupied, Thackeray's narrator is merely preoccupied; the best we can say of his level of mental focus is that he has 'things on his mind'.

Similarly, while the absorbed child plays happily unaware of company, Thackeray's narrative voice disrupts self-engrossed absorption continually in the effort to connect with those who may be listening. In this sense his narrator is less discursive than simply *phatic*: attempting to find social contact, any social contact, to somehow escape the trap of self-enclosure or opacity that is the fate of any of his momentarily absorbed characters.[32] The narrator's distracted attempts to connect, as against the absorption of his miniature child, signal something intriguing about Thackeray's concept of reading: it might be said that reading, unlike the child's card house, is not an autotelic activity, not valuable simply for eliciting a state of immersion; it is a path to something else. Those whom I have previously called cognitive ethicists—from Q. D.

---

[31] Sedgwick reflects upon James's 'ways of negotiating the intersection between absorption and theatricality, between the subjectivity-generating space defined by the loved but unintegrated "inner child," on the one hand, and on the other hand the frontal space of performance'. See Eve Kosofsky Sedgwick, *Touching Feeling: Affect, Pedagogy, Performativity* (Durham, NC: Duke University Press, 2003), 44.

[32] Of interest here is Richard Pearson's account of the sheer oddity of Thackeray's journalistic style, which insists upon the preoccupation, or self-absorption, of the journalist relating the story; as Pearson claims, this voice, capable only of relating an inner world, is 'an unpacking of the journalist persona'. See Pearson, *W. M. Thackeray and the Mediated Text*, 154.

Leavis through to contemporary information scientists—often espouse a kind of debased aestheticism, in which the ability of a pursuit to simply engage attention, whatever its content, is a positive value; attention becomes an end in itself.[33] Thackeray's anxiously phatic narrative voice instead sees the novel as a medium, a path to something else; rapt attention, of the kind Dobbin gives his *Arabian Nights*, is both somehow worthy—Thackeray is not entirely free of the sense that attention is a moral good—and yet limited, an ultimately failed alternative to the social world. This was, as we shall now see, not an uncommon relation to attention in the mid-nineteenth century. Thackeray was not swimming against the current of psychological or physiological approaches to attention, but giving voice and form to a discourse that, for reasons both methodological and political, was suspicious of the value or even possibility of prolonged attentive states.

PHYSIOLOGY AND DIRECTED CONSCIOUSNESS

If it is true, as Jonathan Crary has argued, that dominant regimes of eighteenth- and nineteenth-century neural science such as associationism and physiology did not assign any important role to attention, that fact is part of a general attempt to downplay the role of alert cognition in schemes of mental functioning.[34] The methodologies of physiology in particular often confronted the phenomenon of attentiveness, yet did so only to demonstrate its relatively weak character as an only intermittently possible, and by no means essential, aspect of neural processing, which had powers that ran far deeper than any alert intake of perceptual information. Here Lewes's 1860 *Physiology of Common Life* was paradigmatic. Lewes is first at pains to explain that attention is not coextensive with consciousness, but merely a narrowed version of it: 'We shall do well to hold fast by the maxim that to have a sensation, and to be conscious of it, are one and the same thing; but to have a sensation, and to attend to it, are two different things. Attention is the direction of the consciousness—not the consciousness itself.'[35]

This formulation—attention as a 'directed consciousness', a selection of perceptual channels, but not consciousness *per se*—is in fact not at all far from

---

[33] See esp. Csikszentmihalyi, who voices this oddly aestheticist quality of information science most baldly: 'The key element of an optimal experience is that it is an end in itself.' Elsewhere he discusses what he calls 'the autotelic personality', which sounds remarkably like a Paterian aesthete seeking the fruit of a quickened, multiplied consciousness. See *Flow*, 67, 83–93.

[34] See Crary, *Suspensions of Perception*, 20–1.

[35] G. H. Lewes, *The Physiology of Common Life* (London: Blackwood, 1860), ii. 53.

contemporary approaches to attention, but Lewes's emphasis is surprisingly dismissive in tone; he is eager to point out forms of non-attentive consciousness that are as effective as more focused or alert mental acts.[36]

For this claim Lewes marshals several examples as evidence, such as autonomic actions like respiration and circulation, of which we are conscious but to which we do not pay attention; whereas attention is marshaled only by extremes of bodily pleasure or pain, normal and healthy physical functioning is predicated upon a certain inattentive consciousness of these actions, which Lewes describes as 'a massive and diffusive sensation arising from the organic processes . . . a vast and powerful stream of sensation, belonging to none of the special Senses, but to the System as a whole'.[37] This Lewes proves by recommending a latter-day Cartesian experiment in solitary reverie, describing the act of sitting in front a window, losing oneself in the view, and nonetheless feeling in a sub-attentive manner the quiet presence of one's self as a working organism. Reverie in Lewes's *Physiology* is not an abdication of consciousness but expressive of consciousness in its pure, non-attentive state of undifferentiated intake of information, both external (the view out the window) and internal (the stilled vibrancy of one's body). This is not, however, limited to acts of autonomic bodily functioning. Lewes's most consistent metaphor for the power of inattentive mental processing is, in fact, reading, particularly the familiar—at least to readers of either Victorian physiology or Thackeray—example of sleep-reading.

Describing a sleeping listener of an oral reading, Lewes states: 'Page after page is read aloud, exciting no perception at all in our minds; but has there been no sensation excited? We have not *heard*, but have we not been *affected* by the sounds?'[38] The distinction between reading-as-perception (forming ideas, making mental pictures) and reading-as-sensation (a wave of affect possible without directed consciousness) works toward delineating a kind of absorption that is not exactly attention, and might even be its opposite.[39] By

---

[36] Contemporary psychological approaches, mediating between information science and cognitive science, consider attention primarily as the act of selection: major competing models of attention since the Second World War have been divided between 'early selection' and 'late selection' theories. For early selection theories see Donald Broadbent, *Perception and Communication* (London: Pergamon, 1958); for late selection theories see J. Anthony Deutsch and Diana Deutsch, 'Attention: Some Theoretical Considerations', *Psychological Review* 70/1 (1963), 80–90. Notions of selection are also current in narrative theory; Peter Rabinowitz defines his term 'rules of notice' as textual markers that 'direct' or 'concentrate' the reader's consciousness and therefore screen out irrelevant information. See Rabinowitz, *Before Reading*, 53–6.

[37] Lewes, *Physiology*, 68.   [38] Ibid. 61–2.

[39] Of particular use here is Michael Fried's discussion of why, for French painters of the 1750s, the representation of absorptive states often took the form of 'obliviousness or unconsciousness', particularly sleeping. See Fried, *Absorption and Theatricality*, 31.

virtue of falling asleep, the listener enters a state that is less selective than simply, purely receptive. While Lewes is of course far from recommending sleep as the proper state of textual consumption, he is here attempting to reclaim being 'affected' by text, even in this proto-hypnotic way, as worthy of consideration alongside more alert forms of processing. What the alert listener or reader has in common with the listener or reader in a state of reverie or sleep is, paradoxically, the fact of missing something. The somnolent consumer misses meaning; the alert consumer, or so it seems, may miss affect. This is what Alexander Bain was referring to in calling the epistemological exertions of plot interest, in his *Emotions and the Will*, 'an anesthetic'; forms of alertness, which Bain called 'that entranced attention, under which the mind is debarred from feeling, and from all thoughts extraneous to the situation', often shut off emotional or affective responses.[40]

Which is to say that the attentive reader is missing more than just the host of automatic actions that accompany reading, those actions that Thomas Huxley, in a parallel, 1866 discussion of the reading act, describes as 'a multitude of most delicate muscular actions . . . of which the reader is not in the slightest degree aware', such as muscular contractions in hands, eyes, and lungs.[41] By becoming disembodied—the most important fact of attentive reading for physiologists—the focused reader detaches herself from the more diffusive currents of emotional waves which are known primarily through visceral or central nervous networks. This of course could lead to an emphasis on how attention, which in reading is an 'anesthetic', is a necessary aspect of self-discipline, as it did in the work of Bain, who consistently advocates 'the habitual control of the Attention, as against the diversions caused by outward objects'. As Bain exhorted his readers, 'We have to be put under training to resist those various solicitations, and to keep the mind as steadily fixed upon the work in hand as if they did not happen.' For Bain, this process of attention training could begin as early as the child's tenth month.[42] Bain's theory of attention-as-socialization, however, could not entirely obscure an equal commitment on the part of physiological psychology to register the different forms of intake or

[40] Alexander Bain, *The Emotions and the Will*, 2nd edn. (London: Longmans, Green, 1865), 150–1.

[41] Thomas Huxley, *Lessons in Elementary Physiology*, 2nd edn. (London: Macmillan, 1879), 270.

[42] Bain, *Emotions and the Will*, 460–1, 366. It seems that Victorian parenting began attention training even earlier than Bain's ten-month limit, as Elizabeth Gaskell's diaries indicate; in an entry relating to her 6-month-old daughter Marianne, she writes: 'I try always to let her look at anything which attracts her notice as long as she will, and when I see her looking very intently at anything, I take her to it, and let her exercise all her senses upon it—even to tasting, if I am sure it can do her no harm. My object is to give her a habit of fixing her attention.' See J. A. V. Chapple and Anita Wilson (eds.), *Private Voices: The Diaries of Elizabeth Gaskell and Sophia Holland* (Keele: Keele University Press, 1996), 51.

response common to more vagrant (or autonomic) forms of consciousness; even Bain admits that 'interested, charmed, or stimulated attention to things, is frequently seen in contrast with what may be called the natural retentiveness of the brain, which often inclines towards a different region from the other'.[43] With regards to reading, the collective approach of mid-Victorian physiology could be summarized as follows: attentive reading is essentially a disembodied cortical process, an unselfconscious and highly selective intake of information; inattentive reading, closer to reverie, is self-regarding, physicalized, and more broadly, if less acutely, responsive.

It is also more durable. The physiological investment in attention was, as I have been suggesting, necessarily only partial, given a preference for rooting consciousness in the central nervous system rather than any higher-level cortical functioning; but it is further compromised by an insistence—again based on the physical capacities of the brain—upon the temporal limits to any attentive state. Here physiologists like Lewes, Huxley, and Bain connected to some of the most urgent political and economic questions in Victorian society, particularly the ongoing struggle over the length of the working day and the limits, which were (crucially for physiologists) both physical and cognitive, of laboring attention in any given time span. This was a controversy that initially produced the Ten Hours Bill in 1844, but that by no means died with that legislation. Perhaps the clearest expression of the dilemma was offered by Friedrich Engels, who made the psychological or physiological aspects of the political problem unmistakable:

To tend machinery—for example, to be continually tying broken threads—is an activity demanding the full attention of the worker. It is, however, at the same time a type of work which does not allow his mind to be occupied with anything else. We have also seen that this type of factory work gives the operative no opportunity of physical exercise or muscular activity. This is really no work at all, but just excessive boredom. It is impossible to imagine a more tedious or wearisome existence. The factory worker is condemned to allow his physical and mental powers to becomes atrophied. From the age of eight he enters an occupation which bores him all day long.[44]

In Engels's formulation—a startling one, given the usual bias of cognitive ethicists—'full attention' is a path to mental atrophy: 'It would indeed be difficult to find a better way of making a man slow-witted than to turn him into a factory worker.'[45] The noncorporealized alertness that Bain advocated as a form of self-control is in Engels a form of social and economic control; the

---

[43] Bain, *Emotions and the Will*, 23.
[44] Friedrich Engels, *The Condition of the Working Class in England*, trans. W. O. Henderson and W. H. Chaloner (Stanford, Calif.: Stanford University Press, 1958), 199.
[45] Ibid. 200.

liberty of the worker would involve not only physical exercise but also, perhaps more pertinently, the right to distraction: to nondirected, vagrant forms of consciousness, which are as enlivening as they are unproductive. When Lewes, for instance, denigrated the centrality of attention—particularly in relation to bodily and mental health—he stood on the side of Victorian labor against capital, which, as numerous observers pointed out, sought not only to enforce attention, but also to extend its reach.

Marx has become the most famous of these observers, and his dictum that 'the efficiency of labour-power is in inverse ratio to the duration of its expenditure' is a characteristically Victorian one, based on the wave theory of physiology: the stronger the mental wave, the less time it can extend.[46] What Marx noted as an ongoing process in Britain throughout the 1840s and 1850s was an attempt by factory owners to compensate for shortened working days by expecting ever greater intensities of attention within them, which had the effect of making ten hours more mentally taxing than twelve. In fact, Marx predicted, as new techniques of eliminating distractions were invented, the working day would only get shorter and more intense, as factory owners would seek to increase the relative surplus value of labor by saving on coal and other factory consumables. This tightening of screws on the minds of factory workers—who could face either endless boring durations of numbing attention, or shortened spans of more intense attention—implied not only mental subjection but also physical danger. As noted in a variety of places, the attempt to forbid distraction only brings distraction back in more perilous form: the worker asked to pay strict attention for hours on end finally falls into a state of inattention from which industrial accidents are inevitable. This is a claim frequently made in the Victorian industrial novel. The doomed radical John Barton, in Elizabeth Gaskell's *Mary Barton* (1848), indignantly notes a factory inspection report in which he reads that '*by far th'greater part o' th' accidents as comed in, happened in th' last two hours o' work*, when folk getten tired and careless'.[47] Simply put, factory workers were at the mercy of both management and the iron laws of physiological duration; while owners sought continually to increase the duration or intensity of attention, the nervous system was, as physiologists in the period continually argued, incapable of either extension in time or intensification without needing relief. Attention, for Victorian physiology, was in essence merely one half of a constant oscillation characteristic of consciousness between alertness and

---

[46] Karl Marx, *Capital: A Critique of Political Economy*, i, trans. Ben Fowkes (New York: Vintage, 1976), 535. See Arata, 'On Not Paying Attention', 196–7, for an analogous discussion of attention and factory labor in the period.

[47] Elizabeth Gaskell, *Mary Barton: A Tale of Manchester Life*, ed. Jennifer Foster (Peterborough: Broadview, 2000), 126.

drift, focusing and diffusion. To the extent that attention is intensified or extended, distraction is necessarily more pressing, and will have its revenge. So powerful was this line of reasoning that by the last two decades of the nineteenth century, decades which have normally been taken as the origin of contemporary thought on attention, any enforced attention would come to seem almost a psychic malady; as Théodule Ribot asserted in his *The Psychology of Attention* (1889), the alternations between attention and its opposite 'denote the radical antagonism of attention and the normal psychic life'.[48] From a more openly politicized angle, Marx's son-in-law Paul Lafargue produced in 1880, and in a revised edition in 1883, his famous pamphlet *Le Droit à la paresse* (*The Right To Be Lazy*), which castigated both capitalists and proletariat alike for their enfeebling addiction to labor.[49]

Physiologists like Lewes and Bain did not, of course, directly enter the controversies over the working day, but by insisting upon the limits of human attention spans, they effectively armed more engaged observers with arguments for alleviating the tyranny of 'directed consciousness'. The physiological notion of attention was essentially small-scale: an intense but small wave of light that shines in pulses, not in a steady stream, and that cannot be stretched more tightly, or extended, without being reduced to a flat-lined distraction. Most concisely stated by William Carpenter in his *Principles of Mental Physiology*, (1874), this was the doctrine in which 'its intensity is in a precisely inverse relation to its *extensity*'.[50] Time is the enemy of attention; the wave metaphors of physiology dictated the necessity of its opposite, drift or distraction, as an inescapable part of the oscillations of mental energy. This is the basic argument pressed by Herbert Spencer in his *Principles of Psychology* (1855), where attention becomes a paradigm for the temporal limitations of any affective or cognitive state. In the chapter entitled 'Aestho-Physiology' Spencer insisted that the 'fact that each feeling lasts an appreciable time, introduces us to the allied fact that each feeling produces a greater or less incapacity for a similar feeling, which also lasts an appreciable time'. The fragility of attention, which disappears as soon as its intensity reaches a peak, is for both Carpenter and Spencer a useful model for the temporal dynamics of any affective state. 'Be it in grief, or joy, or tenderness, there is always a succession of rises and falls of intensity—a paroxysm of violent feeling with an interval of feeling less

---

[48] Thédule Ribot, *The Psychology of Attention* (Chicago: Open Court, 1894), 3. For thorough accounts of Ribot's place in the late-nineteenth-century discourse on attention, see Arata, 'On Not Paying Attention', 196–7, and Crary, *Suspensions of Perception*, 11–46. For my purposes, the impact of Ribot's text obscures the interestingly scattered or even dismissive accounts of attention found in mid-Victorian physiological psychology.

[49] Paul Lafargue, *Le Droit à la paresse*, ed. Maurice Dommanget (Paris: Maspero, 1969).

[50] William Carpenter, *Principles of Mental Physiology* 2nd edn. (London: Henry King, 1875), 25.

violent, followed by another paroxysm,' Spencer argues. 'And then, after a succession of these comparatively-quick alternations, there comes a calm—a period during which the waves of emotion are feebler: succeeded, it may be, by another series of stronger waves.'[51] Physiological work on attention in the Victorian era thought primarily in temporal terms, as evidenced by the insistence upon the wave metaphor, and as a result looked crucially different than our own contemporary work on attention, which, by thinking primarily in terms of information overload (bits, processing speed, the number of available channels), spatializes mental processing in a series of metaphors borrowed from computer circuitry.[52]

Our contemporary notions of mental space are, however, much more elastic than past physiological notions of temporalized neural waves; there is no combating the diffusive power of time, expressed as a growing fatigue, upon any strong or consistent mental state in Victorian physiology. The baseline condition of mental functioning, as pictured by Spencer, is therefore essentially *rest*: affectively, a neutral state; cognitively, a state of quiet distraction rather than alert attention. This drifting consciousness, waiting for the arrival of an emotional or intellectual 'wave', has importance in Spencer's account—as, with a slightly different coloration, in Bain's—as the crucible for human desire. 'Desires', he explains, 'are ideal feelings that arise when the real feelings to which they correspond have not been experienced for some time.'[53] Put another way, the formation of desires is possible only when more alert or active states of consciousness have been stilled; the out-of-body focus of attention, or any strong emotion, precludes the gently preoccupied, even partially bored, state of physiological rest that allows desire to form. We constitute ourselves as desiring subjects, therefore, by ceasing to pay outward attention.[54] This helps to explain Bain's frequently stated anxieties, in *The*

---

[51] Herbert Spencer, *The Principles of Psychology*, i (London: Williams and Norgate, 1881), 109, 122.

[52] As one recent psychological textbook has it, research into attention since the mid-twentieth century 'views the mind as an information-processing system'—a model that bears an anxious relation to computer science. The same textbook goes on defensively to insist that 'human information-processing research may provide the clearest evidence about how different the mind and the digital computer are in the underlying modes of function'. See Harold Pashler, *The Psychology of Attention* (Cambridge, Mass.: MIT Press, 1998), 6–7. Despite these denials of similarity, analogies persist: Csikszentmihalyi, in a passage describing the limits of consciousness, states that the upper level of mental processing is somewhere around '126 bits [of information] per second', or half a million bits per hour; attention is therefore the process of limiting the amount of bits processed to produce more streamlined functioning. See Csikszentmihalyi, *Flow*, 29.

[53] Ibid. 126.

[54] Adam Phillips's recent account of boredom, out of an object relations theory perspective, resonates with Spencer's liberal-physiological account; for Phillips, boredom 'returns us to the

Emotions and the Will, about precisely those quiescent or 'diffusive' mental states in which desires take shape. Attention in Bain's work is a habit of self-control that acts to still the dangerously self-regarding and always physicalized waves of mental distraction. To suppress the luxury of drifting, diffuse consciousness, Bain claims, 'is the work of education, and the distinction of mature life'.[55]

The essentially liberal spirit behind Spencer's account of attention and neural waves is made palpable by Bain's discomfort: if liberal subjects are largely constituted by the possession of desires (knowing what one wants), states of distraction are essential to the formation of those subjects; attention, by contrast, is read as a state of self-oblivion in the interests of some kind of social control. Despite the claims made by recent historians of Victorian liberalism that the heroic 'self-overcoming' of desire is at the heart of the liberal project, Spencer and Bain make clear that prior to any self-overcoming—its necessary ground, in fact—is a self-making of desire that overly rapt attention disrupts.[56] The proposition was put more baldly in 1889, by Ribot, who echoed his Victorian predecessors by claiming that attention is usually an 'artificial' state that is 'a product of art, of education, of direction, and of training . . . a product of civilization'—a social demand that we submit ourselves to, albeit partially and uneasily, given that what society demands of us, a constant state of alertness, is essentially impossible except for brief intervals.[57] Distraction or general restful reverie is the ground of any interiority, while attention is the abdication of that set of mental processes—choice, self-communion, even the idle desire to have a desire—upon which the liberal individual bases his right to autonomy. Seen from this vantage point, Spencer's abstract physiological theory is remarkably close to the comments of observers on British factory labor in the same general period: to expect constant attention from a workforce is to deny them the right to their selves. Spencer is a particularly valuable figure here, because he signals overtly what elsewhere is so opaque: the connections between physiology's general disregard of attentive states, a politics that embraces the right of individuals to choose (and thus, to mentally drift, the

---

scene of inquiry, to the poverty of our curiosity, and the simple question, What does one want to do with one's time? . . . Boredom, I think, protects the individual, makes tolerable for him the impossible experience of waiting for something without knowing what it could be.' See Adam Phillips, *On Kissing, Tickling, and Being Bored: Psychoanalytic Essays on the Unexamined Life* (Cambridge, Mass.: Harvard University Press, 1993), 75–7.

[55] Bain, *Emotions and the Will*, 9.

[56] See, e.g., David Wayne Thomas's thorough account of Victorian 'liberal heroics' as 'an ambition to fulfill oneself by denying oneself', in *Cultivating Victorians: Liberal Culture and the Aesthetic* (Philadelphia: University of Pennsylvania Press, 2004), 9.

[57] Ribot, *Psychology of Attention*, 29, 36.

state from which choice becomes possible), and, perhaps unexpectedly, an account of literary form that might reflect both scientific and political notions of attention.

Those connections between literary theory and physiological work on attention are most visible in his 1852 *Westminster Review* essay 'The Philosophy of Style', one of the Victorian period's most overtly physiological theories of literary language. The article's thesis is contained in the idea, which for Spencer is derivable from a host of commonplace theories of rhetoric, of 'the importance of economizing the reader's or hearer's attention'. As he proceeds to explain in more detail:

A reader or listener has at each moment but a limited amount of mental power available. To recognize and interpret the symbols presented to him, requires part of this power; to arrange and combine the images suggested by them requires a further part; and only that part which remains can be used for framing the thought expressed. Hence, the more time and attention it takes to receive and understand each sentence, the less time and attention can be given to the contained idea; and the less vividly will that idea be conceived.[58]

This claim results, initially, in a call for a limpid, transparent, minimally ornamented prose style, one which would avoid elaborate periods, Latinate terms, parentheses, or too much reliance on subordination. As Spencer himself admits, these are not particularly surprising criteria, and much of the charge of the essay lies in its using what he calls a 'psychological ground' for reaffirming more generally held notions of good style; the fragility of attention, particularly across the temporal process of reading, proves how right rhetoricians have always been. Yet, as the essay proceeds, more complicated notions of stylistic practices that might 'economize the reader's attention' are given play, and these notions are not easily assimilable to the insistence upon a direct, simple prose.

Most notably, perhaps, in relation to Thackeray's own form, Spencer takes an interest in what would seem to be the opposite of unornamented directness: plot discursivity. Again he has recourse to physiological notions of neural waves: 'Equally throughout the whole nature, may be traced the law that exercised faculties are ever tending to resume their original states. Not only after continued rest, do they regain their full powers—not only are brief cessations in the demands on them followed by partial re-invigoration; but even while they are in action, the resulting exhaustion is ever being neutralized. The processes of waste and repair go on together.'[59] Mental focusing—which

---

[58] Herbert Spencer, 'The Philosophy of Style', in *Essays: Scientific, Political, and Speculative*, ii (London: Williams and Norgate, 1891), 334–5.
[59] Ibid. 362.

here goes under the term 'waste'—and restorative drift must continually oscillate in any prolonged narrative, in ways both small and large; and, of course, the larger the 'waste' (by some kind of particularly exhausting idea, or plot climax), the longer the period of rest or low-energy diversion required. Here Spencer abandons notions of prose directness and espouses narrative discursivity—anti-climaxes, antitheses, variability between different plots and between moments of emotional pitch and emotional lassitude—as a solution to the temporal qualities of the reader's attention. Like so much physiological literary theory, the recommendations go unsubstantiated by specific examples, but it is an easy leap to multi-plot fiction, which neatly fits Spencer's criteria.

We have arrived, then, at the dominant form of mid-Victorian fiction as the solution to the problem of overburdened attention spans that most physiology of the 1850s routinely claimed. This is, as Spencer's theory of desire formation suggests, a solution with a definite, if abstractly reasoned, political correlate in the 1840s and 1850s: a liberal politics of autonomous subjects left alone to choose their own wants and needs. In physiological terms, these rights were guaranteed—physically, as a form of mental rest—by non-attentive states; in literary terms, as Spencer's essay demonstrates, they were rights permitted by a discursive and continually various narrative practice that allowed space for distraction. Here *The Newcomes*, Thackeray's most openly 'loose' novel of the 1850s, becomes particularly intriguing. Situated in a time bracketed by disputes over the mental exertions of factory labor, scientific claims on behalf of neural rest periods, and even literary theories that took distraction as a necessary ground for any possible attention, Thackeray's long *Familienroman* presents itself as the mid-nineteenth century's most complexly developed response to the formal and political questions raised by attention and distraction.

INSTANTIATING THE READER: *THE NEWCOMES*, I

Unlike its predecessor *Pendennis*, which fully inhabited the chancy, grubby world of early Victorian letters, *The Newcomes* approaches literary production only via parallels with Victorian easel painting, the pursuit of its major character, Clive Newcome, as well as his far more talented, if socially inferior, friend J. J. Ridley. Despite the novel's open admiration for the milieux of visual art, which receive far less skeptical commentary than the bohemian journalistic salons of *Pendennis*, the comparison between literary and visual art is not always flattering to the latter. Most crucially, Thackeray is clear—through the voice of the novelist Arthur Pendennis, who becomes *The Newcomes*'s narrator—that the professionalized, thoroughly alienated market world of literary production is far more relaxed than the premodern tasks of the painter, who must still sell directly to wealthy or aristocratic patrons. 'We sell our wares to the book purveyor, between whom and us there is no greater obligation than between him and his paper-maker or printer. In the great towns in our country, immense stores of books are provided for us, with librarians to class them, kind attendants to wait upon us, and comfortable appliances for study. We require scarce any capital wherewith to exercise our trade. What other so called learned profession is equally fortunate?' (*N*, 937). Doctors require a show of gentility, as do barristers; as for the literary artist: 'If a man of letters cannot win, neither does he risk as much' (*N*, 938). The praise given to the advanced state of the book market here is not entirely, or even primarily, due to the elimination of the courtier's flattery necessary for earlier writers. It is largely because of the book market's ability to protect the writer from the facts of reader response that it is praised, as becomes clear when Pendennis muses on Ridley's own dilemmas.

I have listened to a Manchester magnate talking about fine arts before one of J. J.'s pictures, assuming the airs of a painter, and laying down the most absurd laws respecting the art. I have seen poor Tomkins bowing a rich amateur through a private view, and noted the eager smiles on Tomkins's face at the amateur's slightest joke, the sickly twinkle of hope in his eyes as Amateur stopped before his own picture. . . . And, seeing how severely these gentlemen were taxed in their profession, I have been grateful for my own more fortunate one, which necessitates cringing to no patron; which calls for no keeping up of appearances; and which requires no stock-in-trade save the workman's industry; his best ability; and a dozen sheets of paper. (*N*, 938)

The advantage of the writer is a structural one: he or she need never see their work being read. The low risk of literary art, as Thackeray terms it, is both a financial and an affective safety, since the writer is protected, by the layers of publisher, printer, and bookseller, from viewing the consumption (and possible misconstrual or belittlement) of his work: the writer's profession, unlike the artist's, is non-theatrical. This takes us again to Michael Fried's well-known analysis of Chardin and Greuze, in which the depiction of absorbed figures is meant defensively to screen out the gazes of beholders.[60]

Yet it is surely curious that Thackeray of all Victorian novelists claims this, for he (as we have already seen) was perhaps uniquely obsessed with imagining the consumption of his own work, as if the screen between

---

[60] See Fried, *Absorption and Theatricality*, 67–9. Fried's thesis is usefully complicated for the Victorian novel by Garrett Stewart, who claims that such 'obliviousness to reception and its vocative markers in Victorian texts is not so complete as in an absorptive scene that has foregone all sense of self-conscious spectation and turned in upon its own depicted space'; see Stewart, *Dear Reader*, 60.

writer and audience needed to be continually pierced by an anxious or self-denigrating depiction of reading. In fact that tension—between not having to see, not wanting to see, and yet compulsively picturing nonetheless—is characteristic of Thackeray's relation to the scene of reading, which takes on, particularly in *The Newcomes*, the contours of a primal scene.[61] Most scenes of reading in *The Newcomes* are similarly screened for us: when Clive reads the letter from his beloved cousin Ethel announcing the discovery of a lost bequest to him from his step-grandmother, Pendennis turns his face away out of delicacy, and gazes instead upon Colonel Newcome, whose growing senility ensures that he will not be reflecting Clive's facial expressions of response with even the slightest accuracy. The moment of engagement with a text is invisible in two senses: it is both rude to look too hard, as if to read Clive reading were somehow prurient, and never entirely visible enough to see anyway, for who can see in a reading face any kind of accurate indication of what is being transacted between text and mind? The invisibility, however, provokes constant guesswork on the part of Thackeray and his surrogate narrator Pendennis. It eventually issues in a solution that resonates with the mid-Victorian status of attention: if one cannot really 'see' readerly response at moments of engrossment or real engagement, one can do so at moments when the text has been put down, dropped, abandoned. What *The Newcomes* tells us is that the reader is most visible at the instant reading stops, at the transition between engrossment and release that we might call distraction. As a result, when Thackeray turns to the reader in *The Newcomes*, he does so primarily to encourage us to put the book down—to release us.

That at the very least *The Newcomes* fails to encourage us to keep reading continuously was noted, in a variety of registers, by its initial critics. Immediately after its final serial number in August 1855, the *Athenaeum* proclaimed: 'Few stories are more charming to read in separate pages than tales by the Author of "The Newcomes,"—few, when read in chapters or in volumes, glide out of the grasp of attention with such slippery ease': The reviewer went on to complain of Thackeray's leisurely narrative procedure by stating that Thackeray 'deals unfairly by his own gifts and his own calling as an artist by loitering, be it ever so humorously, philosophically, picturesquely'.[62] During the novel's serial run Margaret Oliphant criticized the chaos of its narrative,

---

[61] See Mary Jacobus, *Psychoanalysis and the Scene of Reading* (Oxford: Oxford University Press, 1999), for the application of psychoanalytic concepts to the description of the reading act. What Jacobus does not consider, however, are the resonances of imagining the reading of one's own work, of picturing the scene that you have made possible and that (in some sense) makes you, your own work, possible.

[62] Anon., 'The Newcomes', *Athenaeum* 1449 (4 Aug., 1855), 895.

and William North mused that 'a cultivated man must find a difficulty in reading it at all'.[63] More sympathetic reviews, of which there were many, found positive ways in which to discuss the dispersal of attention produced by the novel. Whitwell Elwin's long discussion in the *Quarterly Review* protested that its lack of forward-directed plot 'is not to be numbered, in our opinion, among the defects of the tale'; the moral of the novel, for Elwin, was summarized in a remarkably physiological lesson: 'Duration is of more importance than intensity'.[64]

Elwin's analysis spun the usual account of *The Newcomes* in a surprising manner; whereas most reviewers felt that its isolated moments triumphed over the all-too-loose manner of their connection—one representative critic praised its 'incidents, taken separately', but censured the repetitious and tedious 'intervening space'—Elwin privileged the novel's long and constant oscillations between event and non-event, between engaged attention and distraction, and found that oscillation (the 'duration' of experience) more rewarding than any isolated kind of 'intensity'. In this Elwin seems to have responded with more sympathy to Thackeray's own instantiations of his readers in the novel, who are continually imagined in transition, passing in and out of engagement. The first register of these transition moments is boredom, situated either as part of the reader's interaction with Pendennis's narrative voice, or through the reactions of characters to inset narratives. The story of Clive's childhood is cut short with the rueful admission that only one's parents, spouses, and children could possibly care about one's earliest memories; 'shall we weary our kind readers by this infantile prattle', Pendennis asks, 'and set down the revered British public for an old woman?' (*N*, 43). When the Colonel, stationed in India, reads Clive's childish letters to a captive audience of subalterns and their wives, we are told how 'young men would give or take odds that the colonel would mention Clive's name, once before five minutes, three times in ten minutes, twenty-five times in the course of dinner and so on' (*N*, 70). The novel takes pains to map a geography of boredom, such as the gentleman's club, where officers on leave can be caught in the window, looking for anything of interest, 'yawning as widely as that window itself', or the society assembly, where the Colonel has the habit of falling asleep (*N*, 81, 246). This macrogeography—club, assembly, ball—is matched with a microgeography, particularly the interior domestic spaces that trap individuals in a state of almost terrified ennui. One of Thackeray's favorite tropes for this solitary boredom, repeated twice in *The Newcomes*, is the drawing room with

[63] Margaret Oliphant, 'Mr. Thackeray and his Novels', *Blackwood's Edinburgh Magazine* 77 (Jan. 1855), 86–96; William North, 'The Grand Style', *Graham's American Monthly Magazine of Literature, Art, and Fashion* 46/5 (May 1855), 426.

[64] Whitwell Elwin, 'The Newcomes', *Quarterly Review* 97 (Sept. 1855), 361–2.

facing mirrors, in which 'your face (handsome or otherwise) was reflected by countless looking-glasses, so multiplied and arranged as, as it were, to carry you into the next street' (*N*, 825). Its original appearance in *Vanity Fair*—in which the spinster Jane Osborne, doomed to perpetual paternal tyranny, spends her days in an empty drawing room with two large mirrors in which are 'increased and multiplied between them the brown holland bag in which the chandelier hung; until you saw those brown holland bags fading away in endless perspectives, and this apartment of Miss Osborne seemed the centre of a system of drawing rooms' (*VF*, 539)—signals, in its oppressive multiplication of sameness, the boredom of self-preoccupation that is never quite absorption in Thackeray, and that is the assumed ground of most of the novel's actions as well as of most moments of readerly address.

Unlike Jane Osborne, the bored reader has a strategy. It becomes the second register of Thackeray's instantiation of distracted reading: skipping. The novel is prefaced with a long, facetious Aesopian allegory which threatens to give a moral, then retracts: 'But who ever heard of giving the Moral before the Fable? Children are only led to accept the one after their delectation over the other: let us take care lest our readers skip both' (*N*, 6). In fact the very straightforward gerund 'reading' is almost invisible in Thackeray, who prefers the use of slightly imperfect synonyms which reflect discontinuity, such as 'subsiding into' or 'simpering over' a book; to 'turn over the leaves', 'dip into', or 'muse over' a volume; or the virtually constant use of 'peruse' or 'perusal' to stand in for any more continuous 'reading'. Any notation of reading, particularly in *The Newcomes*, assumes its partial, temporary, temporally limited character; 'reading' is primarily described as a distracted grazing process, referenced either by the detached expression of the reader (simpering, musing, smirking) or the physicality of reading (turning, dipping into, or flipping pages). The assumption of skipping is so profound that Thackeray's narrative procedure itself, often improbably, skips: *The Newcomes* is rife with sudden temporal accelerations, as when Sophia Alethea Newcome's funeral prefaces any discussion of her personality; or when the childhood illness of the sickly young Alfred Newcome is immediately undercut by a mention of his future as a Guardsman; or when a chapter describing young Clive's interactions with his father ends with Clive, now aged, looking on with his children at a portrait of the Colonel. As for Clive's dreary European tour with the Colonel, Pendennis spares the reader the trouble of skipping: 'Suppose this part of Mr. Clive's life were to be described at length in several chapters, what dreary pages they would be! In two or three months our friends saw a number of men, cities, mountains, rivers, and what not' (*N*, 735). The paradox of this narrative of considerable, even famous, length is that it is often as rushed as it is leisurely; the operations of what Thackeray calls 'our discursive muse' hurry events into bland summary even more frequently than they dilate them into intense events (*N*, 461).

In either case, however—accelerated summary or lingering narration—the result seems to be inattention. Critics often noted that the novel's length prevented attention to any larger lessons or allegoresis, such as when James Hannay, in the *Leader*, pointed out 'a little fact which might otherwise escape notice': that the two marriages made by the Colonel's father, Thomas Newcome, are neatly allegorical, one a love match (which produces the Colonel) and one a money match (which produces the novel's least morally admirable characters).[65] That such an obvious structuring principle might not be noticed is a curious effect of *The Newcomes*'s technique of inattention: one is either too bored, or too engrossed by minutiae, to see any thematic architecture. That *The Newcomes* is not allegory is a fact due not to its mimetic mode (everyday realism) but instead, it seems, to its temporal form, its inability, or refusal, to structure the reader's attention consistently or continuously enough in order to make allegorical meanings take shape.

These intertwined themes of readerly boredom, periodic inattention, and skipping coalesce in a carefully staged, and crucially interrupted, reading of *Oliver Twist* carried on by Lord Kew, the novel's heroic, manly aristocrat, his saintly mother, and his affectionate brother. Kew, recovering from serious wounds after a duel with a Frenchman, retreats from society (represented by his Machiavellian grandmother Lady Kew) to Strasbourg, where his mother reads him tracts and missionary narratives until his brother smuggles in Dickens's novel. Even the serious-minded mother is entranced: 'it is a fact that Lady Walham became so interested in the parish boy's progress, that she took his history into her bedroom (where it was discovered, under Blatherwick's *Voice from Mesopotamia*, by her ladyship's maid), and that Kew laughed so immensely at Mr. Bumble the Beadle, as to endanger the reopening of the wound' (*N*, 496). During one such reading session, however, Lady Kew dramatically arrives in order to reclaim her grandson for high society, expressly against the wishes of his mother. As Lady Kew prepares for her first interview: 'If the mother and her two sons had in the interval of Lady Kew's toilette tried to resume the history of Bumble and the Beadle, I fear they could not have found it very comical' (*N*, 499). After a climactic series of arguments which results, surprisingly, in Lady Kew's repulse, the reading is resumed: 'Miss Nancy and Fanny again were summoned before this little company to frighten and delight them. I dare say even Fagin and Miss Nancy failed with the widow, so absorbed was she with the thoughts of the victory which she had just won' (*N*, 502).

---

[65] James Hannay, 'The Newcomes', *Leader* 6 (8 Sept. 1855), 871.

Why bracket the scene—a thematically central confrontation between *ancien régime* aristocratic cynicism and the moral rectitude of a bourgeoisified nuclear family, between worldliness and virtue—as an interruption of novel reading? The answer lies, I would suggest, in how the putative absorption of the family as they read *Oliver Twist* is resituated as a discontinuous and inattentive process that occasions or permits other forms of absorption, particularly self-absorption as opposed to worldly ambition. Novel reading is imagined as a background process, a kind of agreeable mental noise, that in its very refusal to insist upon strict attention (unlike the domineering Lady Kew) allows interior reverie to blossom. Nourished and refreshed by the comfortable, familial, half-attentive process of consuming Dickens's narrative, Lady Walham and Lord Kew are both capable of returning to the world to do combat with it. The novel starts; the world interrupts, makes its claims, is vanquished; the novel resumes, and Lady Walham is free to let her mind wander while it continues. To make sure that this process has not gone unnoticed, Thackeray concludes the prolonged scene of interrupted reading with an interruption of his own, which—like Lady Walham's reverie of moral exaltation while Fagin and Nancy do their background business—invites us, in language not far from Lady Walham's usual tone, to make our own personal reflections:

I have said, this book is all about the world and a respectable family dwelling in it. It is not a sermon, except where it cannot help itself, and the speaker, pursuing the destiny of his narrative, finds such a homily before him. O friend, in your life and mine, don't we light upon such sermons daily?—don't we see at home, as well as amongst our neighbours, that battle betwixt Evil and Good? Here, on one side, is Self and Ambition and Advancement; and Right and Love on the other. Which shall we let to triumph for ourselves—which for our children? (*N*, 502)

Oliver Twist's power—like that claimed by Thackeray himself at the end of this episode—is, in other words, its resilient ability to sustain interruption, and as such to occasion moments of personal meditation.[66] Here the bored reader, who puts the book down out of fatigue, merges with the engaged reader, who also puts the book down out of sudden bursts of self-regard or reverie. Far from considering such readerly inattention to be poor reading, lapses from the vigilance of the good reader, Thackeray valorizes it (in such depictions as that of Lady Walham) and, furthermore, openly requests it. His addresses to the reader tend to perform the opposite of their supposed

[66] As Linda Hughes and Michael Lund have shown, *The Newcomes* thematizes interruption most often through the trope of meeting and parting, of 'separation among loved ones', where greeting and farewell are the most common actions; see *Victorian Serial*, 44–58.

function of alerting or hailing attention: they open up instead space for free-roaming thought. More literally, the moments of instantiation in the novel (the narrator saying 'this is you') take the form of envisioning 'you' putting the book down, interrupting its flow. Musing about the hidden recesses in even the people closest to us, Pendennis imagines his own narrative temporarily abandoned:

Who, in showing his house to the closest and dearest, doesn't keep back the key of a closet or two? I think of a lovely reader laying down the page and looking at her unconscious husband, asleep, perhaps, after dinner. Yes, madam, a closet he hath; and you, who pry into everything, shall never have the key of it. I think of some honest Othello pausing over this very sentence in a railroad carriage, and stealthily gazing at Desdemona opposite to him, innocently administering sandwiches to their little boy—I am trying to turn off the sentence with a joke, you see—I feel it is getting too dreadful, too serious. (*N*, 151)

Since the voice addresses figures who have already put him aside, it is hard to say whether Pendennis is talking to these interpolated readerly figures or simply *at* them, since they have already turned away. This would seem to be the opposite of Michael Fried's paradigm of the absorbed pictorial subject ignoring, and thereby figuring, the spectator's own absorption: Thackeray openly hails the reader, interrupts his narrative, and by doing so ensures the inattention of that reader, who will lay the book aside to consider its possible applicability to herself. The narrator's grab for attention becomes the invitation to stop paying it.

For Thackeray, a grazing reading, prepared to halt—a 'perusal' or 'turning over the leaves'—is therefore more productive than a strictly attentive or self-forgetful one. As a result, the moments in *The Newcomes* when Thackeray turns to the reading process exist not to call the reader to attention but instead to call the reader to distraction—to bring absorption to a halt; instantiating the reader means permitting her escape from the fiction. This provides some context, and clarification, for my earlier claim that Thackeray's fiction manages readerly distraction by offering spaces in which the reader can 'opt out' of attention. Those spaces are not periodically recurrent moments of 'filler' or insignificant prattle that we might determine and then bracket off from truly thematically significant material; as in my examples above, they often take the form of precisely the kind of significant material that would seem to call for attention. That is, it becomes impossible in *The Newcomes* to point to 'unimportant' textual moments as a sign of Thackeray's acceptance of distraction. Rather, the Thackerayan narrator gives permission to drift away from the text at even highly charged moments, rooting distraction within seemingly absorptive moments, and encourages that drift—even to the point of putting the book down—as a sign of the novel's power: it sees itself as the instrument by which you pass from mere absorption into productive reverie.[67]

SAVING REVERIES: *THE NEWCOMES*, II

What productive reverie might look like is, in fact, the representational burden of much of *The Newcomes*. To a large extent the novel sketches a pervasive social habit of distraction that, in the way of so many moral lapses in Thackeray's world, is presented as both deeply culpable and also inescapable. Fashion—and in *The Newcomes* the word merges both its social signification as a particular stratum of high society with its temporal signification as something evanescent—is most obviously to blame. It is geographically restless, leading to ripples of restlessness in other social realms; 'after the Fashion chooses to emigrate, and retreats to Soho or Bloomsbury, let us say, to Cavendish Square, physicians come and occupy the vacant houses', and further changes of location for Fashion will lead to even more turnover, Pendennis tells us, so that after the physicians come boarding houses and then artist's studios: gentrification in reverse (N, 214). As such, representatives of the world of Fashion in the novel behave with ridiculous attention deficits, unable to hold an emotion or thought for any length of time. Ethel Newcome's mother, Lady Ann Newcome, 'was constantly falling in love with her new acquaintances; their menservants and their maidservants, their horses and ponies, and the visitor within their gates. She would ask strangers to Newcome, hug and embrace them on Sunday; not speak to them on Monday; and on Tuesday behave so rudely to them, that they were gone before Wednesday' (N, 132). Madame d'Ivry, the narcissistic French aristocrat who plots against Lord Kew, takes in turns to being 'Royalist, Philippist, Catholic, Huguenot', and reminds Pendennis of how 'in a fair, where time is short and pleasures numerous, the master of the theatrical booth shows you a tragedy, a farce, and a pantomime, all in a quarter of an hour, having a dozen new audiences to witness his entertainments in the course of the forenoon' (N, 444). The very recurrence of

---

[67] This is perhaps demonstrated most dramatically when Thackeray rereads Thackeray; in 'A Leaf Out of a Sketch-Book', Thackeray's re-perusal of his old writing occasions a productive distraction: 'In taking up an old book, for instance, written in former days by your humble servant, he comes upon passages which are outwardly lively and facetious, but inspire their writer with the most dismal melancholy. I lose all cognisance of the text sometimes, which is hustled and elbowed out of sight by the crowd of thoughts which throng forward, and which were alive at the time that text was born.' From William Makepeace Thackeray, *Miscellaneous Essays, Sketches, and Reviews*, in *The Works*, xxviii. 432.

the image of the 'fair' should remind us of the centrality of constantly shifting, distracting amusements to Thackeray's conception of the social world; in *The Newcomes* the 'fair' is largely an aspect of the aristocratic and *haut bourgeois* world that his more virtuous characters scorn or avoid. The impact does have ripples, however; even worship becomes a matter of constant distraction, as the crowds that flock to see the fashionable preacher Charles Honeyman abandon him shortly thereafter for newer ecclesiastical sensations.

At other moments, however, distraction seems not a social issue, limited to the frivolities of the *monde*, but a geographical one, a property of London life, and a textual one, a property of the metropolitan reader. Despite the novel's frequent narration of reunions and departures—Clive heads to Europe twice, his father the Colonel returns from India, stays a while, returns, then comes back to Britain—by the end of the novel we are continually reminded that these departures do not signify, since in the mentally taxing world of London nobody even notices:

> To Londoners everything seems to have happened but yesterday; nobody has time to miss his neighbour who goes away. People go to the Cape, or on a campaign, or on a tour around the world, or to India, and return with a wife and two or three children, and we fancy it was only the other day they left us, so engaged is every man in his individual speculations, studies, struggles; so selfish does our life make us:—selfish but not ill-natured. (*N*, 524)

This is the voice of worldly weariness, to be sure, but not one easily distinguished from the attitude that the reader is expected to have. Pendennis's shrug of the shoulders comes after Clive's return from Europe, which had separated narrator and central character for almost five monthly numbers of the novel. What the passage reflects is a certain embarrassment: not that it is odd for Clive and Pendennis to have been apart for so long, nor for the affectionate emotion that their masculine reunion so conspicuously hides, but for the possibility that the reader will have entirely forgotten their separation. Since Pendennis has after all narrated the intervening narrative—supposedly out of material Clive had given him long after the conclusion of the novel's events—we may not have registered their separation in any significant way. We too, as Pendennis happily admits, have things of our own to do; and to put the book down and return to it later without a sensation of elapsed time is both the office of the novel and an example of the temporal foreshortening of urban distraction. When, late in the novel, Pendennis loses contact with Clive, he explains that 'I had a thousand affairs of my own; who has not in London?' (*N*, 951). If I earlier suggested that the narrator of *Vanity Fair* is preoccupied, or has 'things on his mind', Pendennis in *The Newcomes* admits that the reader is most likely similarly distracted.

Whether a property of fashion or urban mental noise, whether castigated, gently lampooned, or helplessly accepted, these pervasive distractions are not what we might call productive: they do not form reverie so much as block it. In several of its central characters, however, *The Newcomes* outlines positive practices of reverie that are predicated, as in the novel's narratorial injuctions to put the book down, on not paying attention to something, or on mental drift. Central in this regard is J. J. Ridley, the dedicated artist and humble son of a boarding-house keeper who stands as a continual rebuke to Clive's dilettantism. He is presented initially as that rarest of things in Thackeray: a true dreamer. We initially meet him listening to one of his family's boarding-house inmates, a Miss Cann, playing Handel and Haydn on an untuned piano: As he listens, he 'beholds altars lighted, priests ministering, fair children swinging censers, great oriel windows gleaming in sunset, and seen through arched columns, and avenues of twilight marble. . . . All these delights and sights, and joys and glories, these thrills of sympathy, movements of unknown longing, and visions of beauty, a young sickly lad of eighteen enjoys in a little dark room where there is a bed disguised in the shape of a wardrobe, and a little old woman is playing under a gas-lamp on the jingling keys of an old piano' (*N*, 154). His is a mind, in other words, capable of endless visual proliferation, a rich field of distractions spurred by the music; he is not paying attention to the music in any rigid way, but instead using it as an occasion for a particularly fecund drift. The facing illustration, by Richard Doyle, attempts a correlative of this description of mental vagrancy over the title 'J. J in Dreamland' (see Figure 2.7). The baroque penumbra of vague, barely outlined fancies in Doyle's image represents not the selection process of attention but the fertile openings of mental vagrancy; they are merely spurred by the piano, from which Ridley turns away in the act of forming his internal images.

This facility for reverie is, as Pendennis later enviously admits, a 'fortunate organization indeed' (*N*, 510). It might be tempting to misread Ridley's artistic prowess as the result of strict application, of trained habits of attention, given that we are told of his constant occupation with his pictures, from which he rarely admits interruptions; but the production of visual art has already been explained by Pendennis as a practice of constant slight interruption, a half-attentive labor that agreeably preoccupies the mind rather than strongly monopolizing it:

It does not exercise the brain too much, but gently occupies it, and with a subject most agreeable to the scholar. The mere poetic flame, or jet of invention, needs to be lighted up but very seldom, namely, when the young painter is devising his subject, or settling the composition thereof. The posing of figures and drapery; the dexterous copying of the line; the artful processes of cross-hatching, of stumping, of laying on lights, and

Figure 2.7. 'J. J. in Dreamland', from chapter 11 of *The Newcomes* (New York: Harper and Brothers, 1856), 73. General Research Division, The New York Public Library, Astor, Lenox, and Tilden Foundations

what not; the arrangement of colour, and the pleasing operations of glazing and the like, are labours for the most part merely manual. (*N*, 507)

Hence Ridley's ability to paint while discussing the vicissitudes of Clive's love life. The passage reads uncannily like Spencer's description of the ideal forms of literary style: an unobtrusive practice of occupying the mind without wearying it, one as comfortably mechanical as strenuously inspired. Continuity is asserted here, but a moderate or tempered one, flexible enough to survive distractions, interruptions, brief halts, switches of procedure or emphasis.[68] If, in other words, attention in the mid-Victorian period is imagined as the mind's (temporary) closure to competing stimuli, Ridley's half-attentive state is characterized by its openness. As a result, it cannot strictly be said what he is thinking *about* during the act of painting; his actions are largely mechanical, and his mind open to influence, suggestion, dream, or even mundane interaction. Painting, which occupies such a strangely sacral space in *The Newcomes*, is a benign process of encouraging the mind's wandering. Painting thus becomes the novel's most valorized trope for novel-reading.

Socially, Ridley's dedication to painting may put him in the camp of *l'art pour l'art*, but psychologically—at least as Thackeray/Pendennis describes it—his art is not autotelic but instrumental toward a wider purpose, that of creating occasions for reverie. Seen this way, Ridley's art connects to the novel's most insistent theme—that of the destructive effects of arranged marriages—which touch virtually every character in the novel: the Colonel, who suffers a lifelong separation from Madame de Florac as a result of her father's insistence on a union with an elderly émigré; Clive, who loses his cousin Ethel because of her family's plans for social advancement; Ethel herself, who is unable to determine her desires when faced with family pressure. As it gets narrated in *The Newcomes*, the oppressive force of socially or financially dictated unions can be critiqued only from the standpoint of a distracted gaze—literally, from not looking at what one is supposed to see. This is vividly apparent in Ethel's most radical and well-known gesture, the act of putting a green ticket marked 'Sold' on her dress prior to a dinner. The idea occurs to her when she is markedly not engaged by a Holman Hunt painting at a Water-Color Exhibition that captures her worldly grandmother:

They came to a piece by Mr. Hunt, representing one of those figures which he knows how to paint with such consummate truth and pathos—a friendless young girl, cowering in a doorway, evidently without home or shelter. The exquisite fidelity of the details, and the plaintive beauty of the expression of the child, attracted old Lady

---

[68] The attempt to describe Ridley's labor is, to use Elaine Scarry's suggestive terms, an attempt to describe an activity that is 'perpetual, repetitive, habitual', so perpetual that it can easily sustain the ruptures or interruptions that Scarry argues are a frequent site whereby novelists represent ongoing activities like work. If for Scarry the ruptures of work in classical fiction require 'repair' or 'rescue', in Thackeray half-attentive work like painting or reading needs no such drastic recovery; it is in the nature of such activities to be continually interrupted and to be continually resumed. See Elaine Scarry, 'Participial Acts: Working: Work and the Body in Hardy and Other Nineteenth-Century Novelists', in *Resisting Representation* (New York: Oxford University Press, 1994), 65–6.

Kew's admiration, who was an excellent judge of works of art; and she stood for some time looking at the drawing, with Ethel by her side. Nothing, in truth, could be more simple or pathetic; Ethel laughed, and her grandmother, looking up from her stick on which she hobbled about, saw a very sarcastic expression in the girl's eyes.

'You have no taste for pictures, only for painters, I suppose,' said Lady Kew.

'I was not looking at the picture,' said Ethel, still with a smile, 'but at the little green ticket in the corner.' (*N*, 361)

Lady Kew's appreciative absorption here alludes only to her insistence on dictating the attention of her granddaughter; Ethel's mocking anti-aesthetic vagrancy, distracted by the market setting of the painting, is actually an effective critique of her own position, a spirited (if somewhat futile) moral blow against the genteel traffic in women to which she usually consents. In the manner of a smart schoolchild, she will not pay attention when and where she is told. If the traditional courtship novel reads love matches as tests of fidelity or prolonged focus, and arranged marriages as worldly distractions, in *The Newcomes* values distribute themselves differently. Here the *mariage de convenance* is described as submitting to the dictates of an instructor—look where I tell you to look—while following the dictates of desire or affection is described as mental vagrancy, wandering, a saving inability to focus. Like Ridley, Ethel at her best simply dreams. As a result, her occasional refusals to play the game for which Lady Kew has assigned her a part are described as 'escapades', not acts of faithfulness to some other ideal; the value is to *stop* paying attention, not to avoid distraction (*N*, 694).

This abstract ethical language of mental vagrancy is condensed in select scenes of Clive's suffering after he consents to marry the pretty but vacuous Rose Mackenzie according to his father's misguided wishes. As Pendennis relates it, Clive's unhappiness in his marriage, and his continuing attraction to Ethel, are signified by his growing mental absence—it is as if he is no longer there; his mind continually wanders. In various scenes Pendennis describes Clive as lost in 'brown studies', in 'lover's reveries', in 'his own meditations'; he habitually 'bites his tawny mustachios, plunges his hands into his pockets and his soul into reverie'; his most characteristic response is a yawn (*N*, 545, 742, 883, 827). Bored abstraction of mind here is panic—a stifled resistance—and also a sign of his moral potential; faced with the dictation of his desires, with being told what it is he should and should not want, he simply stops paying attention. The result is his vanishing as a character. In the manner of *Vanity Fair*'s occasional blank absorptions, Clive resists any kind of narration by Pendennis, who can increasingly note only his friend's restless preoccupation. Similarly, his agency disappears, as his constant distraction results in a practical abstention from plot. No surprise, then, that *The Newcomes* drifts along for its last serial numbers; its central character is too distracted to participate.

Except for those few moments when his distraction can become active reverie. One plot to which Clive reluctantly consents is the parliamentary race run by the Colonel against their Machiavellian relative Barnes Newcome, whom they wish to unseat in order to punish him for his obstruction of Clive's pursuit of Ethel. As part of the election contest, Clive, the Colonel, and their comrade Fred Bayham attend a speech given by Barnes to his constituency, a talk on 'The Poetry of Womanhood, and the Affections; Mrs. Hemans, "L. E. L." ', whose craven hypocrisy is underscored by the known fact of Barnes's illegitimate children. Clive's role is to draw an effective caricature of Barnes for a local newspaper sympathetic to the Colonel's cause, as well as to discomfit the speaker, neither of which he can do effectively, since he is suddenly distracted by the fact that Ethel is in the audience. While staring at her, the assembly disappears for Clive:

And the past and its dear histories, and youth and its hopes and passions, and tones and looks for ever echoing in the heart, and present in the memory—these, no doubt, poor Clive saw and heard as he looked across the great gulf of time, and parting, and grief, and beheld the woman he had loved for many years. . . . Hark, there is Barnes Newcome's eloquence still plapping on like water from a cistern—and our thoughts, where have they wandered? far away from the lecture—as far away as Clive's almost. (*N*, 863)

As so often in Thackeray, this moment of rapt attention (to Ethel's figure) is narrated as a saving distraction: from the sordid plot of electoral revenge his increasingly deluded father is pursuing, from the equally unhappy marital plot that various parental figures have dictated for him, from Barnes's speech and its cynical duplicities. At a moment when there seems to be no escape in the novel's plot—which is worse, the Colonel's needless pursuit of revenge, or Barnes's heartless manipulations of family and electorate alike?—Clive's reverie presents itself as a temporary, if welcome, liberty. Unhappy in allies and enemies alike, he is able temporarily to still their voices and absent himself, to the point of not even hearing, we are later told, the commenting voices of the audience as the speech concludes and everyone exits. This scene is a typical set-piece moment in *The Newcomes*; description and pathos, thematic significance, are marshaled by Thackeray most urgently for moments when a central character disengages him or her self from the immediate situation and drifts off. Characteristically, this particular moment of distraction is caught by the narrator, who 'wanders' with Clive far from the speech, which now no longer has to be repeated, but can be merely an occasion. Distraction as escape: the pessimism of *The Newcomes* can best be registered by its acknowledgment that even its own plot has gone so wrong that the only refuge is in refusing to pay it any mind, in mental vagrancy. In pointing the way to such saving distractions, Thackeray indicates a liberty even from his own narrative's operations.

TOWARD A LIBERAL THEORY OF DISTRACTION

Throughout *The Newcomes*, and even more explicitly in his later sketches for the *Cornhill*, Thackeray imagined the social or ethical function of his narratives in decidedly modest terms. 'Notes of a Week's Holiday', one of his 'Roundabout Papers', offers a particularly self-reflexive example of this narratorial diffidence. Thinking of the propensity of older men to bore their hearers with repetitions of the same anecdotes or jokes, Thackeray addresses a reader with a similar social profile:

This self-indulgence on your part, my dear Paterfamilias, is weak, vain—not to say culpable. I can imagine many a worthy man, who begins unguardedly to read this page, and comes to the present sentence, lying back in his chair, thinking of that story which he has told innocently for fifty years, and rather piteously owning to himself, 'Well, well, it *is* wrong; I have no right to call on my poor wife to laugh, my daughters to affect to be amused, by that old, old jest of mine. And they would have pretended to be amused, to their dying day, if this man had not flung his damper over our hilarity.'. . . I lay down the pen and think, 'Are there old stories which I still tell myself in the bosom of my family?' (*RP*, 224)

The right of those in at least nominal positions of authority—either paterfamilias or, implicitly, narrator—to insist upon the attention of their hearers is here seen as a self-indulgent abuse of that authority. That stern 'moral' is then pressed home in a passage in which Thackeray imagines a guilty reader pausing over his sketch and ceasing to read, as if the intake of this moral (do not claim more attention than you deserve) is dependent upon momentary distraction from the text; even learning to stop enforcing attention requires an initial act of ceasing to pay it elsewhere. Such is the emphasis of the passage upon interruption that even Thackeray's own act of pausing in his composition must be narrated. Distractions ramify in the passage as a way of enacting the limitations of authority's right to attention, so much so that even Thackeray's own desire for his moral to be absorbed must be interrupted with a personal reflection.

However ironically light the moment is—it is, after all, a genial confession of his sketch's own repetitiveness—it condenses and exemplifies what might be called the liberalism of Thackeray's narrative practice, which by dramatizing its production of readerly distraction or inattention calls to mind the limited role of state authority in mid-Victorian liberal political theory. Spencer, whose 'Philosophy of Style' asked that not too much attention be required of the reader, defined liberalism as the 'principle of limitation', the drawing of severe restrictions around any kind of authoritative action; his descriptions of stylist and state are oddly parallel, each falling into difficulties when attempting undue influence.[69] The catalogue of actions permissible to state agency in cases where the individual does not come necessarily into conflict with others is characterized, by Spencer and others, by its severely limited instrumentalism. 'Advice, instruction, persuasion, and avoidance by other people if thought necessary by them for their own good' are, in John Stuart Mill's *On Liberty* (1859), the only permissible means by which social or state disapprobation of most actions can take form. A language of weak instrumentality becomes central to liberal theory: 'encouragement', 'exhortation', and 'stimulation' are the strongest terms Mill can use to describe the force of state power upon the field of individual choice, while Spencer's *Principles of Ethics* (1892) devoted a large portion to a theory of 'negative beneficence', or the ethical virtues of non-interference.[70] For the betterment of society as a whole, in fact, Spencer's and Mill's versions of liberal theory both insist that state encouragement should most often be turned against the state; its power of 'stimulation' should simply remind the individual of his self-sovereignty as a way to release his energy for all manner of beneficial social effects. Seen through the lens of Thackeray's positive valuation of distraction, liberalism's discourse of constrained, attenuated, and self-consuming instrumentalism can seem as much a theory of narration as a theory of limited state agency.[71] The careful, measured, recent reaffirmations of Victorian liberalism carried out by such critics as Amanda Anderson and David Wayne Thomas have tended to concentrate on character subjectivity and agency in the period's fiction; it is perhaps in the interaction between narrative voice and implied reader that such reconsiderations of liberal theory and practice might be profitably resituated.[72]

[69] Herbert Spencer, *The Man* Versus *the State*, in *The Works of Herbert Spencer*, xi (Osnabrück: Otto Zeller, 1966), 292.

[70] See John Stuart Mill, *On Liberty and Other Essays*, ed. John Gray (Oxford: Oxford University Press, 1998), 84, 104; Herbert Spencer, *The Principles of Ethics*, ii (London: Williams and Norgate, 1893), 263–332.

[71] It is of some importance that Thackeray's depictions of the lives of servants often emphasize that they be continually *at attention*, as in 'On a Chalk-Mark on the Door': 'He may be ever so unwell in mind or body, and he must go through his service—hand the shining plate, replenish the spotless glass, lay the glittering fork—never laugh when you yourself or your guests joke—be profoundly attentive, and yet look utterly impassive . . .' (*RP*, 131).

[72] See Amanda Anderson, *The Powers of Distance: Cosmopolitanism and the Cultivation of Detachment* (Princeton: Princeton University Press, 2001); Thomas, *Cultivating Victorians*, esp. 8–14.

Narration in Thackeray is instrumentalist, as we have seen; it imagines its ability to provoke reflection, self-critique, and sometimes resistance; but that instrumentalism is always also described in weak terms, since ultimately it can do no better than get the reader to put the book down, to abandon the text that set off the reflection in the first place. Its instrumentalism, in other words, works toward the dissolution of its claim to require attention, substituting reverie or distraction instead. Encouraging reverie is a characteristically mid-Victorian compromise between reading-as-labor and reading-as-autotelic-activity, between working and an aestheticist working at not working. It is therefore a hesitant, limited, and above all liberal response to the possibility of a novel's impact on reader and world. It might in fact be imagined as a resistance to the allures of either strong instrumentality (doing real work in the world) or aestheticist disengagement (absorbed withdrawal from the world): the production of distracted reverie imagines a limited, partial, and temporary effect on the reader that refuses to insist too long or too much on the reader's attention to it. In the terms provided by liberalism, this is a benign instrumentalism: encouraging but not dictating, only exhorting the reader to release him or her self (via distraction or reverie) from the text that does the exhorting.

For Thackeray and Spencer both, it seems, such limited call upon the reader's attention best defines the benignity of novelistic form. Spencer explicitly used physiological notions of mental and physical waves to support his political theories; he imagined physiological rest states such as reverie or semi-consciousness as integral to the formation of desires, and insofar as his liberalism attempted to set the individual free to choose her own desires, it needed to aim for the limited instrumentalism of leading individuals to states of inattention. It needed, in other words, to liberate them from the strictures of attention. In *The Man* Versus *the State* (1884), Spencer linked the physiological claim that 'animal life involves waste; waste must be met by repair; repair implies nutrition' with the need for the free movement of organisms to achieve this nutrition, which in turn serves Spencer as a metaphor for state agency, which should only encourage the release of its citizens to pursue their own forms of 'repair'.[73] Thackeray's noted looseness might then be the result of an effort to avoid the coerciveness of enforcing attention, and to promote the vagrancy of distraction, a state of mind such that individual responses can form. To imagine as much means to reconceptualize Thackeray's relation to social satire and moral reformation; it means a new understanding of those aspects of his procedure that have always been read as failures of mission, if

---

[73] Spencer, *Man* Versus *State*, 390 ff. Although it was published in book form in 1884, this is a revised collection of essays that had initially appeared as early as 1860.

not also failures of literary form: his digressiveness, his embarrassed appeals to a variety of partially attentive readers, his depictions of individuals in states of distracted reverie. These failures could be reimagined as a particularly liberal kind of formal reticence, an instrumentalism that knows its own limits. It would also mean to imagine alternatives to the powerful claims of what I have termed the tradition of cognitive ethicists, for whom attention, as a good in itself, allows labor and aesthetics each other's virtues. In Thackeray, it would seem, distraction is a good for something, although given the limits of his narratorial agency, it is necessarily open to the individual to decide for what 'something' distraction can be a good.

3

Melodies for the Forgetful: Eliot, Wagner, and Duration (Elongated Form)

Imagine a castle so big that it can't all be seen at once. Imagine a quartet that goes on for nine hours. There are anthropological limits—the limits of memory, for instance—that ought not to be exceeded. When you reach the end of a book you should still find it possible to remember the beginning. Otherwise the novel loses shape, its 'architectonic clarity' is clouded.

Milan Kundera, 'Dialogue on the Art of Composition'

While by no means unique in its length, the size of George Eliot's bulky *Daniel Deronda* seems to have provoked an unusual amount of commentary by the end of its 1876 serial run, as if the weight of Eliot's seriousness compelled reviewers to treat even the novel's undeniably protracted length as a phenomenon to be explained, or a problem to be evaluated, rather than a material fact beneath notice. Henry James, writing for the *Nation* after the novel's first monthly number, proclaimed a gourmand's relish in 'a month to think over and digest any given portion of it'; but later in the novel's run, critics were more prone to write in the language of physiological exhaustion: an anonymous review in the *British Quarterly Review* complained of 'an overstrain' upon the reader's attention, while even R. E. Francillon's laudatory piece in the *Gentleman's Magazine* warned that 'there is a limit to the permissible length of a novel which the most popular of writers must not exceed'.[1] Alongside these more or less uneasy recognitions of the novel's size came more frequent remarks about its repetitiveness. Francillon noted a certain reassuring similarity to the narratorial epigrams; Sidney Colvin,

---

[1] For Henry James's piece, from the 24 Feb. 1876 edn. of the *Nation*, see 'Daniel Deronda', in *Essays on Literature: American Writers, English Writers*, ed. Leon Edel (New York: Library of America, 1984), 973. The anonymous review came after the October completion of the novel's serial run; see Anon., 'Daniel Deronda', *British Quarterly Review* 64 (1876), 472. For R. E. Francillon, see 'George Eliot's First Romance', *Gentleman's Magazine* 17 (Oct. 1876), 422.

otherwise admiring, impatiently cited the use of the word 'claims' in relation
to Gwendolen 'in a hundred passages'. Most famously, James's second, far
less complimentary late 1876 review of the novel poked fun at Eliot's oddly
unconscious use of character tics, such as Deronda's clutching of his coat
collar, or Mirah's crossing of her feet—a stylistic reiteration so embarrassing
that Eliot cut many of them for the novel's 1878 Cabinet edition.[2] Whether the
novel's palpable repetitiveness contributed to the equally palpable exhaustion
of its readers, or whether its repetitiveness helped relieve that exhaustion, is
a debate carried on in the margins of these reviews; what they agree on is
the need to think through the aesthetic and even ethical demands that *Daniel
Deronda*'s length and verbal reiterations may be making upon the reader.
If Eliot is long and repeats herself, so the sentiment runs, then it is for a
reason.

A key to this reason is furnished by the musical analogies that frequently
accompanied discussions of *Deronda*'s form, and it is here that the cultural
significance of the novel's length becomes most evident, and most telling. The
anonymous *British Quarterly* reviewer discussed the novel's main epigraph as
a 'key-note', and spoke of this key-note's frequent repetition, 'the increased
insistence on this theme', or 'the reiteration of this sort of monotone of
melancholy', throughout the novel.[3] Meanwhile, reviewing the initial Bayreuth
Festival, which opened during the August of *Deronda*'s 1876 serial run,
C. Halford Hawkins could find no other analogy for the demanding length of
Richard Wagner's *Ring des Nibelungen* cycle than Eliot herself:

But to say that any one can appreciate its variety, almost endless, in a single hearing
is monstrous. Here is the damning claim, that neither can orchestra be found to
play, nor singers to declaim, nor audience to listen to the work as a whole again.
Herein is chronicled the euthanasia of the *magnum opus* of the advanced school:
for it is evident that not even the riches of the score will induce the ordinary
conductors or executants to rehearse frequently or perform unflaggingly; that no love
of art or disdain of lucre will persuade singers to strain and sacrifice their voices
to the caprice of a theorist; and that finally, no intellectual excitement, however
supreme, will compel average audiences to study (as it must be studied) the minute
development of tone and character painting which makes Wagner the George Eliot of
Music.[4]

Wagner's Eliotism—an inversion of what other critics, James included, read as
Eliot's Wagnerism—is not thematic, or philosophical, but formal. It consists,

---

[2] Francillon, 'George Eliot's First Romance', 425; Sidney Colvin, 'Daniel Deronda', *Fortnightly
Review* 26 (1 Nov. 1876), 603; Henry James, 'Daniel Deronda: A Conversation', in *Essays on
Literature*, 978.

[3] Anon., 'Daniel Deronda', 480.

[4] Halford Hawkins, 'The Wagner Festival at Bayreuth', *Macmillan's* 35 (1876), 63.

as Hawkins's ambivalent piece shows, in a practice of elongated temporal length and insistent complexity, a length without breaks or breathing room, that is both theoretically exhilarating and practically exhausting, an aesthetic desideratum (the *Ring*, Hawkins claimed, 'will modify in a measure all future opera') and an impossibility.

What the Wagner–Eliot comparison reveals, alongside the responses of *Deronda*'s first critics, is a suddenly apparent cultural and artistic concern within Britain in the mid-1870s, one whose initial formulation is worked out in reference to both Eliot's novels and Wagner's music dramas: how the consumption of art over extended time periods takes place, with what possibilities and what sacrifices. Whether the material at hand be opera, symphonic music, or fictional narrative, the following question was increasingly asked: how might temporally elongated forms adapt themselves to consumers? How, in turn, must aesthetic consumers adapt themselves—physically, psychologically, even politically—to these demanding, exhausting forms? The reception of *Deronda*, in which the conditions of repetition, elongation, and unbroken complexity are noted, is part of a moment in the late 1870s in which consumers of high-art temporal forms such as psychological realism or opera are seen as under duress, and spoken of in a rhetoric of nervous fatigue. This is visible most explicitly in the British reception of Wagner and the 'music of the future' that he represented. As the *Punch* illustration from its 1877 'Almanack' demonstrates, the elongation and complexity of contemporary music—its development from Mozartean 'melody' to Romantic 'fantasia' to 'twenty-four independent logarithmic studies for violin and violoncello, with double differential and integral accompaniment on the pianoforte'—not only prevents its audience from either reverie or even casual conversation, but leaves it with two alternatives: aural panic or sleep (see Figure 3.1). It is a tableau of late Victorian musical reception that Eliot knew well; as she notes rather archly during one of *Deronda*'s scenes of avant-garde performance, 'Miss Arrowpoint and Herr Klesmer played a four-handed piece on two pianos which convinced the company in general that it was long' (p. 47).[5] The common account, which Eliot and other British writers of the decade sought to complicate while not disconfirming, was the following: the extravagant demands of elongated form in music disrupted the politely social attentiveness of the drawing room, prostrating or frustrating listeners, turning musical narrative into proliferating, seemingly endless noise. What this made necessary was a retraining of audience expectation, or a series of formal accommodations on the part of the composer.

[5] Citations from Eliot's novel are given parenthetically, from the following edition: George Eliot, *Daniel Deronda*, ed. Terence Cave (Harmondsworth: Penguin, 1995).

Figure 3.1. 'Music at Home', from '*Punch*'s Almanack for 1877'. *Punch*, 72 (14 December 1876). General Research Division, The New York Public Library, Astor, Lenox, and Tilden Foundations

Eliot's thinking on the subject was, like that of many critics and theoreticians, not limited to music. She is, in fact, a unique nodal point in discussions of elongated form during the period, partly because she played a crucial, and deeply ambivalent, role in the British reception of Wagner and Wagnerian avant-gardism, starting in the mid-1850s, but also because her own fictional form worried over the same formal and receptive terrain that Wagner highlighted for British critics and musicologists. As a largely sympathetic commentator on Liszt and Wagner, with access to their work denied to even prominent British music critics, and as the period's most prominent and formally ambitious novelist, Eliot occupied the center of the theoretical terrain we might now call 'temporal form'. To recover the full sense of late Victorian thinking about this terrain, it is therefore necessary to make the move that Eliot herself made so consistently: to place the experience of novel-reading and music-listening side by side as parallel experiences of elongated comprehension. Put another way, in order to think about the problematics of novel-reading *in time* in the mid-to-late nineteenth century, one has to turn to music—particularly because Eliot herself did.

The musicological emphasis of physiological novel theory, as I sketched it in Chapter 1, becomes explicit and fully conscious, no longer just a metaphor, in the Eliot–Wagner nexus of the 1870s. Just as some of the prominent names in British music theory, such as James Sully and Edmund Gurney, turned to physiology to explain musical form, so novelists and novel theorists, with their implicitly physiological methodologies, turned to music as an illustrative, and particularly culturally contentious, example of how temporal form operates, and what (if any) its physical and cognitive limits may be. Not coincidentally, by the late 1870s it was the phenomenon of Wagner that most of this work confronts. That is, if musicology is an apt analogy for physiological novel theory, in the intersection of Wagner and Eliot the cultural and formal stakes of this analogy are startlingly visible. Melody and rhythm; the recurrence or repetition of thematic material over long stretches of intervening time and space (or, the *leitmotiv*); boredom and cognitive exhaustion: these are the topics that music and prose narrative share in this period. These topics are ways of confronting the central theoretical question behind physiological novel theory: how a consumer of temporal art forms cognitively registers a sequence of sensations, and how those cognitive techniques are strained or even altered altogether when the temporal scope of the artwork stretches to demanding new lengths. Or, at what point does elongated length defeat the coherence of temporal forms, and what formal techniques are necessary to maintain coherence in the face of elongated length?

At the center of all this controversy is the musically saturated, intellectually cosmopolitan, and formally elongated *Daniel Deronda*, which, if not

Wagnerism incarnate, is at least a uniquely English solution to the formal questions that Wagnerian music drama raised for physiologically inclined theorists. *Deronda* is drenched with references to Wagner, from the mocking (the callow Clintock telling Gwendolen that croquet is 'the game of the future') to the sinister (Gwendolen comparing her tedious cruises with Grandcourt to the wandering of the Flying Dutchman); the narrative voice references *Tannhäuser* to make a point about 'intensity', while in Klesmer the novel possesses a fully credentialed Wagnerian, fond of ridiculing Meyerbeer and Scribe. Yet the impact of Wagner upon *Deronda* is far more profound than these knowing nods would suggest; it is primarily in the issue of time and form that Wagner's immense cultural influence makes itself felt. From the very first sentence of the novel—'Was she beautiful or not beautiful? and what was the secret of form or expression which gave the dynamic quality to her glance?' (p. 7)—'form' is temporalized, or 'dynamic', making time itself an aesthetic and psychological problem, one to which *Deronda* is sensitive both structurally and thematically. The problem of time in *Deronda* is complicated both by the new anthropological or psychological challenges posed by ambitious, lengthy artworks of the period—of which *Deronda* is a self-conscious example—and by the novel's interest in the political and psychological conditions of what I will call 'lastingness': those affiliations, such as race, nation, or religion, that stretch beyond merely biographical time frames.

Seen this way, it becomes evident that music in *Daniel Deronda* is not simply an activity to be cited in a traditionally realist manner, one with a purely social signification meant to 'place' character like dress or speech habit, but a means by which the deepest questions of aesthetic reception, or human receptivity in general, are thought out. While fine, detailed studies of Eliot and music, Wagner and British culture, or even Eliot and Wagner do exist, their tendency to overlook the dense formal connections between high Victorian realism and Wagnerian music drama—and the physiological language used by Victorians to link the two—finally obscure the stakes really at play in this intersection.[6] Long before Wagnerism became a matter for

---

[6] Alison Byerly puts it most succinctly when she insists that music has no formal importance for Eliot: 'music', she writes, 'is the one art that never appears in [Eliot's] novels as a metaphor for novel-writing'; see *Realism, Representation, and the Arts in Nineteenth-Century Literature* (Cambridge: Cambridge University Press, 1997), 107. Other studies of the social signification of music in Eliot include Delia da Sousa Correa, *George Eliot, Music and Victorian Culture* (Basingstoke: Palgrave, 2003); Alisa Clapp-Itnyre, *Angelic Airs, Subversive Songs: Music as Social Discourse in the Victorian Novel* (Athens: Ohio University Press, 2002); Beryl Gray, *George Eliot and Music* (London: Macmillan, 1989). The recent work of Ruth Solie, however, does offer a more formally and theoretically adventurous consideration of Eliot's relationship to Wagner, taking up the issue of canon formation and artistic 'evolution' that Wagner's polemical version of opera history raised for Eliot; see Ruth Solie, ' "Tadpole Pleasures": *Daniel Deronda* as Music

self-professed 'decadent' aestheticism to emulate and parody, Wagner offered British culture new problems regarding the question of time and aesthetic reception, as well as some controversial solutions to those very problems. As *Daniel Deronda*'s critics are increasingly aware, in perhaps no other Victorian novel is the question of time so prominent, and so vexed.[7] What has not yet been made sufficiently apparent is how rooted *Deronda*'s temporality is in a physiological understanding of Wagnerian musical form, and how that orientation opens up a new understanding of Eliot's attempt to structure novel-reading in time.

The purpose of this chapter, then, is to situate *Deronda* within a particular cultural moment—the mid-1850s to the late 1870s—in which the psychological, social, even anthropological consequences of the collision between ever more harried consumers, and ever more elongated artistic forms, are worked out or given their initial formulations. That these formulations revolved around the example of Wagner, and were most thoughtfully and thoroughly posed by Eliot, is my assumption throughout what follows. By laying out the territory of Wagner's early British reception, and Eliot's important role in it, as a prelude to a reading of *Deronda*, I hope to generate a set of formal categories through which Eliot thought about the reception of elongated forms; to explain the multiple, intertwined historical and generic contexts for those categories, in music, science, and the novel; and to speak to the sociopolitical impact of those categories, and of those receptive practices and demands, which are highlighted in *Deronda* itself. Not least apparent in this inquiry will be the many historical ironies involved in the transference of formal categories from concert hall to reading chair, or from German avant-gardism to British realism—most notably, of course, the fact of Eliot's putting Wagnerian concepts of temporal form in the service of a proto-Zionist narrative project.

THE LAND WITHOUT MUSIC: WAGNER IN ENGLAND, I

Few episodes in cultural transmission reveal as much of the persistent national barriers across Europe in the nineteenth century as that of Wagner's initial contact with Britain in the spring and early summer of 1855. Virtually

Historiography', in *Music in Other Words: Victorian Conversations* (Berkeley: University of California Press, 2004), 153–86.

7 The most prolonged and compelling recent work on *Deronda* and temporality is that of Irene Tucker, who insists that the novel's politics are rooted in a temporal, rather than a spatial, understanding of subjectivity and identity; see Irene Tucker, *A Probable State: The Novel, the Contract, and the Jews* (Chicago: University of Chicago Press, 2000).

unknown to British musical audiences prior to his arrival, except through vague rumors of revolutionary and potentially unsound Continental musical ideas, Wagner managed to rapidly destabilize what had been a settled cultural consensus around the issues of tempo and melody (or, speed and duration, musical form across time), in the process initiating lasting changes in British musical aesthetics. More broadly still, Wagner's 1855 visit, and the series of polemical and critical writings that surrounded it—in which Eliot took a crucial part—was a key and still little-noted episode in the history of aesthetic 'form' in Britain. By discomfiting audiences accustomed to a narrowly familiar range of tempi and melodic lengths, Wagner brought musical form, and by extension all temporal form, into contact with theoretical developments in cognate fields, and spurred research into questions of rate and duration in acts of artistic production and consumption. His polarizing influence also forced British musicians and audiences into closer, and often painfully demoralizing, contact with a cosmopolitan world of musical development that forced his opponents into ever more intricate and heated defenses of 'tradition'—particularly a tradition as manifested in the bodies of listeners, whose comfort zones were under attack. The year 1855, then, marked the opening of the question of elongated form, and also marked Eliot's initial confrontations with it.

The extent of Wagner's British reach was minuscule before 1855; Henry Chorley, the conservative music critic of the *Athenaeum*, had in the early 1850s heard performances of *Tannhäuser* and *Lohengrin* in Weimar and Dresden, and reported negatively in occasional letters from abroad, but none of Wagner's music was performed in Britain until 1854, when the pioneering Louis Jullien, conductor of the New London Philharmonic, offered the *Tannhäuser* overture. Even professional British musicians had limited opportunity to gain first-hand knowledge of Wagner's work. But Eliot had already gained precisely those opportunities, and was in a unique position not only to judge the effect of Wagner's theories but also to help shape British critical opinions about Wagner at an early phase; she was, in effect, Wagner's first major British apologist. Her 1854 trip with G. H. Lewes to Weimar, which extended from late July to early November, involved prolonged contact with various musical luminaries, particularly Franz Liszt, at that time court Kapellmeister, as well as Clara Schumann and Anton Rubinstein. Liszt's role was crucial; he not only played for Eliot and Lewes, but permitted Eliot to translate one of his polemics, 'The Romantic School of Music', as one of Lewes's regular contributions for the *Leader*. From Eliot's journals we know that the translation occupied her for the first two days of October 1854, and that after its completion on 3 October, she and Lewes attended a performance of *Tannhäuser*. 'The overture and the first and second acts thrilled me,' she reported in her journal, using language that prefigured the reception of *Deronda*, 'but the third I felt rather wearisome. The tragedy in this act is very fine, but either I was too much fatigued to relish the music, or it is intrinsically monotonous and spun out beyond any but German patience.'[8] Later in October she and Lewes would also attend *Der fliegende Holländer* and *Lohengrin*, the last occasioning more frustration, particularly on the part of Lewes, who insisted on leaving after two acts. As Eliot noted in her subsequent 'Recollections of Weimar 1854': 'The declamation appeared to me monotonous, and situations in themselves trivial or disagreeable were dwelt on fatiguingly. Without feeling competent to pass judgment on this opera as music, one may venture to say that it fails in one grand requisite of art, based on an unchangeable element in human nature—the need for contrast.'[9]

The ambivalence that Eliot displayed toward Wagner here is instructive, and will characterize her relation to his work for the next two decades. Her private comments are dedicated to reports of exhaustion, weariness, inability to take in a listening experience so prolonged and undifferentiated; her public comments, starting with the *Leader* translation, which predates her actual experiences of Wagner, express admiration for Wagner's theory, which she read as an attempt to solve the formal and thematic problems in earlier operatic practice. Put another way, Eliot finds Wagner theoretically satisfying prior to having heard his work; to the work itself Eliot responds with a self-critical disappointment, the physical experience of Wagnerian exhaustion confirming either her unfitness for new elongated experiences or, possibly, the excesses of Wagnerian theory, which conflict with 'unchangeable' facts of human receptivity. In her *Leader* piece Eliot translates Liszt's account of Wagner as follows: 'so far from making melody an object, he [Wagner] rather rejoices when the melodic motives, which are treated by him in a declamatory and specially dramatic manner, are denied the name of melodies'.[10] Even in Liszt's own voice Eliot registers a conflict between theoretical adventurousness and experiential failure, one that tinges with a rueful, amused, yet admiring irony every subsequent comment she made on the question of Wagner. Yet the practical effect of her visit to Weimar—which exposed her to the forefront of European musical theory—was to place her in what would shortly become the first party of British Wagnerians.

Eliot's visit to Weimar was followed almost immediately by Wagner's visit to Britain. After the late 1854 resignation of Michael Costa, conductor of

---

[8] George Eliot, *The Journals of George Eliot*, ed. Margaret Harris and Judith Johnston (Cambridge: Cambridge University Press, 1998), 26.

[9] Ibid. 233.

[10] George Eliot, 'The Romantic School of Music: Liszt on Meyerbeer—Wagner', *Leader* 5 (28 Oct. 1854), 1028.

the old London Philarmonic Society, and after being turned down by both
Louis Spohr and Hector Berlioz, the Society offered a guest conductorship
to Wagner, who accepted in the hopes of financial benefit. Interwoven issues
of social protocol, nationalism, and anti-Semitism inflect the immediately
negative press response to the Society's choice. James Davison, editor of the
Musical World and chief music critic of *The Times*, himself Jewish and, like
many of his colleagues, an admirer of Felix Mendelssohn, published translated
extracts from Wagner's *Oper und Drama* as well as controversial claims
made by Ferdinand Praeger, one of Wagner's English disciples. Praeger's
comments, initially made to the *New York Musical Gazette* in February
1855, not only proclaimed Wagner's hostility to conventional, conservative
Britain, but revealed him as the author of *Das Judentum in der Musik*, the
1850 pamphlet Wagner had published under the pseudonym 'K. Freigedank'
('K. Freethought'). By publishing Praeger's encomium, Davison thus revealed
for British audiences Wagner's anti-Semitic, anti-British opinions, which
coalesced in Wagner's disdain for Mendelssohn, still in the 1850s the central
reference point for British music critics and audiences alike.[11] If, in other words,
Wagner and followers like Praeger saw Mendelssohn's reputation as evidence
of the Jewish influence in British musical affairs, Davison was prepared to
defend Mendelssohn, confident that the airing of Wagner's anti-Semitism
was enough to discredit his theory as a whole. While many commentators
make much of Wagner's supposed ignorance of normal protocol for visiting
composers—he either failed or refused to make social calls on the critics of
major London publications, Davison included—clearly the issue of Wagner's
anti-Semitism dominated much of his critical reception, particularly prior to
his initial concerts. Wagner did little to avoid it: he ostentatiously conducted

---

[11] Praeger's comments—that Wagner's *Judaism in Music* 'makes a severe onslaught upon
Mendelssohn and Meyerbeer on Judaistic grounds', and that the 'editor of the London *Musical
World*, considering himself one of Mendelssohn's heirs, and Mendelssohn having (so it is said)
hated Wagner, ergo, must the enraged editor also hate him'—explicitly linked Britishness and
Jewishness via the figure of Mendelssohn. For Praeger's text, see William Ashton Ellis's heatedly
pro-Wagnerian *Life of Richard Wagner*, v (New York: Da Capo, 1977), 119. Wagner's 1869
'Appendix to *Judaism in Music*' referred explicitly to this controversy, noting that Davison
'did not hesitate to hold me up to public odium as blasphemer of the greatest composers for
reason of their Judaism', and that 'the English nation . . . seems more grounded on the old
testament, than on the new'. See *Judaism in Music and Other Essays*, trans. William Ashton Ellis
(Lincoln: University of Nebraska Press, 1995), 109–10. In a letter to Otto Wesendonck written
during the height of the 1855 controversy, Wagner most explicitly linked the two, complaining
that 'Mendelssohn is to the English exactly what Jehovah is to the Jews. And Jehovah's wrath
now strikes me, an unbeliever.' See Derek Watson, *Richard Wagner: A Biography* (New York:
Schirmer, 1979), 142. Years later Wagner blamed Davison's animus, and his English reception
in general, upon the discovery of his *Judaism in Music* authorship, stating that Davison's attacks
clearly demonstrated the powerful effect of the pamphlet. See Wagner, *Mein Leben*, ed. Martin
Gregor-Dellin (Munich: List, 1976), 529.

Mendelssohn's *Italian* Symphony wearing kid gloves, removing them before beginning Carl Maria von Weber's *Euryanthe* Overture.[12]

When the concerts began, however, the subject of the attacks on Wagner changed from politics to matters of musical form. Wagner adhered to the parameters of Victorian concert programming, made up of long lists of primarily shorter forms, such as overtures, arias, and duets, that surrounded one longer symphonic work; but his readings of the works in question were radically unfamiliar, particularly in the matter of tempo. Of the Philharmonic's rendition of Mozart's Symphony No. 39 in E flat major, Davison commented:

A stranger performance of Mozart's symphony was never heard. The *allegro* was throughout too slow. . . . The *andante*—of all slow movements the most beautiful, if melody, as we believe, constitutes the principal charm of music—was robbed of its character altogether by the tedious prolixity of the tempo Herr Wagner thought proper to indicate. The *minuetto* and *trio* were equally at variance with the reading consecrated by more than half a century; while the *finale*—singular to relate, after so much provoking slowness in the first three movements—was taken quicker than we ever heard it, so quick, indeed, that the stringed instruments at times could scarcely master the passages allotted them, easy as they are in comparison with those to be found in modern symphonies.[13]

Henry Chorley, writing in the *Athenaeum* of the same concert, found that 'the wind instruments were hardly able to hold out in the middle movement, with such caricatured slowness was that *andante con moto* taken,—and the *finale* was degraded into a confused romp, by a speed as excessive'.[14] Wagner's reading of Mozart's 'Jupiter' Symphony a month later received similar notices; Davison complained that the opening movement was 'tortured and spoiled by every species of affectation that could be expected from an ultra-sentimental boarding-school miss before she had been taught better', and added that the movement, 'dragged back and tormented where its onward [*sic*] course should be impetuous and unimpeded—like a spirited charger, goaded and incensed by the wavering of a timid and inexperienced rider', was 'altogether unlike itself', thanks to what he termed 'the incessant liberties taken with the time'.[15]

---

[12] Watson, *Richard Wagner*, 142.

[13] James Davison, 'Philharmonic Concerts', *The Times*, 16 May 1855, 11.

[14] Henry Charley, 'Music and the Drama', *Athenaeum*, 19 May 1855, 539.

[15] James Davison, 'Philharmonic Concerts', *The Times*, 12 June 1855, 12. So consistent is this opinion of Wagner's conducting that *Punch* could make it the subject of humor: 'He alters Mozart, it appears, if not exactly as a parish clerk once said that he had altered Haydn for the singing gallery, yet in a manner nearly as audacious, altering "*allegro*" to "*moderato*"; "*andante*" to "*adagio*"; "*allegretto*" to "*andante*"; and "*allegro*" again to "*prestissimo*." Wagner would seem to strongly resemble his namesake in Faust, in the particular wherein that *Wagner* differs from

Time was what Wagner's conducting made unnaturally apparent. In his *Über das Dirigiren* [*On Conducting*] (1869), Wagner made explicit reference to his 1855 season with the Philharmonic, commenting at length upon the tendency of British orchestras to play at a level speed and volume. 'The music gushed forth like water from a fountain,' Wagner remembered; 'there was no arresting it, and every Allegro ended as an undeniable Presto. . . . The orchestra generally played *mezzoforte*; no real *forte*, no real *piano* was attained.'[16] For this, Wagner predictably blamed Mendelssohn, who had in fact led the Philharmonic for a series of seasons. That 'the whole duty of a conductor is comprised in his ability to indicate the right tempo', Wagner asserted as dogma; and to indicate the right tempo meant, practically speaking, to call attention to tempo as such, to make time palpable to orchestra and audience alike.[17] In this, Wagner and his critics agreed about the facts but disagreed about their significance. For Davison, Chorley, and others, and (one can reasonably extrapolate) for the Philharmonic's supposedly unhappy 1855 audiences, the traditional readings made time disappear, and made their consumption of an event in time yield to other meanings, particularly shorter melodic units. For Wagner, time itself needed to become a salient aspect of performance and consumption, literally *defamiliarized*, and melody was less a masking or sublimation of time than the passage of time made acutely audible. For this reason, when Wagner performed his own compositions in 1855, critics found them tedious and unstructured: 'an inflated display of extravagance and noise', Davison called the *Tannhäuser* overture, while Chorley termed it 'one of the most curious pieces of patchwork ever passed off by self-delusion for a complete and significant creation'.[18] Making the listener conscious of time seems to have meant—as Wagner and his British critics both understood—three things in particular: an elongation or slowing down of traditional British tempi; a marked alternation between different tempi across one piece; and a refusal, when possible, to fragment melody into smaller, more condensed units. In 1855, this was commonly understood as a foreign, anti-British, anti-traditional, and not incidentally anti-Semitic (because anti-Mendelssohnian) practice. It was also, for reasons that may or

his master—that is, in the circumstance of being no conjuror.' See 'Not a Magic Minstrel', *Punch* 28 (19 May 1855), 204.

[16] Wagner goes on to detail some of the 1855 performances, even the Mozart E flat Symphony program which Davison and Chorley so disliked; he claims that the negative reviews led to his being requested to restore the familiar, 'flabby and colourless' tempi in subsequent performances, 'which, they said, Mendelssohn himself had sanctioned'. Wagner, *On Conducting*, trans. Edward Dannreuther (London: William Reeves, 1897), 23–4.

[17] Ibid. 20.

[18] Davison, 'Philharmonic Concerts', *The Times* (May 16, 1855), 5; Chorley, 'Music and the Drama', 540.

may not have been due to the hostile press accounts of the concerts, a failure, and Wagner retreated to Zurich in late June with the sensation of defeat, not invited by the Society's directors to return.[19]

Around the time of Wagner's departure, however, Eliot added her own voice to the debate, although in a carefully nuanced manner. In June and July issues of *Fraser's Magazine* Eliot offered retrospections on her Weimar visit—'Three Months in Weimar' and 'Liszt, Wagner, and Weimar'—which manage to offer detailed analyses and appraisals of new musical ideas while avoiding the contentiousness of Wagner's British residency. The timing of these pieces could not have been coincidental. They are clearly meant to take advantage of the public controversy surrounding Wagner's tenure with the Philharmonic, as well as Davison's airing of Wagner's polemical writings; and on the whole they offer the most positive reading of Wagner that any British publication would present in the 1850s. Throughout Eliot's account of Wagner, skepticism about the actual performative effect of his work is balanced with a thorough sympathy with his theoretical aims, particularly his confrontation with, and solutions to, the problems of temporal form; the essays offer an uneasily positive account of Wagnerian aesthetics while sidestepping the issues of race and nation that Wagner's critics highlighted.

In particular, 'Liszt, Wagner, and Weimar' concentrates on the temporal organization of Wagnerian opera, using the evidence of the performances that Eliot had witnessed in Weimar. Turning first to Wagner as a theorist, Eliot's summary of his work—seemingly built on a reading of *Oper und Drama*, although none of Wagner's writings are named—reads him as an organicist attempting to solve the problem of relating organicism to a temporal succession of sensations: 'An opera', as Eliot paraphrases Wagner's argument, 'must be no mosaic of melodies stuck together with no other method than is supplied by accidental contrast, no mere succession of ill-prepared crises, but an organic whole, which grows up like a palm, its earliest portion containing the germ and prevision of all the rest.'[20] What interests Eliot about this claim, which she adds is 'surely a theory worth entertaining', is its embedded paradox: that while 'form' is inescapably temporal, the purest forms find a way

---

[19] For decades to come, British critics—and musicologists of a physiological kind—would insist, contrary to Wagner's ideas, that evenness of tempo provides necessary audience comfort; the physiological theorist James Sully, in his *Sensation and Intuition* (1874), explained that the effect of even tempi is to match the usual human pulse rate, thereby creating a pleasurable externalization of inner sensation. Sully added that 'tempo moderato' should be, for this reason, the base tempo, because it matches more closely a base adult heart rate. See *Sensation and Intuition: Studies in Psychology and Aesthetics*, 2nd edn. (London: Kegan Paul, 1880), 193. Recent cognitive psychologists have concurred with Sully; see Bob Snyder, *Music and Memory: An Introduction* (Cambridge, Mass.: MIT Press, 2000), 168.

[20] Eliot, 'Liszt, Wagner, and Weimar', *Fraser's Magazine* 52 (July 1855), 50.

to turn diachrony into synchrony, to make mere succession into accumulative, atemporal wholes. The aria–recitative process of *opera seria* and *opera buffa*, with its disconnected units strung across time, is here contrasted with a more taut musical logic, and as a theoretical claim, Eliot is entirely sympathetic with the logic of synchrony-within-diachrony.

But as throughout her considerations of Wagner, it is in the listening experience that Eliot finds problems, most notably with his lack of familiar melodic structures: 'it is difficult to see why this theory should entail the exclusion of melody to the degree at which he has arrived in *Lohengrin*, unless we accept one of two suppositions: either that Wagner is deficient in melodic inspiration, or that his inspiration has been overridden by his system, which opposition has pushed to exaggeration'.[21] Diachrony must be matched, Eliot insists, with 'a frequent alternation of sensations or emotions', which melody satisfies, insofar as Eliot understands melody as a discernible, bounded unit within a larger structure—a definition, one might note, that Wagner himself did not hold. In the language of contemporary cognitive psychology, Eliot is here discussing the 'chunking' operations of melody: the grouping mechanisms of long-term memory which hold onto discrete units of sensation.[22] In Eliot's largely physiological understanding of musical reception, the fatigue of a (theoretically desirable) organically linked temporal succession is relieved by its (experientially necessary) intervals of melodic distinctness.

However—a point most of the essay's commentators have missed—Eliot's physiological argument is nuanced by her commitment to evolutionary theory, which leads her to admit, with only partial irony, that Wagner's theories may change the facts of human receptivity rather than simply fail to satisfy them.[23] 'As to melody—who knows? It is just possible that melody, as we conceive it, is only a transitory phase of music, and that the musicians of the future may read the airs of Mozart and Beethoven and Rossini as scholars read the *Strabreim*

---

[21] Eliot, 'Liszt, Wagner, and Weimar', 50.

[22] For a definition of 'chunking', see Snyder, *Music and Memory*, 218–22. See also Diana Deutsch, 'The Processing of Pitch Combinations', in *The Psychology of Music*, ed. Diana Deutsch (San Diego: Academic Press, 1999), 370–3, for an account of the assembly of larger musical progressions out of shorter 'chunks'.

[23] The ambivalence in Eliot's discussion here—torn between her theoretical interests and her self-confessedly untutored listening habits and experiences—is usually read as straight sarcasm; Alisa Clapp-Itnyre has recently claimed that Eliot 'detested' Wagner, while Beryl Gray adds, with a bit more justice, that Eliot's attitude to Wagner was 'far less dismissive than that of many of her contemporaries', which nonetheless fails to capture the intensity of her complex relation to Wagner's music and writings. See Clapp-Itnyre, *Angelic Airs, Subversive Songs*, 200; Gray, *George Eliot and Music*, 127. Ruth Solie's ' "Tadpole Pleasures" ' offers a more satisfyingly nuanced approach to Eliot's essay, positioning it in reference to Victorian scientific and historiographical notions of artistic progress.

and assonance of early poetry. We are but in "the morning of the times," and must learn to think of ourselves as tadpoles unprescient of the future fog.' The passage's close—'Still the tadpole is limited to tadpole pleasures; and so, in our state of development, we are swayed by melody'—does not entirely cancel the earlier evolutionary concession: Eliot is both convinced of the fatigue that Wagner's melodic practice makes her feel, and equally convinced, if more abstractly, of the limited horizon of receptivity that she, and others like her, possess.[24] She finds herself, that is, in the position of insisting upon the reality of her disappointment in Wagner's music, while also insisting upon the importance of his conception of the temporality of musical form.

Melody, while a vexed problem for Eliot—a problem that would remain central to the physiological understanding of Wagner, as we shall see—finally, and crucially, yields in her essay to a more satisfying combination of theory and practice in Wagner: the *leitmotiv*. Here Eliot sees a more successful version of synchrony-within-diachrony, and it is here that she is most laudatory:

Certainly Wagner has admirably fulfilled his own requisition of organic unity in the opera. In his operas there is a gradual unfolding and elaboration of that fundamental contrast of emotions, that collision of forces, which is the germ of the tragedy; just as the leaf of the plant is successively elaborated into branching stem and radiant corolla. The artifice, however, of making certain contrasted strains of melody run like coloured threads through the woof of an opera, and also the other dramatic device of using a particular melody or musical phrase as a sort of Ahnung or prognostication of the approach or action of a particular character, are not altogether peculiar to Wagner, although he lays especial stress on them as his own. No one can forget the recurring hymn of Marcel in the *Huguenots*, or the strain of the Anabaptists in the *Prophète*, which is continually contrasted with the joyous song or dance of the rustics. Wagner, however, has carried out these devices much more completely, and in the *Fliegende Holländer* and *Tannhäuser*, with very impressive effect.[25]

The repetition of musical units throughout the work, as a way to bind temporal succession into some kind of loose unity, is for Eliot the most sophisticated aspect of Wagner's method as well as the most experientially satisfying. In the following sections of the essay, which offer prolonged synopses of the *Fliegende Holländer*, *Tannhäuser*, and *Lohengrin*, she attempts a description of purely musical effect, as opposed to scenic or dramatic effect, only when a motif is being used; it is as if the motif has in Wagner perfectly performed its usual function, which is (as in the above examples from Meyerbeer) to be *memorable*.

---

[24] Eliot, 'Liszt, Wagner, and Weimar', 50–1. The reference to *Strabreim* is likely provided by Wagner himself, who in *Oper und Drama* laid great stress on *Strabreim*'s ability to make mixed emotion immediately apparent to the senses. Here and elsewhere in the essay, Eliot reveals a deeper acquaintance with Wagner's theoretical writings than has generally been claimed for her.

[25] Ibid. 51–2.

In the midst of her *Fliegende Holländer* summary, for instance, Eliot pauses to note a striking melodic repetition in the first act: 'As the Hollander slowly descends to land, a strain that rises from the orchestra sounds like a sentence of doom, and recurs throughout the opera whenever his terrible fate is immediately operative' (see Figure 3.2).[26] If Wagner's prolonged melodies vanish in the recollection, thereby failing in their attempt to organically unify temporal form, his motifs—shorter than melodies, mere 'strains' rising from the orchestra—remain, their reiterations altering pure succession into condensed recollections. The *Fliegende Holländer* motif that Eliot singles out is not accidental; it has traditionally been understood as expressing 'weariness of life', particularly the repetitive intervals of the Dutchman's endless seven-year terms of wandering, and as such it is a motif about motifs, centered on the very dilemmas—temporal elongation, repetitive experience—that make motifs necessary.[27] Despite, therefore, the canny political rebuke expressed by the claim that Wagner is elaborating upon a method used by his famous (and Jewish) antagonist Meyerbeer, the terms of Eliot's admiration are clear. The motif, for Eliot, is the *lasting* part of Wagner's work, both historically and psychologically.

Eliot's intervention in the controversy surrounding Wagner's 1855 visit had no immediate impact. It did, however, prefigure the terms of British debate around Wagner that would exist by the 1870s, by producing a reading of Wagnerian theory and practice that was at once physiological (i.e. interested in human receptivity and its conditions) and formal (attuned to the techniques by which Wagner attempted to guide and even change that receptivity). At first glance, this is a remarkable depoliticization of the 1855 controversy, and to an extent Eliot's cosmopolitanism kept her neutral, at least as far as Wagner's well-known disdain for British musical institutions and habits was concerned.

---

[26] Eliot, 'Liszt, Wagner' 52. Of course, generations of Wagner scholars have denied that the term *leitmotiv*, first popularized by Hans von Wolzogen in reference to *Götterdämmerung* in the 1880s, is applicable to operas prior to *Lohengrin*; in these such motifs have tended to be called instead 'reminiscence motives'. As Carl Dahlhaus put it: 'Unlike reminiscence motives, which were restricted to turning points in the plot, the leitmotivs in a music drama form a dense web spread over the whole of the orchestral setting, determining its structure at any given moment.' Carl Dahlhaus, *Nineteenth-Century Music*, trans. J. Bradford Robinson (Berkeley: University of California Press, 1989), 196. Rey Longyear stresses the slightly more melodic quality of this earlier 'reminiscence motive', which 're-inforces the impression of a situation which occurred earlier', while the *leitmotiv* proper, often in the form of a rhythmic or enharmonic modulation rather than a melodic phrase, is more temporally static. See Rey M. Longyear, *Nineteenth-Century Romanticism in Music* (Englewood Cliffs, NJ: Prentice-Hall, 1973), 176. While these categorizations of Wagnerian practice are useful and important, Eliot's relation to Wagner's motivic practices as she found them in his earlier work is general enough to encompass both categories: for Eliot, the motif, insofar as it represents pure repetition, is always about reminiscence.

[27] See, e.g., the canonical description in Ernest Newman's *The Wagner Operas* (Princeton: Princeton University Press, 1949), 31.

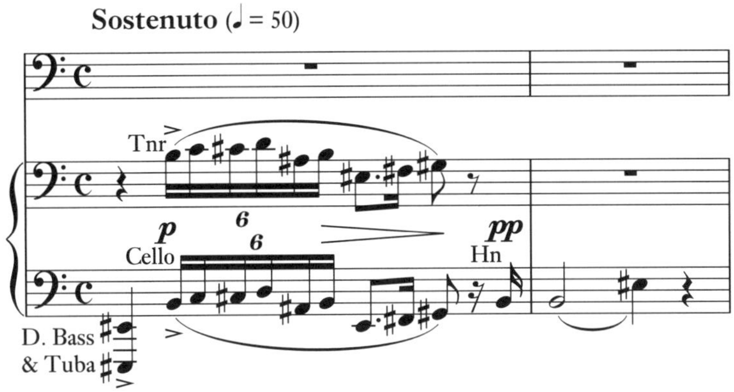

Figure 3.2. The orchestral passage in Act I of *Der fliegende Holländer* noted by Eliot in 'Lizst, Wagner, and Weimar'. The motif, built around the diminished seventh chord in the first, fourth, seventh, and ninth tones, accompanies the Dutchman's landfall prior to the aria 'Die Frist ist um', and has been traditionally understood as expressing weariness or resignation at the endlessness of time

But by *Daniel Deronda* Eliot had thought through the possible politics of Wagnerian form—as opposed to the politics of Wagnerian polemics—and come to her own conclusions. Starting in the mid-1850s, Eliot finds in Wagner a conception of 'form' that is explicitly defined as follows: the temporally sequential sensations which a mind is capable of retaining both during, and after, the unrolling of the full sequence.[28] Both melody and the *leitmotiv* are thus 'formal' operations, technical procedures for making salient memorable aspects of much longer temporal processes, and thereby avoiding the fatigue of a mind attempting to find those aspects without any help from the composer. They are, as Arnold Schoenberg later commented, part of Wagner's 'organizational' aim.[29] The motif, however, is for Eliot organizational in the highest way—it organizes organically. Traces of this can be found in her

[28] This notion of 'form' is very close to that employed by present-day cognitive musicology; as one such definition runs, 'form' in music involves events of greater than 3–5 seconds length—that is, greater than the confines of short-term memory (STM)—that, because of their length, cannot be perceived directly but must instead be made out of representations, or condensations, provided by long-term memory (LTM). 'Formal' operations in music are, therefore, aimed toward the capacities of LTM, which improve with repeated listenings. See Snyder, *Music and Memory*, 193–241.

[29] From Schoenberg's pivotal 1947 essay 'Brahms the Progressive': 'Wagner's *Leitmotiven* usually contain some germinating harmonies in which the urge for modulatory changes is inherent. But simultaneously they fulfill another task, an organizational task, which shows the formalistic side of Wagner's genius.' Arnold Schoenberg, *Style and Idea: Selected Writings of Arnold Schoenberg*, ed. Leonard Stein (Berkeley: University of California Press, 1984), 405.

many uses of the term 'motive' in *Daniel Deronda*, particularly the most charged one, when Deronda offers his farewell advice to Gwendolen: 'What makes life dreary is the want of motive; but once beginning to act with that penitential, loving purpose you have in your mind, there will be unexpected satisfactions—there will be newly-opening needs—continually coming to carry you on from day to day. Your will find life growing like a plant' (p. 769). Motive: a password for organic linkages between past and present, for that which binds otherwise aimless temporality. It is Wagnerian form turned into an ethic.[30]

Eliot's interest in the mnemonic aspects of Wagner's form, however, implicitly raised a problem that is initially psychological, and ultimately (by the time of *Deronda*) political or ethical: did Wagner's motifs exist to aid terminally forgetful listeners, or to mirror the comprehension processes of attentive ones? Does Wagnerian opera slowly raise the listener's sophistication above that of 'tadpole pleasures', or does it in fact capitulate to those listening habits by incorporating reminders? Does the *leitmotiv* signal the triumph of elongated temporal form, or is it a defeat, an admission that no form can extend to the lengths of Wagner's without prosthetic aids for the memory? 'Among the functions of the leitmotiv can be found, alongside the aesthetic one, a commodity-function, rather like that of an advertisement: anticipating the universal practice of mass culture later on, the music is designed to be remembered, it is intended for the forgetful': thus Adorno on Wagner, refusing to take seriously the motif's claims to a Hegelian synthesis of the past in the present.[31] By the time of the composition of

---

[30] Eliot seems, therefore, to have been one of the earliest literary artists to have pondered the significance of the *leitmotiv*, early enough not to have received notice for it; Raymond Furness's standard work on the subject of the literary applications of the *leitmotiv* cites Edouard Dujardin's 1887 *Les Lauriers sont coupés* as the first novel indebted to this aspect of Wagner's practice. See Raymond Furness, *Wagner and Literature* (New York: St Martin's Press, 1982), 16–18.

[31] Adorno's harsh and influential account of the *leitmotiv*—'music abandons the struggle within the temporal framework it mastered in the symphony . . . the motiv is a sign that transmits a particle of congealed meaning'—is contested by Carl Dahlhaus, who insists that for Wagner, 'the child of an age permeated with the philosophy of Hegel, the individual moment receives its meaning from the history accumulated within it, and the present, even as represented on stage, is virtually "inundated" with the past'. This argument between the amnesiac reading of the *leitmotiv* (pointing toward the conditions of commodity culture) and the recollective reading (pointing toward Wagner's Hegelianism) continues to align critics of Wagner. See Theodor Adorno, *In Search of Wagner*, trans. Rodney Livingstone (New York: Verso, 1981), 37, 45; Dahlhaus, *Nineteenth-Century Music*, 197–8. Interestingly, Dahlhaus's account is not consistent across his own writings; elsewhere he writes of the *leitmotiv* as a pure present: 'A motive or theme in an opera must not be referred to a development whereby its import becomes intelligible, but rather must show at once in its exposition what it is all about. Only the present counts; this is one of the laws of operatic music.' Carl Dahlhaus, *Esthetics of Music*, trans. William Austin (Cambridge: Cambridge University Press, 1982), 67–8.

Daniel Deronda in the 1870s—when Wagner's position in British culture had changed entirely—the question would become even more pressing for Eliot: what were the individual's (physiological, psychological) capacities for encountering duration? What did elongated art do to those capacities? And, finally, what kinds of experiences of *lastingness* are possible and desirable?

UNENDING MELODY TRIUMPHANT: WAGNER IN ENGLAND, II

Wagner did not return to London until 1877, by which time almost everything in British musical culture had changed in his favor. The first Wagner Society in Britain was formed in 1872 by the ardent Wagnerian pianist and translator Edward Dannreuther, also a friend of Lewes and Eliot, who in 1873 conducted the Society's first concerts. By the mid-1870s Wagner's orchestral works were familiar fare at the popular Saturday concerts held at the Crystal Palace and conducted by August Manns, Louis Jullien's successor as an advocate for new music.[32] Observers noted the growth of an opera audience willing to move past traditional grand opera, and *Der fliegende Holländer* was first performed—in English—at the Lyceum in 1876, while in 1880 Covent Garden mounted the *Ring* cycle.[33] This was partly the result of the passing of the old, Mendelssohnian guard who wrote in prominent newspapers and periodicals. George Hogarth, the music critic for the *Illustrated London News* (and Charles Dickens's father-in-law) who had played a moderating role in the 1855 controversy, died in 1870; Chorley died in 1872, having stopped active reviewing some years previously; and although Davison retained his post at *The Times* until 1879, his influence was nevertheless rapidly eclipsed by a newer generation of critics, largely German, whose horizon of taste had been formed by Liszt, Berlioz, and Wagner rather than Rossini, Spohr, and Mendelssohn.

[32] See Michael Musgrave, *The Musical Life of the Crystal Palace* (Cambridge: Cambridge University Press, 1995), 102. For an account of Manns's importance to British musical culture in the second half of the nineteenth century—starting in the 1860s, his programs moved to complete symphonies rather than more familiar selected movements, and he championed the work of Brahms, Dvořák, Richard Strauss, and Wagner; see Catherine Dale, *Music Analysis in Britain in the Nineteenth and Early Twentieth Centuries* (Aldershot: Ashgate, 2003), 49. One excellent source on the rise of Wagner's reputation in Britain is Meirion Hughes and Robert Stradling, *The English Musical Renaissance, 1840–1880: Constructing a National Music* (Manchester: Manchester University Press, 1993).

[33] See Ronald Pearsall, *Victorian Popular Music* (Newton Abbot: David & Charles, 1973), 152–4.

Prominent among these was Franz Hüffer, a German expatriate who, later naturalized as Francis Hueffer (and later, father of Ford Madox Ford), was Wagner's most prominent and active British disciple. Hueffer succeeded Davison as *The Times* critic—signal enough, were one needed, of a cultural shift—but he had already, at that point, waged a decade-long periodical campaign in favor of Wagner. His *Richard Wagner and the Music of the Future* (1874), an expanded version of an earlier *Fortnightly Review* article, offered prolonged exegeses of such terms as *unendliche Melodie, Gesamtkunstwerk*, and 'leading motive', and explained Wagner's reforms as 'an energetic protest against the established artificialities of a demoralised operatic stage'.[34] Hueffer's enthusiastic reviews and capsule explanations of Wagnerian aesthetics connected to a growing Hegelian-Darwinian consensus about the nature of artistic 'progress' and 'evolution'. The anonymous 'Lyric Feuds', published in the *Westminster Review* in 1867, was the first sympathetic British piece on Wagner since Eliot's 1855 essay; it argued that musical history ran through important quarrels, such as Handel versus Bononcini, Glück versus Piccini, and Wagner versus various 'purists', which collectively demonstrate that 'the entire history of music . . . points irresistibly in one direction, of developmental progress'.[35]

As Continental revolutionary, Wagner had met resistance in Britain in 1855; recast as avatar of artistic evolution, he was enthusiastically received twenty-two years later. His six Albert Hall concerts in May 1877, intended to help fund the chronically indebted Bayreuth project, took advantage of an enormous orchestra of 169 performers as well as glowing press coverage, which now found ways to sidestep the political pitfalls that had opened up in the 1850s. The popular preacher and Wagnerian H. R. Haweis wrote an anticipatory piece in the *Contemporary Review*, making the familiarly apologetic explanation that although Wagner was a theoretical anti-Semite, 'Wagner's dearest friends have been Jews.'[36] Even *Punch*'s reviews, despite comments about the length of *Das Rheingold* making its audience feel 'an irrepressible "drink-motive" ', added that 'many who went to scoff, returned to praise'.[37] Socially as well as musically, the visit was the obverse of Wagner's first British foray: he was received at Windsor by Queen Victoria and Prince Leopold, and he found a network of admirers willing to entertain and court

---

[34] Francis Hueffer, *Richard Wagner and the Music of the Future: History and Aesthetics* (London: Chapman & Hall, 1874), 74. The earlier version appeared under the name Franz Hüffer as 'Richard Wagner', *Fortnightly Review* 17 (March 1872), 265–87.

[35] Anon., 'Lyric Feuds', *Westminster Review* 32 (1867), 122.

[36] H. R. Haweis, 'Wagner', *Contemporary Review* 29 (May 1877), 995.

[37] See Anon., 'The Wagner Festival', *Punch* 72 (19 May 1877), 221; Anon., 'Our Representative Man', *Punch* 72 (26 May 1877), 237.

him, including Robert Browning, Edward Burne-Jones, and William Morris. Among the contacts renewed during this visit were Lewes and Eliot, who met the Wagners frequently that month, and who heard Wagner read his *Parsifal* libretto at a dinner held by Dannreuther, with whom the Wagners were staying.[38] Whereas Eliot had been one of the few commentators willing in 1855 to commend Wagner's work, by 1877, only a few months after the completion of *Deronda*'s serial run, she was part of a crowd, and perhaps far from its most enthusiastic member. On occasions subsequent to 1855 when she and Lewes had heard Wagner's operas, Lewes's response, voiced as a shared opinion, was severely critical. An 1870 performance of *Tannhäuser* in Berlin led Lewes to remark that 'his operas have failed to give us a moment of rapture; and succeeded in giving hours of noise and weariness'.[39]

Their increasingly negative personal response to Wagner not only bucked the British trend of the 1870s—just as Eliot had bucked it, in the other direction, in 1855—but has tended to occlude the fact that the major force operating in Wagner's favor by 1877 had been prefigured by Eliot twenty-two years earlier: the influence of physiological musicology, which took Wagner as a pivotal, if still controversial, datum for thinking through the reception of elongated temporal forms. As Catherine Dale has claimed, the major trend of Victorian musicology was 'the consideration of musical acoustics as a natural science', one that gathered force only after Hermann von Helmholtz's 1863

---

[38] The Dannreuther dinner, mentioned in Lewes's diary, was, according to Hueffer, the occasion for a charged encounter between Eliot and Cosima Wagner, although no independent confirmation exists for Hueffer's odd anecdote. As Hueffer tells it: 'Madame Wagner, who speaks English perfectly, served as interpreter, and her conversation with the great English novelist—who took a deep interest in music, although her appreciation of Wagner was of a very platonic kind—was both friendly and animated. "Your husband," remarked George Eliot, with that straightforwardness which was so conspicuous and so loveable in her character, "does not like Jews; my husband is a Jew." Needless to add that Wagner's aversion to the Hebrew race was of a purely theoretic kind, and did not extend to individuals—witness his warm friendship for Tausig, one of his staunchest adherents, and the earliest promoter of the Bayreuth idea.' See Francis Hueffer, *Half a Century of Music in England* (London: Chapman & Hall, 1889), 71–2. Hueffer's embarrassment, encapsulated in his 'needless to add', prevents our hearing Cosima Wagner's response, and the episode scarcely reveals the 'straightforwardness' of Eliot that Hueffer claims, given that Lewes had no Jewish ancestry. Cosima Wagner's diaries mention nothing of such a conversation, and only record of Eliot that 'sie macht einen edlen und angenehmen Eindruck' 'she makes a noble and pleasant impression'. See Cosima Wagner, *Die Tagebücher*, i, ed. Martin Gregor-Dellin and Dietrich Mack (Zurich: Piper, 1976), 1048. The strangeness of the moment—was Eliot lying, and bating the rabidly anti-Semitic Cosima? did Hueffer mishear, or misremember?—is increased by the fact that Eliot's biographers have either ignored it, or are unaware of it. Only Frederick Karl notes the irony of the friendship between Eliot, who had just published *Deronda*, and Cosima Wagner, whose anti-Semitism was and is legendary; see Frederick Karl, *George Eliot: Voice of a Century* (New York: Norton, 1995), 580.

[39] Quoted in Gordon Haight, *George Eliot: A Biography* (New York: Oxford University Press, 1968), 424.

Die Lehre von den Tonempfindungen was translated into English as *On the Sensations of Tone as a Physiological Basis for the Theory of Music* in 1875.[40] The trend, however, was not wholly due to Helmholtz, but arose from the deep presence of physiological methodologies among critics of all kinds (and of all media) in the 1860s and 1870s. Eliot's early discussion of temporality in Wagner, and her guarded criticism of the 'frequent alternation of sensations' that his melodies conspicuously lacked, became normative by the 1870s, at which point Wagner galvanized theorists looking for insight into how any sequence of sensations, particularly acoustic sensations, might become 'form'. The lay physiology pervasive in British criticism, that is, found in Wagner's radical reformation of listening habits a model through which to think through the problem of temporal response as a whole.

The idea around which these considerations swirled was, as Eliot had already determined, Wagnerian melody. As Ruth Solie has argued, melody had a central status for Victorian thinkers as the vehicle not only for a listener's emotion but also for the work's moral agency.[41] It also had a unique formal status, as both a temporal, horizontal process (unlike the vertical groupings of harmony) and a mnemonic unit which made recollection possible. Wagner's theoretical writings, at least at first glance, seemed to agree; he had, after all, asserted in 'Zukunftsmusik' that *music's only form is melody*, that it is not even thinkable apart from melody, that music and melody are absolutely indisseverable'.[42] But by placing stress on the horizontality of melody—its temporal reach, rather than its mnemonic groupings—Wagner contested, and therefore challenged, the usual Victorian physiological understanding of melodic functioning as a way to bind elongated forms. One British commentator argued in 1876, with careful physiological reasoning, that by eliminating the cognitively necessary groupings of shorter melodic units, 'infinite melody' produced conditions of extreme fatigue: 'Nor do we believe that the brilliant and powerful points in the work can ever, with any but a very partial audience, adequately atone for the tedium inseparable from a method which allows so little relief and contrast of manner and effect, and

---

[40] C. Dale, *Music Analysis in Britain*, 4. Relevant works mentioned by Dale include George Macfarren's *Six Lectures on Harmony* (1866); John Stainer's *Theory of Harmony, Founded on the Tempered Scale* (1871); and Ebenezer Prout's *Harmony: Its Theory and Practice* (1889). Lewes and Eliot owned Macfarren's volume; see Solie, ' "Tadpole Pleasures" ', 159. For a thorough account of Helmholtz's influence on British thinking, even beyond the field of acoustics, and particularly on Eliot and *Deronda*, see John Picker, *Victorian Soundscapes* (New York: Oxford University Press, 2003), 84–99; Helmholtz and Eliot are also discussed by Kay Young in '*Middlemarch* and the Problem of Other Minds Heard', *Literature Interpretation Theory* 14 (2003), 223–41.

[41] Solie, ' "Tadpole Pleasures" ', 181.

[42] R. Wagner, from 'Zukunftsmusik [Music of the Future]', originally published in 1861. See Wagner, *Judaism in Music and Other Essays*, 333.

which, discarding the resources of amplification and extension of musical form, and emphasising every detail of the words, keeps the musical expression, so to speak, at a white heat throughout, and never allows the listener a moment's repose.'[43] Another protested that Wagner produced 'a constantly strained feeling, a never-ceasing tension . . . it is feverish, effective, exciting, and in the end extremely wearying; it is like the electric light, always brilliant, dazzling, and the same, compared with the tranquil and yet constantly varying daylight; and—to quote a critic who sets Cervantes above Victor Hugo—it "wants dullness, which all great works must have their share of"'.[44] These remarks, which sound oddly like the complaints made at the same time about *Daniel Deronda*, were confirmed by Wagner's own discussions of audience response: in 'Zukunftsmusik' he had described Italian opera as a facilitator of conversation, and added: 'how are we to blame this public if, suddenly confronted with a work which claims a like attention throughout its whole extent and for each of its parts, it sees itself torn from all its habits at musical performances, and cannot possibly take as identical with its beloved melody a thing which in the luckiest event may pass for a mere refinement of that musical noise—that noise whose naïve use before had facilitated the most agreeable interchange of small talk, whereas it now obtrudes the upstart claim of being really heard?'[45]

Of course what was at stake in the British physiological discussions of this idea was the extent to which 'a like attention throughout' was possible—or, put another way, to what temporal limits attention could be stretched, and with what costs of nervous strain or exhaustion. Edward Said has persuasively discussed the change in the shape of musical duration in the second half of the nineteenth century, and argued that concert music became both more abstract and more elongated, as the 'egotistical privilege' of the composer trumped the increasingly powerless audience.[46] Insofar as British musical culture by 1877 seemed to have accepted the privilege of the composer to test an audience's cognitive and physiological limits, the question remained what, in general, those limits might be, and whether Wagner in particular

---

[43] Anon., 'Wagner, and the Modern Theory of Music', *Edinburgh Review* 143 (Jan. 1876), 164.

[44] Edward Rose, 'Wagner as a Dramatist,' *Fraser's Magazine* 19 (April 1879), 529.

[45] Wagner, 'Zukunftsmusik', 332–3.

[46] See Edward Said, *Musical Elaborations* (New York: Columbia University Press, 1991), 66: 'By the time of Brahms and Bruckner musical elaboration has been given a more solid, more assured, less strident texture. Duration is much less frenetic and rushed, there is a greater sense of the composer's egotistical privilege, a deeper awareness, especially in Brahms, of abstract—because socially marginalized and confined to the safe space of the concert hall—patterns and formulas that cannot long sustain inspired eloquence . . . as they did for a beginner like Beethoven.'

had transgressed them. For sympathizers like Hueffer, the unbroken—or, as a cognitive scientist would say, non-chunked—texture of Wagnerian melody was an inescapable part of the theory of *Gesamtkunstwerk*, and an evolutionary advance over outmoded forms of listening.[47] For others, basic physiological theory insisted upon periodicity, or wavelike alternations, in any sequence of sensations, and therefore Wagnerian form was (physically, psychologically) a mistake, or even an impossibility. Lewes was one of the more vocal adherents of this latter sentiment, insisting in his *On Actors and the Art of Acting* (1875) that Wagnerian opera 'wants both form and melody', is generally 'horribly noisy, very monotonous, and wanting in charm', where the absence of 'form', here implicitly a physiological category, is premised upon its monotony.[48]

For physiologically inclined critics, judgments of Wagner tended to fall along what might be called the axis of 'hard' versus 'soft' physiology: 'soft' physiologists included intellection, or higher-level cortical functions, among their discussions of aesthetic pleasure, whereas 'hard' physiologists insisted upon the nervous, or pre-cognitive, root of any sensation, even aesthetic sensations. James Sully is an important example of the former, who not coincidentally wrote sympathetically of Wagnerian melody. In his *Sensation and Intuition* (1874), Sully described melody as a mixed process: 'The gratification afforded by a perfectly harmonious chord, is due, so far as we can discover, to some direct law of nervous action. In the case of melodious sequence, we found that the resulting pleasure involves a nascent intellectual process, namely, the faint perception of a common element of tone in the melodious clangs.'[49] The appreciation of horizontal, or sequential, form means for Sully a partial subordination of 'nervous' or autonomic response to a sense-making mental operation, which means primarily an active recollective process, in which 'calm intellectual consciousness must supplement excited sensuous consciousness; ideal echoes of the swiftly vanishing tones must recur; and amid the innumerable sensations of clang and harmony, their fine-spun threads of continuity and order must disclose themselves to view'.[50] Whereas the nervous system responds to tones in time, therefore, the intellect constructs a spatialized 'order' out of the chaos of sequence; hence Sully's frequent recourse to architectural metaphors in his discussion of acoustic response.

---

[47] See Hueffer, *Richard Wagner*, 108.

[48] G. H. Lewes, *On Actors and the Art of Acting* (London: Smith & Elder, 1875), 196–8. See also his earlier piece 'The Opera in 1833–1863', *Cornhill Magazine* 8 (1863), 295–307, where Lewes's considerations of the state of European opera become explicitly and yearningly nostalgic for a pre-Wagnerian world in which melody is more important than what he sees as the portentiousness of Wagnerian 'meaning'.

[49] Sully, *Sensation and Intuition*, 186.   [50] Ibid. 188.

He held up *Tannhäuser* as an example of a melodic practice which enables the retrospection necessary to 'intellectual' listening, and he praised Wagner's ability to make 'sudden recollection, as in the case of Tannhäuser on the Venusberg', palpable to the listener.[51]

Sully's careful balancing between nerves and intellect, or sequential sensations and spatial form, made little sense to 'harder' physiologists, who insisted instead that the latter, properly speaking, doesn't exist at all, that musical form is purely temporal, and that any notions of forming static wholes out of sequential processes are nonsense. The most carefully argued version of this position was that of Edmund Gurney, the pianist, psychologist, and sometime spiritualist who is now most famous for supposedly being the model for Daniel Deronda himself.[52] As Gurney put it in *The Power of Sound* (1880), his *magnum opus*, 'it is not Harmony or notes in combination, but Melody or notes in succession, which is the prime and essential element in Music . . . there is no simultaneity of impression'.[53] The methodological shift that Gurney implied meant transforming 'the phraseology of *form*' into 'the phraseology of *motion*', in which 'form is perceived by continuous advance along it'.[54] Any structural principle beyond pure contiguity is chimerical, an attempt of commentators to shoehorn music into formal concepts borrowed from nontemporal forms like architecture or visual art. Repetition is the composer's sole means of achieving some kind of link other than contiguity; and 'the notion of a larger and more essential design, in reference to which individual strains are details in the sense of being less essential, has no application. The scheme has no value apart from the bits.'[55] What *The Power of Sound* represents is perhaps the strongest expression that the nineteenth century produced of a purely temporal approach to form.

A sequential progression whose only 'form' is the moment-to-moment processing of melodic 'bits': Gurney's scheme sounds oddly like most British descriptions of Wagnerian *unendliche Melodie*; yet Gurney was a staunch anti-Wagnerian, since in his view Wagner strove for forms of formal coherence—particularly in the repetition of motifs and the elaboration of harmonic material—that were impossible for the listener to appreciate. Wagner is prominent in *The Power of Sound* as an example of the inherent failure of attempts to transcend temporal order. As Gurney stated, using *Lohengrin* as his example,

---

[51] Ibid. 234.

[52] Such, at least, was the guess of Leslie Stephen; see his *George Eliot* (New York: Macmillan, 1902), 191; Haight mentions Gurney among a list of other possibilities, including the young Lewes. See Haight, *George Eliot*, 488–9. Eliot had met Gurney, then an undergraduate, during an 1873 visit to Cambridge, and their acquaintance continued until her death.

[53] Gurney, *The Power of Sound* (New York: Basic Books, 1966), 91–2.

[54] Ibid. 164.   [55] Ibid. 216.

Wagner 'overlooks the humble fact that while melody does not the least want to be infinite, it does very much want to have one bar intelligibly connected with the next, and even with the next but one, and as a rule even the one beyond that; and that the ear's impression of what it is receiving from moment to moment is not the least affected by the knowledge that these present strains belong to a "melody" so large that it will be going on three hours hence'.[56] In a further turn of the analytic screw, Gurney claimed that Wagner's failure is best demonstrated by the average listener's inability to recall any of his melodies—so that Wagner's quixotic attempt at transtemporal coherence is betrayed by his dispensing with the only form that coherence can take, recollection of melodic bits (or 'chunked' melodies). If, as Gurney insisted, it is impossible to appreciate 'something the essence of which is a *succession* of impressions by a *simultaneous* review of all the impressions', memory can, apparently, replay selected units of sense impressions, thereby providing some (rather marginal) escape from strict sequentiality.[57]

This much is clear: that Wagner played a central role in mid-Victorian notions of time and artistic form, primarily through the twinned, if often opposed, concepts of melody and motif, as well as his undeniable length; and that this role was a confused and contested one, with some critics assailing Wagner's formlessness, some praising the genius of his newer notions of form, and some (like Gurney) adding that Wagnerian form is really a pernicious version of formlessness. If Wagner's melodies offered an image of undifferentiated, perhaps exhausting, temporal expansion, and his motifs an image of constant, perhaps wearying repetition, it was never entirely clear how Wagnerian temporality worked—was it a succession of vanishing moments, or a persistent return of identical moments? It was clear, however, that listening to Wagner highlighted the temporality of reception in a way no other composer could. The implied question was perhaps too fundamental to be asked with any clarity at the time: was any kind of prolonged duration possible, either aesthetically or psychologically? Could any coherence premised on duration, or on events that span time, be at all valid or even possible? This is, as I have claimed, a seemingly depoliticized response to Wagner that peaked in the 1870s, one with clear links to the Wagnerian issues of musical tempo in his 1855 visit but without the explicit political context to which those earlier issues referred. Always slightly out of step with the British reception of Wagner, Eliot at this point produced a novel that, as we shall see, is a considered response to the issues of duration that Wagner had made so prominent in physiological aesthetics, a response that not only attempts formal solutions to the problems of temporal form that Wagner illustrated, but also repoliticizes the issues of

---

[56] Ibid. 501.   [57] Ibid. 215.

lastingness, elongation, and duration that critics in the 1870s had cordoned off from Wagner's notorious politics.

Daniel Deronda, in other words, is an extremely *knowing* novel in its representation of duration—particularly the duration of melody, which was such a methodological crux in the mid-1870s. In Klesmer, Eliot produces a pure Wagnerian, one capable of criticizing Gwendolen's choice of music as 'a form of melody that expresses a puerile form of culture—a dandling, canting, see-saw kind of stuff', and of producing a composition described as 'an extensive commentary on some melodic ideas not too grossly evident' (p. 49).[58] Its frequent discussions of melodic form, including various songs, Mirah's Hebrew hymns with their 'quaint melancholy intervals' (p. 374), and the passages that play in Deronda's mind at pivotal moments in the plot, are taken directly from the context of Wagnerian reception and physiological aesthetics which obsessed the higher reaches of British musical culture throughout its mid-century transition from Mendelssohnianism to Wagnerianism. But that knowingness is at the service of goals other than the attempt to achieve a pure or consistent aesthetics of musical form. Melody in *Deronda* is a route into larger questions of duration: into the possibility of elongation in novelistic form, into the possibility of any kind of psychological experience of coherence over time and how that might be achieved, into the political formations and desires premised on protracted temporal spans.[59] Melody is simply *Deronda*'s metalanguage for that set of intertwined concerns.

THINGS REPEAT THEMSELVES IN ME SO: *DERONDA*'S REPETITIONS

Deronda has always been a novel that wears its formal coherence on its sleeve; Eliot's famous comment that 'I meant everything in the book to be related

[58] Attempting to identify a real-life model for Klesmer—and thereby to fix Eliot's complexly ambivalent attitude toward him—has long been a pastime of *Deronda* critics; the most persuasive accounts, those of Ruth Solie and John Picker, have been those that refuse to choose among various possible models (Rubinstein, Liszt, Wagner) but instead take him as a portmanteau character representative of musical modernism in all its aesthetic, political, and even racial complexity. Picker even adduces Franz Mesmer as part of the proliferating suggestiveness of Klesmer; see Picker, *Victorian Soundscapes*, 92, and Solie, ' "Tadpole Pleasures" ', 169.

[59] If, as I am arguing, music is *Deronda*'s slightly displaced mode of considering its own temporal duration, an interesting parallel argument is offered by Garrett Stewart's recent claim that pictured scenes of reading express visual art's 'duration envy', its way of introjecting temporality into stasis. See Garrett Stewart, 'Painted Readers, Narrative Regress', *Narrative* 11/2 (2003), 125–76.

to everything else' has lingered as an expression of its obvious ambitions to
totalizing interconnectedness.[60] Comprehensive relationality, however, means
in practice, at least for *Deronda*, repetition. Recent readings of the novel have
pervasively, if often unconsciously, acknowledged its various repetitions, either
at the structural (type-scenes and actions) or lexical (sentences or phrases)
levels, by finding terms to describe the importance of repetition: for Catherine
Crosby it is 'history', for Catherine Gallagher it is 'circulation', for Jeff
Nunokawa it is 'ongoingness', and for Alexander Welsh it is 'responsibility'.[61]
Each term attempts to find a different, nonaesthetic language—cultural,
economic, psychological, ethical—through which to castigate, or recuperate,
the bald repetitions of Eliot's novel, which permits itself a luxury of reiteration
apparent in none of her earlier novels. *Deronda*, it seems, finds one quite
clear solution to the problem of the organization of prolonged aesthetic
forms, and the solution is the Wagnerian one that Eliot had praised as far
back as 1855: the motif, or the principle of periodically reappearing identical
units. Stressing the musicological, even Wagnerian, roots of this practice
of repetition initially means redirecting our attention back to the concrete
instances of *Deronda*'s repetitions, to their presumed functioning upon the
sense-making operations of readers; ultimately, however, it means attempting
to understand what exactly the necessity of repetition tells us about Eliot's
thinking about those very readers, and the difference between implied reader
and portrayed character. While the various critical terms available for thinking
through *Deronda*'s repetitions are helpful as guides *within* Eliot's fictional
world, placing those repetitions as 'motivic' practices helps us formulate a
guide to the novel as a communicative act aimed at a nonfictional world
of readers—as, in other words, a political/ethical act shaped by attention to
habits of cognition.

   That very formulation—political/ethical acts derived from (attempted)
reshapings of cognitive habits of consumption—was essentially, as I have

---

[60] On its sleeve, or even on its back: Eliot's comment serves as educative blurb for the most
recent Penguin Classics edition of the novel. The line comes from an Oct. 1876 letter to Barbara
Bodichon; see *The George Eliot Letters*, ed. Gordon Haight, vi (New Haven: Yale University Press,
1955), 290.

[61] See Christina Crosby, *The Ends of History: Victorians and 'The Woman Question'* (New
York: Routledge, 1991); Catherine Gallagher, 'George Eliot and Daniel Deronda: The Prosti-
tute and the Jewish Question', in *Sex, Politics, and Science in the Nineteenth-Century Novel*,
ed. Ruth Bernard Yeazell (Baltimore: Johns Hopkins University Press, 1986), 39–62; Jeffrey
Nunokawa, *The Afterlife of Property: Domestic Security and the Victorian Novel* (Princeton:
Princeton University Press, 1994); Alexander Welsh, *George Eliot and Blackmail* (Cambridge,
Mass.: Harvard University Press, 1985). Nunokawa's term is defined with a Wagnerian resonance—he calls *Deronda* 'the endless story of mastery'—but all these critics attempt
to find ways to express the feeling that nothing, in *Deronda*, ever really goes away for
good.

shown, the British understanding of Wagner's impact. It should come as no surprise, then, that repetition is often figured in *Deronda* as a musical practice, as in fact an effect of musical practice, literally understood. As Klesmer explains to Gwendolen: 'Singing and acting, like the fine dexterity of the juggler with his cups and balls, require a shaping of the organs towards a finer and finer certainty of effect. Your muscles—your whole frame—must go like a watch, true, true, true, to a hair' (p. 257). Like the punchline to the old routine about how to get to Carnegie Hall, Klesmer replaces Gwendolen's desire for a set of directions on musical performance with an incantatory insistence upon music as an endless routine of physical mnemonics: practice, practice, practice. That routine extends, apparently, to listeners as well; Mordecai, for instance, recites Hebrew hymns to the child Jacob Cohen in order to 'engrave' them within him through the sheer force of repetition. The idea here is to create an activity so automatic that execution seems to take place outside the self, in some fully externalized space where the issue is less remembrance than preconscious reiteration. The alienated agency of musical performance, in fact, comes to have resonance in later moments of psychological crisis in the novel: Mirah, narrating her escape from her father, states that 'I do believe I could see better than ever I did before: the strange clearness within seemed to have got outside me' (p. 220), while Gwendolen, narrating Grandcourt's drowning, famously explains that 'I only know that I saw my wish outside me' (p. 696). Musical repetition starts in *Deronda* to look like trance: a dwelling in the present moment so intense that the past (practicing a performance, desiring an event) reappears as something outside of the self, happening without any effort or control. It therefore takes on the appearance of a haunting, a possession from without. Gwendolen offers the most plangent expression of this sense of repetition: 'Things repeat themselves in me so. They come back—they will all come back' (p. 770).

There is a connection in *Deronda*, therefore, between the willed repetition of an act in musical practice and the unwilled repetition of a desire or emotion in moments of emergency: both result in an alienated relation to agency; they both create the divided sense of actions that one does, and yet somehow does not, perform. The masterful repetitions of committed musicians like Klesmer, and the helpless sense of recurrence of traumatized characters like Gwendolen, are, however, quite different from the posited novel-reader of *Deronda*, for whom Eliot marshals motivic reminders—identical reappearances of earlier textual moments—in order to supply the remembrance that her major characters, Gwendolen in particular, do not need. That is, if for her characters duration (of learning a piece, of cherishing a desire) is cancelled by unwilled recurrence, for *Deronda*'s readers the duration of the novel is continually stressed by a habit of verbatim reiteration that advertises the gap between what the average reader needs by way of temporal binding and what little the novel's characters need. For characters, motivic recurrence happens as a ghostly revisitation of what has never quite been forgotten; for readers, motivic recurrence is a literal replay of the textual past which we are presumed to have forgotten. 'The audience of these giant works lasting many hours', Adorno commented in relation to Wagner, 'is thought of as unable to concentrate—something not unconnected with the fatigue of the citizen in his leisure time. And while he allows himself to drift with the current, the music, acting as its own impresario, thunders at him in endless repetitions to hammer its message home.'[62] For Adorno, the *leitmotiv* signals the distance between characters who cannot escape the past and an audience that cannot remember it; what signifies *within* the music drama as a Hegelian past-within-the-present (duration's vanishing) works *for* its listeners as a prosthetic *aide-mémoire* (duration's oppressive weight).

Adorno's controversial thesis about Wagner is, at the very least, an accurate description of how motivic recurrence works in *Deronda*. Self-quotation is a normal part of the novel's texture: in the middle of Book 6 we are told that Gwendolen recalls Deronda's description of Mirah being 'capable of submitting to anything in the form of duty' (p. 566)—a replay of a conversation from Book 5—as well as Klesmer's summary of Lush as an 'amateur too fond of Meyerbeer' (p. 567), a replay from Book 2. The reiterations are only slightly imperfect: the first instances are, respectively, 'capable of submitting to anything when it takes the form of duty' (p. 438), and 'an amateur I have seen in town: Lush, a Mr. Lush—too fond of Meyerbeer and Scribe' (p. 119). Gwendolen's recollections are, it seems, so pressing and accurate as to require the use of quotation-marks; they are essentially equivalent to the novel repeating itself, as in fact it does, verbatim, when she recalls in Book 7 Deronda's oracular advice, originally made in Book 5, to turn 'your fear into a safeguard' (pp. 452, 674). They thus offer the reader, thematized as inescapable memories, a way to bridge the prolonged stretches of text between original instance and later iteration.

The most telling instance of such repetition is Eliot's choice to quote more than once, and at length, Lydia Glasher's accusatory letter—'I am the grave in which your chance of happiness is buried'—accompanying the diamonds that she is forced by Grandcourt to relinquish to his new bride. More than half of the original letter, quoted in full in Book 4, is repeated word for word in Book 5 during Gwendolen and Grandcourt's visit to Diplow, the estate of Sir Hugo Mallinger that Grandcourt stands to inherit. The letter itself, we are told, had been burned immediately upon having been read, but

---

[62] Adorno, *In Search of Wagner*, 32.

its physical destruction only results in its being engraved upon Gwendolen's mind: 'The words of that letter kept repeating themselves, and hung on her consciousness with the weight of a prophetic doom' (p. 424). The narrative then promptly quotes the bulk of the letter, an act presumably—but with suspicious exactitude—operating in Gwendolen's thoughts. Only presumably, however; the narrative voice does not situate the quotation as a mental process of Gwendolen, and instead simply offers the chunk of earlier text as an experience for the reader of re-perusing—even reexperiencing—sentences which had appeared in an earlier serial number. Reticence keeps Eliot from announcing the self-quotation as an *aide-mémoire*, and the inferential process of realist procedure would normally lead us to presume that Gwendolen is remembering the burned letter word for word, but the fullness of the 136-word repetition suggests instead that the reader needs a full reminder of a passage so powerful that Gwendolen cannot forget it. What psychological realism depicts as the unwilled return of Gwendolen's traumatic reading experience—its original appearance had caused a nervous collapse—testifies as well to the potential weakness of our original consumption of the letter, since we need what Gwendolen conspicuously does not: an exact copy of Lydia Glasher's message.[63]

Temporal duration, in other words, vanishes for Gwendolen as a result of the constant repetition of Lydia's *j'accuse*, but is accentuated for the reader, who is forced to acknowledge the length of time (and text) between first and second iteration simply because of the unusual exactitude and length of the second appearance, which can only suggest that the original appearance is too far back in the novel's past to retain its hold on us. 'Repetition', Adorno complains of the Wagnerian *leitmotiv*, 'poses as development': the developmental logic of music, the organization of time through what he elsewhere calls 'the most intense effort of memory and anticipation', is via motivic reiteration turned into a static rhythmical practice of periodically recurrent units.[64] In the spirit of Adorno's analysis of Wagner, one might

---

[63] A copy that is material for the reader, while Gwendolen's version of the letter has transcended materiality; for a persuasive reading of the play with textual materiality occasioned by Lydia's letter, see Daniel Hack, *The Material Interests of the Victorian Novel* (Charlottesville: University of Virginia Press, 2005), 171–2.

[64] Adorno, *In Search of Wagner*, 41, 99. Adorno's music theory returns often to the difference between the sequentially unrolling process of thematic development and the identically recurring processes of rhythm, which are for him ideally combined in Beethoven's symphonies: 'On the one hand he remains true to the general ideal of Viennese Classicism with its belief in thematic development and hence the need for a process unfolding in time. On the other hand, his symphonies exhibit a characteristic accentual dialectic (*Schlagstruktur*). By both compressing the unfolding of time and mimicking it, time is abolished and, as it were, suspended and concentrated in space.' Both Wagner and, later, Stravinsky represented to

say, then, that *Deronda*'s repetitions flaunt their lack of development or difference; although it is tempting to read the second appearance of Lydia's letter as somehow contextually altered—as if the more Gwendolen knows of Grandcourt, the more profound the letter becomes—in fact, her second response is largely identical with her first response.[65] The irony of the letter's reappearance is not that its iteration signals a new knowledge ('if I knew then what I know now', etc.), but that from the first its efficacy was premised on what Gwendolen already knew and cannot not know: that by marrying Grandcourt, she broke a promise to Lydia and implicitly consented to the sordid past of her husband. That knowledge is neither supplanted, revised, or added to; it simply persists.

Self-quotation is not the novel's sole motivic practice, only the most unusual one; matching it are a series of recurrent gestures or objects, each with a potentially allegorical meaning or function, which cluster at the beginning and end of the narrative. Deronda's famous 'grasping of his coat-collar' is the most well known of various characterological tics whose stubborn recurrence surprised readers accustomed to Eliot's more usual practice of carefully questioning the significance of visual information.[66] The staged reappearances of objects are even more prominent. The wainscot panel at Offendene, which springs open to reveal a 'picture of an upturned dead face, from which an obscure figure seemed to be fleeing with outstretched arms' during Gwendolen's early performance as Hermione, reappears as a memory after Grandcourt's drowning as 'a white dead face from which she was for ever trying to flee and

---

Adorno the diminishment of this synthesis, which in Beethoven (and later, Schoenberg) makes the idea of 'temporal form' truly possible. See Theodor Adorno, 'Stravinsky', in *Quasi una Fantasia: Essays on Modern Music*, trans. Rodney Livingstone (New York: Verso, 1992), 165–6.

[65] Here I differ somewhat from Irene Tucker's persuasive reading of the novel. For Tucker, the consciousness of time in the reading of *Deronda* is created by jarring discontinuities in repetition, by temporal situatedness: 'Not only does our discovery of the discontinuity jar us into recognizing that reading takes place over time, but it illustrates in no uncertain terms that what we think a given passage in the novel means depends on when we read it and what we already know at that moment.' See Tucker, *Probable State*, 84. As the example of Lydia's letter suggests, the 'already known' informing our (and Gwendolen's) reading of it is present from the start and cannot be changed; Eliot is here not exploring the dangers of moral action without sufficient information, but rather what kinds of moral decisions are made in full possession of the relevant information.

[66] Bryan Cheyette has suggested that the Deronda tic in particular is a solution to the essentially unknowable quality of 'the Jew' in nineteenth-century British discourse: 'hence the need for certain defining traits, such as the routine "grasping of his coat-collar," as if the reader is continually meeting him for the first time'. See Bryan Cheyette, *Constructions of 'the Jew' in English Literature and Society: Racial Representations, 1875–1945* (Cambridge: Cambridge University Press, 1993), 45.

for ever held back' (pp. 27, 674). Deronda's ring is noted frequently, until its theft by Lapidoth precipitates his marriage proposal to Mirah, which presumably necessitates a replacement ring. Finally, the turquoise necklace pawned by Gwendolen in the novel's second chapter, and immediately redeemed anonymously by Deronda, makes important later appearances, notably when she wears it as a bracelet to attract Deronda's attention during the Diplow house party, at which point Grandcourt notices the maneuver and chastises her for her indelicacy. As much as these objects accumulate a history around them, they are possessed from the first by allegorical connotations, which, crucially, do not change. The wainscot panel (guilt? fear?), the ring (Fidelity? Memory?), and the necklace (most Wagnerian of all: Redemption) are precisely what Adorno called particles of 'congealed meaning', evidence of the 'allegorical rigidity' of the *leitmotiv*.[67] Even their allegorical function, however, is subordinate to their ability to simply span the duration of the narrative, to persist despite the vicissitudes of characters; they are principles of temporal endurance that bind the (read) past and the (reading) present. Like the novel's self-quotations, they elaborately point the reader back to earlier situations or events, and they help to mnemonically organize distant thematic and plot material.

Their recurrence, in other words, functions as signposting in an elongated narrative. But as I have suggested earlier, elongation itself takes on different contours for characters within the novel and readers of it. *Deronda* presents a curious temporal paradox: a temporally prolonged investigation into what was always the case (i.e. Deronda's Judaism), in which the sequentiality of the plot underlines a fact that seems to have no temporality at all. Cynthia Chase's influential reading of the novel as presenting 'present causes of past effects', or a skewed sense of causality in time, persuasively delineates the novel's temporal contortions; the contortions, however, are necessitated by the confrontation of an inescapably temporal procedure (elongated narrative) and an extra-temporal fact (racial and religious identity).[68] Resolving this paradox—how to narrate the coming-into-being of an identity that was never not the case?—means for Eliot assigning to character and reader two different experiences of temporality. By creating a discrete division between characters who experience the cancellation of time and readers who experience the weight of time, she turns a paradox into a mere matter of vantage-point.

[67] Adorno, *In Search of Wagner*, 45–6.
[68] See Cynthia Chase, 'The Decomposition of Elephants: Double-Reading *Daniel Deronda*', *PMLA* 93 (1978), 215–25.

Eliot's solution becomes clearer if we return to Wagnerian form as a guide. Famously combining mythical subject matter that seems to exist in a static and ahistorical 'now'—what Adorno called Wagner's 'dazzling present'—and audiences made newly, even oppressively, aware of the temporality of their listening experience, Wagner's operas presented two different forms of duration: the experiential (that of characters) and the reminiscential (that of the audience, which has to be elaborately reminded via the *leitmotiv* of what his characters cannot forget).[69] The difference has been explained more recently by cognitive musicology, which argues that duration in experience and duration in memory are entirely different. As the usual formulation goes, a time period filled with novel or interesting events—with, that is, narrative or melody—will be remembered as elongated, but experienced as quick or truncated.[70] The distinction holds for *Deronda*, if we take its characters as its 'experiential' units and its readers as those undergoing a 'reminiscential' experience; as we have seen, the novel's motivic repetitions constantly reinforce, aid, or refer to a readerly recollection that the novel's characters do not need. Continually, spontaneously, Eliot's characters organize their lives into sudden, atemporal tableaux. Deronda, preparing to listen to Mirah's concert début at Lady Mallinger's music party, having just learned of her connection to Mordecai, 'felt himself on the brink of betraying emotion, Mirah's presence now being linked with crowding images of what had gone before and was to come after—all centring in the brother whom he was soon to reveal to her' (p. 558). What exists for Deronda as a moment combining recollection and anticipation is here narrated for a reader who has instead been consuming delay, long intervals, slow progress. To put it another way: the novel offers us a strenuously temporalized experience of atemporal recurrences and repetitions. This is a Wagnerian solution, learned from Eliot's early attempts to explain and defend Wagner for a British audience. What she saw, as far back as the 1854 performance of *Die fliegende Holländer* in Weimar, was a newly elongated artistic form made tenable by both repetitious motivic reminders, for the ease of listeners seeking to connect time, and the depiction of characters who live outside of that time in a constant 'now'—in the Dutchman's case, the 'now' of what Eliot called his 'terrible fate'; in Gwendolen's case, a constant 'now' of anxious regret; in Deronda's case, the more complex 'now' of a Judaism always dimly palpable if only gradually known. These characters, in other words, experience the repetitions of their narratives as the cancellation of time, even the time of our own listening or reading.

[69] Adorno, *In Search of Wagner*, 98.
[70] See the explanation in Snyder, *Music and Memory*, 213–14. See also Richard Block, 'Models of Psychological Time', in *Cognitive Models of Psychological Time*, ed. Richard Block (Hillsdale, NJ: Erlbaum, 1990), 9–11.

ALWAYS THERE WAS THE SAME PAUSE: *DERONDA*'S INTERVALS

The motif, or the recurrent unit, was for Eliot a persuasive model for the structuring of lengthy temporal forms; but while it had the capacity to link dispersed events and to organize readerly memory, it left unstructured the spaces between repetitions. It worked by replacing progression with repetition, by consigning the time between repetitions—the duration of the experience—to a status of unmarked waiting. But if one aspect of the British understanding of Wagner was his practice of periodic recurrence, another was dedicated, as we have seen, to those stretches of duration between recurrences that went under the contested name of 'melody': to pure sequence. When melody is explicitly thematized in *Deronda*, in fact, it is presented alongside images of progression or seriality, such as the gondolier's song from Rossini's *Otello*, 'Nessun maggior dolore', sung by Deronda while rowing down the Thames; the current of the river pulling Deronda along, as well as the forward movement of the song, will lead him to his first sighting of Mirah. But how is progression to be experienced in forms longer than a song, such as the novel itself—as empty time, which might induce boredom, or as prolonged but nonetheless directed time, which might induce panic, exasperation, anxiety? How, in other words, is duration to be endured in *Deronda*, a novel which gives such a sense of spaciousness to the experience of *waiting*?

Not, we may be sure, by hastening its passing. In the immediate crisis of Gwendolen's decision to marry Grandcourt despite her knowledge of his past, Eliot provides a description of ethical choice figured as accelerated reading, a reading impatient with the *longueurs* of narrative duration:

Quick, quick, like pictures in a book beaten open with a sense of hurry, came back vividly, yet in fragments, all that she had gone through in relation to Grandcourt—the allurements, the vacillations, the resolve to accede, the final repulsion; the incisive face of that dark-eyed lady with the lovely boy; her own pledge (was it a pledge not to marry him?)—the new disbelief in the worth of men and things for which that scene of disclosure had become a symbol. (p. 292)

A series of narrative 'highlights' abstracted from the temporality of her experience of Grandcourt, Gwendolen's retrospects here are not so much inaccurate or self-serving as drained of duration, which would seem to be the ethically problematic aspect of her thought process. It is not that she has Grandcourt wrong, but that she is in a hurry. Foreshortening the remembrance of knowledge acquisition seems to be as self-deluding as reinventing, or explaining away, the knowledge gained. A reader who beats open pages with the intention of accelerating plot sequence may get the plot right, but not the experience—the experience of enduring time; and that time both endures and is something one has to endure, even in recollection, is the primary lesson of the passage, beyond any specifics of Grandcourt's behavior. Pivotal events or crises lose their epistemic centrality, and what Franco Moretti has called 'filler', or the intervals between narrative fireworks, becomes educative in its own right.[71]

Any formal procedure that seeks to do away with the alternation of event and non-event, or the rush to get past the nothing that fills in order to see the something that animates, is in *Deronda*'s moment at least conceptually Wagnerian; it is initiated by Wagner's attempts to do away with the cycle of inattention and riveted attention created by aria–recitative form. In a parallel fashion, Eliot imagined here a novelistic 'reading for the plot' where what is missed is not thematic or philosophical significance but the temporal endurance that gives that significance weight.[72] The result, in Wagner, was a 'through-composed' melodic practice that avoided both end-stopped, self-contained phrases and the empty rest periods of recitative. Eliot was, as we have seen, both theoretically entranced by this notion of endless melodic sequentiality—'an opera must be no mosaic of melodies . . . no mere succession of ill-prepared crises', she had written—and yet disturbingly bored and irritated by its actual sound, an irony increased by the fact that the Wagner operas she knew, such as *Tannhäuser*, were far less through-composed than the later music dramas that seemed to better fulfill Wagner's theory.[73] *Deronda*, however, demonstrates a somewhat Wagnerian formal procedure, in which it is not the significance of the events that make up temporal duration, but the significance of enduring temporality itself, that becomes crucial for the reading experience.

At the figural level, this stress on pure duration is encoded most prominently in the wealth of allusions to seeds, germination, insemination, and the temporality of organic growth that Neil Hertz has most recently, and lavishly, described.[74] Almost all narratorial descriptions of consciousness—such as Gwendolen's 'yeasty mingling of dimly understood facts with vague but deep impressions' (p. 354)—borrow from the language of incremental, largely invisible organic processes, and as such refer to a pervasive surround of temporal delay which is only partly human. But at other levels Eliot attempts

---

[71] See the preface to the second edition of Franco Moretti's *The Way of the World: The Bildungsroman in European Culture*, trans. Albert Spragia (New York: Verso, 2000), p. vi.

[72] For a different account of Eliot's refusals of plot reading—by either her efforts or those of her many editors—see Leah Price, *The Anthology and the Rise of the Novel: From Richardson to George Eliot* (Cambridge: Cambridge University Press, 2000), 137–56.

[73] Eliot, 'Liszt, Wagner, and Weimar', 50.

[74] See Hertz, *George Eliot's Pulse* (Stanford, Calif.: Stanford University Press, 2003).

far stranger methods by which to insist on the intervalic character of experience, as if to say: be aware not only of what happens, but of what passes between the things that happen. The narration of Gwendolen and Grandcourt's first conversation is the most conspicuous of these attempts, in which Eliot gives voice and space to the sinister pauses between Gwendolen's questions about archery and Grandcourt's deliberately vacuous replies:

'Are you converted to-day?' said Gwendolen.

(Pause, during which she imagined various degrees and modes of opinion about herself that might be entertained by Grandcourt.)

'Yes, since I saw you shooting. In things of this sort one generally sees people missing and simpering.'

'I suppose you are a first-rate shot with a rifle.'

(Pause, during which Gwendolen, having taken a rapid observation of Grandcourt, made a brief graphic description of him to an indefinite hearer.)

'I have left off shooting.'

'Oh, then, you are a formidable person. People who have done things once and left them off make one feel very contemptible, as if one were using cast-off fashions. I hope you have not left off all follies, because I practice a good many.'

(Pause, during which Gwendolen made several interpretations of her own speech.)

'What do you call follies?'

'Well, in general, I think whatever is agreeable is called a folly. But you have not left off hunting, I hear.'

(Pause, wherein Gwendolen recalled what she had heard about Grandcourt's position, and decided that he was the most aristocratic-looking man she had ever seen.) (p. 112)

These parenthetical dilations of conversational time transgress normal realist notational practices and become something close to play script, as if only stage direction could give sufficient weight to the not-said of this interaction. As the scene continues, adding seven more significant 'pauses', it becomes clearer that the real value of these asides is less the minute particulars of Gwendolen's psychological response than the insistent oddity of Grandcourt's allowing time to pass. What seems like a making explicit of thoughts running parallel to speech is, in fact, a making strange of the time that passes between speech; what we need to read, in other words, is not the arc of Gwendolen's thinking (which is apparent enough from her speech), but the intention behind Grandcourt's prolonged silences. 'Always there was the same pause before he took up his cue,' Eliot tells us of his conversational technique, which animates time itself. Gwendolen's speech, in fact, reads like nothing so much as the ordinary, nervously compulsive talk of someone uncomfortable with feeling time passing, or of someone in a hurry.

Although Eliot never repeats the typographic and syntactic inventiveness of this scene, she is continually attentive, particularly in moments of dialogue, to the time elapsed between speech, and to rendering the precise affective quality of the duration of a conversational pause. It can be compassionate, as in the interaction between Deronda and Gwendolen at the Diplow house party: 'For what was an appreciable space of time to both, though the observation of others could not have measured it, they looked at each other—she seeming to take the deep rest of confession, he with an answering depth of sympathy that neutralised other feelings' (p. 411). Here again, emotional weightiness is figured by the simple ability to animate, or 'appreciate', a 'space of time', a patch of fugitive duration. Eliot will later give the name 'interval' to the spaces between question and response in Deronda and Gwendolen's final conversation, a word also used prominently in her description of music, such as the 'quaint melancholy intervals' of Mirah's Hebrew hymns (p. 374). Music, in fact, becomes one of the primary means by which the passing of time is made apparent and liveable, as opposed to either absent or unendurable, in *Deronda*. Yet the novel strains to make temporal duration—the time between marked events—visible in a variety of other ways. Deronda's lengthy immersion in the affairs of the Cohen family, for instance, takes place literally between the pawning of his ring as a convenient pretext for acquaintanceship and its continually deferred redemption.

The language of interval is most complexly developed, perhaps, in a passage on Mordecai's enthusiastic conception of Deronda's appearance, which despite some doubt seems to fit his preestablished notion of his 'friend to come':

But the long-contemplated figure had come as an emotional sequence of Mordecai's firmest theoretic convictions; it had been wrought from the imagery of his most passionate life; and it inevitably reappeared—reappeared in a more specific self-asserting form than ever. Deronda had that sort of resemblance to the preconceived type which a finely individual bust or portrait has to the more generalised copy left in our minds after a long interval: we renew our memory, but we hardly know with how much correction. (p. 479)

The time between first and second appearances is given color by the uncertainty surrounding the second appearance: how close is it to the original, how much has it been altered, how accurate was our recollection? Deronda's supposedly Judaic features, his 'resemblance to the preconceived type', are temporalized by the analogy here, and temporality, or 'interval', has become a process of doubt. Hardly knowing how much correction we have undergone, we experience the second iteration of a series of perceptions or sensations as unsettling our sense of the beginning of the series. This is an explanation of recurrence in elongated temporal experiences that partially contradicts the notion of identical repetition generated from Wagnerian motivic practice: we see, hear, or read the same thing twice, often with a prolonged interval in between; but the second time is both like and unlike the first, so that repetition, if the duration of the interval is taken into account, is never entirely the same, while not, of course, entirely different. Intervalic repetition is not, however, progressive; it is a casting back over the time between first and second experiences, an encounter with the force of elapsed time itself.

If, as I have earlier claimed, Eliot's characters often experience iteration as simple identical recurrence, it is open to her readers to feel the duration between recurrences in a way often impossible for her characters, and thereby to disturb the supposedly numbing repetitions of motivic writing. That is, any given repetition might bind dispersed material (remember that?), but might also point out the length of time between appearances of dispersed material (how well do I remember that? is that the same thing?). The difference, essentially, lies in how intensely a given reader experiences intervalic duration, or the simple passing of time. Reading can be either an experience of waiting—either listlessly or agreeably—for the next big event, or an experience of waiting *per se*: a full, deliberate consciousness of how narrative takes time. The latter would seem to be Eliot's choice, but it does not receive in every instance her wholehearted approval. As her responses to Wagnerian opera illustrate, despite her excitement over a musical theory that sought to make time unavoidably apparent to a listener, Eliot's desire, often expressed as an instinctual one, was just as strongly for a musical practice that diverted her from the passing of time, that thwarted boredom or irritation. Instinct, or basic human capacity, was very much part of the problem, and Eliot is continually aware in *Deronda* that certain intervals are too long to occupy comfortably. One significant interval—Deronda's visit to Genoa to meet his mother, which is book-ended by emotional conversations with Gwendolen—is powerful enough to efface any real revival of his interest in Gwendolen or her affairs; he 'had lately been living so keenly in an experience quite apart from Gwendolen's lot, that his present cares for her were like a revisiting of scenes familiar in the past, and there was not yet a complete revival of the inward response to them' (p. 688). As *Deronda* progresses, in fact, intervals become more distinct, and retracing the effects of what they interrupt becomes more and more difficult. It becomes clear, for instance, that Leonora Halm-Eberstein, Deronda's mother, finds herself capable of maintaining her spirited feminist, individualist, artistic ideals in increasingly smaller intervals between attacks of pure abjection. Affect of any kind tends to be described in the physiological language of waves: Eliot speaks of the difference in emotional 'rate' between Grandcourt and

Lydia Glasher, and describes, typically, the 'wave of emotion' that brings
Gwendolen back to desiring Deronda's encouragement after worrying about
the impropriety of their talking (pp. 345, 607). Waves, after all—at least in
the physiological understanding of Eliot's time—are intervals of gradually
diminishing power.

This intervalic question—how do we experience the time between memorable events, or between any kind of events?—gets much of its substance, I
have been arguing, from Wagnerian theory and practice. But it is a particularly
vexed question for the Victorian realist novel, which, by continually shuttling
between different plots, seems to more often than not occupy the space
between: between renewals of former plotlines, between events happening to
other characters or in other spaces, between leaving one plot and returning to
it later. If the usual Victorian multi-plot narrative tried hard to make these
intervals into a seamless present tense, which would not be overly conscious
of what was being left behind or what would be returned to, *Deronda* instead
highlights the process of leavetaking and returning, and particularly the process of *waiting* for the next appearance of that which was already seen. What
Deronda suggests, in fact, is that the central formal problem for the Victorian
novel was its elongation, its sheer time-consuming bulk, which in Eliot's final
novel is worked out with reference to the Wagnerian example. But this is a
problem that has dimensions beyond the formal. Eliot goes so far in *Deronda*
as to propose that the central political problem for Britain, if not for Europe,
was a parallel one: the difficulties, and value, of lastingness, of institutions and
habits that span time.

THE POLITICS OF ELONGATION

The combined formal and political problem of duration expresses itself,
finally, as impatience. One of the novel's longer, and most indulgently fond,
descriptions of Deronda's character—'Daniel had the stamp of rarity in a
subdued fervour of sympathy, an activity of imagination on behalf of others,
which did not show itself effusively'—ends with an oddly terse gesture of
annoyance at the sheer luxury of so much psychological analysis:

It had helped to make him popular that he was sometimes a little compromised by
this apparent comradeship. For a meditative interest in learning how human miseries
are wrought—as precocious in him as another sort of genius in the poet who writes
a Queen Mab at nineteen—was so infused with kindliness that it easily passed for
comradeship. Enough. In many of our neighbour's lives, there is much not only of
error and lapse, but of a certain exquisite goodness which can never be written or even

spoken—only divined by each of us, according to the inward instruction of our own privacy. (p. 179)

Enough—or too much.[75] Eliot's plenitude of description here finds itself faced with a problem of sufficiency—how much is just right to evoke a character?—and ends with a sudden, frustrated admission that extension is often both tiresome and beside the point; better to have said too little, perhaps, about that which cannot really ever 'be written or even spoken'. The novelist famous for her willingness to extend the boundaries of narrative time spent, on analysis of either generalities or particulars, here confronts the possibility of a limit. A series of accusations that are easily enough imagined, and guardedly raised in the novel's reviews—that Eliot's length can be too much of a good thing, that the average reader will not be able to maintain interest or even comprehension over the novel's span—are here openly anticipated. If Wagner's music dramas proudly displayed their refusal to concede to the possible limits of a listener's interest and attention, Eliot in *Deronda* is occasionally moved to precisely those concessions.

The peremptory halt of that 'Enough', unusual in *Deronda* for its jarring frankness, hovers over the novel for reasons that are partly formal and cognitive, in the mode of Victorian novel theory (how long is too long for a reader's attention?), but also, and perhaps more disturbingly for Eliot, political and ethical, given that the burden of duration is prominently placed on the shoulders of the novel's Jewish characters. As Deronda reads in Leopold Zunz, 'if the duration of sorrows and the patience with which they are borne ennoble, the Jews are among the aristocracy of every land—if a literature is called rich in the possession of a few classic tragedies, what shall we say to a National Tragedy lasting for fifteen hundred years, in which the poets and the actors were also the heroes?' (p. 517). Mirah, for one, has 'the thoroughness and tenacity that give to the first selection of passionate feeling the character of a life-long faithfulness' (p. 734); Mordecai speaks, at the Hand and Banner, of seeds growing for centuries unobserved. Undergirding all the particular virtues ascribed to the novel's main Jewish figures (Mordecai, Mirah, Deronda himself) is a fundamentally temporal one: *endurance*, or the ability to feel time as duration. It is a virtue that Gwendolen conspicuously lacks. It is also, as we have seen, a virtue often figured through the act of reading: reading slowly, not skipping 'filler', or its opposite, reading in an accelerated fashion,

---

[75] Catherine Gallagher has recently taken up the question of the 'too much' for Eliot at the time of *Daniel Deronda*, as a problem derived both from Alexander Bain's psychophysiology and William Stanley Jevons's political economics, both of which were interested in questions of satiety and novelty of sensation; as Gallagher memorably puts it, 'the fear of overwriting became an overwritten novel'. See Catherine Gallagher, *The Body Economic: Life, Death, and Sensation in Political Economy and the Victorian Novel* (Princeton: Princeton University Press, 2006), 120.

moving in a hurry. It is symptomatic that by the novel's final third, scenes of reading are restricted to the agonizingly slow, protracted process of Daniel's Hebrew reading with Mordecai, which is an education in duration as much as any particular linguistic tradition. An ethic of reading, one which is rooted in Wagnerian thinking about elongated temporal forms and audience attention, is linked pervasively to a political/religious ethic of lastingness, which is rooted in an image of Judaism that is, it needs hardly be said, opposed to Wagner's anti-Semitic ideology of Judaism as the emblem of cosmopolitan rootlessness.[76]

The problem is that Eliot cannot simply dismiss her culture's pervasive discourse of exhaustion in the face of duration—the drooping, panicked, exhausted listeners of modern music; the overstrained readers of protracted fiction—as blithely or confidently as Wagner did. Her own physiological thinking led her to accept the possibility of innate, psychological or physiological limits to what can be endured, and the very force of her 'Enough', as well as her attraction to the motivic techniques of Wagnerian opera, demonstrate her worry that duration can in fact be too much, even if the scope of those temporal limits is unknown and possibly unknowable. When Deronda chides his mother with the overwhelming force of 'effects prepared by generations' (p. 663), he speaks for the principle of lastingness, and in Eliot's understanding the form of her fiction, in its very elongation, adhered to that same principle: it schooled its reader in the experience of duration. The novel cannot help but acknowledge, however, the opposite: the limits to our endurance or our consent, eloquently expressed by Leonora herself, who is broken by the effort to resist the weight of time, and who remains stubbornly, poignantly unassimilated into the novel's closural culture of durative temporality. Those limits were part of Eliot's own experience as well, most acutely in relation to her thinking about the paramount example of Wagner. To refuse or be unable to endure the length of a musical practice whose theoretical emphasis upon duration remained so attractive meant something problematic: having

---

[76] Which is not to suggest, however, that what I have called 'lastingness' is ultimately an ethic that responds positively to Jewishness. Christina Crosby, Michael Ragussis, and Amanda Anderson have all argued that the identification of Judaism with long duration—what Crosby calls 'history', Ragussis 'unchangeability', and Anderson the projection of 'a prior unity as a future actuality'—not only flattens Judaism, but, in Anderson's words, plays into 'the most dangerous doctrines of modern times', including that of an oppressive assimilationism. See Crosby, *Ends of History*, 13–14; Michael Ragussis, *Figures of Conversion: 'The Jewish Question' and English National Identity* (Durham, NC: Duke University Press, 1995), 24–6; Anderson, *Powers of Distance*, 138. For Anderson this is largely a matter of character, with Deronda representing a self-reflective, dialogical form of Judaism, and Mordecai representing a more sinister attempt to refuse dialogism; I am here arguing that the very form of the Victorian novel, in Eliot's musical/physiological thinking, is implicated in these problems of duration.

to allow for boundaries to our ability to experience durative time. Thinking about reading and listening to prolonged forms, for Eliot as for many others in her moment, led inevitably to thinking about our ability to live in and with other lasting structures, be they national, religious, political, or all three; haunting this thinking was the persistent suspicion that the actual experience of elongated time may result in disappointment, rejection, or even panic, as much as rootedness and belonging.

4

Just Noticeable Differences: Meredith and Fragmentation (Discontinuous Form)

> The hardest sort of judgment, the judgment which strains the attention most (if *that* be any criterion of the judgment's size), is that about the smallest things and differences.
>
> William James, *The Principles of Psychology*

Famous in his time for the disconcerting, confusing, and yet enlivening effects of his prose style, George Meredith was in his novels often given to describing the resonances that different styles could produce in mind and body alike. Reading, in Meredith, is an encounter with stylistic peculiarities, with small, characteristic units of sensation—sentences, phrases, syntactical oddities—that obscure or render irrelevant larger units, such as plot interest. One exemplary instance is an early passage in *Beauchamp's Career* (1875), when the novel's protagonist, Nevil Beauchamp, first discovers Carlyle, a stylist whose syntactical and lexical peculiarities Meredith admired and, in the eyes of many of his contemporaries, sought to emulate. Nevil's family friend, Rosamund Culling, notes Nevil's Carlylean phase with wonder:

His favourite author was one writing of Heroes, in (so she esteemed it) a style resembling either early architecture or utter dilapidation, so loose and rough it seemed; a wind-in-the-orchard style, that tumbled down here and there an appreciable fruit with uncouth bluster; sentences without commencements running to abrupt endings and smoke, like waves against a sea-wall, learned dictionary words giving a hand to street-slang, and accents falling on them haphazard, like slant rays from driving clouds; all the pages in a breeze, the whole book producing a kind of electrical agitation in the mind and the joints. . . . He had dug the book out of a bookseller's shop in Malta, captivated by its title, and had, since the day of his purchase, gone at it again and again, getting nibbles of golden meaning by instalments, as with a solitary pick in a very dark mine, until the illumination of an idea struck him that there was a great deal more in the book than there was in himself. (*BC*, xiii. 24–5)[1]

The strange intent of this passage, strange at least for an artistically self-conscious *Bildungsroman* like *Beauchamp's Career*, is to register the somatic and intellectual effect of a difficult prose style; not to describe the protagonist's wrestling with a dogma, a personality, or a set of ideas, but to describe a reading practice of halting, intermittent, yet forceful engagement. What Meredith finds compelling in Nevil Beauchamp's reading of Carlyle is its fragmentary quality. Carlyle, that is, only makes sense—or only makes sensations—in small bursts or electrical jolts, and the practice of reading for these small bits, the passage implies, is educative in itself. Meredith here uses the language of reading physiology (the 'agitation in the mind and the joints' together), but turns the attention of this physiological theory away from its usual focus, on plot interest, and toward the small scale, the individual units of prose opacity that make Carlyle literally sensational.

Not coincidentally, this practice of discontinuous, small-scale reading, made necessary by a difficult, syntactically peculiar prose style, is precisely how Meredith's initial readers explained their encounters (frustrating or rewarding) with his novels. A series of joltingly crabbed or breathtakingly elongated sentences, a chaotic mixture of different registers, and a jerky, far from seamless accumulation of aphoristic phrases marks Meredith's style, the most overtly 'difficult' style of Victorian prose. As W. E. Henley complained in 1879, 'to read Mr. Meredith straight off is to have an indigestion of epigram'—thus following other Victorian critics in making Meredith's disconnected units of sensation, called epigram, aphorism, maxim, or simply sentence, central to the disconcertingly fragmented experience of reading his novels.[2] As a contemporary critic has termed it, the buildup of such units results in a 'dialogic traffic-jam', in which the usually frictionless forward movement of novel-reading gets stuck in opaque phrases that seem to have no necessary or obvious connection to what came before or what follows.[3] Meredith, it seems, not only slows reading down but detemporalizes it altogether, making the

---

[1] Citations from Meredith's novels are given parenthetically, using the following abbreviations: *BC: Beauchamp's Career*, in *The Works of George Meredith*, xiii–xiv (London: Constable, 1897); *DC: Diana of the Crossways*, in *The Works of George Meredith*, xvii–xviii (London: Constable, 1897); *E: The Egoist*, ed. George Woodcock (Harmondsworth: Penguin, 1968); *OC: One of Our Conquerors*, in *The Works of George Meredith*, xix–xx (London: Constable, 1897); *RF: The Ordeal of Richard Feverel: A History of Father and Son*, ed. Edward Mendelson (Harmondsworth: Penguin, 1998).

[2] W. E. Henley, 'Literature', *Athenaeum* 2714 (1 Nov. 1879), 555.

[3] See Neil Roberts, *Meredith and the Novel* (London: Macmillan, 1997), 152.

causally related, anticipatory momentum of novel-reading-as-usual submit to a series of disconnected flashes of insight or bafflement. As with Nevil's Carlyle, we get in Meredith 'nibbles of golden meaning by instalments' rather than larger wholes. That this is not just the opinion of a set of hostile reviewers, or current critics attuned to modernist experimentation, is evidenced by the practice of reading Meredith's work as nothing *but* a series of choice epigrams. In 1888 an American admirer, Mary Rebecca Foster Gilman, produced with Meredith's reluctant approval *The Pilgrim's Scrip: or, The Wit and Wisdom of George Meredith* (its title taking an oddly unironic cue from the notoriously misogynist collection of paternal aphorisms in *The Ordeal of Richard Feverel*), a compilation of maxims taken indiscriminately from Meredith's characters and narrative voice alike. As Gilman explained it, Meredith's sentences 'are like crystals, the particles grouping themselves together as if in obedience to an inner law'.[4]

What binds accounts of reading Meredith and Meredith's accounts of reading is the stress they both place on the individual unit, on the small moment of sense making or comprehension. This is where Meredith's primary interest to us now might begin: with a detailed consideration, and contextualization, of his interest in producing and describing fragmentary, discontinuous readings. The difficulty of Meredith's style has usually been read as proto-modernist, as a genteel forerunner of the more abstract difficulties of early twentieth-century prose. As this chapter will argue, Meredith's style is more usefully considered as a complex reaction to a cluster of problems that faced both experimental psychology and physiology, as well as physiologically informed literary criticism and theory, starting in the 1860s and extending into the next century: is there such a thing as a 'unit' of consciousness or comprehension, and if so, how large is it, and how can we know when we see one? What is the *size* of the fundamental particles of comprehension that the reading or reacting mind then builds into larger units of knowledge? And what might those units of comprehension tell us about the possible composition, or 'form', of larger structures: arguments, ideas, narratives, reading audiences? These were questions that obsessed the higher reaches of psychological theory and that had a definite, and peculiar, impact on the development of literary formalism in the latter decades of the Victorian period. They receive their most extended articulation in Meredith's novels, which imagine 'form' arising out of a disconnected string of particles. In Meredith, the perfection of larger forms—from the narrative arc of his novels to the polished grandeur of his 1898 De Luxe edition of collected works on which he

---

[4] M. R. F. Gilman, *The Pilgrim's Scrip: or, The Wit and Wisdom of George Meredith* (Boston: Roberts Brothers, 1888), xvii.

worked assiduously—matches uneasily the fragmented, isolated units out of which they are built.[5]

Meredith's interest in fragmentation arises most persistently not from an abstract interest in human cognition, but from a focused interest in the reading act and the materiality of reading—in other words, the psychology of print. No book in Meredith is simply an inert object. Of each book that Meredith mentions, we learn bibliographical detail, as with the different editions of Sir Austin Feverel's *Pilgrim's Scrip* littering *Richard Feverel*; Sir Austin's close friend Lady Blandish, we are told in one instance, carries it 'bound in purple velvet, gilt-edged, as decorative ladies like to have holier books', a description as attentive to material form and social meaning as any latter-day historian of the book might desire (*RF*, 108). In fact, many of the reading practices traditionally of great interest to book historians are given lavish attention in Meredith: his characters are constant users of commonplace books and notebooks for recording witty or otherwise apropos sayings; they circulate books and letters for public reading and private comment; and they employ penknives, paper cutters, and annotating pencils as instruments of courtship and socializing, as when Nevil Beauchamp selectively underlines and annotates a book as a message for his love interest, Cecilia Halkett. They speak in a pervasively bibliographical discourse: Adrian Harley, Richard Feverel's cynical tutor, refers to his charge's infatuation with Lady Judith Felle as 'a second edition' of his childish affection for Lady Blandish, while in *The Egoist* (1879) multiple characters refer to Sir Willoughby Patterne's engagement to Clara Middleton as either 'the same chapter' as his previously unsuccessful engagement to Constantia Durham, or 'the first heading of the chapter' of Clara's life (*RF*, 347; *E*, 70, 244). No different are Meredith's narrators, who can speak, in *Beauchamp's Career*, of 'the bright first chapter' of Cecilia Halkett's life, or, in *One of Our Conquerors* (1891), of an impatient suitor of the young Nesta Radnor as 'an indulgent skipper of parental pages' (*BC*, xiv. 247; *OC*, xix. 207). Even the Braille method of touch reading, first put into use in the 1830s, is mined as a metaphor in Meredith: 'When a person is not read by character, the position or profession is called on to supply raised print for the finger-ends to spell' (*OC*, xix. 225). Few Victorian authors have been as

---

[5] The Constable firm issued the De Luxe edition, thus making a key late-career break from Meredith's three-decade-long association, as house reader and house writer, with Chapman & Hall. For more on the De Luxe edition, see Lionel Stevenson, *The Ordeal of George Meredith: A Biography* (New York: Scribners, 1953), 329–30; for Meredith's break with Chapman & Hall over copyright issues, see his letters to Frederic Chapman in Feb. 1893, in George Meredith, *The Letters of George Meredith*, ed. C. L. Cline, ii (Oxford: Clarendon Press, 1970), 1122–4. Copyright negotiations were particularly protracted because of Meredith's desire to have the De Luxe edition appear simultaneously in Britain and (through Scribners) in the United States.

attuned, in metaphorical or realist registers, to the resonances of book design and manufacture. It is characteristic of Meredith that he once planned essays on both 'Style' and 'The Use of Italic Type'.[6]

This heavy reliance on print and textual culture for Meredith's fictional portrayals has long been noticed, by critics as diverse in their investments as J. Hillis Miller and Garrett Stewart.[7] Its effect, however, has been less well understood, primarily because the diminutive scale of Meredith's bibliographical imagination has yet to be registered. Meredith's interest in print is, pervasively, an interest in fragmentation. His readers are readers of parts; the typographical conventions they consume and use as metaphor are bits, small patches, parts of larger wholes, addenda. They read chapters, not books; they rely, or fail to rely, on the parts of books that permit snatchy, non-sequential reading, as when we learn that Sir Willoughby, in attempting to understand Clara without reading her face, 'dived below the surface without studying that index-page', or when we hear Cecilia Halkett laughing at the image of a book of Nevil Beauchamp's intentions: 'How many erasures! what foot-notes!' (*E*, 80; *BC*, xiii. 199). Print comprehension is in Meredith a discontinuous comprehension, managed through various apparatuses or practices of segmentation. This was a characteristic of Meredith's own novels repeatedly noted by his critics. R. H. Hutton called *Harry Richmond* 'a novel which invites delay rather than prompts rapidity . . . it is very slow reading'; W. E. Henley recommended that Meredith only be read 'at the rate of two or three chapters a day', and called *The Egoist* 'not a novel nor even a romance, but a comedy in chapters'; the *Saturday Review* warned that it 'must be read, not page by page like the ordinary novel, but line by line'; Margaret Oliphant, meanwhile, complained of *The Egoist*'s 'three huge volumes, made up of a thousand conversations, torrents of words in half lines, continued, and continued, and continued . . . to read, and read, and read, till the brain refuses further comprehension, and

---

[6] The projected titles are listed in a notebook that Meredith started in 1863. See George Meredith, *The Notebooks of George Meredith*, ed. Gillian Beer and Margaret Harris (Salzburg: Institut für Anglistik und Amerikanistik, 1983), 58.

[7] Miller argues of *The Egoist* that Meredith's 'social world is already a written record', while Stewart claims that for Meredith's characters 'life is often no more led than read'. What both Miller and Stewart have in common is a desire to dematerialize the bibliographical tropes that in Meredith are so insistently material; Stewart acknowledges as much, insisting that the failure of 'Meredith's mastertrope of the world's book is that it offers no commensurate understanding, no explicit understanding at least, of the books we normally call books'. My argument instead reads Meredith as a historian of the book *avant la lettre*, one deeply interested in the psychic and social effects of real bibliographical technologies and practices. See J. Hillis Miller, ' "Herself Against Herself": The Clarification of Clara Middleton', in *The Representation of Women in Fiction*, ed. Carolyn Heilbrun and Margaret Higgonet (Baltimore: Johns Hopkins University Press, 1983), 99; Garrett Stewart, *Dear Reader: The Conscripted Audience in Nineteenth-Century British Fiction* (Baltimore: Johns Hopkins University Press, 1996), 277, 282.

only a spectrum of broken lines of print remains upon its blurred surface, is cruel'.⁸ Meredith's novels seem to have called overt attention to their small units, as if they were in danger of dissolving—even to the point of Oliphant's *alexia*—into fragments.

That these small units are textual ones (lines of print, footnotes, chapters) means that Meredith understood the psychology of print culture to be a fragmented one. In this he anticipated the work of twentieth-century book history, which seems in both its theoretical and practical work devoted to a charting of a scholarly myth of Babel: a history of constant textual fragmentation. While by no means the only story that book history tells, fragmentation remains its major disciplinary allegory. The milestones of book history are moments of separation into smaller units, starting with the shift from *volumen* to codex; as Henri-Jean Martin has explained it, the scroll encouraged a 'continuous' reading, while the book permitted discontinuous flipping back or jumping ahead.⁹ This initial break with continuity is followed by the replacement of ancient *scriptura continua* with word separation, a prolonged process that was not consolidated until the twelfth century, and is perhaps the major bibliographical narrative of medieval manuscript culture; as one historian has it, word separation prepared the way for 'syntactic punctuation and rapid silent reading which depended on the swift visual recognition of word shape and the perception of larger graphic contours of the page: the clause, the sentence and the paragraph'.¹⁰ With the advent of print, these tendencies of textual fragmentation accelerate and ramify in complexity. Different units proliferate: biblical passages are divided into chapter and verse in the sixteenth century; the paragraph as a textual unit, alongside more advanced forms of punctuation, develops between the sixteenth and eighteenth centuries as part of what Martin memorably calls 'the definitive triumph of white space over black type'; textual innovations like the index and the concordance license non-sequential reading; and fictional narratives from the seventeenth century onwards discover the utility of what Franco Moretti

⁸ Richard Holt Hutton, 'The Adventures of Harry Richmond', *Spectator* 45 (20 Jan., 1872), 79; Henley, 'Literature', 555; Henley, in the *Pall Mall Gazette*, Nov. 1879, quoted in Ioan Williams, ed., *Meredith: The Critical Heritage* (London: Routledge & Kegan Paul, 1971), 217; Anon., 'The Egoist', *Saturday Review* 48 (1879), 607; Margaret Oliphant, 'New Novels', *Blackwood's Edinburgh Magazine* 128 (Sept. 1880), 401–2.

⁹ See Henri-Jean Martin, *The History and Power of Writing*, trans. Lydia Cochrane (Chicago: University of Chicago Press, 1994), 59.

¹⁰ Paul Saenger, 'Reading in the Later Middle Ages', In *A History of Reading in the West*, ed. Guglielmo Cavallo and Roger Chartier, trans. Lydia Cochrane (Amherst: University of Massachusetts Press, 1999), 120. See also Martin, *History and Power*, 54–6, and Malcolm Parkes, *Scribes, Scripts, and Readers: Studies in the Communication, Presentation, and Dissemination of Medieval Texts* (London: Hambledon, 1991), 1–18, 101–12.

has termed an 'extraordinary mechanism of self-segmentation of a text', the chapter.[11] In many ways this careful bibliographical history echoes the more vast theses of media history, in particular those of Marshall McLuhan, who continually stressed 'the fragmented and individualist ways' that Western society learned from Gutenberg: 'The power to translate knowledge into mechanical production by the breaking up of any process into fragmented aspects to be placed in a lineal sequence of moveable, yet uniform, parts', McLuhan argues, 'was the formal essence of the printing press.'[12]

The Babel allegory haunting the history of the book extends to a social history of audiences. Perhaps the most vibrant, if contentious, thesis in the history of reading is Rolf Engelsing's famous account of a shift in the seventeenth and eighteenth centuries from 'intensive' to 'extensive' reading, or from a homogeneous audience devotedly reading a select few books to a heterogeneous audience rapidly scanning many books.[13] Meredith's novels often seem to be pivoting on that very shift; many of his narratives begin as 'intensive' reading communities, groupings possessed by the continual

[11] Martin, *History and Power*, 329; Franco Moretti, *The Way of the World: The* Bildungsroman *in European Culture*, trans. Albert Sbragia (New York: Verso, 2000), 252. For biblical chapter/verse fragmentations, see D. F. McKenzie, *Bibliography and the Sociology of Texts* (London: British Library, 1986), 46–7; on paragraphs, see Roger Chartier, *The Order of Books: Readers, Authors, and Libraries in Europe between the Fourteenth and Eighteenth Centuries*, trans. Lydia Cochrane (Stanford, Calif.: Stanford University Press, 1992), 11; on the index, see Walter Ong, *Orality and Literacy: The Technologizing of the Word* (London: Methuen, 1982), 123–6. Much of this work was anticipated by Lucien Febvre and Martin's seminal *L'Apparition du livre* (Paris: Éditions Albin Michel, 1958), which explained the increasing legibility of the European book as a function of its growing internal separations.

[12] Marshall McLuhan, *Understanding Media: The Extensions of Man* (Cambridge, Mass.: MIT Press, 1994), 111, 116.

[13] See Rolf Engelsing, 'Die Perioden der Lesergeschichte in der Neuzeit: Das statistische Ausmass und die soziokulturelle Bedeutung der Lektüre', *Archiv für geschichte des Buchwesens* 10 (1970), 945–1002; idem, *Der Bürger als Leser: Lesergeschichte in Deutschland, 1500–1800* (Stuttgart: J. B. Metzlersche Verlagsbuchhandlung, 1974). For critiques of Engelsing's notion, see Cathy Davidson's explanation of its inapplicability to antebellum America in Cathy Davidson, ed., *Reading in America: Literature and Social History* (Baltimore: Johns Hopkins University Press, 1989), 16, and Roger Chartier's denial of its usefulness for urban French audiences of the eighteenth century in *The Cultural Uses of Print in Early Modern France*, trans. Lydia Cochrane (Princeton: Princeton University Press, 1987), 223 ff., and idem, *Forms and Meanings: Texts, Performances, and Audiences from Codex to Computer* (Philadelphia: University of Pennsylvania Press, 1995), 17. As Leah Price has recently put it: 'This is not to say that anyone questions the distinction between "intensive" and "extensive" reading practices; rather, what's at issue is the extent to which that contrast can be plotted onto a chronological axis.' See Leah Price, 'Reading: The State of the Discipline', *Book History* 7 (2004), 318. Interesting recent work applies Engelsing's thesis to a history of aesthetics: Martha Woodmansee has explained much eighteenth-century German aesthetic philosophy as an attempt to control reading modes in an age of increasingly extensive reading habits; see Martha Woodmansee, 'Aesthetics and the Policing of Reading', in *The Author, Art, and the Market: Rereading the History of Aesthetics* (New York: Columbia University Press, 1994), 87–102.

re-perusal of a single inset master text such as, in *Richard Feverel*, Austin Feverel's *Pilgrim's Scrip*; in *Beauchamp's Career*, the political letter of the radical Dr Shrapnel whose circulation is the plot's primary engine; in *Diana of the Crossways*, Diana Warwick's novels, which become crucial *romans à clef* to friends and foes of the heroine alike; and, in *One of Our Conquerors*, the satirist Colney Durance's unpopular serial story, 'The Rival Tongues', about the imperialism of European languages. To a large extent, Meredith's characters are scrutinized and differentiated on the basis of the kind and quality of readings they give these master texts; but more importantly, his characters are exhorted finally to understand the only limited utility of the reading of this single text, and to move to either action (social or political) or some wider reading. In the dramatization of a move from the oppressive presence of a single all-important text to a more open, heterogeneous field of reading, Meredith's novels restage the supposed 'reading revolution' of early modern Europe as a narrative of psychological maturation. This is also an anticipation, in many ways, of the political drift of book history, for which fragmentation and popular, individual agency often go hand in hand; the thesis of Carlo Ginzburg's *The Cheese and the Worms*—that 'popular' reading consists of a fragmenting, randomly juxtaposing, and decontextualizing process that works against 'proper' authoritarian sequences—has had a long and influential life within the history of audiences.[14]

The point of Meredith's uncanny anticipation of the methods and pre-dispositions of contemporary book history is the way it helps us see his materialization—in the appearance of books as he knew and described them—of the fragmented consumption of his readers. In Meredith, the material facts of books, and the history of segmentation that they tell, join with a vibrant, late Victorian discourse of discontinuous 'unit' thinking to produce

---

[14] See Carlo Ginzburg, *The Cheese and the Worms: The Cosmos of a Sixteenth-Century Miller*, trans. John and Anne Tedeschi (Baltimore: Johns Hopkins University Press, 1980). New media theory has often (unconsciously or not) turned Ginzburg's thesis into a futurist *cri de coeur*, explaining electronic media as the advent of a liberatory post-authoritarian world of pervasive fragmentary consumption. Paradigmatic here is Jay Bolter's ecstatic claim that electronic texts 'are offered to us as fragmentary and potential texts...a network of self-contained units rather than as an organic whole in the tradition of the nineteenth-century novel or essay'. See Jay Bolter, *Writing Space: The Computer, Hypertext, and the History of Writing* (Mahwah, NJ: Lawrence Erlbaum Associates, 1991), 11. Here, however, book historians often issue cautionary reservations: Roger Chartier has noted that learned reading in the Renaissance was equally a process of fragmented understanding (as in the commonplace book), while Leah Price's work in Victorian reading habits has illustrated that reading for isolated bits, or 'beauties', could function as a way to claim membership in an elite form of consumption. See Roger Chartier, 'Reading Matter and "Popular" Reading', In *A History of Reading in the West*, ed. Guglielmo Cavallo and Roger Chartier, trans. Lydia Cochrane (Amherst: University of Massachusetts Press; 1999), 282; Leah Price, *The Anthology and the Rise of the Novel: From Richardson to Eliot* (Cambridge: Cambridge University Press, 2000).

a fictional practice devoted to the condition of what we might call 'thinking small'. Here Meredith cleverly marries physiological and psychological thinking on fictional form to the materiality of books, which physiological novel theorists tended to ignore or describe in only the most vague terms. He is also trying to redescribe, through the twinned facts of book materiality and psychological theory after 1860, what literary 'form' might look like—particularly what 'form' might look like if we assume that comprehension takes place in small isolated bits. In the eyes of his contemporaries, which have been strangely determining for posterity, Meredith's novels not only exemplified bad form, but a species of bad form tellingly described as *fractured* form. A *Punch* cartoon of 1894 depicts Meredith as a bull in a china shop, recklessly smashing porcelain vases—a cunning reference to a famous scene in *The Egoist*—marked 'Grammar', 'Syntax', 'Construction', and 'Form' (see Figure 4.1). As we shall see, 'form' and 'construction' were keywords for the species of late Victorian literary theory, best exemplified by Vernon Lee, that took inspiration from physiology and Continental psychophysics and sought to understand how the 'units' of readerly comprehension became wholes. For this body of theory, Meredith was a compelling example, an inspiration, and also a problem; his intimate understanding of textual self-segmentation (in

Figure 4.1. Meredith breaking the porcelain of literary form, 'Lord Ormont's Mate and Matey's Aminta, by G***ge M*r*d*th', *Punch*, 107 (July 28, 1894), 37. By permission of the British Library (P.P. 5270)

chapters, scenes, or phrases) seemed to reflect an equally acute understanding of the sheer smallness and slightness of human comprehension. Put another way: Meredith combines the facts of book materiality with an up-to-date psychological understanding of the units of consciousness to produce a fictional practice composed of small parts—aphorisms, flashes of insight, minute scenes—that ultimately describes a silent-reading culture of fragmented or interrupted comprehension.[15]

To read Meredith back into a history of novel theory, and a history of the psychology and physiology of reading, might mean restoring his centrality to the narrative of the British novel in the second half of the nineteenth century. As commentators recurrently note, Meredith now seems less ready for resuscitation than any of his peers.[16] This might be partly ascribed to his difficulty, or to his relatively thin social scope (as in E. M. Forster's remark on Meredith's 'home counties posing as the universe'), or to his lack of congeniality to critical modes based on plot analysis or narrative drive.[17] It is certainly the case that the facts of Meredith's career that might have spoken on his behalf—his political radicalism and feminism, and his central involvement (via his position as chief reader for Chapman and Hall) in the business of Victorian fiction—have largely been ignored. The burden of this chapter is to demonstrate Meredith's importance to an as yet untold story: the development in the late nineteenth century of novelistic 'formalism' out of the mixture of a material history of the book (as exemplified in late Victorian treatises on composition) and a physio-mathematical study of units of sensation or consciousness (called 'psychophysics' in Meredith's time). *The Egoist* is Meredith's most sustained and complex reaction to this early formalism, and its engagement with the issue of fragmented, small-scale comprehension—with form in fragments—offers a unique window onto the problems of novelistic form for late Victorian physiological criticism. A prehistory of fragmented consciousness and literary formalism in the Victorian period, however, is necessary first; as it proceeds, Meredith's mannerisms will

---

[15] Only Gillian Beer has reflected on Meredith's interest in the mechanics of reading: Beer constrasts Meredith's prose, which 'supposes a silent reader, the sentence structures moving in the mind and becoming assimilated to one's own processes of consciousness', to the orality of Dickensian rhetoric, thereby reading Meredith as self-consciously reflecting on the conditions, and perhaps limits, of print consumption. See Gillian Beer, *Meredith: A Change of Masks: A Study of the Novels* (London: Athlone, 1970), 186–7.

[16] See Richard Altick's sardonic remark, in his 1989 assessment of the state of the Victorian canon, that 'George Meredith never appealed to more than a few investors, and despite a small boom in the seventies, trading in him has generally been light'. Richard Altick, 'Victorians on the Move: Or, 'Tis Forty Years Since', In *Writers, Readers, and Occasions: Selected Essays on Victorian Literature and Life* (Columbus: Ohio State University Press, 1989), 323.

[17] E. M. Forster, *Aspects of the Novel* (New York: Harcourt, Brace, & World, 1927), 136.

seem more central to considerations of Victorian literary theory and novel theory, and less a mandarin sensibility than an attempt to produce social cohesion out of textual fragmentation.

UNIT AND MEASUREMENT: A GENEALOGY OF LATE VICTORIAN FORMALISM

Writing in 1894 for *The New Review*, Vernon Lee explained her idea of literary form as a psychological mediation between two consciousnesses, one receptive and one creative:

The impressions, the ideas and emotions stored up in the mind of the Reader, and which it is the business of the Writer to awaken in such combinations and successions as answer to his own thoughts and moods—these, which you must allow me to call, in psychologist's jargon, *Units of Consciousness*, have been deposited where they are by the random hand of circumstance, by the accident of temperament and vicissitudes, and in heaps or layers, which represent merely the caprice or necessity of individual experience. From the Writer's point of view, they are a chaos; and, what is worse for him who wishes to rearrange them to suit his mood, they are the chaos of living, moving things.[18]

The chancy nature of this mediation between reader and writer can be regularized only by what Lee goes on to call 'form', or 'pattern': 'The Writer must select, for the formation of his particular pattern of thought or fact or mood, such as he requires among these living molecules of memory, such and such only as he wants—not one other, on pain of spoiling the pattern.'[19] Formal patterning is a way to guarantee that the units of readerly consciousness activated by a text, the 'living molecules of memory', are precisely those intended; fictional form, in other words, is intersubjective negotiation, or, in the terms of computer science, a neutral protocol language through which two minds communicate with each other. Lee's claim here, which she pressed in a variety of articles on the novel written from the 1890s to the early 1920s, occupies an interesting middle ground between the physiological novel theory of Lewes, Bain, and Dallas and the emerging formalism of James and Lubbock. It is entirely attentive to facts of readerly cognition and affect, unlike Jamesian

---

[18] Vernon Lee, 'The Craft of Words', *New Review* 11 (1894), 575. Renamed 'On Style' and slightly expanded, the essay reappeared (with the cited passage intact) in her 1923 essay collection *The Handling of Words and Other Studies in Literary Psychology* (London: John Lane, Bodley Head, 1923), 34–65.

[19] Lee, 'Craft of Words', 577.

formalism, yet no longer conflates reader response and literary form into the single master metaphor of the wave. 'Form' in Lee emerges, as it would for Lubbock, as a point of contact between reader and writer, although in Lee it retains the temporal, rhythmic quality ('combinations and successions') derived from physiological theory, not yet metamorphosing into Lubbock's spatialized, atemporal mental constructs.

Another way to put Lee's interestingly intermediate position is to say that she struggled to combine two competing discourses: an older notion of literary form deriving from Coleridge—the notion of 'organic form'—with newer notions, informed by physiological psychology, of what 'organicity' might mean. Insofar as theorists like Lewes or Bain brought to their literary theory ideas from live, vivisectionist experimentation, they could and did, as we shall see, consider themselves working toward a more scientifically accurate notion of 'organic form'. But to the extent that the physiological organism was in essence a machine—to the extent, as we have seen, that physiological novel theory could use the machine as a heuristic metaphor for consciousness and affect—it worked directly against Coleridge's famous dichotomy between 'mechanical regularity' and 'organic form'.[20] Physiology, that is, only confounded that dichotomy; the mind and body together constituted a machine that, when functioning optimally, functioned with regularity. Such work therefore forced a rethinking of the organicity of form. The passage from Coleridgean organic form to novelistic formalism required an engagement with physiology, one that Lee sought to work out in the 1890s.

The ground upon which this complicated negotiation was carried out was a surprising one: the argument for the existence of basic organic 'units', or building-blocks, of consciousness. When Lee refers to the 'psychologist's jargon' of '*Units of Consciousness*', she invokes the discourse of psychophysics, the field of half-mathematical, half-biological inquiry founded in Leipzig in the 1850s and 1860s by E. H. Weber and Gustav Fechner, which laid out a careful argument for the existence of basic 'bits' of consciousness. Coleridge had made central to notions of organic form the idea that it presented wholes, fully developed and internally consistent *Gestalten*, while the 'mechanical' offered 'composition (or rather juxtaposition) and decomposition, in short the relations of unproductive particles to each other'—in essence, fragments.[21]

---

[20] Samuel Taylor Coleridge, from *Lectures, 1808–1819: On Literature*, in *The Collected Works of Samuel Taylor Coleridge*, ed. R. J. White (London: Routledge & Kegan Paul, 1972), v. 495.

[21] Samuel Taylor Coleridge, from Appendix C to *The Statesman's Manual*, in *Lay Sermons*, in *Collected Works*, vi., 89. My understanding of the mechanical/organic dichotomy in Coleridge, and its relation to a language of 'construction' in his theory, is indebted to Susan Wolfson, *Formal Charges: The Shaping of Poetry in British Romanticism* (Stanford, Calif.: Stanford University Press, 1997).

If, however, consciousness was both a whole (to naïve introspection) and yet also composed of discernible 'particles', as psychophysics argued, it might be possible to speak of an organic form that was both fragment and whole, both organic and mechanical. This was the gambit around which late Victorian formalism rested: the ability to keep fragment and whole, unit and process, in productive tension with one another while not obscuring either side of the equation.

It is the gambit taken most provocatively by Lee's literary criticism and theory, to which I will return; but a brief detour through Victorian physiology's wrestling with the psychophysical notion of 'units of consciousness' is first necessary to see the scientific and literary stakes of this notion of a fragmented mind made up of additive particles. The precise relation between the small and large scales of mental processing was, throughout Victorian physiology, a vexed one. Physiological experimentation demonstrated the fundamental importance of individual sensations—bursts of neural electricity, impulses traveling from the spinal column to the nerve ganglia—but also insisted upon consciousness as a wave-like motion that subsumed and combined these smaller, discrete sensations. The result was a linguistically nuanced, perhaps over-nuanced, attempt to explain how individual sensations became the holistic sense of being conscious. As Lewes explained it in his *Physiology of Common Life*, 'ganglionic tissue has an inherent property, Sensibility, which serves various functions in various organs; however complex any of these functions, we could find, could we analyse it, that it was a complex of simple sensations. There is an incessant action and interaction of the various parts of the sensitive mechanism: sensations cross and recross, exciting and modifying each other; and the sum total is a feeling of existence.'[22] Consciousness in Lewes becomes the sound of the constant combination and recombination of individual elements or 'simple sensations'. It is notable that the *Physiology of Common Life*, the text that invented the phrase 'stream of consciousness', seems to argue for that stream—the 'wave' of physiological affect—as actually an illusion, composed in reality of the movement of sensational bits. The attempt to marry wave and unit, or the mind as it feels and the mind as it biologically is, produces in Lewes's later work a profusion of metaphors; in his *Problems of Life and Mind* Lewes turns both to an idea of 'mental chemistry', in which simple elements are discoverable but usually found in compound states, and a notion of the mind as a color spectrum, in which certain operations can be performed to 'analyze' mental operations into separate strands.[23] Analysis

---

[22] G. H. Lewes, *The Physiology of Common Life* (London: Blackwood, 1860), ii. 73.

[23] See G. H. Lewes, *The Study of Psychology: Its Object, Scope, and Method* (London: Trübner, 1879), 180, 185. *The Study of Psychology* is the fourth volume, and first volume of the Third

and synthesis mix uneasily in Lewes's work, as it never becomes clear what importance the supposed 'units' of sensation might have: are they the truth of mental functioning, its basis and fundamental fact, or an empirical reality that nonetheless has no real value given the impossibility of introspectively isolating any one 'unit' in our consciousness?

This problem is given a further twist by Alexander Bain, who insisted that consciousness is always already fragmented: 'A plurality of stimulations of the nerves may co-exist, but they can affect the consciousness only by turns, or one at a time. The reason is that the bodily organs are collectively engaged with each distinct conscious state, and they cannot be doing two things at the same instant.'[24] For Bain, mental processing is first a diffusion of a series of sensational units, and then a re-fragmentation in which we can only be 'conscious' (i.e. attentive) of any one kind of sensation at a time. If for Lewes consciousness seems symphonic—the collective sound of individual notes, or sensations—for Bain it is purely serial, a one-thing-and-then-another oscillation among various competing sensations. The physiological models for the interaction of unit and collectivity in mental activity, as instanced by Lewes and Bain, were various and at times overlapping, at times conflicting. Part and whole, in other words, achieve no coherent or consistent articulation in Victorian physiology. In one direction physiology felt itself pulled toward a sensory atomism, or toward the delineation and experimental verification of discrete, 'simple' sensations; in another direction, it was attracted to synthetic theories of consciousness as a magisterially complex organic sublation of these small units.

The work operating behind Lewes's competing metaphors in *Problems of Life and Mind* came from the German field of psychophysics, which exerted a tremendous, if often elusive, influence on British physiological psychology. Weber, along with his more theoretically adventurous student Fechner, seemed by the mid-1860s to have isolated a mathematical formula for determining a fundamental unit of consciousness. Their work arose from Weber's elucidation of the 'just noticeable difference': the amount that had to be added to a given stimulus to create the perception of a difference in the stimulus. For Weber, the just noticeable difference could reliably be expressed as a fraction. For example, if one holds a ten-pound weight and one pound is added to it, the difference may not be registered, but the addition of a further ten-pound weight would

---

Series, of Lewes's *Problems of Life and Mind*. See also Rick Rylance, *Victorian Psychology and British Culture, 1850–1880* (Oxford: Oxford University Press, 2000), 309, for an account of Lewes's 'deployment [in the *Problems of Life and Mind*] of images that suggest energy systems rather than fixed entities'.

[24] Alexander Bain, *The Emotions and the Will*, 2nd edn. (London: Longmans, Green, 1865), 4–5.

certainly be registered. Thus, the just noticeable difference could be expressed as the original stimulus value multiplied by the added stimulus value, divided by the added value: a fraction that, Weber discovered experimentally, was a constant for a large region of the scale of stimulus intensity. The resulting equation, known as the Weber fraction, provided the first definition of the just noticeable difference, or 'jnd':

$$\Delta\Sigma/\Sigma = V,$$

where Σ stands for the stimulus change, and Δ for the original stimulus value. The lesson of Weber's equation was that the jnd—the sensation of difference—was not any particular fixed amount of stimulus increase that created a sensation, but a fractional function of the size of the original stimulus.

Fechner's contribution to this work was to dramatically extend its mathematical possibilities by noticing that it offered a potential key to a measurement system for sensation. The results were published in his 1860 *Elemente der Psychophysik*, which offered the jnd as the 'unit of consciousness'. As Fechner understood it, the jnd could be regarded as a unit by making it the just-perceptible increment over 'threshold', or no sensation. Thus, any given sensation could be 'measured' by adding up the number of jnd increments that it would take to get from 'threshold' to the given sensation. As William James later explained Fechner's logic, 'if we know how much of the stimulus it will take to give a barely perceptible sensation [a jnd], and then what percentage of addition to the stimulus will constantly give a barely perceptible increment to the sensation, it is at bottom only a question of compound interest to compute, out of the total amount of stimulus which we may be employing at any moment, the number of such increments, or, in other words, of sensational units to which it may give rise'.[25] Fechner's equation, called the Psychophysical Law, looked as follows:

$$S = C \log_e R,$$

where R is the stimulus, C a constant, and S the total number of 'sensation units' or 'units of consciousness' present. Put linguistically: sensations increase proportionally to the logarithms of their stimuli. Fechner's equation offered some immediate lessons: it demonstrated first that sensation, and therefore consciousness, worked on a logarithmic (or nonlinear) scale; so that at

[25] William James, *The Principles of Psychology* (Cambridge, Mass.: Harvard University Press, 1981), 508. For a helpful elucidation of Weber's and Fechner's work, see Edward Reed, *From Soul to Mind: The Emergence of Psychology, from Erasmus Darwin to William James* (New Haven: Yale University Press, 1997), 96–8.

low levels of stimuli, small changes will be registered, but at high levels of stimuli, only large stimulus changes will be noticed. Secondly, it offered a mathematical definition for the 'unconscious': the operations of stimuli that fall 'below threshold', or that are not noticed, but that—given the natural-logarithmic curve—when sufficiently accumulated, burst suddenly upon the consciousness. Thirdly—and most importantly—it promised to give consciousness a unit of measurement as constant and useful as the metric system. Consciousness could be expressed numerically.

Fechner's work attracted its skeptics, who saw the Psychophysical Law as a species of mathematical superstition; William James's judgment in 1890 was that 'Fechner's book was the starting point of a new department of literature, which it would be perhaps impossible to match for the qualities of thoroughness and subtlety, but of which, in the humble opinion of the present writer, the proper psychological outcome is just *nothing*'. James's criticism rested on the notion that 'the *mental fact* which in the experiments corresponds to the increase of the stimulus is not an *enlarged sensation*, but a *judgment that the sensation is enlarged*'—in other words, that psychophysics, like physiology, too readily conflated sensation with consciousness.[26] For Victorian physiologists, however, Fechner's work offered possible mathematical proof that consciousness consisted of measurable sensations of difference. As Bain put it in the 1865 edition of *The Emotions and the Will*, 'the basis or fundamental peculiarity of the intellect is Discrimination, or the feeling of difference between consecutive, or co-existing, impressions. Nothing more fundamental can possibly be assigned as the defining mark of intelligence . . . . We are awake, alive, mentally alert, under the discriminative exercise, and accordingly may be said to be conscious.'[27] In his 1868 revision of *The Senses and the Intellect* this became Bain's Law of Relativity, which proclaimed that everything is known relationally as a result of a change from some previous stimulus state.[28] Consciousness could be considered the accumulation of minute mental registrations of difference, or small acts of discrimination (the 'just noticeable difference'); and that accumulation could be given a number.

As abstruse as Fechner's psychophysics was and is, the effect it had on Victorian physiology—which was in search of its own definition of consciousness, and which saw in Fechner's logarithmic equation a possible law for how the small unit became the large sensation—leaked into physiological literary theory, particularly in that body of theory's confusing intersection with notions of the 'organic'. The leakage worked as follows: if 'organic form'

[26] W. James, *Principles of Psychology*, 504, 515.
[27] Alexander Bain, *Emotions and the Will*, 566.
[28] Bain, *The Senses and the Intellect*, 3rd edn. (London: Longmans, Green, 1868), 321.

after Coleridge meant a whole that masked or eliminated the fissures between subordinate parts, and that therefore supposedly better mimicked the workings of organic life, what to do with the psychophysical notion that organic life for humans—in other words, consciousness—consisted of innumerable acts of noticing difference—that is, fractures—in sensation? To what extent would 'organic' literary form be a seamless whole, if the 'organic' was in fact a collection of jnds, or impressions of partial changes? Do the undeniable parts or units of literary form—lines, chapters, scenes, plots—ever become a whole, or do they simply add up mathematically, as Fechner showed, to a sum total? Should the very terms 'organic' and 'mechanical', as they were handed down by Romantic literary theory, be discarded in relation to literature, insofar as the workings of the nervous system—and the reliable constants of Weber's and Fechner's equations—demonstrate an organicity that functions like a machine?

These were complicated questions that never received entirely coherent treatment in the literary criticism and theory produced by physiological scientists. To a large extent, 'organic form' lingered on as a term of approbation, even while its Coleridgean presuppositions were being attacked; theorists like Lewes could both critique certain literary forms and texts with the pejorative term 'mechanical' while using the machine as a model for proper literary functioning. Others would insist, along Coleridgean lines, that fragmentary work was harmful and 'mechanical', while providing theories of reading that intimated that comprehension could only be comprehension of fragmentary differences. Physiological novel theory was entirely comfortable with reading as a temporal process made up of rhythmic waves, but grew confused when presented with a thesis—one that in many respects accorded with physiology's emphases—that consciousness was a pointillist series of bit-like, minute impressions.

The collision between Victorian scientific presuppositions and Romantic literary theory was often dramatic, as in the following passage from Lewes's well-known 1872 account of Dickens, 'Dickens in Relation to Criticism':

When one thinks of Micawber always presenting himself in the same situation, moved with the same springs, and uttering the same sounds . . . one is reminded of the frogs whose brains have been taken out for physiological purposes, and whose actions henceforth want the distinctive peculiarity of organic action, that of fluctuating spontaneity. Place one of these brainless frogs on his back and he will at once recover the sitting posture; draw a leg from under him, and he will draw it back again; tickle or prick him and he will push away the object, or take *one* hop out of the way; stroke his back, and he will utter *one* croak. All these things resemble the actions of the unmutilated frog, but they differ in being *isolated* actions, and *always the same*: they are as uniform and calculable as the movements of a machine. The uninjured frog may or may not croak, may or may not hop away; the result is never calculable, and is rarely a single croak or a single hop. It is this complexity of the organism which Dickens wholly fails to conceive; his characters have nothing fluctuating and incalculable in them, even when they embody true observations; and very often they are creations so fantastic that one is at a loss to understand how he could, without hallucination, believe them to be like reality.[29]

The definition of Dickens's characters as essentially 'brainless' is provocative enough, but the mapping of physiological work directly onto a Coleridgean dichotomy is further reason to pause: here Lewes aligns the organic with the cerebral, the uncalculable, and the complex, and the mechanical with the autonomic nervous system, the calculable, and the fragmentary. This alignment makes a certain sense, but it obscures a methodological catechresis. By adducing the results of physiological experiment—the removal of frogs' brains, a common element in Lewes's researches—as a negative model for the literary-organic (i.e. the brainless frog looks nothing like the 'organic' literary character), Lewes cuts the ground from under his own interdisciplinary intellectual work. If physiology can refer only to the inorganic (in literature), what of its own contention that organicity is essentially as regular as a machine? Lewes's work often turned to images of 'galvanic power' and 'batteries' to explain the conducting power of nerves, the central property of neural processing; here, those nerves are aligned with the inorganic or mechanical, while the organic is cerebral only.[30] In essence, Lewes's analysis of Dickens turned back to a division between psychology as a science of 'Mind' and physiology as a science of 'Life', a division upon which Lewes himself had cast skepticism, claiming that the taxonomies of faculty psychology had no basis in physiological fact.[31] What the passage on Dickens teaches us is that Lewes was occasionally willing in his literary criticism to abandon a battle that he waged vigorously in his scientific work, solely in order to retain the notion of 'organic

---

[29] G. H. Lewes, 'Dickens in Relation to Criticism', *Fortnightly Review* 17 (1872), 149. In some ways Lewes's argument was a critical commonplace; David Masson, in his *British Novelists and their Styles* (1859), differentiated between Dickens and Thackeray on the basis of Dickens's fragmentation into phrases, which 'flashes on the mind of the reader' in an act of what Masson calls 'luminous metonymy', as opposed to Thackeray's 'total effect'. See David Masson, *British Novelists and their Styles: Being a Critical Sketch of the History of British Prose Fiction* (Cambridge and London: Macmillan, 1859), 252–3.

[30] Lewes, *Physiology of Common Life*, 14–19.

[31] 'To cite an example: Psychology announces that the mind has different faculties, and that each of these faculties may have a temporary exaltation, or a temporary suspension. This fact seems established on ample evidence, and is valid in Psychology, although hitherto no *corresponding* fact in Physiology has been discovered—neither the anatomy of the brain, nor any knowledge of the brain's action, can be adduced as furnishing the *evidence*; and if Psychology were absolutely amenable to the conclusions of Physiology, we should here have to doubt one of the most indisputable of psychological facts.' Ibid. 3.

form' intact. One senses in Lewes's appraisal of Micawber an anxiety about the literary effect of physiology's understanding of human consciousness and behavior.

Elsewhere in Lewes the confusion grows. His *Principles of Success in Literature* offers to 'dissect Style, as we dissect an organism, and lay bare the fundamental laws by which each is regulated', and also refers to 'the laws which regulate the mechanism of Style'. This mixture of the mechanical, the organic, and the vivisectionist is entirely in keeping with the physiological emphasis of his theory, but the Coleridgean organic intrudes in a warning that 'the grace and luminousness of a happy talent will no more be acquired by a knowledge of these laws, than the force and elasticity of a healthy organism will be given by a knowledge of anatomy'.[32] Here Lewes shies away from Coleridge's precept that 'form is mechanic when on any given material we impress a pre-determined form, not necessarily arising out of the properties of the material'.[33] Dissect all he wants, he cannot prescribe any particular 'laws' out of the risk of summoning up the ghost of Mechanical Form; the result is the slightly embarrassed quality of Lewes's theory in *Principles*, which solves the conflict between physiology and organic form by deferring to the latter whenever a possible confrontation is sensed.

It is entirely symptomatic of late Victorian formalism that those confrontations tend to circle around the question of the relation of parts to whole. Organicity is most pressingly, and apologetically, invoked by Lewes when the question of subordinate parts of novels is raised. While he differentiates between novel and drama on the basis of the 'prudent prodigality' allowed the novelist in relation to detail and digression, he adds: 'The parts of a novel should have organic relations. Push the license to excess, and stitch together a volume of unrelated chapters—a patchwork of descriptions, dialogues, and incidents,—no one will call that a novel; and the less the work has of this unorganised character the greater will be its value, not only in the eyes of critics, but in its effect on the emotions of the reader.'[34] Characteristically, organicity is evoked by mention of its opposite—fragments—and particularly of the material appearance of fragments (most notably, chapters). The novel posed a formal problem in the attempt to mix physiological response theory with organic form, since, given its usual length, it tended to subdivide naturally into parts (volumes, serial numbers, chapters, scenes) that threatened to call attention to the sutures that organic form ideally masks. At their most practical, physiological theorists could not avoid the necessity of subdivisions; Bain,

---

[32] G. H. Lewes, *The Principles of Success in Literature*, 3rd edn., ed. Fred Scott (Boston: Allyn & Bacon, 1891), 126.

[33] Coleridge, *Lectures, 1808–1819*, 495.   [34] Lewes, *Principles of Success*, 138.

in his *English Composition and Rhetoric* (1866), advised writers on the various uses of chapters, including their ability to make apparent the 'subordination' of subplots and minor events.[35] In their most Coleridgean manner, however, they shied away from such acknowledgment of textual units. Lewes used organicity to insist upon good form's self-erasure: 'Economy dictates that the meaning should be presented in a form which claims the least possible attention to itself as form, unless when that form is part of the writer's object, and when the simple thought is less important than the manner of presenting it.'[36] Yet it is entirely possible for Lewes to phrase this very point—the innocuousness of good form, its smooth erasure of part divisions—as an issue of mechanics, not organics: 'It is the writer's art so to arrange words that they shall suffer the least possible retardation from the inevitable friction of the reader's mind. The analogy of a machine is perfect. In both cases the object is to secure the maximum of disposable force, by diminishing the amount absorbed in the working.'[37]

Lewes's ambivalences around organic form seem to have led to two important attempts to solve the relation between part and whole, machine and living body, in Victorian literary theory. The first was E. S. Dallas's, in *The Gay Science*, which presented a literary formalism, centered on the word 'construction', that solved the psychophysical problem—the thesis that consciousness was a sum of fragmenting discriminations—by demoting consciousness to a sub-artistic rank, a move that Lewes had not envisioned. For Dallas, the mind spontaneously 'takes and makes whole': 'The mind is never content with a part; it rushes to wholes. Where it cannot find them it makes them. Given any fragment of fact, we shape it instantly into a whole of some sort.'[38] Dallas posited three kinds of whole-making activities, which could be mapped onto a system of literary genres: 'intensive' wholes, which turn fragments into symbols, types, or emblems, and which are the essence of lyric poetry; 'protensive' wholes, which turn fragments into constants of human existence, and which characterize epic poetry; and 'extensive' wholes, which connect fragments into psychological portraits or narratives, and which are the primary activity of dramatic and novelistic art. The word proper to the extensive whole, Dallas explains, is 'construction': 'There is the construction of character and all its traits; there is the construction of the personages in relation to each other; there is the construction of events into a consistent plot.'[39] This 'construction', however, is not a property of consciousness, but rather the

---

[35] Alexander Bain, *English Composition and Rhetoric: A Manual* (London: Longmans, Green, 1866), 133.
[36] Lewes, *Principles of Success*, 130.   [37] Ibid. 129.
[38] E. S. Dallas, *The Gay Science* (London: Chapman & Hall, 1866), i. 291.
[39] Ibid. 302.

property of Dallas's famous 'hidden soul' or 'free, unconscious play', a primary process function that sutures what conscious thinking, by discrimination and differentiation, divides into parts. 'It is the nature of voluntary effort to be partial and concentrated in points,' Dallas explains. 'Left to itself the mind is like the cloud that moveth altogether if it move at all; and this wholeness of movement has its issue in that wholeness of thinking which we find in true works of imagination.' Consciousness can produce only 'a want of consistency or construction': a work in fragments.[40]

Dallas's 'hidden soul' theory has a certain fame within a history of nineteenth-century aesthetics, primarily for being the first to link Romantic theories of imagination to nascent Victorian theories of the unconscious. It has yet to be understood, however, as a solution—albeit one without a significant afterlife—to the dilemma of reconciling Romantic organic form, with its dislike for the fragment or unassimilated part, with more contemporary theories of consciousness, which insisted upon the primacy of the mind's disintegrating, differentiating activities. Dallas's hypothesis of a 'hidden soul' parceled out organic whole-making to a metaphysical region of mind, while relegating discrimination and fragmentation to the activity of a suddenly dethroned consciousness. By admitting that consciousness, or the willed, is 'partial and concentrated at points', Dallas could remain consistent with Fechnerian psychophysics while nonetheless exalting seamless organic form as a property of an entirely different realm of mental processing. Dallas's solution leads, by winding avenues, to Lubbock's noetic materialism, in which the reader forms mental wholes out of scattered temporal units of plot. Despite Dallas's commitments elsewhere in *The Gay Science* to a physiologically inflected, temporal/rhythmic reading of the novel, under pressure of the fragment—and the poor reputation of fragments held by Romantic literary theory, which retained influence over the most adventurous Victorian theorists—Dallas ended up with a theory that led in an entirely different direction: toward the atemporal, the assimilating, the mystically 'organic'.

The result of the confrontation between organic form and physiology seems with Lewes and Dallas to have been varieties of compromise that abandoned the more advanced positions on fictional form that these theorists elsewhere held. It is with Vernon Lee's essays on novelistic form in the 1890s that we see a more daring attempt to reconceive what literary criticism might look like—or what novelistic 'form' might be—in the wake of the psychophysical thesis of 'units' of consciousness. Lee's work, initially published in the *New Review* and the *Contemporary Review* from 1885 to 1895 and revised in the early 1920s, openly insists upon the novel's susceptibility to measurement.

---

[40] Ibid. 304–5.

As she argued in her 'A Dialogue on Novels' (1885), the satisfaction we take in novelistic character 'is as purely scientific as the satisfaction in following a mathematical demonstration or a physiological experiment', a claim which made varieties of critical measurement possible for her.[41] Her criticism takes for granted the existence of units or elements of consciousness, and attempts a variety of overlapping but not wholly identical theories and critical practices to connect those units, present in the mind of reader and writer both, to larger notions of form. One such theory was offered in her 1895 article 'On Literary Construction', which borrowed Dallas's term to describe a similar process of building wholes out of fragmented mental and textual units. Here Lee defines it as a 'grouping' or 'manipulation' of 'single impressions, single ideas and emotions, stored up in the reader's mind and deposited there by no act of his own', but by the writer, who must both produce those units of mental awareness and then shape them into coherent form.[42] Lee then proposes an experiment in literary mapping:

Make a stroke with your pen which represents the first train of thought or mood, or the first group of thoughts you deal with. Then make another pen-stroke to represent the second, which shall be proportionately long or short according to the number of words or pages occupied, and which, connected with the first pen-stroke, as one articulation of a reed is with another, will deflect to the right or the left according as it contains more or less new matter; so that, if it grow insensibly from stroke number one, it will have to be almost straight, and if it contain something utterly disconnected, will be at right angles. Go on adding pen-strokes for every new train of thought, or mood, or group of facts, and writing the name along each, and being careful to indicate not merely the angle of divergence, but the respective length in lines. And then look at the whole map. If the reader's mind is to run easily along the whole story or essay, and to perceive all through the necessary connection between the parts, the pattern you will have traced will approximate most likely to a perfect circle or ellipse. . . . But in proportion as the things have been made a mess of, the pattern will tend to the shapeless; the lines, after infinite tortuosities, deflections to the right and to the left, immense bends, sharp angles and bags of all sorts, will probably end in a pen-stroke at the other end of the paper . . . this will mean that you have lacked general conception of the subject, that the connection between what you began and what you ended with is arbitrary or accidental, instead of being logical and organic.[43]

'Pattern' in Lee remains an 'organic' proposition, but the meaning of the spatial exercise she proposes here is an attention to what we might call minimal units: to the individual lines, representing individual textual units ('thought, mood, or group of facts'), that must be carefully delineated before their interrelations

---

[41] Vernon Lee, 'A Dialogue on Novels', *Contemporary Review* 48 (Sept. 1885), 386.
[42] Lee, 'On Literary Construction', *Contemporary Review* 68 (Sept. 1895), 404.
[43] Ibid. 408.

are discovered. It is a purely linear map, a spatial diagram that nonetheless respects the temporality of reading in a way congenial to physiological novel theory, adding to that linearity a heightened regard for the small 'bits' out of which literary construction is built. It is, in fact, oddly premonitory of numerous contemporary textual mapping designs of digital texts which a host of current websites display.[44] This mapping technique (which Lee never herself instantiated) is essentially a formula for close reading along the lines of physiological novel theory; it encourages a focus on minimal units that such theory had never envisioned.

By 1923, after the effects of physiology, psychophysics, and organic form had waned from novel theory, Lee was still honing this idea. The final result was her essay 'The Handling of Words', which proposed, rather than spatial modeling, a quantitative analysis of selected, representative passages in an author's *œuvre* as a way to determine the precise kinds of psychological transactions between reader and writer that different texts call for. In 'The Handling of Words' Lee selected 500-word passages from six different authors and, in each passage, tabulated the words by parts of speech. The process would be a technique of 'statistical experiment' for studying 'the minutest elements to which literary style can be reduced': the just noticeable differences of novel-reading, determined quantitatively, in the manner of Fechnerian psychophysics. Abandoning plot as form, Lee directed her attention to synecdochal patches of text, making the implied claim that the properties of individual units (adjectives, adverbs, prepositions) determined the experience of novel-reading more thoroughly than any larger-order pattern. 'What are the mental attitudes which the Writer forces upon the Reader?', Lee asked by way of preamble; 'what are the mental movements he compels him to execute in that process of evoking and rearranging those past images and feelings?' The result, she noted, would produce a picture of 'the pattern in which an individual author sets his words': a 'pattern' that would arise out of, or take place within, the smallest units of comprehension.[45]

Lee does not list her results in tabular form, although her analyses lend themselves to it; a tabulation of them demonstrates their insistent particularity, as well as a strange general similarity among them, as if salient differences between authors would be statistically small (see Table 4.1).[46] Of special

---

[44] See, e.g., W. Bradford Paley's 'TextArc' (on which an etext of *The Egoist*, among other Meredith novels, can be displayed), at <http://www.textarc.org>; or Ben Fry's 'Valence', at <http://acg.media.mit.edu/people/fry/valence>. Each textual mapping system attempts to maintain a tension between spatialization and a memory of reading's temporality in precisely the same manner as Lee's hypothetical diagram.

[45] Vernon Lee, 'The Handling of Words', in *Handling of Words*, 190.

[46] With the testimony of Meredith's initial reviewers in mind, we might also say that Lee's statistical results are misleading. R. H. Hutton, like many other reviewers, wrote of the

Table 4.1 Vernon Lee's tabulations of novelistic styles in *The Handling of Words*

Author	Nouns/pronouns	Verbs/verbal participles	Adjectives/adjectival participles
Meredith	159	66	25
Kipling	157	59	53
Stevenson	138	70	41
Hardy	108	62	62
James	137	71	48
Hewlett	132	56	54

interest, however, is the fact that she begins with Meredith as the most vivid and representative example of the power of minimal units in novel-reading. Meredith, Lee asserts, lacks expressions of logical connection or subordination, prefers passive to active verb forms, and is given to cryptic personifications of abstract qualities, all of which issue in a reading activity that is given to quick starts and stops, a 'disconnected and discursive' mental activity which Lee explains as the opposite of demanding or taxing readerly memory or 'constructive attention'. 'If anything is claimed, is taxed', Lee writes of Meredith, 'it is the Reader's power of following short, rapid movements, and of "spotting," "twigging," their relation to one another.'[47] Interestingly enough, 'twig' was one of Meredith's chosen terms for accurate, small-scale mental activity; in a notebook filled during the late 1850s and early 1860s, Meredith writes of prophecy that ' 'tis easy to hit the Tree, but not so to transfix one particular twig'.[48] Meredith, that is, is useful for Lee's study because his novels require the very activity—short, sharp, fragmented, discontinuous attention—that her notion of the study of novelistic form in minimal units makes central. He is the instantiation of reading as a process of discriminating just noticeable differences.

Lee's gambit, here and in 'On Literary Construction', was to take the 'Units of Consciousness' she wrote of elsewhere and apply them to minute notions of novelistic patterning. 'Pattern', 'construction', and 'form', key words of Victorian literary formalism, were primarily for Lee properties of small units. This was both a consequence of, and a challenge to, physiological literary theory; she accepted its legacy of a psychological study of reader cognition as a

importance of 'his subtlety in the matter of adverbs and adjectives', a category in which Meredith, in Lee's tabulation, is oddly underrepresented. See Richard Holt Hutton, 'Mr. George Meredith's New Novel', *Spectator* 52 (1 Nov. 1879), 1383. Of further interest is the general reluctance of Meredith's reviewers to quote long passages of text in the manner in which other Victorian authors were treated; it is as if Meredith's insistent fragmentariness made the leisurely citations of most Victorian criticism inoperable. If, in other words, most Victorian citation exists to demonstrate a wave (of affect, of plot), Meredith's units disrupt any such waves.

[47] Lee, 'Handling of Words', 195–6.   [48] *Notebooks of Meredith*, 43.

guide to novelistic form, but refocused the frame of that study to a smaller scale. She therefore introduced, if belatedly, close reading as a possible technique of novel theory, at a moment when physiological novel theory yielded to Jamesian formalism, which, at least in Lubbock's hands, had similarly little use for close reading. For Lee, using Meredith as an inspiration, the novel was a practice of brief units of comprehension, a form of cognition pitched at a minimal scale. With Lee's example, reading back into the late 1870s, when Meredith began work on *The Egoist*, we can better see his place within a history of novel-reading: Meredith seems to have exemplified the problems and possibilities of fragmented, minimal comprehension. *The Egoist* can, in fact, be read as a condensation of the entire history of Victorian literary-critical formalism, from its origins in Romantic organic form through its physiologically inflected engagement with psychophysics and new definitions of pattern and construction. Its key difference, however, is in its imagination of a social context, and social meaning, for the practice of fragmented comprehension.

THE EGOIST, I: MINIMAL FORM

Meredith's references to literary 'form' are as complex and contradictory, at least in the collision between his critical writing and his fiction, as that of Victorian physiological novel theory. In his 1877 lecture 'On the Idea of Comedy, and the Uses of the Comic Spirit' (known later as the *Essay on Comedy*), he was capable of a fairly straightforward application of organic form, as in his praise of Molière: 'His moral does not hang like a tail, or preach from one character incessantly cocking an eye at the audience, as in recent realistic French Plays, but is in the heart of his work, throbbing with every pulsation of an organic structure.'[49] Throughout the *Essay on Comedy*, Meredith's appeals to classic formal arbiters—Greek drama, French comedy—present him as the most fastidious and scholarly of literary formalists, for whom the fragmentariness of modern literature cannot hope to match the perfections of older models. This use of organicity as a weapon of the Classics in their battle against the Moderns, however, is parodied in *The Egoist*, which is often considered to be merely an application of the ideas in the *Essay on Comedy*. Clara Middleton's father, the scholar Dr Middleton, is seduced into

---

[49] George Meredith, 'On the Idea of Comedy, and the Uses of the Comic Spirit', in *George Meredith's* Essay on Comedy *and Other* New Quarterly Magazine Publications: A Critical Edition, ed. Maura Ives (Lewisburg, Va.: Bucknell University Press, 1998), 122.

ignoring his daughter's plea for escape from Sir Willoughby by the quality of Sir Willoughby's port, eulogized in much the same manner that Meredith reserved for Molière: 'Senatorial Port! we say. We cannot say that of any other wine. Port is deep-sea deep. It is in its flavour deep; mark the difference. It is like a classic tragedy, organic in conception' (*E*, 239). Nothing more comically blinkered, it seems, than the scholar inebriated on praise of the organic.

When not parodied, form in *The Egoist* is fragmented, as if ostentatiously flouting the rules of organic form. The central moment is the one picked up by *Punch* in 1894: the accidental shattering of a porcelain vase intended as a wedding present to Clara and Sir Willoughby by the voluble Irish interloper, Sir Willoughby's friend and rival Colonel Horace De Craye. In the attempt to save Clara from a runaway cart, Horace's fly, driven by the servant Flitch, hurries to pick her up, causing the destruction of the vase inside the fly; as Flitch narrates it: 'the vaws it shoots out against the twelfth mile-stone, just as though there was the chance for it! for nobody else was injured, and knocked against anything else, it never would have flown all to pieces, so that it took Bartlett and me ten minutes to collect every one, down to the smallest piece there was' (*E*, 214). Horace, answering a hostile question from Sir Willoughby, turns the accident into an occasion for a comic meditation on form:

> 'Wasn't it packed in a box?'
> 'No, it was wrapped in paper, to show its elegant form. I caught sight of it in the shop yesterday and carried it off this morning, and presented it to Miss Middleton at noon, without any form at all.' (*E*, 217)

The punning linkage between social form and physical form—both, here, broken into pieces—condenses what the novel is in the process of displaying: the fragility and artificiality of elegant wholes, be they artifactual (like the vase) or social (like Clara's engagement to Sir Willoughby). Of course, Clara herself has already been labeled 'a dainty rogue in porcelain' by the epigrammatic Mrs Mountstuart Jenkinson, leading to Horace's later proclamation: 'I'm haunted by the idea that porcelain always goes to pieces' (*E*, 313). Ostensibly invested in formal completeness, *The Egoist* turns into a study of fractures.

In this sense, the novel is far from the world of the *Essay on Comedy*; where the *Essay* is unapologetically classicist in its references to form, *The Egoist* is cunningly up-to-date, reducing form to its minimal units.[50] It is, then, a novel built on a ruse. The elegance of its formal arrangement is everywhere palpable: the novel is restricted physically and socially, to the limits of Sir Willoughby's estate, and based on the form of a quadrille, in which two

---

[50] For a useful discussion of the disconnect between the *Essay*'s and *The Egoist*'s notions of form, see David McWhirter, 'Imagining a Distance: Feminism and Comedy in Meredith's *The Egoist*', *Genre* 22/3 (1989), 263–86.

putative couples—the egoist Sir Willoughby and his promised bride Clara Middleton, and the tutor Vernon Whitford and the past-her-prime poet Laetitia Dale—must reverse their intended positions, as the wealthy Clara must link herself to the masculine, penniless tutor, while Sir Willoughby must be humbled by a union with a disillusioned Laetitia. The novel is staged in scenes that carefully arrive at all possible dialogic combinations of the small set of participants; it observes the unities of time and place, with the exception of a central, abortive escape attempt to the nearby railway station by Clara. In short, it is the Victorian novel least interested in using what Lewes called the novelist's right to a 'prudent prodigality'. Yet this carefully wrapped package is composed of fragments, small notations of difference, disconnected minute parts.

The ruse might better be expressed as the difference between what cognitive scientists call 'top-down', or 'frame-determined', and 'bottom-up', or 'data-determined' strategies of mental processing.[51] Seen from above, *The Egoist* presents a series of all-too-visible formal patterns, winkingly alluded to by Sir Willoughby's surname, Patterne. Seen from below—that is, seen from the perspective of the moment-to-moment detailed transactions of reading, rather than retrospective or distanced assessment—the novel offers a series of disconnected bits. Take, for example, the most immediately notable feature of Meredith's prose in the novel: the constant presence of unusual and virtually euphuistic vocabulary, strange or obsolete coinages, *hapax legomena*. The *OED* lists *The Egoist* as the sole source of nine words—including 'basiation' (kissing), 'epitonic' (overstrained), and 'bradypeptic' (slow of digestion)—while a mass of other terms, such as 'longinquity', 'fustigation', 'percoct', 'atrabiliar', 'cramoisy', 'anachronic', 'latrons', 'planguncula', and 'deglutition', to mention only the most obvious—are resurrected by Meredith from sixteenth- and seventeenth-century obscurity. In the effort to perform the etymological work necessary to construe Meredith's lexical oddities, larger ideas of form (plot, character symmetry) yield to unusually minute efforts at comprehension. It might be usefully remembered that Patterne Hall, throughout the novel, houses two forms of work: the unspecified scientific experiments of Sir Willoughby, which take place in the estate's laboratory, and the scholarly debates between Vernon Whitford and Dr Middleton on ancient Greek lexical and grammatical cruxes, which take place in the estate's library. Both are analytic pastimes, the breaking down of larger forms into smaller units, and both emblematize the act of reading the novel itself, in their seclusion and their careful minuteness.

---

[51] The terms are borrowed from the now-canonical sketch of a cognitive narrative theory by Manfred Jahn, 'Frames, Preferences, and the Reading of Third-Person Narratives: Towards a Cognitive Narratology', *Poetics Today* 18/4 (Winter 1997), 441–68.

On a less rarified level, the novel continually punctuates its elaborately peri-odic sentences and politely composed dialogues with single-word exclamatory bursts, minimal and nongrammatical explosions that virtually summarize a movement of plot or a psychological tendency of character without any appended narratorial comment. Starting with Sir Willoughby's haughty 'Not at home' to his unfashionable relative Lieutenant Crossjay Patterne—an exclamation that, observed by his then-fiancée Constantia Durham, leads to the end of his first engagement—a series of increasingly inarticulate units (as opposed to the hyperarticulacy of Meredith's *hapax legomena*) seizes the text. Sir Willoughby interrupts Clara's first formal request for freedom with an outraged call to a trespassing former servant: 'Flitch!' (*E*, 147). This is followed later by more distressed ejaculations, as Sir Willoughby successively utters 'Fooled!' and 'Deceit!' in relation to his (misguided) surmise that Clara and Horace have formed an intimacy; finally he is reduced, during Laetitia Dale's rejection of his first marriage proposal to her, to the simple phoneme 'Oh!' (*E*, 353, 372, 477). Other characters break out into similar monoverbal bursts: Clara frustratedly screams 'Marriage!'; the normally epigrammatic Mrs Mountstuart Jenkinson can only manage a wondering 'Twice!' at the imminent spectacle of Sir Willoughby being jilted again; and Laetitia must summon up a firm 'No!' to Sir Willoughby's marriage proposal (*E*, 273, 452, 475). Joining Meredith's flaunted lexical obscurities on the level of the minimal unit are a series of heatedly emotional ordinary terms that encapsulate, or condense, strong affect in what we might call a prearticulate manner. At its strongest, affect in *The Egoist* erupts into the simplest of isolated sounds.

This, then, is the first level of the novel's fragmented form: its tendency, at the level of the word, phrase, or sentence, to present units detached from the flow of reading-as-usual. In the novel's 'Prelude', Meredith explains this as the central function of Comedy (an idea not present in the *Essay on Comedy*): a practice of condensation, in both writing and reading, as an aid to understanding. Meredith begins the novel by summoning up the ghost of the largest and most spectral of his inset texts, 'a certain big book, the biggest book on earth; that might indeed be called the Book of Earth; whose title is the Book of Egoism', a Book that, 'to be profitable to us,' needs 'a powerful compression' (*E*, 33). The vast windiness of narcissism is deflated and made comprehensible by the puncturing precisions of comic wit. Yet the metaphor—Egoism as Book, Comedy as saving compression of that book—stubbornly refuses to stay metaphorical. As the Prelude proceeds, in fact, the Book of Egoism merges into the contemporary novel. Citing an archetypal 'humourist,' Meredith adds:

In other words, as I venture to translate him (humourists are difficult: it is a piece of their humour to puzzle our wits), the inward mirror, the embracing and condensing spirit, is required to give us those interminable milepost piles of matter (extending well-nigh to the very Pole) in essence, in chosen samples, digestibly. I conceive him to indicate that the realistic method of a conscientious transcription of all the visible, and a repetition of all the audible, is mainly accountable for our present branfulness, and that prolongation of the vasty and the noisy, out of which, as from an undrained fen, steams the malady of sameness, our modern malady. (*E*, 34)

The narcissism of the Book of Egoism becomes the sheer length and detail of the Victorian novel of the 'realistic method', figured by endless mileposts (upon one of which Horace's porcelain vase will shatter), digestive obstruction, and swampy agriculture. The turn in the Prelude—from metaphorical Book to ubiquitous novel—pivots on the notion of comprehension. What makes the Book of Egoism akin to the realistic novel is its 'unvaried length', which defeats efforts of understanding; both must yield to what Meredith calls the Comic Spirit, which is invoked in the language of textual materiality: 'it condenses whole sections of the book in a sentence, volumes in a character; so that a fair part of a book outstripping thousands of leagues when unrolled may be compassed in one comic sitting' (*E*, 35). The Book of Egoism, mirrored by the contemporary novel, becomes here a *volumen* that, via comedy, becomes a readable, short codex.

Readable because short: comedy, in the novel's Prelude, is not merely a mode of presentation but a mode of consumption, a hunting for small differences. 'Why, to be alive, to be quick in the soul, there should be diversity in the companion throbs of your pulses,' Meredith proclaims, using organic language—crucially the updated organicity of physiology: nerves and recurrent pulsations—to describe the effects of small-scale penetration. This practice of detecting the minute is what goes under the name of Comedy. 'Comedy', Meredith summarizes, 'he pronounces to be our means of reading swiftly and comprehensively' (*E*, 35–6). The argument of the Prelude is condensed, in fact, in the embedded pun in the final word: to be 'comprehensive', or to understand, one should not be 'comprehensive', or large-scale. The comprehensible is the small, the slightly shifting, the minutely discriminatory. This is a theory of novelistic form and reading cognition masked as a theory of Comedy and Egoism; however abstract the terms of the Prelude, the contemporaneity and materiality of the argument (novels, the 'realistic method', reading in a sitting, diversity of pulsations) erupts from underneath.

Caveats lurk everywhere in *The Egoist* about small-scale units, however, most notably in Meredith's career-long concern about the value and utility of aphorisms. In *The Egoist* they are often monuments to stupidity or malice: 'Frequently indeed, in the contest between gentlemen and ladies, have the maxims of the Book stimulated the assailant to victory. They are rosy with blood of victims' (*E*, 495). When not simply misogynistic—we are reminded that 'the Book' is largely the work of men—they are misleading; in one of the novel's more veiled parables, Vernon Whitford is sent by Mrs Mountstuart Jenkinson, the novel's primary aphorist, to the railway station to pick up a Professor Crooklyn, armed only with a putatively precise description of his appearance. Her witty description of his face ('complexion of a sweetbread, consistency of a quenelle, grey, and like a Saint without his dish') is literally one-sided, however, and Vernon, who sees only the back of what he takes to be 'an old gentleman of dark complexion', leaves the station without the professor, who promptly catches cold on the rainy platform (*E*, 370). The epigrammatic fails to be plainly referential, and instead remains sealed in self-referentiality; at real-world work, it conspicuously fails.[52] The smallness of epigrams is also loosely associated in the novel with the work of 'cutting': of cleverly wounding, of minutely separating, and of socially disregarding in a cruel manner. Sir Willoughby, we are told, was 'supremely advanced at a very early age in the art of cutting' (*E*, 41).[53] By worrying so visibly about the social or political impact of verbal forms like epigrams, Meredith sets the stage for what has been the dominant critical argument about *The Egoist*: whether or not the novel's avowedly feminist content—the liberation of Clara Middleton from strangulating male egoism—is belied by a formal polish that conservatively shuts doors that Meredith's content would wish to open.[54]

The liberatory/conservative poles might not, however, be the most profitable through which to view the social effects of Meredith's chosen textual practices. Instead, a coding of what literary forms and reading practices had what

[52] See John Goode for a reading of *The Egoist* as a critique of Comtean positivism, with its ideology of progress through self-conscious egoism or self-realization; for Goode, 'the novel sees the psychology of self-consciousness primarily in terms of reflection and therefore of enclosure'. See John Goode, '*The Egoist*: Anatomy or Striptease?', in *Meredith Now: Some Critical Essays*, ed. Ian Fletcher (New York: Barnes and Noble, 1971), 212.

[53] This discourse of 'cutting', as Margaret Tarrant has noticed, links in complex ways with the occupations of Meredith's father and grandfather, who were both Portsmouth tailors, a fact that Meredith took pains to conceal during his lifetime. See Margaret Tarrant, ' "Snips," "Snobs," and the "True Gentleman" in *Evan Harrington*', in *Meredith Now*, 95–113. The discourse of cutting recurs uncannily in much Meredith criticism, as in Virginia Woolf's assessment: 'His teaching seems now too strident and too optimistic and too shallow. It obtrudes; and when philosophy is not consumed in a novel, when we can underline this phrase with a pencil, and cut out that exhortation with a pair of scissors and paste the whole into a system, it is safe to say that there is something wrong with the philosophy or with the novel or with both.' See Virginia Woolf, 'The Novels of George Meredith', in *The Second Common Reader* (New York: Harcourt, Brace, 1932), 211.

[54] The most cogent argument for the ideological conflict between form and content in the novel is offered by Carolyn Williams in 'Unbroken Patternes: Gender, Culture, and Voice in *The Egoist*', *Browning Institute Studies* 13 (1985), 45–70. McWhirter's 'Imagining a Distance' offers a subtle argument that rehabilitates Meredithian 'form' as a process rather than a conservative structure.

social meaning in Meredith's time might offer a clearer view of the stakes of Meredith's form, and might help dissolve the form/content dichotomy that most critics of *The Egoist* rely upon. The example of the aphorism is particularly telling. The practices of the small-scale that Meredith most disavows (aphorisms, maxims, 'cutting') derive, in his account, from a desire to remain pure or uncontaminated, to have polish or finish—ultimately, from a 'high' aesthetic of formal perfection. Against these practices of the minute, Meredith insists instead on a fragmented comprehension that dispenses with polish or formal 'pattern', aligning himself with a disreputable habit of 'bit' reading—skimming, dipping, skipping—that was often coded as a low aesthetic of mass consumption. Assessments of the reading of the mass public, particularly in the 1870s and 1880s, turned frequently to the problem of reading in bits; in one such piece from 1886 in the *Quarterly Review*, the author warily admits that some books—Horace, Boswell's *Life of Johnson*—could be profitably read by a 'snatchy method of perusal', but that 'such moments should as a rule be devoted to books which are already more or less familiar. The habit of frivolously taking up, and as frivolously casting aside, a book is, however, one which should be guarded against with the utmost care. . . . This thoughtless, fragmentary reading has debilitated the contemporary mental fibre of the nation; and has so absorbed the time, we cannot say the attention, of the immense majority of the reading public, that many of them are ignorant even of the existence of the standard works of literature.'[55] As Leah Price has recently argued, the question of part versus whole cut in confusing and often arbitrary ways across a social landscape of the Victorian novel-reading public.[56] Here, symptomatically, a discontinuous reading of parts is sanctioned for learned audiences, as a kind of humanist contemplation, while discountenanced for a mass audience as a commodified consumption. The cunning irony of *The Egoist*'s form is that it is aligned with what could be taken as nonstandard, or 'low', reading practices—the novel's Prelude virtually calls for the 'fragmentary reading' and 'snatchy perusal' that this commentator laments—but that it veils these fragments in an elaborate armature of self-parodically high obscurity and literariness. Meredith's vaunted difficulty might be the mask for a populist notion of novel-reading: hence, perhaps, the energy that the novel expends in disavowing more elite practices (such as aphoristic wit) that look like fragments but are actually still embedded in formalist perfection. This irony, if present, has been so successful that Meredith's reviewers fall into its trap without exception: when

[55] Anon., 'Books and Reading', *Quarterly Review* 162 (1886), 515–18.
[56] See Price, *Anthology and the Rise of the Novel*, 149–56, for a discussion of the social valences of part reading before and after George Eliot.

they extol the ways in which his novels force a reader into a 'line by line', bit-by-bit reading, they miss the connection that this reading practice has with its more disreputable cousins in the Victorian mass literary market. Nowhere is this more evident than in Meredith's textual metaphors, as when he envisions, in his Prelude, a scholarly 'scroll' metamorphosing, via Comedy, into the comfortable and more temporally limited confines of a 'book'.

Shattering comfortable, and comfortably deluded, wholes into fragments is, after all, the novel's psychological work and the occasion of its most charged moments. When Clara tests Sir Willoughby's resolve to never release a spouse by asking 'not if she ran . . . ?', his understanding of the possibilities of female psychology is tested: 'His ideal, the common male Egoist ideal of a waxwork sex, would have been shocked to fragments had she spoken further to fill in the outlines of these awful interjections' (*E*, 195). Laetitia, her admiration of Sir Willoughby enlightened by his frantic attempts at managing Clara's defection, no longer thinks of him as a whole: 'But now she admired him piecemeal. When it came to the putting of him together, she did it coldly' (*E*, 391).[57] Clara herself, thinking over her sudden and unanswerable desire to flee her engagement, finds herself 'disintegrating and crumbling' (*E*, 423).[58] The ironic intent of *The Egoist*'s plot is to continually take Sir Willoughby, who considers his actions and motives as massively consistent and of a piece, and subject him to a recognition of his warring impulses, ambivalences, and inconsistencies—not simply to make his actions at war with his motives, but to show the very motives as self-conflicting, fragmented. Hence the relish with which Meredith charts the 'mood of hugging hatred' with which Sir Willoughby approaches Clara, a mood that is explained with reference to a dramatic instance of piecemeal, fragmentary reading:

(For these mysteries, consult the sublime chapter in the Great Book, the Seventy-First on Love, wherein nothing is written, but the Reader receives a Lanthorn, a Powder-cask, and a Pick-axe, and therewith pursues his yellow-dusking path across the rubble of preceding excavators in the solitary quarry: a yet more instructive passage than the overscrawled Seventieth, or French Section, whence the chapter opens, and where hitherto the polite world has halted.) (*E*, 347)

The mining metaphor takes us back, in fact, to Nevil Beauchamp reading Carlyle, 'getting nibbles of golden meaning by instalments'. Digging for

---

[57] R. H. Hutton plays off this line in his review of the novel, writing that Meredith 'describes his characters admirably, piecemeal; when it comes to the putting of them together, he does it coldly', thereby making of Meredith the same charge that Lewes makes of Dickens: the fragmentary, unorganic quality of his characters. See Hutton, 'Mr. George Meredith's New Novel', 1384.

[58] Clara's 'disintegrations' are the occasion of J. Hillis Miller's classically deconstructive reading of the novel, which reads the chapter 'Clara's Meditations' as a paradigm for the slippage of a unitary 'self' into its multiple determinations; see Miller, ' "Herself Against Herself" '.

valuable bits seems consistently to have been Meredith's image for worthwhile reading, and it is an image with a definite relation to the 'fragmentary' or 'snatchy' reading that commentators on mass reading denigrated.

One objection to this linkage might run as follows: that the 'snatchy' reading condemned in the *Quarterly Review* is only half-attentive, whereas Meredith's reading-as-mining image pictures a total, if locally fixated, attention, and that therefore the two kinds of fragmentary comprehension are radically different in quality. Following this logic, the snatchy reader takes up only in order to cast aside, whereas Meredith's reader is stuck in the mine, resolutely pursuing treasure. That difference is dissolved, however, in *The Egoist*, which consistently refers to the claustrophobia and panic of, in essence, not being able to put a book down. Sir Willoughby's triumphant paean to the virtue of shutting oneself off from the world is one telling instance. 'I am, we will say, riding home from the hunt,' he tells Clara; 'I see you awaiting me; I read your heart as though you were beside me. And I know that I am coming to the one who reads mine! You have me, you have me like an open book, you, and only you!' To this invitation to read and keep reading, Clara asks the agonized question: 'I am to be always at home?' (*E*, 99). Or: I am to never put that book down? The submergence of total, immersive, continuous reading in *The Egoist* suddenly seems like being trapped, while fragmentary reading seems imbricated with the world, ventilated by the air of life's other activities. Much in line with Anthony Trollope's admission in his *Autobiography* that reading novels for more than an hour and a half continuously disrupts any pleasure, Clara's question implies that the rhythm of starting and stopping reading, the rhythm of interrupting fiction with life, is preferable to the insistence upon the whole made by formalists and cultural commentators.[59] Meredith's minimal form works against the claustrophobia of continuous reading; it promises instead the rewards of small-scale attention, of the shock of quick, even if shattering, discovery over the confirmations of monolithic cultural narratives. Seen as *minimal* form, Meredith's form is far less at war with his content than most of his critics have assumed, and far more of a challenge to hierarchies of status than it has usually seemed.

---

[59] See Anthony Trollope, *An Autobiography*, ed. P. D. Edwards (Oxford: Oxford University Press, 1980), 158. As Franco Moretti has argued, it is the chapter, among the many features of the novel form, which best reflects this fact of novel-reading: 'the chapter balances our satisfaction with what we have learned (the meaning that has been attributed to an event) and our curiosity for what we still do not know (that meaning is as a rule always imcomplete). We can thus continue our reading (giving in to our curiosity) or interrupt it (declaring ourselves satisfied). The narrative structure authorizes both choices and thereby renders symbolically plausible the irregular rhythm of interruptions and resumptions to which the reader is in any case constrained by the size of the novel.' See Moretti, *Way of the World*, 252.

THE EGOIST, II: LOGARITHMIC AFFECT

There is in *The Egoist* a persistent temporal mystery, masked by the swiftness and constriction of the novel's time scheme: when, exactly, is Clara disillusioned enough with Sir Willoughby to desire her freedom? The novel refuses to narrate this affective shift as either a climactic occurrence or an accretive series of gradual disillusionments. Instead, it narrates the frustration of Clara's several foiled, gradually more drastic, attempts at escape, and leaves open the question when, or how, her change of heart happened; it can even seem as if the change predates the events of the novel itself, given that her first cited words are the 'chilling' addendum 'as far as I am concerned' to Sir Willoughby's declaration that their engagement 'is written above' (*E*, 73). This sequential opacity of her emotion (when did it happen?) makes Clara a common type among Meredith's characters, who are rapid, not carefully rational, thinkers, given to sudden illuminations that make invisible the determining conditions of those illuminations. The motto for Meredith's protagonists might be given by Diana Warwick in *Diana of the Crossways*, who admits that 'she read rapidly, "a great deal at one gulp," and thought in flashes—a way with the makers of phrases' (*DC*, xvii. 9); or Richard Feverel, of whom Meredith claims that 'the true hero . . . does not plot: Fortune does all for him. He may be compared to one to whom, in an electric circle, it is given to carry the battery. We caper and grimace at his will: yet not his the will, not his the power' (*RF*, 228).

Thought in Meredith seems to come in surges: unpredictable, unaccountable leaps or explosions, less a 'stream' of consciousness than the stream plunged into briefly and selectively.[60] One of Meredith's most enthusiastic critics, the poet and journalist Alice Meynell, reassessed *The Egoist* in 1895 as an attempt to provide, within narrative, the illusion of sudden thought. Meynell argued that in Meredith

the thought of the thinker and the speaker in his drama of passions seems to reflect itself like a mirror that faces a mirror. You look and know not whether you see a certain thing reflected directly or for the third time; nor how many times, visibly, the shuttlecock of thought is returned by opposing shocks. . . . The reflection of mirrors takes no time, the reflection of motives little, the narrative more; but the suggestion,

---

[60] Gillian Beer's formulation is instructive: 'Meredith is particularly successful in his portrayals of articulate people: and he repeatedly shows that intelligence does not automatically bestow self-knowledge. The act of analysis is in itself an act of dramatisation. It is set apart from the amorphousness of continuous being.' See Beer, *Meredith*, 142.

at least, of instantaneousness is given in the long phrase that includes so many actions of the mind.[61]

Discussions of Meredith's style often turned to images of 'flashes' or brief 'shocks'; Geraldine Jewsbury lamented the 'fatiguing' quality of Meredith's prose, calling it 'the succession of sharp blows eliciting sparks'.[62] The shocks, however, are minor, slight readjustments of sensation or perception, rather than pivotal occurrences that could be classified as nodes or turning-points of plot. That they resist narrative conscription is best illustrated by the 1898 play script of *The Egoist* on which Meredith collaborated with the dramatist Alfred Sutro. In its stage form, which remained unproduced, the final ten chapters of the novel, starting with Sir Willoughby's abortive first marriage proposal to Laetitia—the novel's final fifth—are expanded into two and a half of the play's five acts; most of the novel's actions are compressed into a little over two acts, as its carefully minute notations of Clara's reactions to Willoughby's egoism disappear.[63] One might deduce that Meredith believed that the stage could not display the flashes of seemingly instantaneous thought and sensation that occupy much of the novel's texture—flashes that, we might say, are the 'just noticeable differences' of Meredith's characters.

The Fechnerian unit of consciousness, the jnd, is the structuring principle of most of *The Egoist*'s attenuated confrontations. We know from the outset that both Clara and Sir Willoughby are minutely perceptive; Clara has the gift of 'quickness at catching the hue and shade of evanescent conversation', while Sir Willoughby 'could be preternaturally acute in reading any of his fellow-creatures if they crossed the current of his feelings' (*E*, 76, 127). This dance of minimal perceptions is expressed in a series of deliberately subtle interactions between the two which hinge on the notation of minute, or 'just noticeable', perceptions. One representative scene is Clara's reaction to Sir Willoughby's plan to take on the young Crossjay Patterne as a protégé rather than educate him for the Navy:

> 'I propose to make a man of him,' said Sir Willoughby.
> 'What is to become of him if he learns nothing?'
> 'If he pleases me, he will be provided for. I have never abandoned a dependent.'
> Clara let her eyes rest on his and, without turning or dropping, shut them.
> The effect was disconcerting to him. He was very sensitive to the intentions of eyes and tones; which was one secret of his rigid grasp of the dwellers in his household. They

---

[61] Alice Meynell, 'Mr. George Meredith's New Book', *Illustrated London News* 107 (14 Dec., 1895), 734.

[62] Jewsbury, 'New Novels', *Athenaeum* 1905 (30 April, 1864), 610.

[63] See George Meredith, *The Egoist [A Play]: From the Novel by George Meredith, Arranged for the Stage by George Meredith and Alfred Sutro*, ed. Lewis Sawin, (Athens: Ohio University Press, 1981).

were taught that they had to render agreement under sharp scrutiny. Studious eyes, devoid of warmth, devoid of the shyness of sex, that suddenly closed on their look, signified a want to comprehension of some kind, it might be hostility of understanding. Was it possible he did not possess her utterly? He frowned up.

Clara saw the lift of his brows, and thought, 'My mind is my own, married or not.'

It was the point in dispute. (*E*, 113)

The slightest of physical movements—the shutting of eyelids, the lifting of a brow—are the scene's determinants, far more so than the spoken dialogue, which, while balder than the minute adjustments of facial expression, is less effective at conveying intention. In such moments, Meredith dramatizes the psychophysical question: what is the smallest change in perception that can be noticed? In other scenes, we hear of even more precise measurements of such perceptions, as when Sir Willoughby boasts of his acuteness to Laetitia: 'I dread changes. The shadow of the tenth of an inch in the customary elevation of an eyelid!—to give you an idea of my susceptibility.' When Laetitia responds coldly to this boast, Meredith describes his (barely registered) disappointment: 'he was not less acutely sensitive to the fractional divisions of tones than of eyelids' (*E*, 182). A precise definition of the jnd—a 'fractional division' of sensation—explains both the fractures in Sir Willoughby's stranglehold over his estate and Clara's eventually effective rebellion against it. Like psychophysical mathematics, the affective paths of Meredith's characters are broken down into the smallest isolated units. At moments like these the minimal habits of Meredith's prose (*hapax legomena*, monoverbal bursts) join the minute registrations of difference of his characters in depicting a world of disjointed, sudden perceptions. Clara's resolution to remain free is formed in such moments: when she 'reviews' Sir Willoughby, the review 'was all in one flash . . . occupying about a minute in time, and reached through a series of intensely vivid pictures'; the result of which is the ejaculation, 'I cannot!' (*E*, 251).

Here, however, we return to the temporal mystery of the novel: when exactly do the minute sensations (or jnds) of Clara's dislike burst into a determination to oppose Sir Willoughby? This is the central question of Fechnerian psychophysics as well: what do we make of the units of sensation that are not noticed (the slight additions to a weight, for instance) prior to the one final slight addition that brings extra weight to our consciousness? Fechner's answer was to describe these preconscious differences, or below-threshold stimuli, as evidence of a collective unconscious, a 'world mind'. Meredith's answer is to provide a new temporality for the buried or below-threshold units of consciousness, one that is essentially unnarratable until after the fact of its bursting upon consciousness: a temporality of sudden affect that, following Fechnerian lines, is essentially logarithmic, a curve of exponentially exploding sensation that starts slowly and builds with sudden power; a temporality that paradoxically mixes the gradual and the instantaneous. It is best explained by Clara in her response to Mrs Mountstuart Jenkinson's outraged catechism, in a statement that reads as both childishly confused and maturely precise:

> 'I have found that I do not . . .'
> 'What?'
> 'Love him.'
> Mrs Mountstuart grimaced transiently. 'That is no answer. The cause!' she said.
> 'What has he done?'
> 'Nothing.'
> 'And when did you discover this nothing?'
> 'By degrees; unknown to myself; suddenly.' (*E*, 424)

Clara's paradox—later exasperatedly caricatured by Mrs Mountstuart as '*gradually* you *suddenly* discovered' (*E*, 429)—is as exact a description of the logarithm at the heart of Fechner's Psychophysical Law as could be desired. By a series of additive but below-threshold stimuli, a gradual fact builds until it suddenly becomes evident in one, potentially quite small, perception. The result is a confused temporality, one that feels instantaneous and isolated but that nonetheless bears hints of its long preconscious formation. The burst, or spark, or fractional division, or fragmented sensation, has a history, but not a history that can be known. Meredith's narrative can then perform two functions: mimic the instantaneousness of thought, as in Meynell's formulation, or suggest (through paradoxes like Clara's) the temporality of affect that feels too sudden to have a temporality. To the question, when did it happen?, the novel responds cunningly: it just happened; it was always happening.

This, it bears remarking, is close to, but crucially different from, the novels of James as read by Lubbock, where (as in Lubbock's analysis of *The Wings of the Dove* discussed in Chapter 1) revelation takes the form of an 'enlightening word' that 'did not seem peculiarly emphatic as it was uttered, it was not announced with any particular circumstance; and yet, presently—there was the piece of knowledge that I had not possessed before': in other words, sudden revelation masking a gradual accumulation of perceptions.[64] What stood for Lubbock as the perfect *Gestalten* of James's plots—temporality canceled in the moment of discovery—tends in Meredith to work instead as the elaborate description *of* the hidden temporality of discovery. Lubbock's James, in other words, could become the paradigm for noetic materialist novel theory, for static formalist structure, whereas Meredith's notations of

---

[64] Percy Lubbock, *The Craft of Fiction* (New York: Viking, 1957), 176.

discovery as a psychophysical threshold crossing seek to hold in tension both the newness and the long lineage of any perception. We are asked in *The Egoist* to recognize the gradual accumulation of what happens suddenly, whereas for Lubbock, James makes our recognition of gradual accumulation (i.e. of time passing, of our past reading) unnecessary in one magnificent gesture of sudden summarization. Slight as the difference may seem, it is the key distinction between Lubbock's '*now* I understand' and Meredith's 'now I understand what I was *always* understanding' that separates twentieth-century novelistic formalism from late Victorian formalism.

The psychophysical formulation of *The Egoist*—affect that gradually happens suddenly—is a narrative solution (modeled on a mathematical one) to the problem that lurked within physiological novel theory's engagement with organic form: how to combine the single, fragmented, and 'mechanical' unit with the seemingly organic wave signature beloved of physiologists. In Meredith's work, the wave becomes a logarithmic curve, while the discontinuous moment or unit, represented as a jnd, stands in for a mute and invisible history of steady accretion over time. Emotion, passion, affect, all happen at once, pointing nonetheless to a largely unknowable process of formation. Crucially, these sudden perceptions—built out of small adjustments of sensation—are finally, in *The Egoist*, liberatory. The minute, the fragmented—in essence, unit comprehension—carries in Meredith the burden of release, a release that is always both psychological and social: the long-unnoticed coming to consciousness.

THE DISCONTINUOUS PUBLIC

Fragmentary comprehension and popular audiences: the linkage is a well-trodden one in the history of reading. In a 1983 dialogue between Pierre Bourdieu and Roger Chartier the point is made explicitly. As Bourdieu puts it first: 'un texte à longs paragraphes s'adresse à un public plus choisi qu'un texte découpé en petits paragraphes. Cela repose sur l'hypothèse qu'un public plus populaire demandera un discourse plus discontinu, etc. Ainsi l'opposition entre le long et le court, qui peut se manifester de multiples façons, est une indication sur le public visé et, du meme coup, sur l'idée que l'auteur a de lui-même, de son rapport aves les autres auteurs' ('a text with long paragraphs is aimed at a more select public than one divided into short ones. This is based on the hypothesis that a lower-class public requires a more discontinuous discourse. Hence the opposition between long and short, which can take many different forms, is an index to the envisioned public of a text and, at the same time, of the image the author has of himself and of his relation to other authors').[65] Chartier responds affirmatively, with a general claim about printing history: 'Quand un texte passe d'un niveau de circulation à un autre, plus populaire, il subit un certain nombre de transformations dont l'une des plus claires est la fragmentation opérée dans la mise en livre, aussi bien au niveau de chapitre qu'au niveau du paragraphe, et destinée à faciliter une lecture point virtuose' ('When a text goes from one level of circulation to another, more lower-class one, it undergoes a certain number of changes, one of the most evident being fragmentation in its textual presentation, at the chapter and paragraph level both. These changes are meant to facilitate a less virtuosic reading').[66] Backed up by an enormous range of evidence across the study of the European book, the claims made here are essentially canonical. The more discontinuous the form or appearance of a text, the lower its intended audience in the social scale of the time.

Yet, in regards to Meredith, this central dictum of book history seems initially inapplicable. His novels are thoroughly fragmented at the level of plot (which veers away from seamlessness to discontinuity), of diction (which tends toward the epigrammatic, the gnomic, and the agrammatical), and of character psychology (which, as we have seen, becomes a matter of sudden lurches and discoveries); yet they were, by virtually unanimous consent, viewed as the most rarified example possible of the Victorian novel. Meredith's emphasis on the minute and the fragmentary courted the accusations of the most censorious observers of popular reading habits, who (as in one anonymous piece from 1861) inveighed against 'the importance which a large part of the popular literature of the day attaches, and encourages those who read it to attach, to trifles'; or who complained, like Arnold Haultain in his 1896 essay 'How to Read', about 'discursive and indiscriminate' reading, a practice of understanding parts and not wholes of books.[67] The small and the partial receive largely poor press in late Victorian literary criticism and theory, as the province of ignorant audiences only. John Ruskin saw danger in the contemporary novel's tendency toward fragmentation, warning in his 1865 lecture 'Of Queen's Gardens' that 'the temptation to picturesqueness of statement' of modern novelists rendered the ethical teachings of their novels inoperable.[68] It is no accident, perhaps, that Meredith named his

---

[65] Pierre Bourdieu and Roger Chartier, 'La lecture: une pratique culturelle', in *Pratiques de la lecture*, ed. Roger Chartier (Paris: Rivages, 1985), 222.

[66] Ibid. 223.

[67] Anon., 'Dignity', *Cornhill Magazine* 3 (1861), 589; Haultain, 'How to Read', *Blackwood's Edinburgh Magazine* 159 (1896), 250.

[68] John Ruskin, 'Of Queen's Gardens', in *Sesame and Lilies*, ed. Harold Bloom (New York: Chelsea House, 1983), 95.

most politically radical figure, in *Beauchamp's Career*, 'Shrapnel'. By so ostentatiously fragmenting his discourse, and by so visibly concerning himself with fragmentary comprehension, Meredith would seem to have risked these charges of a too-popular discourse. Instead, however, he was seen as abstract and obscure, an example of the almost decadent development of the Victorian novel toward ever more rarified and mandarin segments of the market.

It is this paradox, in fact—Meredith's appeal to supposedly popular reading practices in the guise of elaborately experimental, difficult prose form—that argues most for his importance in any history of novel-reading in Britain. What we might say is that Meredith attempted the use of literary fragmentation as a means to social reintegration. As aware as any contemporary historian of reading of the constantly subdividing form of the book and of audiences, Meredith openly appeals to the devices of textual and psychological fragmentation that were seen, then as now, as the effects of mass reading; but by connecting those devices to an older, more elite notion of literary 'parts', such as aphorisms and epigrams, Meredith sought to connect the part reading of privileged readers with the part reading of the new Victorian reading public. Haultain's 'How to Read', for instance, laments the discursive reading habits of the masses while advocating, for educated readers, skipping, skimming, the transcription of important passages, and marking crucial phrases—an ideological division that Meredith's novels, formally and thematically, seek to heal.[69] The *hapax legomena*, in other words, is no different from the incoherent exclamation; Clara's supposedly childlike, feminine confusion is no different from her acute, swift perception. Meredith's minimal form attempts to straddle high and low, abjected and consecrated. Vernon Lee's later novel theory followed Meredith by using as a heuristic a practice (partial or minute notations of small patches of text) that, socially, was potentially disreputable; by starting with the minimal unit, Lee's criticism sought the same kind of destratification of reading modes as Meredith's fiction.

The vision of Meredith's novels, like Lee's theory after it, is therefore of a reading public made whole by virtue of a culture-wide practice of reading in parts, an 'extensive' public made into a community by virtue of the fragmentary 'intensities' of their reading.[70] The attempt was, of course, a

[69] See Haultain, 'How to Read', 264–5: 'Never read a book without pencil in hand . . . the careful transcription of striking, beautiful, or important passages is a tremendous aid to the memory . . . learn the "accomplishments of skipping and skimming"; learn, in short, how to "eat the heart out of" such books.'

[70] In this I concur, although with a significantly different emphasis, with Judith Wilt's claim that Meredith sought not the 'coterie reader' or the 'class reader' but the 'civilized reader', a reader trained out of narrow self-identifications. See Judith Wilt, *The Readable People of George Meredith* (Princeton: Princeton University Press, 1975), 53–4.

failure; ideological blindnesses like those in Haultain's article continued neatly to separate the approved skipping of the educated reader from the inattentive scrappy perusals of the uneducated reader, the one grasping the pith of an argument, the other hurriedly digesting bits of text. Social codes, that is, continued to mark differently reading practices that bore striking similarities to each other. The result was Meredith's posthumous disappearance from popular and elite canon alike: too difficult and idiosyncratic to represent the Victorian novel-as-usual, too fragmented and sloppily organized to be treated as a *chef-d'œuvre* of Victorian narrative art, as the renascence of 'organic form' in the early twentieth century doomed Meredith's different notions of organicity to neglect. It is the chastening lesson of Meredith's career that his attempt to indicate the uncanny similarity between ostensibly disparate and stratified reading modes resulted in a drastic example—perhaps the preeminent such example—of subsequent effacement from reading lists, reprints, and general cultural currency.

5

The Eye as Motor: Gissing and Speed-Reading (Accelerated Form)

> 'If Steam has done nothing else, it has at least added a whole new Species to English Literature!'
>
> 'No doubt of it,' I echoed. 'The true origin of all our medical books—and all our cookery-books—'
>
> 'No, no!' she broke in merrily. 'I didn't mean *our* Literature! *We* are quite abnormal. But the booklets—the little thrilling romances, where the Murder comes at page fifteen, and the Wedding at page forty—surely *they* are due to Steam?'
>
> 'And when we travel by Electricity—if I may venture to develop your theory—we shall have leaflets instead of booklets, and the Murder and the Wedding will come on the same page.'
>
> Lewis Carroll, *Sylvie and Bruno*

Although exact figures by word or page count are unavailable and most likely unattainable, the evidence is nonetheless fairly clear: in the last two decades of the nineteenth century, the British novel began to contract in size. As the familiar and reassuring girth of Eliot and Trollope yielded to the comparative brevity of Stevenson, Kipling, and Wells—a reduction in size accelerated by the demise of the three-volume novel in 1894—observers of the phenomenon of literary shrinking began to wonder if the decline was caused by a reading public less interested in prolonged texts, or was instead gradually creating a public without the cognitive equipment necessary for their consumption. The atmosphere of textual condensation was only exacerbated by the wave of short, wildly successful periodical digests, such as George Newnes's well-known *Tit-Bits*, which started in 1881 and, by 1890, was reaching circulation figures upwards of 500,000 a week.[1] As media historians such as Laurel Brake

---

[1] For circulation figures, see Richard Altick, *The English Common Reader: A Social History of the Mass Reading Public* (Chicago: University of Chicago Press, 1957), 396; Terence Nevett, 'Advertising', in *Victorian Periodicals and Victorian Society*, ed. J. Don Vann and Rosemary

have noted, the brevity of the press was matched by the decreasing intervals of publication, 'from quarterlies to monthlies to weeklies, to more than once a week, to dailies and to evening dailies', a rate compression that, Brake claims, altered 'the perception of time in relation to print culture'.[2] Whether these shorter and faster-appearing texts were merely responding to a general incapacity for lengthy reading, or were wholly responsible for the lack of sustained reading abilities, their effect was pervasively bemoaned. 'That their general tendency is to stimulate superficial, cursory, and scrappy reading can scarcely be questioned,' wrote Joseph Ackland in *The Nineteenth Century* in 1894, shortly before the publishing industry would be forced to abandon the large novels of the past.[3] The solid, respectable bulk of mid-Victorian publishing formats and literary forms, from the multi-plot, three-volume novel to the dense monthly periodical, was clearly yielding to less imposing packages, a development as apparent as it was difficult to quantify or explain. An era of the 'cursory' or the 'scrappy' in reading habits was widely proclaimed as a result.

Another way of phrasing it—which adds considerably to the complexity of the cultural and literary-historical situation—is that the era saw a notable acceleration of both textual forms and consumption habits: that *speed*, alongside size, was a key factor here, and that starting in the 1880s the British novel, along with periodical publications, entered into a modern dynamics of continual speed-rate increases that we tend to associate with industries such as transportation (the railroad and automobile) and information (the telegraph, telephone, and microprocessor).[4] The shortening of forms was conceived of as a manifestation of an ever growing rapidity of consumption, of scanning, skimming, or the reading of 'bits'; the reader envisioned by commentators on publishing changes in the 1880s and in the 1890s was, for the first time, a 'speed-reader'. The anachronism of that term is in fact only apparent: the

VanArsdel (Toronto: University of Toronto Press, 1994), 223. Nevett's figure of 900,000 per week is significantly higher than Altick's more conservative sum, but not for that reason impossible.

[2] Laurel Brake, *Print in Transition, 1850–1910: Studies in Media and Book History* (Basingstoke: Palgrave, 2001), 11.

[3] Joseph Ackland, 'Elementary Education and the Decay of Literature', *Nineteenth Century* 35 (March 1894), 421. Ackland's piece was part of the *Nineteenth Century*'s sustained interest in the question of mass literacy in the 1880s and 1890s; see also Edward Salmon, 'What the Working Classes Read', *Nineteenth Century* 20 (July 1886), 108–17; and George Humphery, 'The Reading of the Working Classes', *Nineteenth Century* 33 (April 1893), 690–701.

[4] Relevant here are two widely noted structures to the modern interest in speed-rate increases: a search for either a physical limit to the acceleration (e.g. the speed of light), or a mathematical law governing the rate of increase, such as 'Moore's Law', the pronouncement by engineer Gordon Moore in 1965 that the capacity (or speed) of microprocessors is doubled every eighteen months. Insofar as the novel began to enter into the rhetorics of both natural limit and inevitable exponential increase, it entered the temporal world of industrial technology.

last two decades of the century saw the invention of the technologies of, and the cultural demand for, speed-reading, which this chapter will claim was tied intimately to changes in the form and content of fiction. As tends to be the case in charged moments in the history of speed, lamentations over the inevitability of acceleration were matched with attempts to adapt individuals to new regimes of velocity. While observers like Ackland discussed a readership already given over to the pleasures of rapid consumption, the physiology of optics, for all intents born in the late 1870s, proclaimed a need for methods to train faster readers, primarily by producing faster, more efficient eyes and bodies. This new field of inquiry constructed the reader as a body turned into a machine by the act of reading, a wholly different object of knowledge from the participant in a literate endeavor envisioned by literary criticism or sociology.

To the cultural historian, the picture is a confused one: the late-century British reader is either far too fast or not nearly fast enough, and speed-reading is either a *fait accompli* or a distant goal. That confusion, however, is typical of the phenomenon of acceleration, which tends to produce a sense not only of 'too much' but also of 'not enough', and that precise contradiction characterizes the relationship between those who considered speed-reading from the perspective of class (concerned with mass readership) and those who considered it from the perspective of physical science (concerned with the capacity of the eye). Mediating between these two perspectives—their shared ground, in fact—was the materiality of the novel, which in the period of its sudden shortening became the site where the politics of speed and literacy was first hammered out.

What this chapter will explore, then, is the coalescence of two key moments in the history of novel-reading: the period in the 1890s which saw not only the collapse of the three-volume novel in Britain, a relatively well-studied moment, but also the effloresence of ophthalmologic physiology and its attendant techniques for measuring and accelerating the rates of readers, which has remained almost completely neglected. It will do so through the unlikely figure of George Gissing, who perhaps most stubbornly among major British novelists of the late nineteenth century held out against the pressure to decrease the size, or increase the speed, of his narratives. In Gissing's fiction, an acute awareness of the acceleration of reading rates—in fact, accelerations of perception generally—is set alongside a wounded self-consciousness about changes in publishing formats and changes in the composition of the audience for novels. Never an enthusiast for change, Gissing's dislike of the new regimes of speed becomes a topic of his mature fiction, from *New Grub Street* (1891) to *Born in Exile* (1892), *The Odd Women* (1893), *In the Year of Jubilee* (1894), and *The Whirlpool* (1897). In each of these novels, the conditions and processes of rapid comprehension—the birth of speed-readers—are overtly thematized even as they are formally resisted by a conservative narrative apparatus that retards rather than accelerates, and that anatomizes rather than satisfies, the desire for speed.

One result of this contextualizing is to recast Gissing as a novelist of textual consumption, not simply a novelist of production. His interest in the milieux and typical personalities of the late-century literary marketplace—novelists, journalists, publishers, editors, agents, hacks—is of course vivid and consistent. But that topical concern is always matched with an equally acute depiction of styles and manners of consumption, with reading his particular interest. Even those of his characters who are most obviously literary producers are still largely described through their ways of apprehending the world rather than reproducing it textually; those forms of apprehension are always figures for the kind of readers they are likely to be. Our introduction to *New Grub Street*'s Jasper Milvain occurs prior to his beginning his writing career, and situates him as someone with the cognitive and emotional abilities to appreciate tremendous speed:

'Will you indulge me in a piece of childishness?' he said. 'In less than five minutes a London express goes by; I have often watched it here, and it amuses me. Would it weary you to wait?'

'I should like to,' she replied with a laugh.

The line ran along a deep cutting, from either side of which grew hazel bushes and a few larger trees. Leaning upon the parapet of the bridge, Jasper kept his eye in the westward direction, where the gleaming rails were visible for more than a mile. Suddenly he raised his finger.

'You hear?'

Marian had just caught the far-off sound of the train. She looked eagerly, and in a few moments saw it approaching. The front of the engine blackened nearer and nearer, coming on with dread force and speed. A blinding rush, and there burst against the bridge a great volley of sunlit steam. Milvain and his companion ran to the opposite parapet, but already the whole train had emerged, and in a few seconds it had disappeared round a sharp curve. The leafy branches that grew out over the line swayed violently backwards and forwards in the perturbed air.

'If I were ten years younger,' said Jasper, laughing, 'I should say that was jolly! It inspirits me. It makes me feel eager to go back and plunge into the fight again.' (*NGS*, 63)[5]

Apprehension precedes production: if Jasper ends up becoming a writer whose primary talent is for quickness (of wit and of composition), his place in the

---

[5] Citations from Gissing's novels are given parenthetically, in the text, using the following abbreviations: *BE: Born in Exile*, ed. David Grylls (London: Everyman, 1993); *IYJ: In the Year of Jubilee*, ed. Paul Delany (London: Everyman, 1994); *NGS: New Grub Street*, ed. Bernard Bergonzi (Harmondsworth: Penguin, 1968); *OW: The Odd Women*, ed. Arlene Young (Peterborough: Broadview, 1998); *W: The Whirlpool*, ed. William Greenslade (London: Everyman, 1997).

literary field is securely predicted by his ability to consume speed as spectacle, to both see and enjoy velocity. As is characteristic of Gissing, exhilarations of speed are thoroughly mixed with a distate for that exhilaration; and the passage presents in miniature a further problem for Gissing, which is the extent to which speed can be described without being enacted. Put simply, do passages like this depict, or cater to, a desire for acceleration, for the pleasures of onrushing force? Can the two ever be severed?

Gissing's mature novels, then, offer not only sociologies of the late-nineteenth-century reading public of deserved interest, but also a curious formal balancing act with respect to the shortenings of texts and the acceleration of their consumption. A narrative technique of old-fashioned deliberateness, set in a material form (the three-volume novel) to whose unwieldy mass Gissing remained ambivalently yoked, sets itself the task of describing without necessarily courting a culture of speed, while continually aware that it is being consumed by readers in haste, by skimmers, skippers, the 'cursory' and 'scrappy'. As we shall see, Gissing's novels are also aware of the mechanical aspect of speed-reading—its tendency to turn readers into more efficient machines for scanning text—and, although they attempt to resist that technologizing of the body and of narrative, are also seduced by the appeal of the mechanical. Gissing, that is, confronts in ways both revealing and revealingly confused the embarrassing fact of rapid reading and its effect upon the novel, which would seem in its length the form most poised to resist that speed, but which in fact has tended to accommodate itself to it. That embarrassment is nowhere more apparent than in contemporary scholarship's silence on the subject of speed-reading, which for even the most liberal-minded historian or critic has been too vulgar to mention.[6] With Gissing and the crises of speed and consumption that occur in the 1890s, that silence becomes harder to maintain, and more necessary to lift.

TIMING THE EYE: THE PSYCHOMETRICS OF READING

During 1878 and 1879 the French physiologist and ophthalmologist Émile Javal published eight ground-breaking articles in the *Annales d'Oculistique* under the omnibus title 'Essai sur la Physiologie de la Lecture', thereby initiating

---

[6] Typical here is Robert Darnton, who writes in his seminal 1982 essay 'What is the History of Books?': 'Reading was a passion long before the *"Lesewut"* and the *"Wertherfieber"* of the romantic era; and there is *Sturm und Drang* in it yet, despite the vogue for speed-reading and the mechanistic view of literature as the encoding and decoding of messages.' See *The Kiss of Lamourette: Reflections in Cultural History* (New York: Norton, 1990), 132.

the serious study of the motor processes involved in reading.[7] Javal was a
pioneering researcher into diseases of the eye such as strabismus and an early,
devoted Esperantist, but his largely accidental discovery of the movements of
the eye during reading would become his primary contribution to European
science. His discovery was a deceptively simple one, observed with a mirror:
that the passage of the eyes across a line of text is not continuous, but instead
broken into a succession of pauses (later termed 'fixations') and rapid leaps,
which would come to be called 'saccades', a reference to the sudden jerking
of a ship's sail when caught by the wind.[8] As Javal himself would summarize
the discovery almost thirty years later, 'La lecteur divise la ligne en un certain
nombre de sections d'environ dix lettres, qui sont vues grâce à des temps de
repos rythmés; le passage d'une section à la suivante se fait par une saccade
très vive, pendant laquelle la vision ne s'exerce pas' ('The reader divides a line
into a certain number of sections of around ten letters each, which are seen
during rhythmically recurring rest periods; the movement from one section
to the next happens in an extremely rapid leap, during which vision does not
happen').[9]

The consequences of Javal's finding were enticing to physiologists. Not a
steady or uniform process, reading for Javal was jumpy, irregular, essentially
nervous. This was in essence a confirmation of physiological novel theory's
emphasis on the rhythms or wave signatures of comprehension, which could
now be rooted in the eye itself. By virtue of the complex motor skills put to use,
reading after Javal could be understood as less a state (of repose) and more an
act (of rapid scanning), an act whose physical trace would look like a skittish and
almost electrically wired line rather than a smooth flow (see Figure 5.1). Javal,
that is, fundamentally altered reading as an object of knowledge, moving it
decisively away from epistemology or sociology and toward ocular physiology.
More exciting still to nineteenth-century psychology, Javal opened up reading
to the emerging field of psychometrics—the study of the timing of cognitive
processes—which was the major focus of work in what would come to be

[7] See Émile Javal, 'Essai sur la Physiologie de la Lecture', *Annales d'Oculistique* 79 (1878),
97–117, 155–67, 240–74; 80 (1879), 135–49; 81 (1879), 61–73; 82 (1879), 72–81, 159–70,
242–53. Of interest is also the seminal and better-known work that preceded Javal's work
on reading and precipitated the physiological interest in the eye, Hermann von Helmholtz's
Handbuch der physiologischen Optik (Leipzig: Voss, 1867). Still a well-known name to cognitive
psychologists and ophthalmologists alike, Javal remains largely unknown to historians of reading,
who have ignored late-nineteenth-century work on the timing and acceleration of reading motor
skills. For an exception, see Alberto Manguel, *A History of Reading* (Harmondsworth: Penguin,
1996), 37.

[8] Although he would eventually use it, 'saccade' is not initially Javal's term; its first use
seems to have been by that of a colleague, Edmond Landolt, in his 'Nouvelles recherches sur la
physiologie des mouvements des yeux', *Archives d'Ophthalmologie* 11 (1891), 385–95.

[9] Émile Javal, *Physiologie de la lecture et de l'écriture* (Paris: Félix Alcan, 1906), 127.

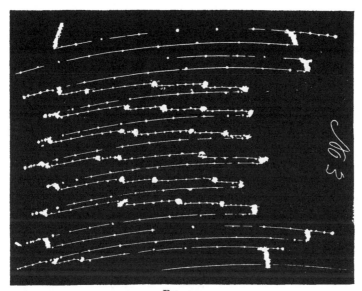

FIG. 2.

Specimen Curve of 'Spark' Record.

This reproduction, cut by a careful engraver upon a block on which the original tracing had been photographed, shows with great accuracy the sort of record from which the times of the eye movements have been determined. The chief difference between the original and the reproduction is in the breadth of the horizontal lines which are finer in the original.

The curve shows the movements of the eye in reading six lines, preceded and followed by two free movements of the eye each way, in which it was swept from one end of the line to the other, the beginning and end alone being fixated. The broad vertical lines and the round blurs in the reading indicate pauses in the eye's movements, the successive sparks knocking the soot away from a considerable space. The small dots standing alone or like beads upon the horizontal lines, show the passage of single sparks, separated from each other by 0.0068 sec. The breaks in the horizontal lines indicate that the writing point was not at all times in contact with the surface of the paper though near enough for the spark to leap across, as shown by the solitary dots.

The tracing shows clearly the fixation pauses in the course of the line, the general tendency to make the "indentation" greater at the right than at the left, and the unbroken sweep of the return from right to left.

NOTE. The cut and description are reproduced from the *American Journal of Psychology*, Vol. XI.

Figure 5.1. The path of the eye during reading, as recorded by an apparatus attached to the cornea of a reader. From Edmund Huey, *The Psychology and Pedagogy of Reading* (New York: Macmillan, 1908), 28. General Research Division, The New York Public Library, Astor, Lenox, and Tilden Foundations

recognized as the first psychological laboratory, founded by Wilhelm Wundt in Leipzig in 1879. Reading presented an ideal subject matter: an observable human act combining both cognitive and motor elements that moved at a speed too fast for ordinary measurement but not so fast that newer technologies could not arrive at some quantification. Curiously enough, therefore, the modern psychological study of reading and the modern psychological interest in speed dovetailed from the beginning. Reading psychologists thought first about achieving correct base times for the various components of the act, while psychometricians used reading as a standard for honing their theories and laboratory practices.

The American James McKeen Cattell, Wundt's first assistant from 1883 to 1886, was the first and most persistent investigator into the timing of neural processes; as he stated in his seminal 1886 paper on the subject, his goal was 'to inquire into the time needed to bring about changes in the brain, and thus to determine the rapidity of thought'.[10] Cattell's choice of subject was word perception, or the time necessary to see and name a word. The methodological problem for Cattell was the construction of an apparatus that could both display the text to the laboratory subject and accurately time responses to the text. His solution was the 'gravity chronometer', which—more than any of the specific times that emerged from his experiments—became his legacy for reading psychology and, eventually, for the development of modern speed-reading pedagogy. The gravity chronometer consisted of an electromagnetized iron screen held between two brass columns, which could be adjusted to fall at specific speeds, with a variation of 1/500 of a second (see Figure 5.2). A timing mechanism attached to the gravity chronometer started with the fall of the screen, displaying a single word, and stopped when the subject spoke the word into a mouthpiece.[11] Cattell's apparatus was, in short, the first sophisticated machine constructed to measure both neural speed and the speed of literacy, and was premised upon the mechanical workings of the eye during reading.

In its later incarnations—used by a generation of psychologists and, later, specialists in training Air Force pilots as well as common readers—the apparatus would come to be known as a tachistoscope, the fundamental tool for determining not simply visual acuity but also neural speed in general. It uncovered an entirely new dimension to speed: the world of micro-rapidity, in which speeds too fast to be experienced (such as the saccades of the eye), if nonetheless rooted in the body, could be quantified. While the humbler

---

[10] James McKeen Cattell, 'The Time Taken Up by Cerebral Operations', *Mind* 11 (1886), 220.
[11] For full descriptions of the gravity chronometer, see ibid. 221–30; see also his essentially identical description in James McKeen Cattell, 'Psychometrische Untersuchungen', *Philosophische Studien* 3 (1886), 305–55.

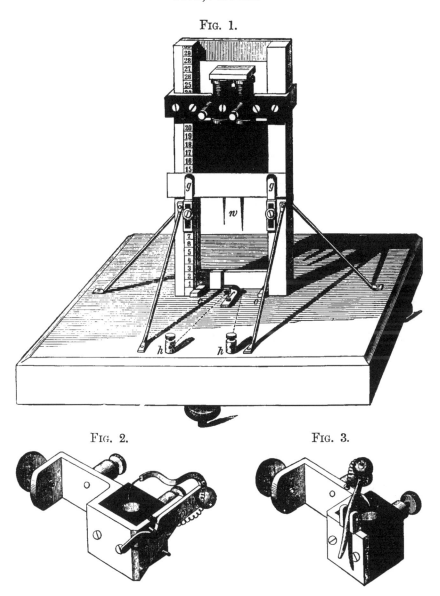

Figure 5.2. The first 'Literary Machine': a diagram of Cattell's gravity chronometer, the prototype of the tachistoscope, speed-reading's first training device. 'The Time Taken Up by Cerebral Operations', *Mind* 11 (1886): 223. General Research Division, The New York Public Library, Astor, Lenox, and Tilden Foundations

measures of words per minute or pages per hour would eventually become part of the later tradition of speed-reading, physiologists produced an image of reading far closer to the world of contemporary nanoscience. A series of investigations during the 1880s and 1890s by experimenters in Germany and the United States successively honed the general times of the movements first observed by Javal, and produced results of surprising regularity and alarming speed. Cattell suggested that the perception time for English words varied from 132σ(milliseconds) to 158σ. The later American reading psychologists Edmund Huey and Walter Dearborn established that the average duration of the fixations, or pauses, in the eye's movements during reading lasted from 160σ to 400σ, with $190-200\sigma$ the most common time; the saccades were timed at the almost unimaginably rapid pace of $40-60\sigma$. The average number of fixations was also studied, with between 4 and 7 pauses per line of text found to be common.[12] This meant, as Cattell had suggested, that the eye was not aware of individual letters—the time necessary to identify a letter was not significantly shorter than that necessary to identify a word—but instead took in larger groups: words, phrases, syntactical units. In its rapidity, the eye skimmed and made inferences, rather than moving carefully across each textual unit. The gravity chronometer, in other words, envisioned an eye that moved with more speed than accuracy, more concern for forward momentum than precision.

This was particularly evident during the saccades of the eye, where a consensus gradually developed that no perception happened at all. Javal had been circumspect about this point originally, but later work by Cattell and the influential German-American team of Benno Erdmann and Raymond Dodge established for optical physiology what the contemporary cultural critic Paul Virilio has recently insisted upon: that 'movement is blindness'.[13] Too fast to actually see when moving, the eye therefore habitually skips text, or observes only a proportion of text in the relatively blurred 'parafoveal' zone adjacent to the point of fixation; to 'read' did not, then, necessarily always mean to 'see'. The process of reading, as studied by psychometricians like Cattell or ophthalmologists like Javal, suddenly seemed like a scientifically validated version of its own worst caricature: a quick, intermittently

---

[12] See Edmund Huey, 'On the Psychology and Physiology of Reading: II', *American Journal of Psychology* 12 (1901), 292; Walter Fenno Dearborn, *The Psychology of Reading: An Experimental Study of the Reading Pauses and Movements of the Eye* (New York: Science Press, 1906), 130–1.

[13] Paul Virilio, *The Art of the Motor*, trans. Julie Rose (Minneapolis: University of Minnesota Press, 1995), 68. For the early work on perceptual blindness during saccades, see Dearborn, *Psychology of Reading*, 10; Benno Erdmann and Raymond Dodge, *Psychologische Untersuchungen über das Lesen auf experimenteller Grundlage* (Halle: Niemeyer, 1898).

attentive skimming process that was largely blind much of the time. As yet not claiming to make any changes to the way individuals actually read, reading physiology made wholesale changes in the cultural image of reading, primarily through the two practical applications that developed from it: the hygiene of reading and the impetus toward developing speed-reading techniques.

The hygienics of reading naturally followed from the extreme speed at which the eye was found to move: if reading was this fast, it was dangerous. As historians like Richard Altick have noted, the lighting conditions for much nineteenth-century reading were often perilous; but for reading physiologists excessive speed, not insufficient illumination, was the problem.[14] 'The increasing part played by reading in the life of civilized man is a striking characteristic of modern culture,' wrote Harold Griffing and Shepherd Franz in the *Psychological Review* in 1896. 'In fact, the man of today might be defined as a reading animal. The result of this strain upon the eye has been the wide prevalence of myopia, astigmatism and kindred disorders.'[15] Edmund Huey similarly announced that reading, 'one of the more frequently performed psycho-physiological operations', was 'fatiguing, often disastrously so'.[16] This led most reading psychologists, particularly Huey and Javal, to a serious and sustained interest in the materiality of the book: typography, textual layout and design, and the modernization and standardization of spelling. As the American psychologist Edmund Sanford commented in 1888, 'The problem is to get the greatest amount of matter with the greatest ease in reading on the least space; or, as it has been phrased, to get the greatest legibility to the square inch.'[17] Huey's interpretation of reading physiology led him to conclude that the horizontal arrangement of text was inferior to the vertical presentation of Asian languages, where, it was claimed, two to three times as many words could be seen in a single fixation.[18] Typefaces, font sizes, and orthographic practices were evaluated carefully with an eye toward ease and efficiency, with the claim that 'a total rearrangement of our printed symbols' was likely to be imminent.[19] In his utopian fervor, Huey went even further, imagining

---

[14] Altick, *English Common Reader*, 93–4.

[15] Harold Griffing and Shepherd Ivory Franz, 'On the Conditions of Fatigue in Reading', *Psychological Review* 3 (1896), 513.

[16] Edmund Huey, 'On the Psychology and Physiology of Reading: I', *American Journal of Psychology* 11 (1900), 283.

[17] Edmund Clark Sanford, 'The Relative Legibility of the Small Letters', *American Journal of Psychology* 1 (1888), 402.

[18] See Edmund Huey, *The Psychology and Pedagogy of Reading* (New York: Macmillan, 1908), 424–6. Javal concurred with this assessment, although he wondered if a Sinologist would agree; see Javal, *Physiologie de la lecture*, 136–7.

[19] Huey, *Psychology and Pedagogy*, 424.

something like multimedia technology, and championing the demise of the printed page:

Indeed there are those who go further than any of these legitimately warranted prophecies of future economy in the time and effort of the reader, and predict the displacement of much of reading, *in toto*, by some more direct means of recording and communicating. Just as the telegrapher's message was at first universally read from the tape, by the eye, but has come to be read far more expeditiously by the ear; so, it is argued, writing and reading may be short-circuited, and an author may talk his thought directly into some sort of gramophone-film book which will render it again to listeners, at will; reproducing all the essential characteristics of the author's speech, which, as we have seen, are not recorded by written language and which the reader must construct for himself at a considerable expense of energy.[20]

Not accidentally, the utopian desires of reading psychologists tended to issue in the death of reading itself, and its replacement by more efficient, direct, and safe communication technologies. Admittedly arising out of the impetus provided by the spread of mass literacy, the hygienic concern of psychologists like Huey saw in future invention the solution to the dangers of reading, as if the eye was finally too sensitive for what Huey called 'this most universal and artificial of habits'.[21]

These millennial prophecies of the end of reading aside, most reading physiologists abandoned the unlikely reforms of hygienics to concentrate on more practical, immediately observable reforms, of which the most culturally consequential and lasting was the development of speed-reading. That some individuals had the talent to read quickly was a matter of much anecdotal discussion; Javal mentioned a friend who could read Paul Bourget's *Cruelle énigme* in an hour, or 550 words a minute, while Huey discussed a mathematician friend who read 'the whole of a standard novel of 320 pages in two and one-fourth hours'.[22] More typically, however, the waste and inefficiency of typical reading was lamented. Huey compared the act of reading-as-usual to photographing successive but considerably overlapping sections of the text, suggesting thereby that the eye moved quickly, but often moved not far enough or moved too often, and paused for too long.[23] Experimental results that showed far greater variability in the speed of fixations than in the speed of saccades suggested something fundamental: that during saccades the eye always operated at close to optimum speed, whereas fixations not only took

---

[20] Huey, *Psychology and Pedagogy*, 429–30.   [21] Ibid. 9.

[22] For Javal's anecdote, see *Physiologie de la lecture*, 162; Huey, *Psychology and Pedagogy*, 180.

[23] This analogy bears a suggestive relation to the photographic motion studies that early Taylorists such as Frank Gilbreth carried out in the first years of the twentieth century. For a useful description, see Stephen Kern, *The Culture of Time and Space, 1880–1918* (Cambridge, Mass.: Harvard University Press, 1983), 116–17.

up a large proportion of the time of reading but contained a large amount of room for improvement. As Huey claimed, 'passages read at maximum speed show a decrease in the length of the reading pause, and as the speed of movement is not increased it would seem that increase in speed is brought about solely, or at least mainly, by decreasing the number and duration of the reading pauses'.[24] As Dearborn more succinctly put it, 'rapid readers make fewer fixations'.[25]

It would not be entirely fanciful to compare the theory of early speed-reading to that of industrial travel: like trains, faster readers stop less often and for less time, while actually traveling between stops at more or less the same speed as slower versions. But a more accurate and telling analogy would be industrial labor, to which the act of reading in physiological theory bears a remarkable resemblance. A kind of Taylorism *avant la lettre*, the physiology of reading broke down the act into component parts and identified the inefficient elements in order to produce a faster and more accurate overall performance. As Laurel Brake has noted, periodical culture of the late Victorian era was an exercise in mechanical time regularity: 'weekly *numbers*, monthly *parts*, bi-annual *volumes* echoing and reinforcing the regularity of time, the passing of which itself creates the material and desire for another number'.[26] Ocular physiology rooted this temporal regularity within the consumption of single texts, rather than the timing of their publication. It was therefore a form of what E. P. Thompson, in relation to clock time, has called 'technological conditioning': with the new measurements of the gravity chronometer or tachistoscope, the motor skills of reading could be separated, stripped of useless motions, and recombined in a more self-aware battle against the clock.[27] As with Taylorism, speed directly equated to accuracy; in the words of J. O. Quantz, an early speed-reading enthusiast, 'rapid readers not only do their work in less time, but do superior work. They retain more of the substance of what is read or heard than do slow readers.'[28] With speed-reading, the supposed leisure of textual perusal disappears entirely, and is replaced by a resolute determination to extract meaning without loss or distortion in as fast and painless a manner as possible. Paradoxically, the intensified speed recommended by Huey and others was seen to compliment, not contradict, the hygiene of reading; fatigue of the eye arose, so it was claimed, from inefficiency (operating fast machinery without care) rather than rapidity.

---

[24] Huey, 'On the Psychology and Physiology of Reading: I', 293.
[25] Dearborn, *Psychology of Reading*, 27.   [26] Brake, *Print in Transition*, 31.
[27] E. P. Thompson, 'Time, Work-Discipline, and Industrial Capitalism', in *Customs in Common* (New York: New Press, 1991), 382.
[28] J. O. Quantz, *Problems in the Psychology of Reading* (New York: Macmillan, 1897), 49–50.

If speed-reading tended to treat the text as information to be consumed, this did not mean, however, that it took as its basis the usual material of nineteenth-century information culture, such as newspapers or periodicals. Instead, repeatedly, physiologists turned to the novel as the form most amenable to testing, observation, and improvement, both in the manner in which it was read and the manner in which it was composed. A sustained experiment run by Huey in 1899 and reported in the *American Journal of Psychology* in 1901 tested twenty-eight readers with a common text: 'eleven pages, each containing 405 words, were selected from an interesting novel which presented no peculiar difficulties to the reader,' suggesting that the stylistic ubiquity of novelistic prose could serve as a general representation of textuality as a whole, 'novel' substituting neatly for 'book'.[29] Each subject was then asked to read pages from the unnamed 'interesting novel' in a variety of ways, from auditory reading to lip-movement reading to what Huey called the 'silent own method', in which the subject was asked to 'fall into the mood in which he would do such readings in an easy-chair at home'.[30] Not surprisingly, the 'silent own method' was repeatedly the fastest method, proving that novel-reading-as-usual had already adapted itself to a culture of speed. In addition, this 'silent own method' was, Huey observed, remarkably rhythmic: 'A strong rhythmic tendency was observed, and this aspect of reading merits a careful study. Readers fall into a natural state, which gives almost exactly the same times for page after page.'[31] Novel reading was therefore a standard, but a fast standard: consumption at the quickest rate possible for the culture at present.

Not, however, the fastest rate imaginable. Huey's conclusion was that speed increases were still possible, given the sloppiness of even the rhythmic novel-reader in the easy chair, whose eyes covered 'three or four times as much ground as is necessary to get its data'. Huey's recommendation is sufficiently shocking for the literary critic: 'From the interpretation side, one of the serious objections is that the present arrangement [of typography as well as of reading habits] makes "skimming" difficult and unsatisfactory. We have noticed the progressive tendency to read in larger and larger units; and this should go on until much of our reading could be done by a skimming process. This skimming should be but an enlargement of normal reading, proceeding by a somewhat regular series of omissions and resting places, in which, however, all the matter could be taken account of in some degree.' Although the novel-reader using the 'silent own method' skimmed more than

---

[29] Huey, 'On the Psychology and Physiology of Reading: II', 295. The experiment is also reported in Huey, *Psychology and Pedagogy*, 174 ff.

[30] Huey, 'On the Psychology and Physiology of Reading: II', 295.   [31] Ibid. 297.

other readers, given their faster times, more skimming was thought necessary: 'At present, however, one who attempts to "skim" down a page must proceed in a kind of hurdle-race fashion, breaking across lines of which the full content is necessarily unknown; and violating at every instant reading habits which it has taken years to form. The arrangement that is finally found to be the best for ordinary reading, will, I believe, facilitate skimming as well.'[32] This meant, first, two major changes: the redesign of Western typography, which became Huey's obsession, but also a retraining of motor skills which would become speed-reading's primary goal. Speed-reading, following Huey's suggestions, became an organized, methodized form of skimming, of consuming larger and larger units in a single glance.

It also meant a third, more speculative change, one which Huey felt would be inevitable as soon as his science was disseminated: a compositional practice geared toward skimming readers. Huey writes: 'The reader's habits of word and phrase association and expectation have not been consulted in composing in the past as they will be when the psychology of style has become a matter of common knowledge. The fact that subject-matter arranged to accord with the reader's reading-habits is read in one-half the time of matter arranged contrary to these habits, suggests the immense advantage that may come from studies in this field.'[33] What Huey presents here is a remarkably intertwined set of suggestions for the acceleration of textual communication: faster, better-trained skimming readers, using more efficiently designed textual objects, which were to be composed with greater attention to the rapidity of consumption, presumably with a syntactically simplified and unornamented style. Reader, writer, and printer could ideally all collaborate in the goal of shortening the time devoted to the act of reading. The novel, already in the vanguard of fast textuality, could become the experimental laboratory in which the theories of speed could be tested and observed.

The 'psychology of style' which Huey desired, at least if the later example of Vernon Lee is taken as representative, never devoted itself to speed; and the developments in the materiality of the book, however drastic, have not taken the shape that Huey imagined. But out of the work of Huey, Javal, Dearborn, and their colleagues, the pedagogy of speed-reading grew rapidly. From the

---

[32] Ibid. 310–11.

[33] Ibid. 311. Javal offers a similar suggestion: 'Rendre la lecture plus rapide, tel est le but principal de mes remarques. On verra, chemin faisant, que les moyens propres à accélérer la lecture auraient pour conséquence accessoire de diminuer la grosseur de nos livres, et d'abréger le premier enseignement de la lecture et de l'écriture' 'Making reading faster is the primary goal of my observations. One can see, on the way, that the means suitable to accelerating reading will have the secondary consequence of decreasing the bulk of our books, and of shortening the initial instruction of reading and writing'. Javal, *Physiologie de la lecture*, 276.

1920s, a burgeoning field of lay texts on methods of speed-reading developed, such as John O'Brien's *Silent Reading: With Special Reference to Methods for Developing Speed* (1922), Walter Pitkin's *The Art of Rapid Reading: A Book for People Who Want to Read Faster and More Accurately* (1929), and Norman Lewis's *How to Read Better and Faster* (1944). The apotheosis of speed-reading as a defined pedagogy came, however, with the development at the University of Utah, in the late 1950s, of the 'Reading Dynamics' program invented by Evelyn Wood.[34] The methods are still based on the insights and rhetorical moves of early reading physiology and psychometrics: an industrialization of the reading act, in which motor skills are broken down into the smallest possible units to eliminate waste, while the goal of 'comprehension' is measured solely by an ethic of utility (portable information, summarizable 'gist') rather than diversion, pleasure, reflection, or reverie. While Wood's innovation was to eliminate the tachistoscope as a measuring device, most speed-reading theorists depended upon its training capacity well into the 1950s, as the primary psychometric apparatus became a true 'reading machine'.

The ambiguous lesson of reading physiology was that neural processing—particularly textual consumption—either needed to get faster to adapt to a culture of acceleration, or that it was already remarkably swift, an organic technology of extraordinary speed in need of faster texts to elicit its full capacity. A pervasive mid-to-late Victorian interest in neural speed, particularly via the 'shocks' of the sensation novel, had already addressed some of these same issues. Gissing himself was fond of such descriptions, as with *Born in Exile*'s Godwin Peak's rapid, psychometrically calculated ratiocination when his masquerade as a theological student is discovered by one of his former rationalist friends: 'Tumult of thought was his only trouble; it seemed as if his brain must burst with the stress of its lightning operations. In three seconds, he re-lived the past, made several distinct anticipations of the future, and still discussed with himself how he should behave this moment' (*BE*, 249). But the discourses of speed-reading, either physiological or, as we shall see, part of the world of novel publishing, made these merely descriptive moments less relevant. Given that the novel had evolved the capacity to depict neural speed, how could it generate the capacity to satisfy neural speed? How, in other words, could it

---

[34] Although clearly indebted to late-nineteenth-century work on optical physiology, speed-reading manuals in general cite less and less of the work of Javal, Huey, Dearborn, and Erdmann and Dodge, as the twentieth century progresses. O'Brien's *Silent Reading* contains an excellent survey of psychometrics and reading physiology from Cattell onwards, while manuals such as Pitkin's or Lewis's concentrate less on the mechanics of eye movement and more on posture and the avoidance of lip-movement or vocalization. Furthermore, the later manuals begin to avoid fiction as test material for the beginning speed-reader, replacing it with short informational articles often reprinted from news magazines.

move from a representation (often quite deliberate) of quick processing to a technology *for* rapid consumption? The question was not theoretical; it was, for Gissing and those situated like him in the 1880s and 1890s, a practical, financial one as well, as it existed in the area where the materiality of the novel met the formal practices of working novelists. This was the area that naturalism was well-adapted to investigate. If, as Rachel Bowlby has claimed, naturalist fiction both rendered and critiqued the experience of observing 'a social reality that appears simply as a succession of separate images or scenes'—the reality troped by the gravity chronometer and the tachistoscope—it was well poised to consider the sudden speeding-up of those images or scenes.[35]

SHORTENED SPANS: THE END OF THE THREE-DECKER

Writing in his diary on 3 July, 1894, Gissing recorded his first response to the news that, only six days earlier, the set of unofficial business arrangements buttressing the long-lived edifice of three-volume British fiction had collapsed: 'Announcement that Mudie's and Smith's will give the publishers only 4/- a vol. for 3-vol. novels after end of this year. Grievous outlook for some unfortunate authors.—Am thinking of making my next book a vol. of essays.'[36] A month later he returned to the issue, after having read the novel that sparked the collapse, Hall Caine's *The Manxman*: 'The publishers seem disposed to give up the 3-vol. publication altogether, and the Author's Society has passed a resolution to the same effect. My own interests in the matter are entirely dubious.'[37] Gissing's dubiety about the effects of the change was not unusual, although it is perhaps unexpected from the author whose *New Grub Street* had, three years earlier, devoted so much space to discussing 'that well-worn topic, the evils of the three-volume system' (*NGS*, 235). But the political and psychological affect accompanying the end of the three-volume novel—a fear of liberation from hateful, but familiar, restraints—was not unique to

[35] Rachel Bowlby, *Just Looking: Consumer Culture in Dreiser, Gissing and Zola* (London: Methuen, 1985), 16.

[36] See George Gissing, *London and the Life of Literature in Late Victorian England: The Diary of George Gissing, Novelist*, ed. Pierre Coustillas (Lewisburg, Pa.: Bucknell University Press, 1978), 341.

[37] Ibid. 343. In his letters Gissing tended more to straightforward pessimism than dubiety about the Mudie/Smith ultimatum: in July 1894 he wrote to Clara Collet that the change 'means a very serious diminution of payment for the author' and that it had 'strengthened my intention to write something other than fiction, as soon as I feel able to write anything at all'. See George Gissing, *The Collected Letters of George Gissing*, ed. Paul Mattheisen, Arthur Young, and Pierre Coustillas, iv (Athens: Ohio University Press, 1994), 214–15.

Gissing. It expressed a concern that the social and economic forces that had clashed so oddly with the antique three-decker were now to be unleashed, with unforeseen results for those novelists who had enjoyed the insulation provided by the three-volume format. No small part of those forces was a new culture of speed in textual consumption, against which the novelist no longer had immunity.

The tale of the three-decker's long rule and sudden collapse in 1894 has usually been narrated as a strictly economic story, one of artificial price stability and market inflexibility—a kind of genteel protectionism—replaced, quickly but inevitably, with a culture of multiple, cheap formats that finally managed to emerge from under the blanket of the library novel. That story is sufficiently well known that only its broader outlines need recounting: on 27 June, 1894, the two major circulating library firms, Mudie's and W. H. Smith's, issued a joint ultimatum to the effect that they would not be accepting three-volume novels from publishers at their previously high wholesale price, given that the increasing prevalence of cheaper reprints, often immediately following the first more expensive edition, had made the proposition a losing one from the perspective of the libraries. Since the libraries were the only sizable market element able to afford the exorbitant price of 31s. 6d. that a novel carried, the format disappeared almost immediately: whereas 184 such novels were issued in 1894, by 1897 only four were published, and the form became a relic of Victoriana.[38] The arrangement had ensured a captive market for publishers, in which much of a print run was sold to libraries before the day of publication, and it had ensured the cultural hegemony of the libraries, who, as the largest buyer of new fiction by far, were able to act as *de facto* censor. It had also, in its minimalization of risk, created what John Sutherland has called 'a very benign state of affairs for the production of fiction', since the publishers who were virtually guaranteed a small profit on each print run stood to lose little on lesser-known or novice authors.[39] In each version in which it is told, the moral of the story seems to be that the riskier ventures of speculative capitalism

---

[38] For the publication figures, see Royal Gettman, *A Victorian Publisher: A Study of the Bentley Papers* (Cambridge: Cambridge University Press, 1960), 262.

[39] John Sutherland, *Victorian Novelists and Publishers* (Chicago: University of Chicago Press, 1976), 17. The point is also made in somewhat different terms by Simon Eliot, who stresses how the risk management of the three-volume novel enabled the existence of a cadre of minimally successful novelists, like *New Grub Street*'s Reardon, who could make a subsistence living in selling three-deckers to publishers; see Simon Eliot, 'The Business of Victorian Publishing', in *The Cambridge Companion to the Victorian Novel*, ed. Deirdre David (Cambridge: Cambridge University Press, 2001), 50. Thinking of Reardon and his like as artisans, laboring for a subsistence living, we can make sense of N. N. Feltes's claim that the three-decker was a 'petty-commodity' form of literary production, oriented around monopolies of distribution: see N. N. Feltes, *Modes of Production of Victorian Novels* (Chicago: University of Chicago Press, 1986), 27.

tend to disturb even the most stable of protectionist arrangements, with the mixed results of ending any effective centralized cultural censorship while also making life difficult for those less capable of catering to the market's fluctuating tastes. Gissing's own dubiety is echoed in our standard accounts of three-volume fiction, as critics seem torn between the market immunity provided by the form and its undeniably procrustean demands made upon novelists.

Most famous of those demands was its excessive length. Critics since Richard Altick have blamed 'the verbosity, inordinate length, qualitative unevenness, and sometimes the sheer formlessness' of Victorian fiction on its usual material container.[40] Like so much else in Victorian book history, the complaint goes directly back to Gissing himself. *New Grub Street*'s vivid presentation of Edwin Reardon's prolonged difficulty in filling three volumes has remained lodged in the minds of literary historians: 'Description of locality, deliberate analysis of character or motive, demanded far too great an effort for his present condition. He kept as much as possible to dialogue; the space is filled so much more quickly, and at a pinch one can make people talk about the paltriest incidents of life' (*NGS*, 154). It is not just Reardon's style that is unhinged by such an insatiable demand for fictional copy; the hack journalist Sykes, during a conversation in a dingy reading-room, explains that 'in an evil day I began to write three-volume novels': 'I persevered for five years, and made about five failures' (*NGS*, 415). At a year per novel—a speed which the impecunious Reardon has to more than double, to the detriment of his health—the three-decker was, for the novelist, slow enough in the production to be barely worth the effort of selling.

Temporal over-extension is also the key-note of its material form. At a little over 300 pages per post-octavo volume, and with word counts generally running between 150,000 and 200,000, three-deckers were slow going, all the more so given the prevalent way in which they were read, with one volume at a time—the limit to the standard guinea-per-year subscription—taken out from the circulating library.[41] Here textual materiality, and the consequent habits of textual consumption, rejoin economics in a simple fact that has gone little noted: for publishers, slow reading made money. Richard Bentley, for one, admitted as much when he claimed to an author that the longer books were kept out of the library by readers, the more copies libraries would

---

[40] Richard Altick, 'Publishing', in *A Companion to Victorian Literature and Culture*, ed. Herbert Tucker (Oxford: Blackwell, 1999), 295.

[41] For the word counts, see Gettman, *Victorian Publisher*, 233–4. Guinevere Griest, however, stresses the form's elasticity, as it was able to encompass novels as short as 120,000 and as large as 250,000 words. See Guinevere Griest, *Mudie's Circulating Library and the Victorian Novel* (Bloomington: Indiana University Press, 1970), 163–4.

have to buy to satisfy customers; short books, books that could be consumed quickly, made no economic sense under the circulating library system.[42] The precarious arrangement between publishers and libraries only worked if the texts produced by authors were of a sufficient size to encourage, even demand, dilatory or prolonged reading. Thus, for Bentley (and, presumably, other major publishers), there was no compelling economic incentive to publish shorter one-volume novels. N. N. Feltes's claim that the three-decker was a 'commodity-book', produced, discussed, and consumed with overt attention to its physical packaging, is never clearer than in these hard-headed calculations about how large size, translated into long reading time, maintained the increasingly outrageous 31s. 6d. list price and kept major publishing firms going.[43] Like most installment plans, the library system of three-volume novels depended upon delay on the part of the consumer or borrower to produce profit, with length of delay tied directly to size of profit. It is no coincidence that all such installment plans in Gissing's fiction, such as Beatrice French's South London Fashionable Dress Supply Association in *In the Year of Jubilee*, are patently fraudulent in intent, if not in the eyes of the legal system.

The economic viability of the three-decker for publishers was tied, then, to slowness of consumption. For novelists, as Reardon bitterly explains to Milvain, it was hard to detach oneself from this system, given the widespread assumption that should libraries be replaced by a culture of sales, the willingness of publishers to buy from lesser-known novelists would vanish: 'Do you suppose the public would support the present number of novelists if each book had to be purchased? A sudden change to that system would throw three-fourths of the novelists out of work.' When Milvain offers the understandable objection that libraries could just as well circulate one-volume novels, Reardon offers the standard contemporary response: 'Profits would be less, I suppose. People would take the minimum subscription' (*NGS*, 236). Slowness kept novelists working and minimally paid, but, as *New Grub Street* continually reiterates, it also made their labor protracted, tedious, and artistically disastrous, given the pressure to fill the 900 pages that the market preference for slow consumption required. Hence Gissing's dubiety about the virtues of the form, usually expressed in the fatigued tones of assembly-line

---

[42] See Gettman, *Victorian Publisher*, 240, who quotes the Bentley letter at length, although without considering the consequences for the form of Victorian fiction of this key economic/material fact. Of interest here is also Walter Besant's claim in 1894 that the circulating library was the economic consequence of the acceleration of reading rates in the late eighteenth century: 'People read faster as well as more; they devoured books. No purse was long enough to buy all the books that one could read; therefore they lent to each other; therefore they combined their resources and formed book clubs; therefore the circulating libraries came into existence.' See Walter Besant, 'The Rise and Fall of the "Three Decker"' *Dial* 17 (Oct. 1894), 185.

[43] See Feltes, *Modes of Production*, 26–7.

production: 'When I read to you the MS. of "Workers in the Dawn"', he wrote to Eduard Bertz in 1891, shortly before commencing *New Grub Street*, 'we did not foresee this endless series of 3-Vol. novels. I suppose you possess them all? Alas! there will be many more.'[44]

There would, however, be only four more for Gissing: after *In the Year of Jubilee*, published in December 1894 (shortly before the Mudie/Smith ultimatum was scheduled to go into effect, in January 1895), the three-decker was over both for Gissing and for the British novel in general, while the market pressure for slow consumption evaporated. The reasons for the 1894 collapse are many, and had been long in preparation, but in the public debate surrounding the form dating from the 1880s it is clear that speed, particularly speed of consumption, is at the heart of the issue. What is evident from these debates is how both defenders and critics of the three-decker appealed to speed as a rationale for their positions. Initially, as one might expect, the defenders of the three-decker wrote in a conservatively ironized relation to speed, as did the anonymous author of a *Tinsley's Magazine* piece in 1882: 'Has life become so fast that we cannot afford to read *in extenso* the stories which enthralled our fathers or our grandfathers?'[45] Later commentators, however, employed a physiological defense for the necessity, even the rapidity, of the three-volume novel. A *Spectator* critic in 1894 proclaimed that the rush to end the three-decker was based on the faulty assumption that 'the great public reads novels from pure love of fiction, and because of delight in skilful narrative, witty reflections, and crisp, natural dialogue'. Novel-reading is instead a matter of nervous system palliation:

What enables so many novels to be printed is the semi-physical need which so large a number of people have for a constant supply of fairly readable new novels. There are thousands of men and women who merely use novels as mental sedatives,—who simply want them to steady their nerves. Almost all people who use their brains much, or otherwise exhaust their nervous energies, want some form of mental sedative. . . . In order to quiet the thinking organism it must be kept gently at work. The easier and more mechanical that work is the better, but the mental powers must be kept running.[46]

Since this need is constant, even the cheapest editions would be too much; the novel-reader, like any addict of speed, requires so reliable a supply that only circulating libraries are cost-efficient. Furthermore, the inherent ephemerality of the novel makes an affordable purchase price beside the point, since what

---

[44] *Gissing, Collected Letters*, iv. 289–90.

[45] Anon., 'Is the Novel Moribund?', *Tinsley's Magazine* 30 (April 1882), 389.

[46] Anon., 'Novels as Sedatives', *Spectator* 73 (28 July 1894), 108. The point is made in an even more exaggerated fashion by *Punch*, which parodied the three-decker as an infallible cure for insomnia. See Anon., 'In Three Volumes', *Punch* 107 (1 Sept., 1894), 101.

true novel-reader requires ownership of volumes that are worthless the minute
they are over? However jaundiced the thought process here, the reliance upon
a lay physiology operated to demonstrate the rapidity of the three-decker
system.

Indeed, as even the *Spectator* writer acknowledged, the 1894 controversy
tended to involve considerations of neural operations: 'The Author's Society
has been stirred to its foundations,' the article begins drily, 'and deep has
called to deep, romance to analytical psychology, in the literary page of the
Daily Chronicle.'[47] Here public debate over publishing matters joined the
contemporaneous inquiry into the physiology of vision. Voiced as early as
1872, one key concern of the three-decker's proponents was the size of its
type, which was judged 'easy to read, even to the weakest sight; whereas
the cheap edition, being in smaller type and on inferior paper, is necessarily
more difficult to read'.[48] No small part of the three-volume novel was its
clear and large typography, motivated to a considerable extent by the need to
'bump out' inadequate manuscripts to the required page length. The printer's
art in massaging small amounts of text into large page counts was never
more elaborately or successfully displayed, perhaps, than in the heyday of the
three-decker: margins were widened, leading between lines increased, typeface
expanded, blank space before and after chapters used liberally, all in an effort
to fit manuscript to form. 'Procrustean' might even be a misleading metaphor,
since novel manuscripts were rarely squeezed into the form; stretching tended
to be by far the more necessary operation.[49] For Gissing's Reardon, this
meant that 'sixty written slips of the kind of paper he habitually used would
represent—thanks to the astonishing system which prevails in such matters:
large type, wide spacing, frequency of blank pages—a passable three-hundred
page volume' (*NGS*, 151).

Critics attuned to the physiology of reading, in its flowering in the 1880s
and 1890s, understood therefore that this bright and spacious page design
meant that the three-decker was not slower (because of its girth) but actually
faster: more easily consumed, less fatiguing to the eyes. And the necessary
condensation of type that would go into one-volume novels would actually
slow consumption and create the problem of reading hygienics currently
preoccupying Javal and Huey, among others. One popular complaint about

---

[47] Anon., 'Novels as Sedatives', 108.

[48] Anon., 'On the Forms of Publishing Fiction', *Tinsley's Magazine* 10 (May 1872), 412.

[49] For accounts of this typesetting process, see Gettman, *Victorian Publisher*, 234, and Altick,
'Publishing', 295. Anthony Trollope asserted that this system, which 'stretched my pages by means
of lead and margin into double the number I had intended', was a 'literary short-measure',
equivalent to any other kind of consumer fraud. See Anthony Trollope, *An Autobiography*
(Oxford: Oxford University Press, 1980), 336.

the 1894 collapse was that this new fiction would not be consumed as easily by the elderly or the very young, and that even for the merely mature the novel would become a slower proposition.[50] A purely visual comparison of the typefaces of *In the Year of Jubilee*, published in three volumes in 1894, and *The Whirlpool*, published in one volume in 1897, illustrates the difference (see Figure 5.3). Furthermore, the hygienic requirements of reading physiology, as they were elaborated beginning in the 1890s, bear a striking (if coincidental) resemblance to a measurement of the page design of three-deckers like *New Grub Street*, while *The Whirlpool*'s design falls far short of the general recommendations, which for ophthalmologic physiologists would not only make it slow reading but potentially injurious as well (see Table 5.1). The

---

192   IN THE YEAR OF JUBILEE

with tangle of leaf and bloom, solitude is safe from all intrusion—unless it be that of flitting bird, or of some timid wild thing that rustles for a moment and is gone. From dawn to midnight, as from midnight to dawn, one who would be alone with nature might count upon the security of these bosks and dells.

By Nancy Lord and her companions such pleasures were unregarded. For the first few days after their arrival at Teignmouth, they sat or walked on the promenade, walked or sat on the pier, sat or walked on the Den—a long, wide lawn, decked about with shrubs and flower-beds, between sea-fronting houses and the beach. Nancy had no wish to exert herself, for the weather was hot; after her morning bathe with Jessica, she found amusement enough in watching the people—most of whom were here simply to look at each other, or in listening to the band, which played selections from Sullivan varied with dance music, or in reading a novel from the book-lender's,—that is to say, gazing idly at the page, and letting such significance as it possessed float upon her thoughts.

THE WHIRLPOOL   381

CHAPTER VI

In these days Rolfe had abandoned even the pretence of study. He could not feel at home among his books; they were ranked about him on the old shelves, but looked as uncomfortable as he himself; it seemed a temporary arrangement; he might as well have been in lodgings. At Pinner, after a twelvemonth, he was beginning to overcome the sense of strangeness; but a foreboding that he could not long remain there had always disturbed him. Here, though every probability pointed to a residence of at least two or three years, he scarcely made an effort to familiarise himself with the new surroundings; his house was a shelter, a camp; granted a water-tight roof, and drains not immediately poisonous, what need to take thought for artificial comforts? Thousands of men, who sleep on the circumference of London, and go each day to business, are practically strangers to the district nominally their home; ever ready to strike tent, as convenience bids, they can feel no interest in a vicinage which merely happens to house them for the time being, and as often as not they remain ignorant of the names of streets or roads through which they pass in going to the railway station. Harvey was now very much in this case. That he might not utterly waste his time, he had undertaken regular duties under Cecil Morphew's direction, and spent some hours daily in Westminster Bridge Road. Thence he went to his club, to see the papers; and in returning to Gunnersbury he felt hardly more sense of vital connection with this suburb than with the murky and roaring street in which he sat at business. By force of habit he continued to read, but only books from the circulating library, thrown upon his table pell-mell—novels, popular science, travels, biographies; each as it came to hand. The intellectual disease of the time took hold upon him: he lost the power of mental concentration, yielded to the indolent pleasure of desultory page-skimming. There remained in him but one sign of grace: the qualms that followed on every evening's debauch of

---

Figure 5.3. The 'astonishing system which prevails in such matters': a comparison of the typesetting and legibility of Gissing's novels before and after the 1894 shift to one-volume production, with compression of the text evident in the later novel. From *In the Year of Jubilee*, i (London: Lawrence and Bullen, 1894), 192, and *The Whirlpool* (London: Lawrence & Bullen, 1897), 31. General Research Division, The New York Public Library, Astor, Lenox, and Tilden Foundations

---

[50] See Griest, *Mudie's Circulating Library*, 165, 193, for examples of these complaints.

Table 5.1 Typeface specifications of Gissing's novels compared to hygienic recommendations

Factor	*New Grub Street* (1891) Smith and Elder, 3 vols.	*The Whirlpool* (1897) Lawrence and Bullen, 1 vol.	Physiological desiderata (Huey, Griffing and Franz)
Leading	5 mm	3.5 mm	No specifics; more recommended
Line length	84 mm	88 mm	75–85 mm
Lines per page	27	38	No specifics; fewer recommended
Small letter height	2 mm	1 mm	Above 1.5 mm
Type size	12 point	10 point	11 point min.

possibility existed, in other words, that the three-volume novel was actually a technology of safe speed, and that a misunderstanding of reading physiology was leading to an only putatively faster technology that might have ruinous consequences for the reading public.

The argument, of course, did not succeed, any more than did the hygienic suggestions of Javal and Huey, although two British governmental commissions, the Committee on Type Faces in 1922 and the Medical Research Council in 1926, did investigate the question of print legibility from the standpoint of ophthalmologic hygiene.[51] But what is important to note is that the ground for argument between detractors and critics of the three-decker stood now on a shared agreement about the virtues of speed; having ceded that much to modernity, the defenders of the three-decker were less able to mount successful counter-arguments to what seemed like the self-evidently faster one-volume novel. What Arjun Appadurai has called an 'aesthetic of ephemerality' in relation to more recent forms of consumption seems actually to have become a consensus by the 1890s, at least in relation to British fiction, where it both hastened the demise of the Victorian era's most stable literary form and engaged the energies of its defenders.[52] For those who, like Gissing, looked with more skepticism or fear on the culture of acceleration, the problem of the three-volume novel would become intractable, undecidable, part of a larger dubiety about the rate of cultural change and the extent to which it should

[51] See Marjorie Plant, *The English Book Trade: An Economic History of the Making and Sale of Books* (London: George Allen & Unwin, 1965), 449.
[52] From Appadurai's essay 'Consumption, Duration, and History', in Arjun Appadurai, *Modernity at Large: Cultural Dimensions of Globalization* (Minneapolis: University of Minnesota Press, 1996), 85.

or could be resisted. Although Gissing published solely in one volume after 1894, that choice could not have been his, and in fact the continuing size of his novels made the change in format seem largely cosmetic; *The Whirlpool*, for instance, is as large as his earlier three-deckers, and considerably longer than many three-volume novels of the 1880s. Gissing did, however, condense and revise some of his earlier novels, such as *The Unclassed*, and he occasionally expressed a belated exasperation at the size and languorousness of his earlier work and the material constraints that made those qualities inevitable.[53] For Gissing, the combination of a lifelong involvement with a single material form (the three-decker and its controversial demise) and a cultural consensus on the need to increase and protect the speed of consumption (expressed by the work of reading physiology) led to a marked ambivalence about speed that would be played out in the intersection between theme and form, between a realist commitment to depicting an accelerated world and a conservative desire to retard the speed of readers who exist in it.

TECHNOLOGIES OF SPEED: TIME AND SPACE IN GISSING

New Grub Street is undeniably a 'slow' novel in the sense in which the term was understood by the 1890s: a three-volume library novel devoted to character analysis and the gradual working out of destinies, without the shocks or telegraphic brevity of newer fictions. Within it, however, as a matter of the first thematic importance, time accelerates uncomfortably. The standard units of time measurement for classical narrative (seasons, months, days) are compressed to a compulsive, and not wholly unobtrusive, notation of hours, minutes, and seconds. Jasper's accurate sense that the Great Western express

---

[53] Gissing's ambivalence is best signaled by an 1898 letter to Grant Richards in which he envisioned writing 'two kinds of novel: one running to about 150,000 words [i.e. the usual three-volume length], the other to some 80,000'. See George Gissing, *The Collected Letters of George Gissing*, ed. Paul Mattheisen, Arthur Young, and Pierre Coustillas, v (Athens: Ohio University Press, 1995), 107. In other words, Gissing never entirely surrendered his attachment to the three-decker form, even after its demise and all of his published criticism on the subject. Given that he detected a similar ambivalence in Dickens's relation to serial publication in his *Charles Dickens: A Critical Study* (London: Blackie and Sons, 1898), Gissing may have felt that an inherent part of a novelist's vocation was an uneasy, lovingly hostile relation toward a particular format. This almost neurotic relation to publication mode has long been read into *New Grub Street*, most recently by Patrick Brantlinger, who characterizes it as torn between nostalgia for 'Dickens, Mudie's, three volumes, and mid-Victorian realism' and a gloomy, suspicious anticipation of 'modernist and avant-garde liberation from the constraints of "the masses"'. See Patrick Brantlinger, *The Reading Lesson: The Threat of Mass Literacy in Nineteenth-Century British Fiction* (Bloomington: Indiana University Press, 1998), 184–5.

train passes through Wattleborough 'in less than five minutes' is echoed by a narrative procedure that rarely fails to cite, and wonder at, the bewildering rapidity of experience. The breakup of Reardon's marriage to Amy Yule is a matter, we are told, of hours: two hours for the removal of furniture to a secondhand dealer, two more hours to find an affordable garret, a few minutes to write a letter to his estranged wife enclosing money and his new address. The narrative of Reardon's sudden journey to Brighton in heavy snow to see his dying son is related with a timetable-like precision: it begins at 6.55 p.m., too late to catch a 7.20 p.m. train, and ends at exactly 11.00 p.m. (according to a public clock) when he arrives at his wife's door. Within this 4 hours and 5 minutes a variety of experiences of temporality are evoked, from impatient hurry as a cab struggles to make it to the station on time, to helpless delay as Reardon waits for the next train, to exhaustion on his arrival. Even processes that could have been narrated with less attention to small time units are funneled through them; the first financial crisis of the novel for Reardon is not a matter of gradual pressure, such as the onset of winter and its extra expenses, but a two-day emergency in which the quarter-rent must be somehow obtained. The profusion of 'in a few minutes', 'half an hour later', 'a couple of hours', and the like—the watch-on time-consciousness of Gissing's prose—suggests an acute awareness of speed, despite the banality of the notation, at least to readers habituated to such literally prosaic details. After all, the most famous put-down of novelistic prose—Paul Valéry's apocryphal comment that he could never bring himself to write the sentence 'La marquise sortit à cinq heures'—depends entirely on the novel's addiction to the everydayness of clock time.[54] It is part of the effect of *New Grub Street* to make this innocuous novelistic chatter about time into something more psychologically pressing and claustrophobic.

The thematics of speed in Gissing are involved with more than just suddenness or shock, the discourses of industrial trauma, although his mature novels are dotted with instances of these familiar *topoi*, from the accidental death of Doctor Madden in *The Odd Women* to the railway crash that kills the family of Victor Duke, the homeless eye doctor, in *New Grub Street*. What makes speed, and technologies of speed, so troubling in Gissing is scarcely a secret, since it is present from the novel's opening lines: the disappearance of viable notions of 'space' because of speed. *New Grub Street* starts with two collapses of space via temporal simultaneity: the first a rather antique one (a church clock, two miles away, striking eight in the morning), the second depending on more contemporary technologies. 'There's a man being hanged

---

[54] As related in André Breton's *Manifeste du surréalisme* (1924), in *Oeuvres Complètes*, i (Paris: Gallimard-Pléiade, 1988), 314.

in London at this moment,' Jasper announces, conflating (thanks both to newspaper information and the widespread adoption of Greenwich Mean Time from the 1840s onward) church, house, and metropolis into a single unit (*NGS*, 35). Space in Gissing can more reliably be discussed in temporal terms; even Reardon's struggles to produce bulky novels become questions of time, as the meaning of 'three volumes' dangerously contracts over the course of the novel, from the seven months that Reardon took to write his one success, 'On Neutral Ground', to the matter of weeks necessary to produce 'Margaret Home', the last of his novels. Smaller time–space calculations (manuscript pages per day, weeks to the volume) are equally prevalent. On a larger scale, the technologies of acceleration make a symbolic map of literary and professional space, such as the centrality of London, obsolete, as Reardon argues:

'We form our ideas of London from old literature; we think of London as if it were still the one centre of intellectual life; we think and talk like Chatterton. But the truth is that intellectual men in our day do their best to keep away from London—when once they know the place. There are libraries everywhere; papers and magazines reach the north of Scotland as soon as they reach Brompton; it's only on rare occasions, for special kinds of work, that one is bound to live in London.' (*NGS*, 474)

The first effect of this consciousness of spatial collapse via speed technologies is to render Gissing's London a largely empty, characterless landscape, as has often been noted, most memorably by Fredric Jameson.[55] A larger effect is to render any description of place unnecessary and symbolically inert. True *places* in Gissing—locales with symbolic weight and descriptive richness—achieve significance only by being cut off from the grid of speed networks (railroads, telegraphs) which have already emptied London of its historic function; they tend to be rural *loci amoeni* like Exeter (*Born in Exile*), the Lake District (*The Odd Women*), and the fictional 'Greystone' (*The Whirlpool*). In *New Grub Street* the most lovingly evoked place is, in fact, Greece, described by Reardon in a Ruskinian rhapsody that marks its unreality. Significantly, the immunity of these places to the encroachment of speed is marked by a combination of leisured reading and premodern temporality: in both *The Unclassed* and *The Whirlpool*, retreat is signaled by outdoor reading next to a sundial.[56]

[55] Borrowing to some degree from Raymond Williams's characterization of Gissing's London in *The Country and the City*, Jameson calls it a Dickensian city 'little by little drained of its vitality and reduced to the empty grid of calls by one character to another, visits to oppressive rooms and apartments, and intervals of random strolls through the streets. The city therefore no longer functions as the molar unity of these narratives, as their outer emblem of "totality," as the external sign of the meaningful unity of their social content.' Fredric Jameson, *The Political Unconscious: Narrative as a Socially Symbolic Act* (Ithaca, NY: Cornell University Press, 1981), 190.

[56] Gissing's career ends, in fact, on precisely such a note of rural withdrawal: *The Private Papers of Henry Ryecroft* (1903), published serially under the title 'An Author at Grass', is the

But perhaps the largest effect of this notion of 'spatial collapse' is to make simultaneity—the synchronous occurrence of events in different spaces—one of Gissing's primary formal and psychological problems. *New Grub Street* begins with the question, should it matter that a man is being hanged in London 'at this moment', and if so, how? Does the speed of technology and of consciousness capable of making this fact a pressing one mean the expansion or contraction of human sympathy? David Harvey's well-known suggestion that simultaneity, or 'time–space compression', is the major crisis for European realism after 1848 is borne out by Gissing, who finds not a radical solution to the problem in the mode of modernism but instead a primarily conservative one.⁵⁷ When technologies of speed are marshaled as objects of description in Gissing's mature novels, their effect upon fictional form is neutralized by a narrative procedure that disperses their effect and refuses to find formal equivalents for the simultaneity they necessarily produce. This is, one might say, a more deeply embedded version of the paradox of *New Grub Street*: if London is as obsolete as Reardon claims, why does the novel refuse to leave it?

Take, for instance, two telegraphic announcements in *New Grub Street*, the first relating the news of the death of Jasper's mother, the second the far more consequential news of John Yule's death, which will lead to an ultimately delusive legacy for Marian Yule and a large, real one for Amy Reardon. Both pieces of news arrive via telegram, but both arrive *twice*, at widely dispersed intervals in different homes, so that the simultaneity of the announcements—presumably sent out to interested parties at roughly the same time—is disrupted and delayed. The Yule telegram arrives first to his brother Alfred, who relates the news to Marian; Gissing sticks with this particular family through the funeral, the reading of the will giving Marian £5,000, the relation of this news to Jasper, Alfred Yule's attempts to get Marian to invest the money in a new literary journal, and Jasper's proposal to Marian. Only five chapters later, across the divide between volumes two and three, does the telegram arrive at Amy's refuge with her mother, when all the news that it contains, including Amy's own £10,000 legacy, has already been learned, digested, and acted upon by every other character in the novel except Amy and Reardon. Put another way: that a single, dramatic announcement

---

final development of the pastoral vision which, in his mature fiction, is Gissing's only means of accessing place description.

⁵⁷ See David Harvey, *The Condition of Postmodernity: An Enquiry into the Origins of Cultural Change* (Oxford: Blackwell, 1990), 240, 265. 'Time–space compression' has become a category of major interest for historians, sociologists, and philosophers, and is a cornerstone of the 'dromology' of Paul Virilio; but Harvey's claims about simultaneity and novelistic realism have yet to be fully engaged within literary criticism.

(via high-speed technology) of news in the novel's *fabula* is reiterated and protracted in the novel's *sjuzet* means that narrative presentation in *New Grub Street* acts primarily to retard the accelerated pace of events and to disable simultaneity. Gissing will report speed as a 'fact of the fiction', but will refuse to mimic it; the novel will not move with the speed of a telegram.[58]

The struggle of Gissing's mature fiction, then, is to oppose referential fact with narratorial value, to refuse to let the narrated world contaminate the stubbornly measured tread of narration. Machinery of any kind, particularly machines of speed, are introduced to be counteracted: the dystopic efficiency of Marian's imagined 'Literary Machine', an automaton capable of reducing and blending older books for modern consumption, dissolves into her headaches, produced by 'the sputtering whiteness of the electric light, and its ceaseless hum', in which the pages turn 'blue and green and yellow before her eyes' in a vivid description of ophthalmologic fatigue (*NGS*, 138). By the time of *The Whirlpool*, Gissing largely refuses any direct description of machines such as trains, and instead prefers to linger on the nervous disorders of Alma Frothingham, whose similar headaches are brought on by the cognitive disruptions of underground travel.[59] As a matter of principle, however, this strong dichotomy between modernity within the text and a self-consciously traditional narrative procedure cannot at all moments hold. The suggestions that accelerated technologies would eventually influence literary style and plotting were accumulating by the 1890s, not simply in the relatively parochial world of reading physiology, but in literary-critical surmises as well.[60] Perhaps their most immediately discernible impact on Gissing is in the relation of a new set of characters, those who with a wide set of connotations are often called 'fast'.

By the mid-1890s Gissing had accumulated a gallery of such portraits. *The Odd Women*'s Mrs Luke Widdowson, who 'lived at the utmost pace compatible with technical virtue' (*OW*, 137), joins *In the Year of Jubilee*'s Beatrice French and Luckworth Crewe, both modern entrepreneurs, as exemplars of a certain kind of accelerated personality. That the term 'fast' had recently come to

---

[58] For the phrase 'fact of the fiction', see Ann Banfield, *Unspeakable Sentences: Narration and Representation in the Language of Fiction* (Boston: Routledge & Kegan Paul, 1982), 217.

[59] Gissing did in 1892 begin writing a novel, called 'Gods of Iron', on 'the degree to which people have become *machines*, in harmony with the machinery amid which they spend their lives', although one imagines that the de-anthropomorphizing procedure of this now-lost novel, by making narrated fact and narratorial procedure come too close together, was finally too different from Gissing's normal process to be completed. See Gissing, *Collected Letters*, v., 76.

[60] See, e.g., Robert O'Brien, 'Machinery and English Style', *Atlantic Monthly* 94 (Oct. 1904), 464–72, which evaluates the impact of shorthand, typewriting, and telegraphic communication upon contemporary prose; O'Brien's assessment is notably evenhanded, and finds as many gains (in clarity and force) as losses (in ornamentation or variety).

signify moral looseness, particularly in relation to women, is in Gissing no
hindrance to its literal sense; Crewe is notable both for his careless dress, which
'bore the traces of perpetual hurry', and for his walking pace, which outstrips
all but the most determined (*IYJ*, 85). Far from taking 'fast living' as a dormant
metaphor for immorality or modernity, Gissing reendows it with all the force
of descriptions of embodied acceleration. His 'fast' characters age quickly, are
possessed of more rapid heartbeats and sensitive nervous systems, and talk
and act more quickly, and less deliberately, than others. Straining to describe
their rapid way of life, Gissing's narratives catch a reflected sense of exhilarated
speed from them. *New Grub Street*'s Jasper is the first of such figures, and his
account of his daily activities is a testament to modern acceleration:

'My word, what a day I have had! I've just been trying what I could really do in
one day if I worked my hardest. Now just listen; it deserves to be chronicled for the
encouragement of aspiring youth. I got up at 7:30, and whilst I breakfasted I read
through a volume I had to review. By 10:30 the review was written—three-quarters of
a column of the *Evening Budget*. . . . The book was Billington's "Vagaries"; pompous
idiocy, of course, but he lives in a big house and gives dinners. Well, from 10:30 to 11,
I smoked a cigar and reflected, feeling that the day wasn't badly begun. At eleven, I
was ready to write my Saturday *causerie* for the *Will o' the Wisp*; it took me till close
upon one o'clock, which was rather too long. I can't afford more than an hour and
a half for that job. At one, I rushed out to a dirty little eating-house in Hampstead
Road. Was back again by a quarter to two, having in the meantime sketched a paper
for *The West End*. Pipe in mouth, I sat down to leisurely artistic work; by five, half the
paper was done; the other half remains for to-morrow. From five to half-past I read
four newspapers and two magazines, and from half-past to a quarter to six I jotted
down several ideas that had come to me whilst reading. At six I was again in the dirty
eating-house, satisfying a ferocious hunger. Home once more at 6:45, and for two
hours wrote steadily at a long affair I have in hand for *The Current*. Then I came here,
thinking hard all the way. What say you to this? Have I earned a night's repose?'
    'And what's the value of it all?' asked Maud.
    'Probably from ten to twelve guineas, if I calculated.' (*NGS*, 213)

As Rachel Bowlby has pointed out, Jasper's day is the successfully maximized
version of the notations in Gissing's diaries, which describe with similar
temporal exactness days of writer's block and wasted hours.[61] It represents
a perfect adaptation of bodily and mental rhythms to the demands of a
certain kind of routinized craft labor, and in Jasper's awareness of the smallest
movements of the clock, as well as his easy ability to convert space ('three-
quarters of a column') into time ('an hour and a half') into money ('ten to
twelve guineas'), we see the mind turning into a timed industrial machine. In

---

[61] See Bowlby, *Just Looking*, 108–12.

this sense Jasper becomes what Paul Virilio has recently called 'hyperactive man', for whom the elimination of wasted time 'will now be pursued right inside living matter, this time by the reconstitution of vital dynamics, the phagocytosis of what is alive, of the subject's vitality itself'.[62] Technology *per se* is far less important to this kind of speed than the technologizing of the body itself, just as the machinery of the tachistoscope was, for reading physiologists, only a means toward the transformation of the eye into an efficient motor.

The breathlessness of Jasper's narration is, as I have claimed, the kind of experience of acceleration that Gissing's novel strives to describe without enacting. But here the techniques of delay and elongation that slow the speed of *New Grub Street*'s telegrams are powerless: Jasper's narration is even faster than the speed of what he narrates, and Gissing offers us no account of the gaps or lassitudes in Jasper's day that might counteract the rate of his machine-like production. Here Jasper poses his most sustained problem for the novel. At moments—concentrated, generally, on Jasper—the novel achieves what narratologists have long termed 'speed': a relation, in the words of Gerald Prince, between 'the duration of the narrated' and 'the length of the narrative (in words, lines, or pages, for example)', in which the time of reading is presumably shorter than the time of the narrated action.[63] What I want to suggest here is that the force of Jasper's narration, as with most of his appearances, has less to do with the unusual rapidity of his production, and the envy and envious ridicule that it might occasion, than his acceleration of the narrative's speed; by forcing the novel to become faster, in narratological terms, and thereby forcing the reader's experience to accelerate, Jasper pulls the reader with him. While Reardon narrates in pages what took a moment to experience (an Athenian sunset), Jasper quickly narrates a day of quick work. The speeds of production and consumption are here aligned.

There is, however, a problem with the narratological definition of speed, one that its more acute practitioners have noted, and one that takes us further into Gissing's attempts to describe a culture of rapid responses. Any true measurement of speed requires a spatial unit—*miles* per hour, *meters* per second—not simply a comparison of two different speeds over what is surely very different terrain (reading about, as opposed to performing, an action or series of actions). Without any common spatial unit between narrated action and reading time, the narratological measure of speed is only a relation between vague abstractions. As Gérard Genette has pointed out, the only common spatial unit possible is text itself: the materiality of words, lines, and

[62] Virilio, *Art of the Motor*, 105.

[63] See Gerald Prince, *A Dictionary of Narratology* (Lincoln: University of Nebraska Press, 1987), 89.

pages, precisely the materiality that reading physiologists began to study in the late nineteenth century.[64] To get from the duration of a narrated action to the duration of the reading experience, the mediating point of textual materiality is necessary. Not coincidentally, *New Grub Street* concentrates its account of accelerated reading habits on the bibliographical facts of shortened, choppier texts, and turns repeatedly to the materiality of text as a way of making more exact its description of rapid consumption. Like the reading physiologists contemporary with it, *New Grub Street* can best explain the impact of speed through a description of paper and ink, lines and pages.

HE WHO RUNS MAY READ: THE ADVENT OF RAPID CONSUMPTION

Few nineteenth-century novels, with the exception, perhaps, of Balzac's *Illusions perdues*, are as rooted in the materiality of text as *New Grub Street*. Paper is the common element of the novel's central family, the 'house of Yule', whose three brothers are engaged in relations to paper that are neatly divisible, from industrial production (John Yule, the wealthy paper manufacturer), to retail sales (Edmund Yule, deceased father of Amy, was a stationer), to cultural reproduction (Alfred Yule, the critic and 'man of letters'). As the relation to paper becomes more abstract and reified, however, the financial rewards decrease, which is perhaps why the novel's cadre of novelists, journalists, and occasional writers is obsessed with removing the veil of artistic ignorance and discussing the procedural facts of how texts are assembled for the market. Primary among these facts is something that one might call the New Brevity: the fragmentation and shortening of reading material as well as readerly attention which is the novel's constant concern. Gissing arranges a gallery of opinions about this New Brevity, starting with Alfred Yule's conservative

---

[64] As Genette realizes, this spatial unit would have to be specified with care, and would have to be common to many different texts; thus, for his account of the 'speed' of Proust's *À la recherche de temps perdu*, he relies on the common measure of the Pléiade series. It scarcely needs adding that such a common measure is largely unavailable for the Anglo-American novel, let alone Gissing's novels, which exist in a bewildering variety of texts without an 'authoritative' version. See Gérard Genette, *Narrative Discourse Revisited*, trans. Jane Lewin (Ithaca, NY: Cornell University Press, 1988), 34–5. Genette is responding here to a tradition of narratological speculation that is comfortably imprecise about what 'time of consumption' really is; in Seymour Chatman's influential account, 'discourse-time' is defined as 'the time it takes to peruse the discourse', without an exact measure of how to measure, or time, 'discourse' itself. See Seymour Chatman, *Story and Discourse: Narrative Structure in Story and Film* (Ithaca, NY: Cornell University Press, 1978), 62.

claim that the 'evil of the time is the multiplication of ephemerides', of 'essays, descriptive articles, fragments of criticism' (*NGS*, 67–8). Jasper is, as one might expect, neutral with regard to this phenomenon, except insofar as it gives him opportunity for an article on 'Typical Readers'; his comment about the new publication 'The Current', that 'the tone is to be up to date, and the articles are to be short; no padding, *merum sel* from cover to cover' (*NGS*, 104), is a fine balance of commercial approval and in-the-know mockery. But the novel's most enthusiastic appraisal is given by Whelpdale, the fledgling literary agent, who proposes a thinly disguised version of Newnes's *Tit-Bits*:

> 'Let me explain my principle. I would have the paper address itself to the quarter-educated; that is to say, the great new generation that is being turned out by the Board schools, the young men and women who can just read, but are incapable of sustained attention. People of this kind want something to occupy them in trains, and on 'buses and trams. As a rule they care for no newspapers except the Sunday ones; what they want is the lightest and frothiest of chit-chatty information—bits of stories, bits of description, bits of scandal, bits of jokes, bits of statistics, bits of foolery. Am I not right? Everything must be very short, two inches at the utmost; their attention can't sustain itself beyond two inches.' (*NGS*, 496–7)

If time largely eliminates the force of space in Gissing's narrative procedure, within Whelpdale's ruminations we find space (the 'two inches' that he proclaims the maximum duration of readerly interest) troping time. Both a serious proposal and a self-parody, Whelpdale's idea is to aid accelerated comprehension by producing a style wholly fitted to rapid reading, for scanning and skimming. It is a technological proposal, matched to cognate technologies of speed—Dora Milvain remarks in approval that 'one knows by experience that one can't really fix one's attention in traveling' (*NGS*, 497)—and expressed with a mathematical clarity: not only is no article to be longer than two inches, but each inch, Whelpdale claims, must contain at least two paragraphs. In later work Gissing will make this kind of material a sociological index of suburban vulgarity, as with the textual detritus of the Peachey family from *In the Year of Jubilee*, whose drawing room is littered with 'illustrated weeklies, journals of society, cheap miscellanies, penny novelettes, and the like', including 'half-a-dozen novels of the meaner kind'; Ada Peachey's reading is composed entirely of fragments, of 'instalments of a dozen serial stories, paragraphs relating to fashion, sport, the theatre, answers to correspondents (wherein she especially delighted), columns of facetiae, and gossip about notorious people' (*IYJ*, 8). In *New Grub Street*, however, the production of such fragmented, accelerated text is still a matter for resentful admiration, at least toward the ingenuity with which it is designed and executed.

This is, for Gissing, the new horizon of reading: a demand for speed that can only be satisfied finally by such mechanical expedients. It demands fragmentation of content and style at every moment, a fact that even Harold Biffen's tutee, one Mr Baker, can discern with unintentional irony: 'The thoughts come in a lump, if I may say so. To break it up—there's the art of compersition' (*NGS*, 242). It is the accelerated scanning that all literary composition now faces, and that therefore threatens the standard size and traditional procedures of narrative fiction. In this, Gissing adheres closely to the analyses of many contemporary observers, particularly those, such as Ackland, who took the 1870 Education Act as the precipitating cause of the cultural situation.[65] Here Gissing arrives at a double, and somewhat contradictory, diagnosis: the habitual slowness of the novel and the new rapidity of the mass reader. The latter is continually adduced by all corners of the literary field as Gissing represents it; it is not a matter for dispute, only for resistance, like Yule's, or adjustment, like Whelpdale's. Neither of these examples, however, directly concerns the novel, which remains discreetly offstage in *New Grub Street*'s discussions of rapid consumption. What is a matter for comment is the novel's ponderous slowness, the vast and resented bulk of its usual three-volume form that makes such demands upon the novelist's capacity for inventive padding, and that makes it unfit for a landscape of omnibus or train readers. 'Reardon's story was in itself weak,' we are told, 'and this second volume had to consist almost entirely of laborious padding' (*NGS*, 161). The speed of literary forms, like all cultural speeds, is in Gissing discontinuous; but in *New Grub Street* the discontinuities are in the process of flattening themselves out into a more homogeneous world of rapidity, and narrative fiction is in danger of losing its cultural centrality.

We meet, therefore, with a contradiction. Is the dilemma excessive slowness, as in the novel form that Reardon practices, or excessive speed, as in the often

---

[65] The accuracy of *New Grub Street* as a cultural history of the literary market has long been a live issue, at least since Raymond Williams's proclamation that 'it is so representative and so thorough that it is extraordinary that it should not be more generally read'. See *Culture and Society, 1780–1950* (London: Chatto & Windus, 1958), 174. Recent work has suggested that the novel is anachronistic, importing back into the early 1880s the concerns of the early 1890s: see Nigel Cross, *The Common Writer: Life in Nineteenth-Century New Grub Street* (Cambridge: Cambridge University Press, 1985), 204–40; John Sloan, *George Gissing: The Cultural Challenge* (New York: St Martin's, 1989), 89. Adrian Poole's nuanced claim that Gissing's depiction of the literary market is not so much anachronistic as partially misguided is persuasive; Poole argues that Gissing misread a fragmentation of the market into several new niches (one of which guaranteed the small success of *New Grub Street* itself) as instead a wholesale orientation of the market toward the mass publication, and thus saw as an elimination what was really his compartmentalization as a 'minority' writer. See Adrian Poole, *Gissing in Context* (London: Macmillan, 1975), 140–6. Gissing's depiction, however, hews fairly closely to what many contemporaries claimed about the marketplace and the mass reader, and is thus, if not wholly accurate, at the very least representative of his moment.

asserted tastes of the new output of public education, the mass reader? Is the evil castigated by *New Grub Street* the 'padding' of Reardon's novels—the uninspired length that a misguided publishing industry requires him to produce—or the new breed of skimmers and skippers who have turned away from the novel to such forms as Whelpdale's two-inches-or-less gossipy bits? When both novelistic 'padding' and journalistic 'ephemerides' come in for sustained critique, it is possible that no middle ground can be found between an outmoded, slow narrative form and an undereducated, rapid readership. As a result, *New Grub Street* offers solutions that are only fantasies. One such is a retreat to an impossibly distant past: the intimate oral reading of Homer that temporarily bonds Reardon and Amy; the debates over Sophoclean metrical effects between Reardon and Biffen; Reardon's sedate, 'a canto each day' reading of Dante's *Commedia* (*NGS*, 234). Another is Biffen's novelistic experiment, 'Mr. Bailey, Grocer', the practice of 'absolute realism in the sphere of the ignobly decent' which is, significantly, to appear in one volume, 'the length of the ordinary French novel' (*NGS*, 173, 244). Biffen's avowed purpose looks like nothing so much as Reardon's 'padding' without the accompanying narrative context, an utterly transparent depiction of ordinariness that will be, as Biffen admits, 'unutterably tedious' but nonetheless veracious (*NGS*, 174). As a means toward reconciling accelerated audience and lethargic novel, Biffen's attempt is a self-proclaimed failure, less a proto-modernist manifesto than a violent caricature or harsh distillation of the Victorian novel as usual. Neither old practices nor new forms can solve the dilemma.

The refusal to specify a solution is part of a larger resistance or resentment in *New Grub Street* toward both the novel's languorous bulk and the audience's desire for rapid sensations. For a novel constantly citing a variety of embedded texts—'Mr. Bailey', Reardon's novels, Alfred Yule's 'English Prose in the Nineteenth Century', Clement Fadge's devastating review of Yule's book, any of the poor reviews of Reardon's 'Margaret Home', the textbooks for youth composed by Dora and Maud Milvain, any of Jasper's many occasional pieces—Gissing significantly abstains from any pastiche. The novel resolutely silences its many referenced texts, in a move as bold as it is timid; one has only to think, again, of Balzac's many pastiches in his *Illusions perdues* to think of the opportunities for parody and biting stylistic analysis that are foregone in *New Grub Street*. This refusal might be, in fact, Gissing's sense of the novel's only remaining cultural role: to resist incorporation into the new, more rapid or telegraphic styles of the day. Here Gissing's vision of the novel is at odds with that imagined by reading physiology, for which the novel represented consumption at its potentially fastest. With the exception of Yule's ponderous book, almost all of *New Grub Street*'s cited texts would have to be more epigrammatic, witty, or terse than Gissing's own style, and as a result they are only paraphrased, their rapid styles quarantined from the novel's own deliberate pace. *New Grub Street* poses itself against the new speed-reader, and offers itself as a counterexample to the kind of modernized styles imagined by reading psychologists, but recognizes that this stance is an isolated and eventually defeated one.[66] Its acerbity is a result of its obstinate preference for the vanishing world of slow reading—it is, finally, a three-volume novel that refuses to relinquish that status—but that acerbity is also caused by the helpless recognition that 'slowness' is relative, and finally not entirely an authorial choice. As readers get faster, what had been normal speeds would become increasingly slow, and *New Grub Street* is possessed by the knowledge that, over time, it will only seem slower.

What kind of reading, then, does this slow novel in a world of speed-readers imagine that it can get? At best, it seems, it can serve as a respite in a world of exhaustion; readers in Gissing, from *New Grub Street* onward, are either so drained by hopeless competitive effort, or so thoroughly trained by the constant demand for faster comprehension and consumption, that novels are read only in a distracted daze, or in a state akin to sleep. Reardon turns away from narrative altogether, its duration no longer something he has patience for: 'He could not read continuously, but sometimes he opened his Shakespeare, for instance, and dreamed over a page or two' (*NGS*, 376). In later novels Gissing is more explicit about the quality of neural processing involved in modern novel-reading. *In the Year of Jubilee*, Nancy Lord, who carries books on evolution and pretends to read Helmholtz's 'Lectures', spends most of her leisure time 'reading a novel from the book-lender's—that is to say, gazing idly at the page, and letting such significance as it possessed float upon her thoughts' (*IYJ*, 92). Harvey Rolfe of *The Whirlpool*, at his lowest ebb in the narrative, retreats to the safety of the circulating library to read novels and books of travel: 'he lost the power of mental concentration, yielded to the indolent pleasure of desultory page-skimming' (*W*, 355). These instances, and many others like them in Gissing's later fiction, are only ostensibly sociologies of reading. We might better understand them as physiologies of reading traced through the sociological choices of texts made by various characters; cognitive and physiological training is usually adduced as the fundamental

---

[66] This reading of *New Grub Street*'s affective tone is, of course, indebted to both Raymond Williams's account in *Culture and Society* of Gissing's 'negative identification' and Fredric Jameson's analysis in *The Political Unconscious* of Gissing's 'authentic *ressentiment*'. I am suggesting here that these nuanced appraisals of Gissing's political stance need to be put in the context of the debates over the reading public's changing nature, particularly its new desire for speed, throughout the 1890s.

cause underlying the kind of books selected. Samuel Barmby, *In the Year of Jubilee*'s suburban piano-dealer and representative of mass literacy, might jumble Matthew Arnold with Samuel Smiles and George Eliot with Ellen Wood, but his inability to make discriminations amidst the literary field of his day is the effect, largely physiological, of his earliest textual training: 'much diet of newspapers rendered him all but incapable of sustained attention' (*IYJ*, 180). Gissing's reliance upon psychological, rather than purely sociological, reasoning is not surprising for his moment; what are distinctive, at least within the tradition of physiological theorizing about reading and narrative, are his conservative conclusions, which tend to imagine the accelerations of consumption that Barmby (and others) evoke as cultural disasters rather than cognitive adaptations. Barmby is, in fact, a reader very much like that called for by reading physiologists of his time: skilled in quick evaluations, wide-ranging and undiscriminating in his habits, a skimmer rather than a prolonged reader. This is the reader, to a large extent, that *New Grub Street* exists both to describe and to frustrate.

By the mid-1890s, a further source of mental dispersal comes to Gissing's notice: advertising. *In the Year of Jubilee* is dotted with references to billboards, placards, posters, and signs of all sorts, and the novel's fascination is less with the vulgarity of their slogans or the banality of their products than with the ways in which they are consumed—primarily with how they are consumed in transit. Luckworth Crewe, the British novel's first advertising agent, plans a series of billboards along the South-Western Railway, in 'a certain particular place, where the trains slow, and folks have time to meditate upon it' (*IYJ*, 63). Taken along with the novel's descriptions of the advertisements on Underground platforms, the description here speaks to a fascinated horror at the time–space calculations of *mobile reading*, a literal form of speed-reading that men like Crewe had to know how to cater to and that linked uneasily with the novel, particularly the railway novel, as another form of material for mobile consumption. Seen in a flash, the advertisements that Crewe plans are identical, in cognitive form, to the experiments performed by physiologists on the tachistoscope or gravity chronometer: they are signs, seen in shortened exposures, that train the eye in the most rapid forms of comprehension. Alongside the sheer size and speed of these advertisements (which relied upon physiological work on legibility and speed for their precise dimensions), the novel has, in Gissing, become a form only for lethargy, for the nervous reactions ensuing upon such rapid exertions. One might even speak of the novel form in late Gissing as a light entertainment, where the lightness derives not so much from the presumed frothiness of content as from the form's cognitive permissiveness, which asks for nothing more than an occasionally fixated, intermittent, idle attention.

As for dreams of devoted, immersed reading, in Gissing they are almost parodies. The following, from *Born in Exile*, is one significant instance:

After a little dallying, he became absorbed in this work, and two or three hours passed before its hold on his attention slackened. He seldom changed his position; the volume was propped against others, and he sat bending forward, his arms folded upon the desk. When he was thus deeply engaged, his face had a hard, stern aspect; if by chance his eye wandered for a moment, its look seemed to express resentment of interruption. (*BE*, 149–50)

The work being read here is F. H. Reusch's *Bibel und Natur*, an attempt to reconcile revelation and science; the reader is Godwin Peak, one of Gissing's most skeptical readers. Peak's attention is recruited not by any simple interest or credulity, but because he plans to use Reusch as a textbook of hypocrisy, as a guide for his plan to pass himself off as an Anglican believer in order to gain entry to the Warricombe household, home of Sidwell Warricombe, his object of (class and erotic) desire. The intensity of his reading gaze is entirely self-interested, entirely disbelieving, at once immersed and utterly removed. It seeks in the text nothing but utility, with a ruthlessness that makes Gissing's rapid, inattentive readers, like Samuel Barmby, sympathetic by comparison. It is, lastly, the most protracted description of readerly immersion that we have from Gissing in the 1890s, when all of his other readers have turned to scanning, skimming, and dreaming over the page of text. It is as if, in an age of speed-reading, the obverse—submerged, prolonged engagement in the mental act of reading—has warped into something sinister, something no longer a cultural commonplace but a sign of deeper, anti-social disturbance.

TOWARD THE READER OF THE FUTURE

Lewis Carroll's *Sylvie and Bruno* (1889) furnishes a parable which, one imagines, would have been congenial to Gissing during the composition of *New Grub Street*. One of the narrator's several interlocutors, an earl, advises taking pleasures quickly rather than slowly: 'It takes *you* three hours and a half to hear and enjoy an opera. Suppose *I* can take it in, and enjoy it, in half-an-hour. Why, I can enjoy *seven* operas, while you are listening to one!' When the narrator expresses doubt that an orchestra can be found to perform such a feat, the earl replies that he has already found one, albeit a mechanical one: a music-box with a broken regulator, which played complete airs in three seconds. Asked if the air was enjoyable in so short a form, the earl responds enthusiastically that it wasn't particularly, but of course 'I hadn't been trained to that kind of music!'[67] What Gissing saw in mass readership by the 1890s was a public increasingly trained to speeds that might excite ridicule or disbelief—the half-hour opera, the three-second air, and the shortened novel—but that much cultural energy was devoted to normalizing. Gissing was as interested as Carroll in describing the increasing cultural value of compression and brevity, and as prone as Carroll to seeing it as a by-product of technological rapidity.

The earl was, of course, one possible reader of the future, the self-confident speed-reader, 'trained' to acceleration, gradually turning the eye into a machine of greater efficiency. As a dream of the body's technologizing, speed-reading has remained remarkably alluring, down to the present, even if continually embarrassing for the profession of literary criticism, centered as it is on the reading act. But Gissing's proto-speed-readers, from Jasper to Barmby to Crewe, are only one version of the envisioned reader of the future; the other version, left in the wake of reading's acceleration, is the blind reader. It should not be surprising, therefore, that one of *New Grub Street*'s narrative strands ends in blindness, when Alfred Yule finally succumbs to what the novel suggests, but never confirms, is cataract in both eyes. The description of his failing sight, however, is straight from the worst-case scenarios of reading physiologists interested in ophthalmologic hygiene: 'While standing thus he noticed that the objects at which he looked had a blurred appearance; his eyesight seemed to have become worse this morning. Only a result of his insufficient sleep perhaps. He took up a scrap of newspaper that lay on the stall; he could read it, but one of his eyes was certainly weaker than the other; trying to see with that one alone, he found that everything became misty' (*NGS*, 442). Yule's rapidly fading eyesight, however it is diagnosed, and however terminal it may be, is not far from the occasional headachy, blurred vision that afflicts both Marian and Reardon, and that always looms for all of the novel's many professional readers. Once Yule's vision goes, everything in his life, his reading included, slows almost to a halt; limited to large print, and to only a few hours a day of reading, Yule is incapable of reaching the speeds he needs to do his work, and he thus dwindles into absolute debility. The imperative for speed, in reading as in so much else, has its casualties, and Yule's catastrophic blindness is the other version of the reading of the future: the breakdown of the motorized eye.[68] Here again, Gissing's devotion to disastrous binaries is evident: accelerate or die.

---

[67] Lewis Carroll, *Sylvie and Bruno* (London: Macmillan, 1889), 338–9.

[68] The imperative for speed was such that Javal, himself blind from glaucoma at the time of his *Physiologie de la lecture et de l'écriture* (1906), suggests that Braille is an insufficient textual method for the blind because of its 'excessive lenteur'. See Javal, *Physiologie de la lecture*, 275. Narrowing the gap between the accelerating speeds of sight reading and the persistent slowness

The novel, likewise, began in the rhetoric of the 1890s to occupy an uneasy middle ground between technologized strenuousness and pre-technological exhaustion and lassitude. For reading physiologists, it was prime ground upon which to experiment with new capacities for rapid consumption. For Gissing, it was a form threatening to become both a condensed, accelerated caricature of itself, a doomed competitor of the chatty newspaper, and a form that, in its persistent slowness, could find a cultural home only as an occasion for dreamy, vacuous mental abstraction, for the occasional tired intervals in a world of quick scanning. Seeing too quickly, or not really seeing at all ('gazing idly at the page'): the alternatives of speed-reading and *alexia*, which for Gissing constituted the stark binary of late-nineteenth-century literary consumption, offer no real way out. Either alternative, it becomes clear, means the eventual minoritizing of the novel; 'adjust and accelerate, or die' means, for Gissing, 'adjust and accelerate, and die'. In this sense, the ambivalence of Gissing's relation to the novel, the mixed hatred and affection that animates *New Grub Street* and his later fiction, can be seen as a depressive-position state, one that desired to protect the novel from the depredations of its consumers, from the increasingly distorting ways it was being read in a culture of speed. In many ways, that depressive position has lingered for readers, writers, and critics of novels, to our own day.

of reading by hand was Javal's primary reason for suggesting a range of orthographic reforms to the Braille system; his concern was less for the range of texts available in Braille than for the disabilities of the blind in a culture of acceleration.

Coda: I. A. Richards and the End
of Physiological Novel Theory

These damned 400-page novels take such a lot of time, and they are very
rarely worth it. 31 hours for twopence!

Richards in a letter to Mansfield Forbes, August 1919

The strange story of the Victorian physiology of the novel—as that of
physiological aesthetics generally—has a final, brief moment of efflorescence
and withering. That moment occurred in a single place, the University of
Cambridge, and in a small span of time, between the initial formation in 1917
of what would become the English Tripos and the publication in 1924 of I. A.
Richards's *Principles of Literary Criticism*. Those years saw the foundation of
the academic study of literature along lines receptive to a physiological inquiry
into reading, cognition, and literary form, as well as to fiction in general; they
also saw Richards, eventually the most well known of Cambridge's early literary
theorists, invent a form of physiological criticism that could not, and cared not
to, study the novel. The story of how the study of English dissociated itself from
both Anglo-Saxon philology and the discipline of Classics has been told in
many different ways, but the main outlines are clear: in the unsettled wartime
atmosphere of Cambridge, four men primarily—Sir Arthur Quiller-Couch,
second holder of the recently founded chair of English; H. M. Chadwick,
Professor of Anglo-Saxon; the belletrist A. C. Benson; and Mansfield Forbes,
fellow in history, teacher of Old English, and magnetic attractor of young
literary and scholarly talent—informally devised a plan whereby the study of
English literature would be detached from the Medieval and Modern Language
Tripos into its own Honours course of study.[1] Crucially, it was Forbes who
insisted that lectures on the contemporary novel be given in this new academic

---

[1] For three different accounts of these formative years in the discipline of English studies
at Cambridge, see Hugh Carey, *Mansfield Forbes and his Cambridge* (Cambridge: Cambridge
University Press, 1984); F. R. Leavis, *English Literature in Our Time and the University* (London:
Chatto & Windus, 1969); and E. M. W. Tillyard, *The Muse Unchained: An Intimate Account
of the Revolution of English Studies at Cambridge* (London: Bowes & Bowes, 1958). While each

pursuit, and who, in the spring of 1919, recruited Richards to give those initial lectures.

To an observer versed in Victorian novel physiology, the choice was not as strange as it would later seem, given Richards's subsequent aversion to fiction. Since taking his degree in Moral Sciences in 1915, and barred from participation in the war because of recurrent tuberculosis, Richards had struggled to find an outlet for his intellectual energy. Ultimately he returned to Cambridge in 1918 to do two things: to study and read physiology at the Cavendish Laboratory, and to begin writing two novels which were never completed and whose fragments do not survive. Richards, that is, in these formative years for English literary studies, was occupied in a characteristically Victorian activity: cross-fertilizing inquiries into fictional form and physiological theory. His version of this activity was of course updated, replacing the worn names of Bain, Maudsley, and Lewes with Charles Sherrington's *The Integrative Action of the Nervous System* (1906), William James, and G. E. Moore. As he would put it half a century later: 'I was someone really saturated in psychology and neurology making up a book about the literary approaches. That was a bit of luck really. Two quite different concerns crossing at a crucial point.'[2]

The initial fruits of that crossing appear, although only in hints and detached musings, in Richards's letters to Forbes in the spring of 1919. Having been engaged to teach two courses—one called 'The Principles of Literary Criticism', the other 'The Contemporary Novel'—Richards was clearly thinking through a possible synthesis of novel studies, critical theory, and his reading in physiology and neurology. In May he hinted to Forbes that he had 'a doctrine of Types of Novel, which at last has come out of the mangle ready for wear, very quickly and straight'; in mid-1920 he wrote that he had completed 'the introductory chapter of the book on "The Novel" which I was writing; with a few addenda it has got the main thing which *I* say stated'.[3] Neither Richards's lectures nor his book on the novel have survived; all that remains of this period of his development is a reading list—comprising Hardy, Conrad, Joyce, Bennett, Moore, Wells, and Lawrence—that illustrates

version is essentially a celebration of the discipline's formal origin, Leavis's version is the most anxious to make Richards's contribution, and physiological aesthetics, an unhappy accident of the time, rather than a key element of the early English Tripos; Richards's interest in literature, Leavis insists, 'was not intense and was never developed', and *Principles of Literary Criticism* is attacked for the 'insistent pretension' of its 'pseudo-scientific pseudo-psychological' claims. See Leavis, *English Literature*, 16–17.

[2] See Reuben Brower, 'Beginnings and Transitions: I. A. Richards Interviewed by Reuben Brower', in *I. A. Richards: Essays in his Honor*, ed. Reuben Brower, Helen Vendler, and John Hollander (Oxford: Oxford University Press, 1973), 28.

[3] I. A. Richards, *Selected Letters of I. A. Richards, C. H.*, ed. John Constable (Oxford: Clarendon Press, 1990), 9, 20.

Richards's notion of the 'contemporary' novel of 1919.[4] Even without much textual evidence from this period, however, the nature of Richards's critical thinking at this time is clear, and it is unmistakably Victorian. It is, first, a study of the novel through its current avatars; it is not a history of the genre. It is also a study based in recent physiologies of response—in other words, it is a communication theory of genre. This is the tradition of Lewes, Bain, Dallas, and others, unexpectedly reappearing in postwar Cambridge, reinvented for an academic rather than a journalistic or belletristic pursuit. Seen this way, Richards—at least at this point in his career—could with justice be called the last Victorian novel theorist.

In fact, the reading that Richards pursued in these years seems to have been far more rooted in Victorian physiology than any biographer has previously noted, or that Richards himself was willing to admit. While Richards gave due homage in his later years to William James and Charles Sherrington, and the influence of G. E. Moore's philosophical psychology is clear, his published writings from the 1920s contain ample traces of an earlier tradition. Within *Principles of Literary Criticism* one can find citations from Vernon Lee, Gustav Fechner, Thèodule Ribot, and Edmund Gurney, while his later *Practical Criticism* (1929) mentions Alexander Bain, whose *Emotions and the Will*—so crucial a text for Victorian physiologies of the novel—Richards had clearly studied.[5] Even if these citations are often dismissive or critical (particularly those of Lee), they demonstrate that Victorian physiologists and physiological aestheticians were still, at least until 1920, part of the background that a serious student of physiological aesthetics needed to possess. It is not the case, in other words, that Richards leapt from Coleridge to Sherrington; he used Victorian theorists as well, in order to construct his guiding notion in the 1920s, that—as Paul Fry has recently put it—the soul is neurological.[6] Furthermore, his embryonic theory of the novel, written as lectures for the equally embryonic English Tripos, was, it seems, formed along the disciplinary lines that Victorian critics had already pursued.

Given these facts, why did Richards never finish or publish his 'book on "The Novel"', the book that might have pushed physiological novel theory into the twentieth century? And why, when the eventual outcome of his early English Tripos courses—*Principles of Literary Criticism*—appeared, did it contain no trace of this novel theory? The absence of the novel within

---

[4] See John Paul Russo's comprehensive account of this period in *I. A. Richards: His Life and Work* (Baltimore: Johns Hopkins University Press, 1989), 66.

[5] Ibid. 319–20.

[6] Paul Fry, 'I. A. Richards', in *The Cambridge History of Literary Criticism*, vii: *Modernism and the New Criticism*, ed. A. Walton Litz, Louis Menand, and Lawrence Rainey (Cambridge: Cambridge University Press, 2000), 191.

Principles of Literary Criticism suggests that at some point between 1919 and 1924 Richards found his physiological or neurological approach to literature inapplicable to the novel, or that his distaste for the novel grew strong enough that he refused to write on fiction. A third possibility is even more likely: that the reasons for his distaste coalesced neatly with the reasons why the novel failed to fit his physiology. A look at some early comments to Forbes, along with a consideration of the places in *Principles* where the novel makes its presence felt in a ghostly manner, suggests that this third possibility is correct, and that one fact above all—the length of the novel form—motivated both Richards's dislike for it and his inability to treat it theoretically. This most obvious or banal of facts, the one that had driven so much Victorian novel theory—the size of the novel, its increasing bulk, its implicit demand for more and more of our time, spread out over days and weeks—is for Richards the fundamental stumbling block.

Even in 1919, while constructing his syllabus and his theory of the novel, his complaints are consistent. To Forbes he writes: 'That brings me to the Novels. They are going to be a bother. So many of those which one cannot help mentioning are just tiring things dropsically blown out. The novel in its typical form, Beresford, Cannon, Smith, Sidgwick, Walpole, Bennett, George, is a diseased thing.'[7] His comments about 'damned 400-page novels' are only partly the laments of a time-pressed instructor constructing a course from scratch; they are also recognitions that the scale of the novel, and the scale of his preferred critical mode, are incommensurable. This scale difference, and the theoretical issues it raises, is perhaps the only salient difference between Richards's project in *Principles* and the projects of Lewes, Bain, and Dallas, although it is important enough to rule the novel out of consideration. In other fundamental matters, Richards is in essential agreement with his forebears. That there is no difference in kind between aesthetic experiences and everyday experiences, that the facts of everyday reading are of theoretical importance, that notions of 'machinery' are useful analogies for aesthetic objects: Richards's open assertion of these positions is different from those of his Victorian predecessors only in his greater forthrightness. The famous opening line of *Principles*—'A book is a machine to think with'—is elaborated later on:

It is no less absurd to suppose that a competent reader sits down to read for the sake of pleasure, than to suppose that a mathematician sets out to solve an equation with a view to the pleasure its solution will afford him. The pleasure in both cases may, of course, be very great. But the pleasure, however great it may be, is no more the aim of the activity in the course of which it arises than, for example, the noise

---

[7] Richards, *Selected Letters*, 8.

made by a motorcycle—useful though it is as an indication of the way the machine is running—is the reason in the normal case for its having been started.[8]

The aim of literary machinery, as Richards argues, is instead a 'modification' of our experiences, a modification created by 'a diffused reaction in the organs of the body brought about through the sympathetic nervous system', or by 'extensive changes in the visceral and vascular systems' (pp. 92–3). In intent and vocabulary these assertions are in essential agreement with mid-Victorian novel physiologies. They imply that a study of the physicality of reader response and a neurologically based epistemology of how reading occurs are essential for any developed critical account of literature. As Richards puts it, 'enough is known for an analysis of the mental events which make up the reading of a poem to be attempted. And such an analysis is a primary necessity for criticism' (p. 74).

'A poem': this is the crucial adjustment in Richards's approach that signals his significant break with the Victorian theorists whom he elsewhere echoes so closely. The key-note of Richards's deployment of physiology is his caution, particularly as to scale: 'Only the simplest human activities are at present amenable to laboratory methods. Aestheticians have therefore been compelled to begin with as simple a form of "aesthetic choice" as can be devised. In practice, line-lengths and elementary forms, single notes and phrases, single colours and simple collocations, nonsense syllables, metronomic beats, skeleton rhythms and metres and similar simplifications have alone been open to investigation' (p. 4). Any more temporally protracted aesthetic experience—in fact, any more prolonged experience at all—quickly becomes, for Richards, too complex to investigate, too resistant to the kinds of isolations and experimental controls that science needs. As an illustration of this methodological limit, Richards turns to music:

Every element in a form, whether it be a musical form or any other, is capable of exciting a very intricate and widespread response. Usually the response is of a minimal order and escapes introspection. Thus a single note or a uniform colour has for most people hardly any observable effect beyond its sensory characteristics. When it occurs along with other elements the form which they together make up may have striking consequences in emotion and attitude . . . The separate responses which each element in isolation would tend to excite are so connected with one another that their combination is, for our present knowledge, incalculable in its effects. Two stimuli which, when separated by one interval of time or space, would merely cancel one another, with another interval produce an effect which is far beyond anything which either alone could produce. And the combined response when they are suitably arranged may be of quite another kind than that of either. (p. 158)

[8] I. A. Richards, *Principles of Literary Criticism* (London: Routledge, 2001), 88. Subsequent citations are given parenthetically in the text.

The theoretical terrain here is familiarly Victorian: the notion of a temporal form that is not simply additive but either logarithmic or wavelike in its effects; the concept of 'intervals' which are as important as events in any consideration of temporal form; the problem of how to assess stimuli both in themselves and in the context of a shifting, accumulative process of stimuli. It is the problem that preoccupied Victorian theorists; it is the problem that Percy Lubbock would solve, in 1921, by recourse to a readerly memory that transforms time into spatial arrangements. For Richards, however, it remains insoluble, at least in the temporally elongated examples of prose fiction and musical composition. As a result, *Principles of Literary Criticism* turns for examples to the shortest instances: Richards's centerpiece reading is of one line of verse ('Arcadia, Night, a Cloud, Pan, and the Moon'), a line without even any necessary syntactic directionality—the words could be transposed without loss of sense or effect—and thus without time. Richards's diagram of the line's effect is patently atemporal: 'Nor are temporal relations intended,' he explains (p. 106). This is, as one of Richards's chapter titles names it, the 'impasse of musical theory'.

It is also, of course, the impasse of longer literary forms. In one of the very few references to prose in *Principles*, Richards asserts that prose produces a 'very much vaguer and more indeterminate expectancy than verse' (p. 123). In this too he does not disagree with his Victorian predecessors; the very vagueness and dispersal of prose effects are the motivations behind the wave metaphors of Lewes and Bain, and that vagueness licensed a series of investigations into states of mental abstraction: drift, inattention, unconscious cerebration, accelerated comprehension. The Victorian physiologies used by the period's novel critics were, on the whole, friendlier to notions of diffused or vague affect than those employed by Richards. Sherrington's physiology was based upon the notion of the 'common path', or the coordination of reflexes in a single direction, a coordination called 'attention' as opposed to 'interference' in his 1906 magnum opus:

Expressed teleologically, *the common path, although economically subservient for many and various purposes, is adapted to serve but one purpose at a time. Hence it is a co-ordinating mechanism and prevents confusion by restricting the use of the organ, its minister, to but one action at a time. . . . The resultant singleness of action from moment to moment is a keystone in the construction of the individual whose unity it is the specific office of the nervous system to perfect.* The interference of unlike reflexes and the alliance of like reflexes in their action upon their common paths seem to lie at the very root of the great psychical process of 'attention.'[9]

---

[9] Charles Sherrington, *The Integrative Action of the Nervous System* (New Haven: Yale University Press, 1946), 234–5; emphasis original.

As we have seen, attention is an ambiguous and not always positive phenomenon in Victorian physiologies; it is limited, fragile, partial. In Sherrington's physiology it is central, the very purpose of mental operations, and those neural effects that combat it—reverie, distraction, competition of multiple stimuli—are only 'interference'. We pass, in other words, from a psychology friendly to multi-plot prose fiction to one best adapted to lyric condensation. The consequences of Sherrington's revision of Bain are everywhere palpable in Richards's choice of literary subjects and the scale of his readings. His *Science and Poetry* (1926) produces a reading of Wordsworth's 'Westminster Bridge' sonnet as paradigmatic because of its brevity; it is only 'an experience, ten minutes of a person's life'.[10] Three years later, *Practical Criticism*'s famous 'protocols' modeled reading on the basis of short, contextually isolated verse passages. The title of Richards's 1942 handbook, *How to Read a Page: A Course in Efficient Reading with an Introduction to a Hundred Great Words*, sufficiently expresses its investment in small-scale reading practices.

The consequences of Richards's reading of Sherrington for the new discipline of literary studies were just as profound. Modes of reading that fell short of full, 'integrated' attention were elaborately taxonomized and critiqued in *Practical Criticism*, under such terms as 'illegitimate expectation', 'irrelevant association', and, more colloquially, 'swoon-reading', as with readers 'content to loll at ease swinging softly in the hammock of the rhythm, satisfied to find at last something that sounded like poetry', or 'rapid persuals', against which Richards counseled a consciously exaggerated slowness.[11] Full attention became the *sine qua non* of the New Criticism, and subsequent schools of theory supposedly in combat with New Critical presuppositions have paradoxically maintained the status of attention in their otherwise different approaches. Sherringtonian physiology was far less rapidly abandoned in literary criticism than it was within neurology. With its triumph in Richards—and, given Richards's extraordinary influence in the middle decades of the twentieth century, in literary studies as a whole—it came to underwrite critical schools whose practitioners had no real interest in physiology or neurology. Only recently has this continued influence been recognized; as Andrew Elfenbein phrased it recently, 'Academic literary criticism institutionalized and continues to be fostered by many of the specific cognitive strategies and standards demanded by Richards.'[12]

---

[10] I. A. Richards, *Science and Poetry* (London: Kegan Paul, Trench, Trubner, 1926), 10.

[11] Richards, *Practical Criticism* (New York: Harcourt, Brace, & World, 1966), 154–5, 222.

[12] Andrew Elfenbein, 'Cognitive Science and the History of Reading', *PMLA* 121/2 (March 2006), 498.

What, then, of the novel, that form that Richards first tried to theorize and then abandoned? At the end of *Practical Criticism* Richards gestures to a standard *topos* of Victorian criticism—the similarity of novel and machine, the novel's status as a technology—in order to separate literary criticism from a host of interrelated concepts, including 'information', diffused consciousness, wide circulations of ideas, and (by implication) prose fiction:

It is arguable that mechanical inventions, with their social effects, and a too sudden diffusion of indigestible ideas, are disturbing throughout the world the whole order of human mentality, that our minds are, as it were, becoming of an inferior shape—thin, brittle and patchy, rather than controllable and coherent. It is possible that the burden of information and consciousness that a growing mind now has to carry may be too much for its natural strength. If it is not too much already, it may soon become so, for the situation is likely to grow worse before it is better. Therefore, if there be any means by which we may artificially strengthen our minds' capacity to order themselves, we must avail ourselves of them. And of all possible means, Poetry, the unique, linguistic instrument by which our minds have ordered their thoughts, emotions, desires . . . in the past, seems to be the most serviceable.[13]

At the very least, such a passage serves to remind us that Richards was the supervisor of the dissertation that became Q. D. Leavis's *Fiction and the Reading Public*, the century's most sustained attack upon prose fiction's cognitive and social effects. Yet it also provides an ironic conclusion to a history of physiological theories of the novel. What began in the nineteenth century as a way to consider, perhaps even celebrate, the technology of fiction, its widespread appeal and undeniable success, its way of finding temporal rhythms adapted to industrial existence, became in Richards's time yet another way of condemning fiction for its vitiating effects upon modern consciousness. The Victorian engagement with physiology and fiction was, in its own way, an engagement with the social—an attempt to understand what, in a machine age, 'the social' might look like, how consciousness operated in such an age and in such a society, and how (and why) the novel reflected and catered to the kinds of cognition demanded by new social facts. Richards's Sherringtonian physiological aesthetics refused a logic of engagement, and instead sought an antidote, a cure, a retreat, and set up literary critics as physicians for diseased modern cognitions. It is a temptation that continues to this day, wherein newer textual media and newer inventions than Richards knew are consistently posed as diseases for which a more purely 'literary' cure must be found. Sometimes, as this book has shown, the novel returns as the cure rather than the disease. Both approaches, however, do a disservice to the real, complicated engagements that the novel has had with social norms

---

[13] Richards, *Practical Criticism*, 301.

of cognition. Perhaps a renewed study of the physical, psychological, even neural effects of reading different literary forms in different ways might free us from the urge to attach ethical weight to cognitive categories; perhaps it might free literary critics from the burden of being the unappointed guardians of human attention; perhaps it might make us better understand why, even in our own time, the novel has become the preeminent modern literary form. It would certainly force us to acknowledge the real and productive place of drift, inattention, rhythm, and speed in our consumption of novels, and the complex ways in which reverie and attention oscillate to produce that curious and curiously compelling act we call reading a novel.

Bibliography

1. Novels and Fiction

Carroll, Lewis. *Sylvie and Bruno*. London: Macmillan, 1889.

Eliot, George. *Daniel Deronda*. 1876. Ed. Terence Cave. Harmondsworth: Penguin, 1995.

Gaskell, Elizabeth. *Mary Barton: A Tale of Manchester Life*. 1848. Ed. Jennifer Foster. Peterborough: Broadview, 2000.

———J. A. V. Chapple, and Anita Wilson, *Private Voices: The Diaries of Elizabeth Gaskell and Sophia Holland*, ed. Keele: Keele University Press, 1996.

Gissing, George. *Born in Exile*. 1892. Ed. David Grylls. London: Everyman, 1993.

——— *In the Year of Jubilee*. 1894. Ed. Paul Delany. London: Everyman, 1994.

——— *New Grub Street*. 1891. Ed. Bernard Bergonzi. Harmondsworth: Penguin, 1968.

——— *The Odd Women*. 1893. Ed. Arlene Young. Peterborough: Broadview, 1998.

——— *The Private Papers of Henry Ryecroft*. London: Constable, 1903.

——— *The Whirlpool*. 1897. Ed. William Greenslade. London: Everyman, 1997.

Lewes, G. H. *Ranthorpe*. Leipzig: Tauchnitz, 1847.

Meredith, George. *Beauchamp's Career*. 1875. In *The Works of George Meredith*, xiii–xiv. London: Constable, 1897.

——— *Diana of the Crossways*. 1885. In *The Works of George Meredith*, xvii–xviii. London: Constable, 1897.

——— *The Egoist*. 1879. Ed. George Woodcock. Harmondsworth: Penguin, 1968.

——— *One of Our Conquerors*. 1891. In *The Works of George Meredith*, xix–xx. London: Constable, 1897.

——— *The Ordeal of Richard Feverel: A History of Father and Son*. 1859. Ed. Edward Mendelson. Harmondsworth: Penguin, 1998.

Thackeray, William Makepeace. *Miscellaneous Essays, Sketches, and Reviews*. In *The Works of William Makepeace Thackeray*, Kensington Edition, xxviii. New York: Scribners, 1904.

——— *The Newcomes: Memoirs of a Most Respectable Family*. 1855. Ed. Andrew Sanders. Oxford: Oxford University Press, 1995.

——— *Roundabout Papers, Little Travels, and Roadside Sketches*. In *The Works of William Makepeace Thackeray*, Kensington Edition, xxvii. New York: Scribners, 1904.

——— *Vanity Fair: A Novel without A Hero*. 1848. Ed. John Sutherland. Oxford: Oxford University Press, 1983.

2. Primary Sources in Victorian Physiologies, Sciences, and Novel Criticism and Theory

Ackland, Joseph. 'Elementary Education and the Decay of Literature.' *Nineteenth Century* 35 (1894), 412–23.

Allen, Grant. *Physiological Aesthetics*. London: Henry King, 1877.

Anon. 'The Art of Storytelling.' *Fraser's Magazine* 53 (1856), 722–32.

—— 'Books and Reading.' *Quarterly Review* 162 (1886), 501–18.

—— 'Daniel Deronda.' *British Quarterly Review* 64 (October 1876), 472–92.

—— 'Dignity.' *Cornhill Magazine* 3 (1861), 584–97.

—— 'The Egoist.' *Saturday Review* 48 (1879), 607–8.

—— 'In Three Volumes.' *Punch* 107 (1 September 1894), 101.

—— 'Is the Novel Moribund?' *Tinsley's Magazine* 30 (April 1882), 389–94.

—— 'The Newcomes.' *Athenaeum* 1449 (4 August 1855), 895–6.

—— 'Novels as Sedatives.' *Spectator* 73 (28 July 1894), 108–9.

—— 'On the Forms of Publishing Fiction.' *Tinsley's Magazine* 10 (May 1872), 411–14.

—— 'The Reading of the Working Classes.' *Nineteenth Century* 33 (1893), 690–701.

—— 'What and How to Read.' *Westminster Review* 126 (1886), 99–118.

Austin, Alfred. 'The Vice of Reading.' *Temple Bar* 42 (1874), 251–7.

Bagehot, Walter. *Literary Studies*. Ed. R. H. Hutton. 2 vols. London: Longmans, Green, 1895.

Bain, Alexander. *The Emotions and the Will*. 2nd edn. London: Longmans, Green, 1865.

—— *English Composition and Rhetoric: A Manual*. London: Longmans, Green, 1866.

—— *The Senses and the Intellect*. 3rd edn. London: Longmans, Green, 1868.

Besant, Walter. *The Art of Fiction*. Boston: Cupples, Upham, 1885.

—— 'The Rise and Fall of the "Three Decker".' *Dial* 17 (October 1894), 181–9.

Bulwer-Lytton, Edward. 'The Critic.—No. 2: On Art in Fiction.' *Monthly Chronicle* 1 (1838), 138–49.

Carpenter, William. *Principles of Mental Physiology*. 2nd edn. London: Henry King, 1875.

Cattell, James McKeen. 'Psychometrische Untersuchungen.' *Philosophische Studien* 3 (1886), 305–55.

—— 'The Time Taken Up by Cerebral Operations.' *Mind* 11 (1886), 220–42, 377–92, 524–38.

Collins, Wilkie. 'The Unknown Public.' *Household Words* 18 (21 August 1855), 217–22.

Colvin, Sidney. 'Daniel Deronda.' *Fortnightly Review* 26 (1 November 1876), 601–16.

Dallas, E. S. *The Gay Science*. 2 vols. London: Chapman & Hall, 1866.

—— 'Great Expectations.' *The Times*, 17 October 1861, 6.

Dearborn, Walter Fenno. *The Psychology of Reading: An Experimental Study of the Reading Pauses and Movements of the Eye*. New York: Science Press, 1906.

Dowden, Edgar. 'Fiction and its Uses.' *Fraser's Magazine* 72 (1865), 746–60.

Eliot, George. *Selected Essays, Poems, and Other Writings*. Ed. A. S. Byatt. Harmondsworth: Penguin, 1991.

Elwin, Whitwell. 'The Newcomes.' *Quarterly Review* 97 (September 1855), 350–78.

Erdmann, Benno, and Raymond Dodge. *Psychologische Untersuchungen über das Lesen auf experimenteller Grundlage*. Halle: Niemeyer, 1898.

Francillon, R. E. 'George Eliot's First Romance.' *Gentlemen's Magazine* 17 (October 1876), 411–27.

Gissing, George. *Charles Dickens: A Critical Study*. London: Blackie, 1898.

Gissing, George. *London and the Life of Literature in Late Victorian England: The Diary of George Gissing, Novelist.* Ed. Pierre Coustillas. Lewisburg, Pa.: Bucknell University Press, 1978.

Griffing, Harold, and Shepherd Ivory Franz. 'On the Conditions of Fatigue in Reading.' *Psychological Review* 3 (1896), 513–30.

Gurney, Edmund. *The Power of Sound.* New York: Basic Books, 1966.

Hannay, James. 'The Newcomes.' *Leader* 6 (8 September 1855), 870–1.

Haultain, Arnold. 'How to Read.' *Blackwood's Edinburgh Magazine* 159 (1896), 249–65.

Helmholtz, Hermann von. *Handbuch der physiologischen Optik.* Leipzig: Voss, 1867.

Henley, W. E. 'Literature.' *Athenaeum* 2714 (1 November 1879), 555–6.

Hennequin, Émile. *La Critique scientifique.* Paris: Perrin, 1888.

Huey, Edmund. 'On the Psychology and Physiology of Reading: I.' *American Journal of Psychology* 11 (1900), 283–302.

——— 'On the Psychology and Physiology of Reading: II.' *American Journal of Psychology* 12 (1901), 292–312.

——— *The Psychology and Pedagogy of Reading.* New York: Macmillan, 1908.

Humphery, George. 'The Reading of the Working Classes.' *Nineteenth Century* 33 (April 1893), 690–701.

Hutton, Richard Holt. 'The Adventures of Harry Richmond.' *Spectator* 45 (20 January 1872), 79–80.

——— 'Ineffectual Novels.' *Spectator* 35 (22 February 1862), 218–19.

——— 'Mr. George Meredith's New Novel.' *Spectator* 52 (1 November 1879), 1383–4.

——— 'The Tension in Charles Dickens.' *Spectator* 45 (16 November 1872), 1456–8.

Huxley, Thomas. *Lessons in Elementary Physiology.* 2nd edn. London: Macmillan, 1879.

James, William. *The Principles of Psychology.* 1890. Cambridge, Mass.: Harvard University Press, 1981.

Javal, Émile. 'Essai sur la Physiologie de la Lecture.' *Annales d'Oculistique* 79 (1878), 97–117, 155–67, 240–74.

——— 'Essai sur la Physiologie de la Lecture.' *Annales d'Oculistique* 80 (1879), 135–49.

——— 'Essai sur la Physiologie de la Lecture.' *Annales d'Oculistique* 81 (1879), 61–73.

——— 'Essai sur la Physiologie de la Lecture.' *Annales d'Oculistique* 82 (1879), 72–81, 159–70, 242–53.

——— *Physiologie de la lecture et de l'écriture.* Paris: Félix Alcan, 1906.

Jeaffreson, John Cordy. *Novels and Novelists from Elizabeth to Victoria.* 2 vols. London: Hurst & Blackett, 1858.

Jewsbury, Geraldine. 'New Novels.' *Athenaeum* 1635 (26 February, 1859), 284.

——— 'New Novels.' *Athenaeum* 1654 (9 July, 1859), 48–9.

——— 'New Novels.' *Athenaeum* 1745 (6 April, 1861), 465–7.

——— 'New Novels.' *Athenaeum* 1905 (30 April, 1864), 610–11.

——— 'New Novels.' *Athenaeum* 1966 (3 July, 1865), 12–13.

——— 'New Novels.' *Athenaeum* 2066 (1 June, 1867), 720–1.

——— 'New Novels.' *Athenaeum* 2068 (15 June, 1867), 783–4.

Landolt, Edmond. 'Nouvelles recherches sur la physiologie des mouvements des yeux.' *Archives d'Ophthalmologie* 11 (1891), 385–95.

Lee, Vernon [Violet Paget]. 'Aesthetics of the Novel.' *Literature* 5 (11 August, 1899), 99–100.

_____ 'The Craft of Words.' *New Review* 11 (1894), 571–80.

_____ 'A Dialogue on Novels.' *Contemporary Review* 48 (September 1885), 378–401.

_____ *The Handling of Words, and Other Studies in Literary Psychology*. London: John Lane, Bodley Head, 1923.

_____ 'On Literary Construction.' *Contemporary Review* 68 (1895), 404–19.

_____ and Kit Anstruther-Thomson. *Beauty and Ugliness, and Other Studies in Psychological Aesthetics*. London: John Lane, 1912.

Lewes, G. H. 'Dickens in Relation to Criticism.' *Fortnightly Review* 17 (1872), 143–51.

_____ *The Letters of George Henry Lewes*, i. Ed. William Baker. Victoria, Canada: English Literary Studies, 1995.

_____ 'The Novels of Jane Austen.' *Blackwood's Edinburgh Magazine* 84 (1859), 99–113.

_____ *On Actors and the Art of Acting*. London: Smith & Elder, 1875.

_____ 'The Opera in 1833–1863.' *Cornhill Magazine* 8 (1863), 295–307.

_____ *The Physical Basis of Mind*. London: Trübner, 1877.

_____ *The Physiology of Common Life*. 2 vols. New York: Appleton, 1860.

_____ *Principles of Success in Literature*. 3rd. edn. Ed. Fred Scott. Boston: Allyn & Bacon, 1891.

_____ *The Study of Psychology: Its Object, Scope, and Method*. London: Trübner, 1879.

_____ 'A Word about Tom Jones.' *Blackwood's Edinburgh Magazine* 87 (1860), 331–41.

Mansel, Henry. 'Sensation Novels.' *Quarterly Review* 113 (1863), 481–513.

Masson, David. *British Novelists and their Styles: Being a Critical Sketch of the History of British Prose Fiction*. London: Macmillan, 1859.

Meynell, Alice. 'Mr. George Meredith's New Book.' *Illustrated London News* 107 (December 1895), 734.

North, William. 'The Grand Style.' *Graham's American Monthly Magazine of Literature, Art, and Fashion* 46/5 (May 1855), 418–28.

O'Brien, Robert. 'Machinery and English Style.' *Atlantic Monthly* 94 (October 1904), 464–72.

Oliphant, Margaret. 'Mr. Thackeray and his Novels.' *Blackwood's Edinburgh Magazine* 77 (January 1855), 86–96.

_____ 'New Novels.' *Blackwood's Edinburgh Magazine* 128 (September 1880), 378–404.

_____ 'Sensation Novels.' *Blackwood's Edinburgh Review* 91 (May 1862), 564–85.

Olmsted, John Charles. *A Victorian Art of Fiction: Essays on the Novel in British Periodicals*. 3 vols. New York: Garland, 1979.

Quantz, J. O. *Problems in the Psychology of Reading*. New York: Macmillan, 1897.

Raleigh, Walter. *The English Novel: Being a Short Sketch of its History from the Earliest Times to the Appearance of Waverly*. 1894. 5th edn. New York: Scribners, 1905.

Ribot, Théodule. *The Psychology of Attention*. Chicago: Open Court, 1894.

Robertson, John. *Essays Towards a Critical Method*. London: Unwin, 1889.

Robinson, Solveig, ed. *A Serious Occupation: Literary Criticism by Victorian Woman Writers*. Peterborough: Broadview, 2003.

Roscoe, William Caldwell. *Poems and Essays*. Ed. R. H. Hutton. 2 vols. London: Chapman & Hall, 1860.

Ruskin, John. *Sesame and Lilies*. 1865. Ed. Harold Bloom. New York: Chelsea House, 1983.

Salmon, Edward. 'What the Working Classes Read.' *Nineteenth Century* 20 (1886), 108–17.

Sanford, Edmund Clark. 'The Relative Legibility of the Small Letters.' *American Journal of Psychology* 1 (1888), 402–35.

Sherrington, Charles. *The Integrative Action of the Nervous System*. 1906. New Haven: Yale University Press, 1946.

Simcox, Edith [H. Lawrenny, pseud.]. 'Recent Novels.' *Academy* 2 (15 December 1871), 552–4.

Spencer, Herbert. *The Man Versus the State*. In *The Works of Herbert Spencer*, xi. Osnabrück: Otto Zeller, 1966.

—— 'The Philosophy of Style.' In *Essays: Scientific: Political, and Speculative*, ii. London: Williams & Norgate, 1891 333–69.

—— *The Principles of Ethics*, ii. London: Williams & Norgate, 1893.

—— *The Principles of Psychology*, i. London: Williams & Norgate, 1881.

Sully, James. *Sensation and Intuition: Studies in Psychology and Aesthetics*. 2nd edn. London: Kegan Paul, 1880.

Taine, Hippolyte. *History of English Literature*. Trans. H. Van Laun. 4 vols. Edinburgh: Edmonston & Douglas, 1874.

Trollope, Anthony. *An Autobiography*. 1883. Ed. P. D. Edwards. Oxford: Oxford University Press, 1980.

3. Secondary Sources

Adorno, Theodor. *The Culture Industry: Selected Essays on Mass Culture*. Trans. J. M. Bernstein. London: Routledge, 1991.

—— *In Search of Wagner*. Trans. Rodney Livingstone. New York: Verso, 1981.

—— *Quasi una Fantasia: Essays on Modern Music*. Trans. Rodney Livingstone. New York: Verso, 1992.

Allen, James. *In the Public Eye: A History of Reading in Modern France, 1800–1940*. Princeton: Princeton University Press, 1991.

Altick, Richard. *The English Common Reader: A Social History of the Mass Reading Public*. Chicago: University of Chicago Press, 1957.

—— 'Publishing.' In *A Companion to Victorian Literature and Culture*, ed. Herbert Tucker, Oxford: Blackwell, 1999 289–304.

—— *Writers, Readers, and Occasions: Selected Essays on Victorian Literature and Life*. Columbus: Ohio State University Press, 1989.

Ames, Van Meter. *Aesthetics of the Novel*. Chicago: University of Chicago Press, 1928.

Anderson, Amanda. *The Powers of Distance: Cosmopolitanism and the Cultivation of Detachment*. Princeton: Princeton University Press, 2001.

Anon. 'Lyric Feuds.' *Westminster Review* 32 (1867), 119–60.

_____ 'Not a Magic Minstrel.' *Punch* 28 (19 May 1855), 204.

_____ 'Our Representative Man.' *Punch* 72 (26 May 1877), 237.

_____ 'The Wagner Festival.' *Punch* 72 (19 May 1877), 220–1.

_____ 'Wagner, and the Modern Theory of Music.' *Edinburgh Review* 143 (January 1876), 141–76.

Appadurai, Arjun. *Modernity at Large: Cultural Dimensions of Globalization*. Minneapolis: University of Minnesota Press, 1996.

Arata, Stephen. 'On Not Paying Attention.' *Victorian Studies* 46/2 (Winter 2004), 193–205.

Ashton, Rosemary. *G. H. Lewes: A Life*. Oxford: Clarendon Press, 1991.

Baldick, Chris. *The Social Mission of English Criticism, 1848–1932*. Oxford: Clarendon Press, 1983.

Banfield, Ann. *Unspeakable Sentences: Narration and Representation in the Language of Fiction*. Boston: Routledge & Kegan Paul, 1982.

Barbauld, Anna. 'On the Origin and Progress of Novel-Writing.' In *The British Novelists*, i. London: Rivington, 1810 1–62.

Barthes, Roland. *The Pleasure of the Text*. Trans. Richard Miller. New York: Noonday, 1975.

Beer, Gillian. *Meredith: A Change of Masks: A Study of the Novels*. London: Athlone, 1970.

_____ *Open Fields: Science in Cultural Encounter*. Oxford: Oxford University Press, 1996.

Benjamin, Walter, *Illuminations: Essays and Reflections*. Trans. Harry Zohn. New York: Schocken, 1968.

Bennett, Tony. 'Texts in History: The Determinations of Readings and their Texts.' In *Reception Study: From Literary Theory to Cultural Studies*, ed. James Machor and Philip Goldstein. London: Routledge, 2001 61–74.

Birkerts, Sven. *The Gutenberg Elegies: The Fate of Reading in an Electronic Age*. New York: Ballantine, 1994.

Block, Richard, ed. *Cognitive Models of Psychological Time*. Hillsdale, NJ: Erlbaum, 1990.

Bolter, Jay. *Writing Space: The Computer, Hypertext, and the History of Writing*. Mahwah, NJ: Lawrence Erlbaum Associates, 1991.

Booth, Wayne. *The Company We Keep: An Ethics of Fiction*. Berkeley: University of California Press, 1988.

Boring, Edwin. *A History of Experimental Psychology*. New York: Appleton-Century-Crofts, 1957.

Bourdieu, Pierre, and Roger Chartier. 'La lecture: une pratique culturelle.' In *Pratiques de la lecture*, ed. Roger Chartier. Paris: Rivages, 1985 218–39.

Bowlby, Rachel. *Just Looking: Consumer Culture in Dreiser, Gissing and Zola*. London: Methuen, 1985.

Brake, Laurel. *Print in Transition, 1850–1910: Studies in Media and Book History*. Basingstoke: Palgrave, 2001.

Brantlinger, Patrick. *The Reading Lesson: The Threat of Mass Literacy in Nineteenth-Century British Fiction*. Bloomington: Indiana University Press, 1998.

Breton, André. *Œuvres complètes*, i. Paris: Gallimard-Pléiade, 1988.

Broadbent, Donald. *Perception and Communication*. London: Pergamon, 1958.

Brooks, Cleanth, and Robert Penn Warren. *Understanding Fiction*. New York: F. S. Crofts, 1943.

Brooks, Peter. *Reading for the Plot*. New York: Knopf, 1984.

Brower, Reuben. 'Beginnings and Transitions: I. A. Richards Interviewed by Reuben Brower.' In *I. A. Richards: Essays in his Honor*, ed. Reuben Brower, Helen Vendler, and John Hollander. Oxford: Oxford University Press, 1973 17–41.

Brown, Homer. *Institutions of the English Novel: From Defoe to Scott*. Philadelphia: University of Pennsylvania Press, 1997.

Byerly, Alison. *Realism, Representation, and the Arts in Nineteenth-Century Literature*. Cambridge: Cambridge University Press, 1997.

Carey, Hugh. *Mansfield Forbes and his Cambridge*. Cambridge: Cambridge University Press, 1984.

Chambers, Ross. *Loiterature*. Lincoln: University of Nebraska Press, 1999.

Chartier, Roger. *The Cultural Uses of Print in Early Modern France*. Trans. Lydia Cochrane. Princeton: Princeton University Press, 1987.

_____ *Forms and Meanings: Texts, Performances, and Audiences from Codex to Computer*. Philadelphia: University of Pennsylvania Press, 1995.

_____ *The Order of Books: Readers, Authors, and Libraries in Europe between the Fourteenth and Eighteenth Centuries*. Trans. Lydia Cochrane. Stanford, Calif.: Stanford University Press, 1992.

_____ 'Reading Matter and "Popular" Reading.' In *A History of Reading in the West*, ed. Guglielmo Cavallo and Roger Chartier, trans. Lydia Cochrane. Amherst: University of Massachusetts Press; Cambridge: Polity, 1999 269–83.

Chase, Cynthia. 'The Decomposition of Elephants: Double-Reading *Daniel Deronda*.' *PMLA* 93 (1978), 215–25.

Chatman, Seymour. *Story and Discourse: Narrative Structure in Story and Film*. Ithaca, NY: Cornell University Press, 1978.

Cherry, Colin. 'Some Experiments on the Recognition of Speech, with One and with Two Ears.' *Journal of the Acoustical Society of America* 25/5 (September 1953), 975–9.

Cheyette, Bryan. *Constructions of 'the Jew' in English Literature and Society: Racial Representations, 1875–1945*. Cambridge: Cambridge University Press, 1993.

Chorley, Henry. 'Music and the Drama.' *Athenaeum* 1438 (19 May 1855), 539–40.

Clapp-Itnyre, Alisa. *Angelic Airs, Subversive Songs: Music as Social Discourse in the Victorian Novel*. Athens: Ohio University Press, 2002.

Colby, Vineta. *Vernon Lee: A Literary Biography*. Charlottesville: University of Virginia Press, 2003.

Coleridge, Samuel Taylor. *Lay Sermons*. In *The Collected Works of Samuel Taylor Coleridge*, vi. Ed. R. J. White. London: Routledge & Kegan Paul, 1972.

_____ *Lectures, 1808–1819: On Literature*. In *The Collected Works of Samuel Taylor Coleridge*, v. Ed. R. J. White. London: Routledge & Kegan Paul, 1972.

Crary, Jonathan. *Suspensions of Perception: Attention, Spectacle, and Modern Culture.* Cambridge, Mass.: MIT Press, 1999.

Crosby, Christina. *The Ends of History: Victorians and 'The Woman Question'.* New York: Routledge, 1991.

Cross, Nigel. *The Common Writer: Life in Nineteenth-Century New Grub Street.* Cambridge: Cambridge University Press, 1985.

Csikszentmihalyi, Mihaly. *Flow: The Psychology of Optimal Experience.* New York: Harper & Row, 1990.

Dahlhaus, Carl. *Esthetics of Music.* Trans. William Austin. Cambridge: Cambridge University Press, 1982.

___ *Nineteenth-Century Music.* Trans. J. Bradford Robinson. Berkeley: University of California Press, 1989.

Dale, Catherine. *Music Analysis in Britain in the Nineteenth and Early Twentieth Centuries.* Aldershot: Ashgate, 2003.

Dale, Peter Allan. *In Pursuit of a Scientific Culture: Science, Art, and Society in the Victorian Age.* Madison: University of Wisconsin Press, 1989.

Dames, Nicholas. 'Reverie, Sensation, Effect: Novelistic Attention and Stendhal's *De l'amour.' Narrative* 10/1 (January 2002), 47–68.

Danzinger, Kurt. 'Mid-Nineteenth-Century British Psycho-Physiology: A Neglected Chapter in the History of Psychology.' In *The Problematic Science: Psychology in Nineteenth-Century Thought,* ed. W. R. Woodward and M. G. Gash. New York: Praeger, 1982 119–46.

Darnton, Robert. *The Kiss of Lamourette: Reflections in Cultural History.* New York: Norton, 1990.

da Sousa Correa, Delia. *George Eliot, Music and Victorian Culture.* Basingstoke: Palgrave, 2003.

Davidson, Cathy, ed. *Reading in America: Literature and Social History.* Baltimore: Johns Hopkins University Press, 1989.

Davison, James. 'Philharmonic Concerts.' *The Times,* 16 May 1855, 11.

___ 'Philharmonic Concerts.' *The Times,* 12 June 1855, 12.

Deutsch, Diana, ed. *The Psychology of Music.* San Diego: Academic Press, 1999.

Deutsch, J. Anthony, and Diana Deutsch. 'Attention: Some Theoretical Considerations.' *Psychological Review* 70/1 (1963), 80–90.

Diderot, Denis. *Œuvres esthétiques.* Ed. Paul Vernière. Paris: Garnier, 1965.

Doane, Mary Ann. *The Emergence of Cinematic Time: Modernity, Contingency, the Archive.* Cambridge, Mass.: Harvard University Press, 2002.

Du Bos, Jean Baptiste. *Réflexions critiques sur la poésie et la peinture.* 2 vols. Paris, 1719.

Dunlop, John Colin. *The History of Fiction: Being a Critical Account of the Most Celebrated Prose Works of Fiction, from the Earliest Prose Romances to the Novels of the Present Day.* 3 vols. London: Longman, Hurst, Rees, Orme & Brown, 1814.

Edgar, Pelham. *The Art of the Novel from 1700 to the Present Time.* London: Macmillan, 1933.

Eigner, Edwin, and George Worth. 'Introductory Essay.' In *Victorian Criticism of the Novel.* Cambridge: Cambridge University Press, 1985 1–21.

Elfenbein, Andrew. 'Cognitive Science and the History of Reading.' *PMLA* 121/2 (March 2006), 484–502.

Eliot, George. *The George Eliot Letters*, vi. Ed. Gordon Haight. New Haven: Yale University Press, 1955.

——— *The Journals of George Eliot*. Ed. Margaret Harris and Judith Johnston. Cambridge: Cambridge University Press, 1998.

——— 'Liszt, Wagner, and Weimar.' *Fraser's Magazine* 52 (July 1855), 48–62.

——— 'The Romantic School of Music: Liszt on Meyerbeer—Wagner.' *Leader* 5 (28 October 1854), 1027–8.

——— 'Three Months in Weimar.' *Fraser's Magazine* 51 (June 1855), 699–706.

Eliot, Simon. 'The Business of Victorian Publishing.' In *The Cambridge Companion to the Victorian Novel*, ed. Deirdre David. Cambridge: Cambridge University Press, 2000 37–60.

Ellis, William Ashton. *The Life of Richard Wagner*, v. New York: Da Capo, 1977.

Engels, Friedrich. *The Condition of the Working Class in England*. Trans. W. O. Henderson and W. H. Chaloner. Stanford, Calif.: Stanford University Press, 1958.

Engelsing, Rolf. *Der Bürger als Leser: Lesergeschichte in Deutschland, 1500–1800*. Stuttgart: J. B. Metzlersche Verlagsbuchhandlung, 1974.

——— 'Die Perioden der Lesergeschichte in der Neuzeit: Das statistische Ausmass und die soziokulturelle Bedeutung der Lektüre.' *Archiv für geschichte des Buchwesens* 10 (1970), 945–1002.

Fahnestock, Jeanne. 'Geraldine Jewsbury: The Power of the Publisher's Reader.' *Nineteenth-Century Fiction* 28 (1973), 253–72.

Febvre, Lucien, and Henri-Jean Martin. *L'Apparition du livre*. Paris: Éditions Albin Michel, 1958.

Feltes, N. N. *Modes of Production of Victorian Novels*. Chicago: University of Chicago Press, 1986.

Flint, Kate. *The Woman Reader, 1837–1914*. Oxford: Clarendon Press, 1993.

Forster, E. M. *Aspects of the Novel*. New York: Harcourt, Brace, & World, 1927.

Freedman, Jonathan. *Professions of Taste: Henry James, British Aestheticism, and Commodity Culture*. Stanford, Calif.: Stanford University Press, 1990.

Fried, Michael. *Absorption and Theatricality: Painting and Beholder in the Age of Diderot*. Chicago: University of Chicago Press, 1980.

Fry, Ben. 'Valence.' <http://acg.media.mit.edu/people/fry/valence>.

Fry, Paul. 'I. A. Richards.' In *The Cambridge History of Literary Criticism, vii: Modernism and the New Criticism*, ed. A. Walton Litz, Louis Menand, and Lawrence Rainey, 181–99. Cambridge: Cambridge University Press, 2000.

Fryckstedt, Monica. *Geraldine Jewsbury's* Athenaeum *Reviews: A Mirror of Mid Victorian Attitudes to Fiction*. Uppsala: Acta Universitatis Upsaliensis Anglistica Upsaliensia, 1986.

Furness, Raymond. *Wagner and Literature*. New York: St Martin's Press, 1982.

Gagnier, Regenia. *The Insatiability of Human Wants: Economics and Aesthetics in Market Society*. Chicago: University of Chicago Press, 2000.

Gallagher, Catherine. *The Body Economic: Life, Death, and Sensation in Political Economy and the Victorian Novel*. Princeton: Princeton University Press, 2006.

——— 'Formalism and Time.' *Modern Language Quarterly* 61/1 (March 2000), 229–51.

——— 'George Eliot and *Daniel Deronda*: The Prostitute and the Jewish Question.' In *Sex, Politics, and Science in the Nineteenth-Century Novel*, ed. Ruth Bernard Yeazell. Baltimore: Johns Hopkins University Press, 1986 39–62.

Garrett, Peter. *The Victorian Multiplot Novel: Studies in Dialogical Form*. New Haven: Yale University Press, 1980.

Genette, Gérard. *Narrative Discourse Revisited*. Trans. Jane Lewin. Ithaca, NY: Cornell University Press, 1988.

Gerrig, Richard. *Experiencing Narrative Worlds: On the Psychological Activities of Reading*. New Haven: Yale University Press, 1993.

Gettmann, Royal. *A Victorian Publisher: A Study of the Bentley Papers*. Cambridge: Cambridge University Press, 1960.

Gilman, M. R. F. *The Pilgrim's Scrip: or, The Wit and Wisdom of George Meredith*. Boston: Roberts Brothers, 1888.

Ginzburg, Carlo. *The Cheese and the Worms: The Cosmos of a Sixteenth-Century Miller*. Trans. John and Anne Tedeschi. Baltimore: Johns Hopkins University Press, 1980.

Gissing, George. *The Collected Letters of George Gissing*, iv. ed. Paul Mattheisen, Arthur Young, and Pierre Coustillas. Athens: Ohio University Press, 1994.

——— *The Collected Letters of George Gissing*, v. ed. Paul Mattheisen, Arthur Young, and Pierre Coustillas. Athens: Ohio University Press, 1995.

Goode, John. '*The Egoist*: Anatomy or Striptease?' In *Meredith Now: Some Critical Essays*, ed. Ian Fletcher. New York: Barnes & Noble, 1971 205–30.

Grabo, Carl. *The Technique of the Novel*. New York: Scribners, 1928.

Graff, Gerald. *Professing Literature: An Institutional History*. Chicago: University of Chicago Press, 1987.

Graham, Kenneth. *English Criticism of the Novel, 1865–1900*. Oxford: Clarendon Press, 1963.

Gray, Beryl. *George Eliot and Music*. London: Macmillan, 1989.

Griest, Guinevere. *Mudie's Circulating Library and the Victorian Novel*. Bloomington: Indiana University Press, 1970.

Hack, Daniel. *The Material Interests of the Victorian Novel*. Charlottesville: University of Virginia Press, 2005.

Haight, Gordon. *George Eliot: A Biography*. New York: Oxford University Press, 1968.

Hale, Dorothy. *Social Formalism: The Novel in Theory from Henry James to the Present*. Stanford, Calif.: Stanford University Press, 1998.

Hall, David. *Cultures of Print: Essays in the History of the Book*. Amherst: University of Massachusetts Press, 1996.

Hartman, Geoffrey. *The Fate of Reading and Other Essays*. Chicago: University of Chicago Press, 1975.

Harvey, David. *The Condition of Postmodernity: An Enquiry into the Origins of Cultural Change*. Oxford: Blackwell, 1990.

Haweis, H. R. 'Wagner.' *Contemporary Review* 29 (May 1877), 981–1003.

Hawkins, C. Halford. 'The Wagner Festival at Bayreuth.' *Macmillan's* 35 (1876), 55–63.

Hearnshaw, L. S. *The Shaping of Modern Psychology*. London: Routledge & Kegan Paul, 1987.

Herman, David. 'Scripts, Sequences, and Stories: Elements of a Postclassical Narratology.' *PMLA* 112 (1997), 1046–59.

Hertz, Neil. *George Eliot's Pulse*. Stanford, Calif.: Stanford University Press, 2003.

Hueffer, Francis [Franz Hüffer]. *Half a Century of Music in England*. London: Chapman & Hall, 1889.

——— 'Richard Wagner.' *Fortnightly Review* 17 (March 1872), 265–87.

——— *Richard Wagner and the Music of the Future: History and Aesthetics*. London: Chapman & Hall, 1874.

Hughes, Linda, and Michael Lund. *The Victorian Serial*. Charlottesville: University Press of Virginia, 1991.

Hughes, Meirion, and Robert Stradling. *The English Musical Renaissance, 1840–1880: Constructing a National Music*. Manchester: Manchester University Press, 1993.

Iser, Wolfgang. *The Act of Reading: A Theory of Aesthetic Response*. Baltimore: Johns Hopkins University Press, 1978.

——— *The Implied Reader: Patterns of Communication in Prose Fiction from Bunyan to Beckett*. Baltimore: Johns Hopkins University Press, 1974.

Jacobus, Mary. *Psychoanalysis and the Scene of Reading*. Oxford: Oxford University Press, 1999.

Jahn, Manfred. 'Frames, Preferences, and the Reading of Third-Person Narratives: Towards a Cognitive Narratology.' *Poetics Today* 18 (1997), 441–68.

James, Henry. *The Art of the Novel*. Ed. R. P. Blackmur. New York: Scribners, 1934.

——— *Henry James: Literary Criticism: Essays on Literature, American Writers, English Writers*. Ed. Leon Edel. New York: Library of America, 1984.

Jameson, Fredric. *The Political Unconscious: Narrative as a Socially Symbolic Act*. Ithaca, NY: Cornell University Press, 1981.

Jauss, Hans-Robert. *Toward an Aesthetic of Reception*. Trans. Timothy Bahti. Minneapolis: University of Minnesota Press, 1982.

Johns, Adrian. *The Nature of the Book: Print and Knowledge in the Making*. Chicago: University of Chicago Press, 1998.

Johnson, Julian. *Who Needs Classical Music?* Oxford: Oxford University Press, 2002.

Jordan, John, and Robert Patten, eds. *Literature in the Marketplace: Nineteenth-Century British Publishing and Reading Practices*. Cambridge: Cambridge University Press, 1995.

Karl, Frederick. *George Eliot: Voice of a Century*. New York: Norton, 1995.

Kern, Stephen. *The Culture of Time and Space, 1880–1918*. Cambridge, Mass.: Harvard University Press, 1983.

Kernan, Alvin. *The Death of Literature*. New Haven: Yale University Press, 1990.

Klancher, Jon. *The Making of English Reading Audiences, 1790–1832*. Madison: University of Wisconsin Press, 1987.

Kracauer, Siegfried. *The Mass Ornament: Weimar Essays*. Trans. Thomas Levin. Cambridge, Mass.: Harvard University Press, 1995.

Lafargue, Paul. *Le Droit à la paresse*. Ed. Maurice Dommanget. Paris: Maspero, 1969.

Leavis, F. R. *English Literature in Our Time and the University*. London: Chatto & Windus, 1969.

—— *The Great Tradition*. Garden City, NY: Doubleday, 1954.

Leavis, Q. D. *Fiction and the Reading Public*. London: Chatto & Windus, 1932.

Levine, Caroline. *The Serious Pleasures of Suspense: Victorian Realism and Narrative Doubt*. Charlottesville: University of Virginia Press, 2003.

Longyear, Rey M. *Nineteenth-Century Romanticism in Music*. Englewood Cliffs, NJ: Prentice-Hall, 1973.

Lubbock, Percy. *The Craft of Fiction*. New York: Viking, 1957.

Lynch, Deidre, and William Warner, eds. *Cultural Institutions of the Novel*. Durham, NC: Duke University Press, 1996.

Lyons, Martyn. *Readers and Society in Nineteenth-Century France: Workers, Women, Peasants*. London: Palgrave, 2001.

McKenzie, D. F. *Bibliography and the Sociology of Texts*. London: British Library, 1986.

McLuhan, Marshall. *Understanding Media: The Extensions of Man*. Cambridge, Mass.: MIT Press, 1994.

McWhirter, David. 'Imagining a Distance: Feminism and Comedy in Meredith's *The Egoist*.' *Genre* 22/3 (1989), 263–86.

Maltz, Diana. 'Engaging "Delicate Brains": From Working-Class Enculturation to Upper-Class Lesbian Liberation in Vernon Lee and Kit Anstruther-Thomson's Psychological Aesthetics.' In *Women and British Aestheticism*, ed. Talia Schaffer and Kathy Alexis Psomiades. Charlottesville: University Press of Virginia, 1999 211–29.

Manguel, Alberto. *A History of Reading*. Harmondsworth: Penguin, 1996.

Martin, Henri-Jean. *The History and Power of Writing*. Trans. Lydia Cochrane. Chicago: University of Chicago Press, 1994.

Marx, Karl. *Capital: A Critique of Political Economy*, i. Trans. Ben Fowkes. New York: Vintage, 1976.

—— *Grundrisse: Foundations of the Critique of Political Economy (Rough Draft)*. Trans. Martin Nicolaus. London: Pelican, 1973.

Mellor, Anne. *Mothers of the Nation: Women's Political Writing in England, 1780–1830*. Bloomington: Indiana University Press, 2000.

Menke, Richard. 'Fiction as Vivisection: G. H. Lewes and George Eliot.' *ELH* 67/2 (2000), 617–53.

Meredith, George. *The Egoist [A Play]: From the Novel by George Meredith, Arranged for the Stage by George Meredith and Alfred Sutro*. Ed. Lewis Sawin. Athens: Ohio University Press, 1981.

—— *George Meredith's* Essay on Comedy *and Other* New Quarterly Magazine *Publications: A Critical Edition*. Ed. Maura Ives. Lewisburg, Va.: Bucknell University Press, 1998.

—— *The Letters of George Meredith*, ii. Ed. C. L. Cline. Oxford: Clarendon Press, 1970.

Meredith, George. *The Notebooks of George Meredith*. Ed. Gilliam Beer and Margaret Harris. Salzburg: Institut für Anglistik und Amerikanistik, 1983.

Mill, John Stuart. *On Liberty and Other Essays*. Ed. John Gray. Oxford: Oxford University Press, 1998.

Miller, Andrew. *Novels Behind Glass: Commodity Culture and Victorian Narrative*. Cambridge: Cambridge University Press, 1995.

Miller, D. A. *The Novel and the Police*. Berkeley: University of California Press, 1988.

Miller, J. Hillis. ' "Herself Against Herself": The Clarification of Clara Middleton.' In *The Representation of Women in Fiction*, ed. Carolyn Heilbrun and Margaret Higgonet. Baltimore: Johns Hopkins University Press, 1983 98–123.

Montgomery, Robert. *Terms of Response: Language and Audience in Seventeenth- and Eighteenth-Century Theory*. University Park, Pa.: Penn State University Press, 1992.

Moretti, Franco. 'Conjectures on World Literature.' *New Left Review* 1 (2000), 54–68.

—— *The Way of the World: The* Bildungsroman *in European Culture*. Trans. Albert Spragia. New York: Verso, 2000.

Muir, Edwin. *The Structure of the Novel*. London: Hogarth Press, 1928.

Murray, Janet. *Hamlet on the Holodeck: The Future of Narrative in Cyberspace*. Cambridge, Mass.: MIT Press, 1997.

Musgrave, Michael. *The Musical Life of the Crystal Palace*. Cambridge: Cambridge University Press, 1995.

Nell, Victor. *Lost in a Book: The Psychology of Reading for Pleasure*. New Haven: Yale University Press, 1988.

Nevett, Terence. 'Advertising.' In *Victorian Periodicals and Victorian Society*, ed. J. Don Vann and Rosemary VanArsdel. Toronto: University of Toronto Press, 1994 219–34.

Newman, Ernest. *The Wagner Operas*. Princeton: Princeton University Press, 1949.

Nunokawa, Jeffrey. *The Afterlife of Property: Domestic Security and the Victorian Novel*. Princeton: Princeton University Press, 1994.

Nussbaum, Martha. *Love's Knowledge: Essays on Philosophy and Literature*. Oxford: Oxford University Press, 1990.

—— *Poetic Justice: The Literary Imagination and Public Life*. Boston: Beacon Press, 1995.

O'Brien, John Anthony. *Silent Reading: With Special Reference to Methods for Developing Speed*. New York: Macmillan, 1922.

Ong, Walter. *Orality and Literacy: The Technologizing of the* Word. London: Methuen, 1982.

Orel, Harold. *Victorian Literary Critics: George Henry Lewes, Walter Bagehot, Richard Holt Hutton, Leslie Stephen, Andrew Lang, George Saintsbury and Edmund Gosse*. London: Macmillan, 1984.

Paley, W. Bradford. 'TextArc.' <http://www.textarc.org>.

Parkes, Malcolm. *Scribes, Scripts, and Readers: Studies in the Communication, Presentation, and Dissemination of Medieval Texts*. London: Hambledon, 1991.

Pashler, Harold. *The Psychology of Attention*. Cambridge, Mass.: MIT Press, 1998.

Pavel, Thomas. *La Pensée du roman*. Paris: Gallimard, 2003.

Pearsall, Ronald. *Victorian Popular Music.* Newton Abbot: David & Charles, 1973.

Pearson, Jacqueline. *Women's Reading in Britain, 1750–1835.* Cambridge: Cambridge University Press, 1999.

Pearson, Richard. *W. M. Thackeray and the Mediated Text: Writing for Periodicals in the Mid-Nineteenth Century.* Aldershot: Ashgate, 2000.

Peregrini, Matteo. *Della acutezze.* Genoa, 1639.

Phillips, Adam. *On Kissing, Tickling, and Being Bored: Psychoanalytic Essays on the Unexamined Life.* Cambridge, Mass.: Harvard University Press, 1993.

Picker, John. *Victorian Soundscapes.* New York: Oxford University Press, 2003.

Plant, Marjorie. *The English Book Trade: An Economic History of the Making and Sale of Books.* London: George Allen & Unwin, 1965.

Poole, Adrian. *Gissing in Context.* London: Macmillan, 1975.

Poovey, Mary. 'The Model System of Contemporary Literary Criticism.' *Critical Inquiry* 27 (Spring 2001), 408–38.

Price, Leah. *The Anthology and the Rise of the Novel: From Richardson to George Eliot.* Cambridge: Cambridge University Press, 2000.

——— 'Reading: The State of the Discipline,' *Book History* 7 (2004), 303–20.

Prince, Gerald. *A Dictionary of Narratology.* Lincoln: University of Nebraska Press, 1987.

Rabinowitz, Peter. *Before Reading: Narrative Conventions and the Politics of Interpretation.* Ithaca, NY: Cornell University Press, 1987.

Radway, Janice. 'Reading is Not Eating: Mass-Produced Literature and the Theoretical, Methodological, and Political Consequences of a Metaphor.' *Book Research Quarterly* 2/3 (Fall 1986), 7–29.

Ragussis, Michael. *Figures of Conversion: 'The Jewish Question' and English National Identity.* Durham, NC: Duke University Press, 1995.

Raven, James, Helen Small, and Naomi Tadmor, eds. *The Practice and Representation of Reading in England.* Cambridge: Cambridge University Press, 1996.

Reed, Edward. *From Soul to Mind: The Emergence of Psychology, from Erasmus Darwin to William James.* New Haven: Yale University Press, 1997.

Reeve, Clara. *The Progress of Romance, Through Times, Countries, and Manners; with Remarks on the Good and Bad Effects of It, on Them Respectively: in a Course of Evening Conversations.* 2 vols. Colchester: W. Keymer, 1785.

Richards, I. A. *How to Read a Page: A Course in Efficient Reading with an Introduction to a Hundred Great Words.* New York: Norton, 1942.

——— *Practical Criticism.* 1929. New York: Harcourt, Brace, & World, 1966.

——— *Principles of Literary Criticism.* 1924. London: Routledge, 2001.

——— *Science and Poetry.* London: Kegan Paul, Trench, Trubner, 1926.

——— *Selected Letters of I. A. Richards, C. H.* Ed. John Constable. Oxford: Clarendon Press, 1990.

Richardson, Alan. *British Romanticism and the Science of the Mind.* Cambridge: Cambridge University Press, 2001.

——— *Literature, Education, and Romanticism: Reading as Social Practice, 1780–1832.* Cambridge: Cambridge University Press, 1994.

Roberts, Neil. *Meredith and the Novel*. London: Macmillan, 1997.

Rorty, Richard. *Contingency, Irony, and Solidarity*. Cambridge: Cambridge University Press, 1989.

Rose, Edward. 'Wagner as a Dramatist.' *Fraser's Magazine* 19 (April 1879), 519–32.

Rose, Jonathan. *The Intellectual History of the British Working Classes*. New Haven: Yale University Press, 2001.

Rossetti, Dante Gabriel. *The Correspondence of Dante Gabriel Rossetti*, iv. Ed. William Fredeman. Cambridge: D. S. Brewer, 2002.

Russo, John Paul. *I. A. Richards: His Life and Work*. Baltimore: Johns Hopkins University Press, 1989.

Rylance, Rick. *Victorian Psychology and British Culture, 1850–1880*. Oxford: Oxford University Press, 2000.

Saenger, Paul. 'Reading in the Later Middle Ages.' In *A History of Reading in the West*, ed. Guglielmo Cavallo and Roger Chartier, trans. Lydia Cochrane, 120–48. Amherst: University of Massachusetts Press; Cambridge: Polity, 1999.

Said, Edward. *Humanism and Democratic Criticism*. New York: Columbia University Press, 2004.

——— *Musical Elaborations*. New York: Columbia University Press, 1991.

Scarry, Elaine. *Dreaming by the Book*. New York: Farrar, Straus, Giroux, 1999.

——— *Resisting Representation*. New York: Oxford University Press, 1994.

Schoenberg, Arnold. *Style and Idea: Selected Writings of Arnold Schoenberg*. Ed. Leonard Stein. Berkeley: University of California Press, 1984.

Secord, James. *Victorian Sensation: The Extraordinary Publication, Reception, and Secret Authorship of* Vestiges of the Natural History of Creation. Chicago: University of Chicago Press, 2000.

Sedgwick, Eve Kosofsky. *Touching Feeling: Affect, Pedagogy, Performativity*. Durham, NC: Duke University Press, 2003.

Shklovsky, Viktor. *Theory of Prose*. Trans. Benjamin Sher. Normal, Ill.: Dalkey Archive Press, 1990.

Sloan, John. *George Gissing: The Cultural Challenge*. New York: St Martin's Press, 1989.

Snyder, Bob. *Music and Memory: An Introduction*. Cambridge, Mass.: MIT Press, 2000.

Solie, Ruth. *Music in Other Words: Victorian Conversations*. Berkeley: University of California Press, 2004.

Spacks, Patricia Meyer. *Boredom: The Literary History of a State of Mind*. Chicago: University of Chicago Press, 1995.

Spolsky, Ellen. *Gaps in Nature: Literary Interpretation and the Modular Mind*. Albany, NY: SUNY Press, 1993.

Stang, Richard. *The Theory of the Novel in England, 1850–1870*. New York: Columbia University Press, 1959.

St Clair, William. *The Reading Nation in the Romantic Period*. Cambridge: Cambridge University Press, 2004.

Stephen, Leslie. *George Eliot*. New York: Macmillan, 1902.

Stevenson, Lionel. *The Ordeal of George Meredith: A Biography*. New York: Scribners, 1953.

Stewart, Garrett. *Dear Reader: The Conscripted Audience in Nineteenth-Century British Fiction*. Baltimore: Johns Hopkins University Press, 1996.

———. 'Painted Readers, Narrative Regress.' *Narrative* 11/2 (2003), 125–76.

Sutherland, John. *Victorian Fiction: Writers, Publishers, Readers*. Basingstoke: Macmillan, 1995.

——— *Victorian Novelists and Publishers*. Chicago: University of Chicago Press, 1976.

Tarrant, Margaret. ' "Snips," "Snobs," and the "True Gentleman" in *Evan Harrington*.' In *Meredith Now: Some Critical Essays*, ed. Ian Fletcher. New York: Barnes & Noble, 1971 95–113.

Taylor, Jenny. '*The Gay Science*: The "Hidden Soul" of Victorian Criticism.' *Literature and History* 10/2 (1984), 189–202.

Tesauro, Emmanuele. *Il Cannocchiale aristotelico*. 1670. Turin: Einaudi, 1978.

Thomas, David Wayne. *Cultivating Victorians: Liberal Culture and the Aesthetic*. Philadelphia: University of Pennsylvania Press, 2004.

Thompson, E. P. *Customs in Common*. New York: New Press, 1991.

Tillyard, E. M. W. *The Muse Unchained: An Intimate Account of the Revolution of English Studies at Cambridge*. London: Bowes & Bowes, 1958.

Trilling, James. 'My Father and the Weak-Eyed Devils.' *American Scholar* 68/2 (Spring 1999), 17–41.

Tucker, Irene. *A Probable State: The Novel, the Contract, and the Jews*. Chicago: University of Chicago Press, 2000.

Turner, Mark. *Reading Minds: The Study of English in the Age of Cognitive Science*. Princeton: Princeton University Press, 1991.

Valéry, Paul. *Œuvres*, i. Paris: Gallimard, 1957.

Vincent, David. *The Rise of Mass Literacy: Reading and Writing in Modern Europe*. Cambridge: Polity, 2000.

Virilio, Paul. *The Art of the Motor*. Trans. Julie Rose. Minneapolis: University of Minnesota Press, 1995.

Wagner, Cosima. *Die Tagebücher*, i. Ed. Martin Gregor-Dellin and Dietrich Mack. Zurich: Piper, 1976.

Wagner, Richard. *Judaism in Music and Other Essays*. Trans. William Ashton Ellis. Lincoln: University of Nebraska Press, 1995.

———— *Mein Leben*. Ed. Martin Gregor-Dellin. Munich: List, 1976.

———— *On Conducting*. Trans. Edward Dannreuther. London: William Reeves, 1897.

Warner, William. *Licensing Entertainment: The Elevation of Novel Reading in Britain, 1684–1750*. Berkeley: University of California Press, 1998.

Watson, Derek. *Richard Wagner: A Biography*. New York: Schirmer, 1979.

Watt, Ian. *The Rise of the Novel: Studies in Defoe, Richardson, and Fielding*. Berkeley: University of California Press, 2001.

Wellek, René. *A History of Modern Criticism, 1750–1950: The Age of Transition*. New Haven: Yale University Press, 1965.

Welsh, Alexander. *George Eliot and Blackmail*. Cambridge, Mass: Harvard University Press, 1985.

Williams, Carolyn. 'Unbroken Patternes: Gender, Culture, and Voice in *The Egoist.*' *Browning Institute Studies* 13 (1985), 45–70.

Williams, Ioan, ed. *Meredith: The Critical Heritage*. London: Routledge & Kegan Paul, 1971.

Williams, Raymond. *The Country and the City*. New York: Oxford University Press, 1973.

—— *Culture and Society, 1780–1950*. London: Chatto & Windus, 1958.

—— *The Long Revolution*. New York and London: Columbia University Press, 1961.

—— *Politics and Letters: Interviews with* New Left Review. London: Verso, 1981.

Wilt, Judith. *The Readable People of George Meredith*. Princeton: Princeton University Press, 1975.

Winter, Alison. *Mesmerized: Powers of Mind in Victorian Britain*. Chicago: University of Chicago Press, 1998.

Wolfson, Susan. *Formal Charges: The Shaping of Poetry in British Romanticism*. Stanford, Calif.: Stanford University Press, 1997.

Wood, Jane. *Passion and Pathology in Victorian Culture*. Oxford: Oxford University Press, 2001.

Woodmansee, Martha. *The Author, Art, and the Market: Rereading the History of Aesthetics*. New York: Columbia University Press, 1994.

Woolf, Virginia. *The Second Common Reader*. New York: Harcourt, Brace, 1932.

Young, Kay. '*Middlemarch* and the Problem of Other Minds Heard.' *Literature Interpretation Theory* 14 (2003), 223–41.

Index

Note: Italic numbers denote reference to illustrations.